IN
PLAIN
SIGHT

ALSO BY
D. S. BUTLER

Lost Child
Her Missing Daughter

DS Karen Hart Series:

Bring Them Home
Where Secrets Lie
Don't Turn Back
House of Lies
On Cold Ground
What She Said
Find Her Alive
Before the Dawn
Leave No Trace

DS Jack Mackinnon Crime Series:

Deadly Obsession
Deadly Motive
Deadly Revenge
Deadly Justice
Deadly Ritual
Deadly Payback
Deadly Game
Deadly Intent

East End Series:

East End Trouble
East End Diamond
East End Retribution

Harper Grant Mystery Series:

A Witchy Business
A Witchy Mystery
A Witchy Christmas
A Witchy Valentine
Harper Grant and the Poisoned Pumpkin Pie
A Witchy Bake Off

IN PLAIN SIGHT

D.S. BUTLER

THOMAS & MERCER

Text copyright ©2025 by D. S. Butler
All rights reserved.

Published by Thomas & Mercer, Seattle

www.apub.com

Amazon, the Amazon logo, and Thomas & Mercer are trademarks of Amazon.com, Inc., or its affiliates.

ISBN-13: 9781662512292
eISBN: 9781662512308

Cover design by @blacksheep-uk.com
Cover images: © Vitaliy Kriuchkov © Nikolay Vlasenko © Ghost Bear © s_oleg © travellight / Shutterstock

Printed in the United States of America

For Yvonne. Thank you for being such a lovely neighbour.
We wish you and John every happiness!

Prologue

The bus is almost empty. Its headlights shine on a dark country road and a grey wall of rain.

Christie is sitting at the back with Leo, Mason and Mia. Mason is telling another rude joke – something about two girls in a bar – but Christie has tuned him out. She is starting to worry about getting home tonight. Her parents will kill her if she's not home by midnight. She stares out of the rain-splattered window, her breath misting the glass.

Leo takes a swig from a small bottle of vodka and passes it across to Christie. 'Go on, Christie,' he says, lifting his eyebrows. 'You're shivering. It'll warm you up.'

'I'm fine,' Christie says, shaking her head. He's right. She is shivering. That's because she didn't want to wear her coat out tonight. It's the one she had for school last year, and it's so baby-ish. It makes her look even younger than seventeen, and she wants to look older, like Mia with her bangles and heavy eyeliner. But instead of looking sophisticated like Mia, Christie just looks ridiculous in her black cardigan that's not warm enough for this cold, rainy October evening.

Leo shrugs and takes another drink.

'Give me some of that,' Mason says, grabbing the bottle from his hand.

'Hey!' Leo says, trying to get it back.

'I can't understand why they didn't let us into Imporium, as you're clearly so mature!' says Mia, rolling her eyes and laughing as Mason struggles with Leo.

Christie's fingers tighten around her mobile phone. Should she call her parents now and warn them she might be late? But then they'll worry about her, and she doesn't want that. She'll be fine. She's with friends. And anyway, they'll be back at Mia's soon and everything will be okay. Her parents will have no idea she wasn't where she told them she would be tonight. They think she's studying at Mia's.

The bus driver pulls up to a junction, the engine idling as he waits for a gap in the traffic so he can pull out on to the main road.

As Leo manages to get the vodka back from Mason, Mia takes out a packet of cigarettes, removes one and then offers the pack to Christie. 'Want one?'

Christie shakes her head. She doesn't smoke and hates the smell. 'We can't smoke on the bus, Mia.' The words leave her mouth before she has time to think about them, and she immediately regrets speaking. She sounds like a child.

Mia shrugs and takes out a lighter. 'We're the only passengers. No one will care.'

Christie's not so sure about that. The driver keeps glancing in his rear-view mirror, keeping a close eye on them. She doesn't blame him.

Mason takes a big swig from the vodka bottle and wipes his hand across his mouth. 'Little Miss Perfect,' he says to Christie. 'Do you ever do anything wrong?'

Christie stares at him, feeling her cheeks flush red. 'Of course, sometimes,' she mutters.

'Like what? What's the worst thing you've ever done?' Mason asks, looking at her with bloodshot eyes, clearly expecting an answer.

'Um . . .' Christie can't think of anything to say. Mason is right. She never does anything wrong. *Ever*. Her parents would kill her if she got into trouble. Telling her mum and dad that she's spending the evening studying with Mia while actually going drinking is pretty much the worst thing she's ever done. Pathetic really.

Mason snorts and shakes his head at Leo, as if Christie's the most boring person alive.

'Leave her alone,' Leo says, his voice low and quiet. 'She's okay.'

Christie feels her cheeks flush even more, and she looks down at her lap so no one can see her face. She holds her breath. Leo is so good-looking, with his mischievous smile and black hair that falls in front of his eyes. She catches herself sneaking glances at him all the time. He makes her feel like she matters. She used to feel invisible at her old school, where everyone ignored her.

They moved to the area from Hampshire just before the start of term, after Christie's father accepted an academic post at the university. She was so nervous about starting college. But then Mia and Mason started talking to her in English and they introduced her to Leo. They've been so nice to her and made her feel welcome. Even Mason when he's not drunk. She's glad she met them. But even so, she feels out of place, like an imposter or something. They're all so confident and know how to dress right, and she . . . doesn't.

She's awkward, childish and boring.

'Ignore Mason,' Leo says, leaning back in his seat and taking another gulp from the vodka bottle before offering it to her again. 'He can't handle his drink and gets a bit lairy.'

Before Christie can take the bottle from him, Mason snatches it away. 'I *can* handle my drink.'

'Hey!' Leo says, reaching for the vodka.

'You want it back?' Mason taunts.

His eyes are wild, and Christie's starting to feel very uncomfortable. She glances at Mia, but she only throws her head back and laughs, like she's seen it all before.

Leo stands and tries to grab the bottle from Mason, but Mason is taller than Leo and holds it high above his head, out of Leo's reach. 'Come on,' he says, grinning. 'You want it? Come and get it.'

Leo lunges forward, but Mason steps back. Leo stumbles against the seats in front, almost falling on to the floor.

The driver glances in his rear-view mirror again, his face tight with concern. 'Oi! You kids. Sit down!' he shouts over his shoulder.

'Or what?' Mason shouts back at him. 'What are you going to do about it?' He collapses into a seat in a fit of giggles.

'I'm warning you!' the driver yells, as he pulls the bus over to the side of the road and slams on the brakes.

Mason stands up again, still laughing. 'What are you going to do, you old git?'

The driver turns around in his seat and glares at them. Then he slowly gets to his feet. He's a big man. Mason is tall, but the bus driver is much broader, and the muscles in his forearms bulge as he clenches and unclenches his fists.

Mason squares up to him. 'You going to make me sit down?'

'Stop it, Mason,' Mia mutters.

The bus driver looks at her and his eyes narrow as he spots the cigarette in her hand. 'You're smoking?'

'Sorry,' she says, quickly stubbing it out on the back of the cigarette packet.

But the driver has already turned his attention back to Mason, who is still standing there, swaying slightly, with a grin plastered across his face. 'I want you all off my bus. Now.'

'We can't get off here,' Leo says. 'We're in the middle of nowhere.'

'Get. Off. My. Bus,' the driver says through gritted teeth.

'No!' Mason shouts back at him, stepping forward until his face is just inches from the driver's.

The driver grabs Mason by the scruff of the neck and drags him towards the door.

'Hey!' Mason yells. 'Let me go!'

The driver opens the doors with one hand while holding on to Mason with the other. Then he pushes Mason out, sending him sprawling on to his hands and knees in a puddle.

'You can't leave us here,' Mia says, and Christie's impressed by how calm her voice is. She watches Mia challenge the irate bus driver with a mixture of envy and admiration. How can she be so fearless? The thought of standing up to an authority figure like that makes Christie's chest feel tight. What if the driver calls the police? She can already imagine the disappointed looks on her parents' faces, and the inevitable grounding.

She can't believe they're going to be thrown off the bus in the middle of nowhere. Christie's nails dig into her palms as she clenches her fists, the sharp sting reminding her that this may feel like a nightmare, but she is wide awake. This is really happening. Mia continues to stare down the bus driver, as though getting into trouble is the furthest thing from her mind. Christie wishes she could be that unafraid.

Mia crosses her arms and adds, 'It's not right to leave young women out here alone in the dark. It isn't safe.'

The driver looks at Mia, then at Christie and Leo, before turning his attention back to Mason, who has got to his feet and is now standing on the verge, muttering expletives under his breath. The driver shakes his head. 'You're not alone. You have these two young . . . *gentlemen* with you.'

He jerks a thumb at the open door.

'Fine,' Leo grumbles as he steps down from the bus.

Mia stalks along behind him and Christie follows meekly, murmuring apologies, but the driver pays her no attention. As soon as she steps off the bus, the door closes, and he accelerates away.

'What are we going to do now?' Mia asks, looking around at the dark fields that surround them.

'I don't know where we are,' Leo says, staring at his mobile phone. 'I've got no signal.'

They all check their phones. None of them have any service. They're stranded on a country road in the middle of nowhere with no way of getting home.

Leo swears under his breath. 'This is your fault, Mason.'

But Mason ignores him and starts walking up the road back in the direction they've just come from, stumbling slightly as he does so.

Mia clears her throat. 'You're going the wrong way.'

'You know where we are?' Christie asks hopefully.

Mia nods confidently. 'If we take the road, we'll be at mine in about an hour. We can be there in fifteen minutes if we cut across the fields.'

They all turn to look at the dark fields that stretch out on either side of them.

'It's muddy,' Mia says. 'And it's a bit creepy, but it's not far.' She looks at Mason, who is still walking away from them along the middle of the road. 'Mason! It's this way!'

Christie looks down at her low-heeled boots. Definitely not designed for rain-soaked fields. 'I don't know,' she says tentatively. 'Maybe we should stick to the road and keep checking for a phone signal. We could call one of our parents to pick us up.'

Mia grimaces. 'Your mum and dad think you're studying at my house tonight, and my parents would not be impressed if I called them at this time on a school night to come and collect me. They'd ground me for months.'

'Mine too,' Leo agrees.

'Doubt mine would even answer the phone,' Mason says when he finally joins them.

'But we're going to get in trouble with our parents anyway,' Christie says. 'We're going to be late getting home.'

'We'll be even later if we walk along the road,' Mia says, fiddling with her bangles. 'Look, it's up to you, Christie. But I'm going home across the fields.'

Christie looks around at the dark landscape again and shivers. It's cold out here and starting to drizzle again. She doesn't want to walk through soggy fields in the dark, but she doesn't want to walk alone down a country road either.

'I'll come with you,' Christie says quietly.

Mia smiles at her. 'Come on then.'

She leads them off the road and into the field. The ground is muddy and uneven and water seeps into Christie's boots. She tries to keep up with Mia, but she's walking fast, and Christie breaks into a jog to catch her. 'Are you sure you know the way?' Christie asks.

'Positive,' Mia says without turning around.

Mason stumbles behind them, muttering to himself as he walks.

'Are you struggling to keep up, Mason?' Leo asks, his voice dripping with sarcasm.

'I'm fine,' Mason slurs back.

Christie uses the light on her phone to see where she's going, but the beam isn't strong, and it just makes the surroundings seem even darker and scarier. Now and then a car passes by on the road behind them. Christie feels more vulnerable and exposed as the traffic sounds lessen, and she's glad when they reach the other side of the field.

'This way,' Mia says as she points to another field.

'Hey!' Leo calls after her. 'How many of these fields do we have to cross?'

Mia ignores him and keeps walking.

The rain has soaked through Christie's cardigan and jeans, and her feet are wet inside her boots. She's shivering again. And tired. It's been a long day, and she just wants to get home, take a hot shower, put on her fleecy pyjamas and go to bed.

They squeeze through the hedge dividing the fields, and the branches scratch at Christie's face, catching on her hair. She stumbles down the other side into a ditch full of water. 'Mia!' Christie calls after her, but she doesn't turn around or slow down.

Leo helps Christie up and out of the ditch. 'You okay?' he asks her as they follow Mia across the next field. Christie nods, even though she's not. Her eyes prick with tears, and she furiously blinks them away. She can't show herself up in front of Leo and the others by crying.

'What are you doing?' Leo shouts at Mia, who is climbing over a wall. 'This can't be the way.'

'It is,' Mia says confidently as she jumps down on to the other side of the wall.

The rain is falling harder now, and Christie thinks she hears thunder rumbling in the distance. *Great*. Could things get any worse?

They trudge along in silence for a while. The only sounds are the wind rustling through the hedges, Mason's heavy breathing as he stumbles along behind them, and their footsteps squelching in the mud.

'How much further?' Leo asks.

'Ten minutes or so,' Mia says with a shrug.

Ten minutes isn't so bad. Christie can cope with another ten minutes. Leo offers her his arm for support, and she takes it gratefully.

'I'm sorry,' he says to Christie quietly as they walk along. 'You shouldn't have had to get off the bus. You didn't do anything wrong.'

'It's okay,' she says. Maybe they'll laugh about it tomorrow. But right now, she just wants to be warm and dry again.

They reach a gate and climb over it, Mason almost falling flat on his face as he does so, and then they're in another field, with a dark wood on the other side.

Then Mia stops so suddenly that Christie bumps into her.

'What's wrong?' Christie asks, her voice shaking. 'Why have you stopped?'

'Look,' Mia says, pointing at something ahead of them. Christie shines the light from her phone along the grass and sees what she's pointing at.

There's a large white trailer and a couple of small white tents. Beside the tents are huge blue tarpaulins, staked low and covering the ground. A massive JCB digger is parked close to the trailer.

'Everything looks different in the dark,' Mia says.

Christie suddenly knows where she is. Although she hasn't been here before. This is the project her father has been working on.

'It's an archaeology site. A dig. My father's working here,' she says. 'They're filming a TV show about discovering the Roman remains. *Britain's Biggest Treasure Hunt*—'

She stops speaking abruptly as Mason pushes past her and walks towards the site.

'Mason! Don't go near it!' Leo calls after him, but Mason ignores him and keeps walking.

They watch in silence as he reaches the site and pulls at one of the tarpaulins covering the ground.

'Stop it, Mason!' Christie shouts. 'You'll get us all into trouble.'

But Mason doesn't stop, and with one more tug, the tarpaulin comes away. 'Let's have a look,' he calls back.

'No! Mason!' Mia shouts, running towards him.

Leo follows and Christie rushes behind them as fast as she can, her heart thudding against her ribs. She hopes there is no one in the trailer or those tents. If her father finds out about this, he'll be disappointed. Her mother will be livid.

There is a sign right in front of them warning people not to enter the area. But Mason ignores it and leans forward to look into the hole that has been excavated.

'Just a load of mud, as far as I can see.' Mason angles the light from his phone towards the hole.

Christie is surprised at its size. The trenches she's seen before have never been this deep.

Then Mason stumbles on a tuft of grass, his arms flailing as he tries to regain his balance.

They all rush forward, Leo reaching him first but not fast enough to stop Mason tumbling into the deep trench. He lands with a thump. And then there's silence. Mason isn't moving.

'Are you hurt?' Mia asks, kneeling and trying to peer down into the darkness.

'Mason!' Leo shouts, leaning over and shining the light from his phone into the trench.

Mason's face is smeared with mud. His eyes are open wide, but he seems unnaturally still. And when he looks up at them, the expression on his face sends a shiver shooting down Christie's spine.

Mason lets out a shuddering breath.

Christie's mouth is dry, and her pulse is racing.

'There's something down here,' Mason says, his voice cracking with emotion as he stares into the darkness. He looks up at them again, his eyes wide with fear. 'You need to see this. I think I've found a body.'

'Don't touch anything,' Mia warns. 'Of course there'll be bones down there. It's a site of archaeological interest.'

'It's not bones,' Mason says, pointing along the trench.

Leo shines a light across the mud, and there, just a few feet from Mason, is a woman's body; her face is obscured, but Christie can see her blonde hair. Her limbs are twisted and bent in an unnatural way and there are dark stains on her clothes. Maybe mud, maybe blood. There's something clamped around her throat and attached to her wrists. It's made of wood and reminds Christie of a mini version of the stocks. She has never seen anything like it before.

Leo swears, and the light shakes as his arm starts to tremble. 'What's that around her neck?'

'She's not . . . I mean . . . Is she still alive?' Mia asks in almost a whisper.

Mason jerks back. 'What?'

'Check for a pulse.' Mia nods towards the blonde woman, who still hasn't moved.

'I don't think I can. I've hurt my ankle.'

'You have to,' Mia insists.

'If you're so keen, why don't you come down here and do it?' Mason glares up at them but then reluctantly shuffles closer to the woman. He suddenly seems very sober as he reaches out a tentative hand and touches her neck. The woman rolls back slightly as if trying to pull away from him.

Christie wraps her arms around her body, trying to stop shivering.

Mason tries again, and after a few seconds, he shakes his head. 'No pulse.'

Christie can't speak. Her hands are trembling so much that she almost drops her phone.

'She's dead, and this isn't a Roman burial,' Mason says, stating the obvious. 'I'm pretty sure they didn't wear jeans back then.'

Leo takes a few steps back from the edge of the hole. 'We need to call the police. Anyone got a signal?'

11

They all check their phones again, but there's still no reception.

'We have to go back to the road,' Mia says, her voice calm. 'That's the best chance of getting a signal.'

Leo turns to her with a frown. 'I thought we were nearly at your house. You said you knew where we were?'

Mia looks sheepish. 'Everything seems different in the dark . . . I'm not really sure how to get to my house from here. I think we should head back to the road.'

'Hey, don't leave me!' Mason shouts. He tries to scramble up but winces in pain. The mud is too slippery, and he falls on to his backside. 'You can't leave me here alone with a dead body.'

'We'll come back for you,' Leo promises him. 'We just need to call the police.'

To Christie's surprise, Mason starts to cry. '*Please* don't leave me here. *Please*.'

'We won't be long,' Mia says, her voice soft. 'We'll come back as soon as we can.'

Christie looks down at the body of the woman again. Someone left her here. The person who dumped her body could still be around. She doesn't blame Mason for not wanting to stay here alone.

'I'll stay with him,' she says suddenly.

Mason looks up at her, his eyes red and wet with tears. 'You will?'

Christie nods, then turns to Leo and Mia. 'You two go back to the road and call the police.'

Leo leans in close so Mason doesn't hear him. 'But what if whoever killed this woman is still around?'

Christie swallows hard. She doesn't want to dwell on that possibility. 'We'll be all right,' she says, hoping she sounds more confident than she feels. 'Go quickly and get help.'

Leo nods and turns to go.

'Wait!' Mia says, taking off her long scarf and handing it to Christie. 'You'll get cold fast if you're not moving.'

Christie takes it gratefully and wraps it around her shoulders. It smells of Mia's perfume, and for some reason, that is comforting. 'Thank you,' she says, as Mia and Leo turn to go back across the fields.

'Thanks for staying,' Mason says when they're gone. He looks up at Christie with wide eyes. 'I don't want to be here alone with her. Not even for a minute. It's creepy, you know?'

Christie nods and sits on the wet grass. 'It's okay,' she says, trying to sound brave. 'We won't be alone for long.'

As they sit there, Mason babbles on about Imporium and how many times he's been in the past and that he can't believe they didn't get in this time. It's as though he's scared of the silence. But all Christie can think about is the dead woman. There was something about her – something familiar.

Christie pulls out her phone, and the beam from the light trickles slowly over the uneven ground at the bottom of the trench, casting eerie shadows that flicker in the darkness.

'What are you doing?' Mason squirms, recoiling and pushing himself back against the damp earth. 'I don't want to see it again.'

'I just need to check something,' Christie explains, keeping her voice low. She doesn't want to upset Mason. But she needs to see the body. Because there was something about the victim . . . something familiar.

Pale light glints off the woman's green jacket, then illuminates the strange wooden clamp fastened around her slender neck.

Mason lets out a low moan. 'Please just turn it off, Christie,' he pleads, his voice higher and reedier than usual.

'Just a minute.' Christie squints into the darkness as the light hits the victim's face. Strands of blonde hair have fallen forward, partially obscuring her features. But Christie can see enough. The victim's glassy eyes are cold and empty.

With a sudden shock of horror, Christie realises she was right. She knows exactly who this woman is. And that makes everything much, much worse.

Chapter One

Detective Sergeant Karen Hart sat curled up on the sofa with a book in her lap and the TV on low in the background. The clock on the mantelpiece ticked steadily towards midnight. She was home alone.

Her partner, Mike, and his dog, Sandy, were away on a residential course in Staffordshire, and she missed them. The house felt empty. It still surprised her how quickly Mike had come to fill a space in her life. When she'd lost her husband and daughter, Karen hadn't been able to imagine sharing her home with anyone else, but now it felt natural to have Mike there. He understood what she'd been through, having lost his own son. They both knew that the pain of their grief would never disappear, but were trying to find a balance between holding on to their memories and building a new life together.

Except that he'd seemed distracted lately. Karen had put it down to him wanting to know more about his biological father; something that had only recently become more important to him. His mum shutting down the conversation whenever Mike brought it up had only added to his frustration. But maybe there was more to his recent low moods? Was there something else on his mind?

Last week, they'd both been so busy at work that they'd only managed to have dinner together once. She'd tried to talk to him, but Mike had dismissed her questions, saying he was fine. He'd never been one to talk about his feelings.

When Mike returned from the course, they'd have a proper chat. No more dismissals. No more *I'm fine*. She would find out what was bothering him. And together, they'd work through it.

She sighed, stretched, and looked at the clock again. Nearly time for bed. Just enough time to squeeze in one more chapter.

Her mobile phone chirped and started buzzing along the coffee table. Was that a new ringtone? She could have sworn she hadn't changed it. It must have happened when the phone updated. Modern technology was getting more and more intrusive. Karen didn't *want* a new ringtone. She liked the old one.

She leaned forward and picked up the phone, expecting it to be Mike calling to say goodnight. But the screen displayed a different number. One that Karen recognised all too well.

She answered the call. 'DS Hart.'

'Evening, Sarge,' the duty officer said. 'I've got a job for you.'

Karen sat up straight, and her book slid off her lap on to the floor. 'Go ahead.'

'A body's been found at an archaeological dig site in Stow.'

'At this time of night? It's a bit late for digging for antiquities, isn't it?' Karen asked.

'It wasn't the archaeology team who found it. A group of teenagers stumbled across the body about an hour ago.'

Karen tightened her grip on the phone. 'You're telling me this is a fresh body, not ancient remains?'

'Afraid so, Sarge.' The duty officer's tone was grave. 'The teenagers reported it looked . . . well, recent. Very recent.'

'What were the teenagers doing there?'

There was a pause. 'Er . . . I don't know.'

'What do we know? Is the body male? Female?'

'Female. It's a bit of an odd one. Apparently, she has something around her neck.'

'What?'

Karen heard him shuffling papers. 'That I can't tell you. I only have a few notes. Can you get there? I'll send you the address. It's a field just outside Stow. A crime scene team have been assigned, and the pathologist has been informed.'

'I'll head there now.'

After ending the call, Karen went upstairs and pulled on a pair of dark trousers and a warm wool jumper, then went back downstairs and tugged on her boots.

Stow was a small village between Lincoln and Gainsborough. If Karen took the Eastern Bypass, she could be there in twenty-five minutes.

The night was damp and drizzly. As she drove along the empty roads, she wondered why teenagers would have been wandering around a muddy field in this weather. Maybe some kind of dare? Or perhaps they had heard about the dig and wanted to explore when no one was around.

The discovery of an ancient Roman settlement in the area had been hailed as one of the most important in years, causing quite a stir in the local news and online. Two TV presenters, Trevor Barker and Molly Moreland, were recording at the site for *Britain's Biggest Treasure Hunt*. The programme involved the two running around the country, visiting various dig locations and interviewing experts. Trevor and Molly were far from history experts themselves. Trevor was a former radio DJ, and Molly was a model who had appeared briefly in a reality show a decade ago and now made a living presenting terrible documentaries.

Having previously hosted cookery shows and home improvement shows, without success, Molly had struck gold with archaeology. The show was in a primetime slot on Sunday evenings. Karen had tried watching it once, but both the presenters had grated on her nerves with their fake, over-the-top enthusiasm, and she'd switched it off after ten minutes. She preferred *Time Team*.

Karen turned off the main road and followed the directions to the site. She'd envisaged having trouble finding it, but the SOCOs had made it there before her, and the floodlights lit the place up like a football pitch. She parked her car in a pull-in area and got out. It was cold, but it had at least stopped raining.

A lone uniformed officer stood on duty by the entrance to the field. He was huddled next to the gate, shivering. When Karen showed him her ID, he perked up a bit and offered a smile.

'Can you give me any more details?' she asked.

His smile soured. 'I can't tell you much. My partner is the one to ask. He's in the field doing *actual* police work. I get the exciting job of standing guard by a gate.'

'You don't sound too happy about that.'

'Would you be?'

'Who's your partner?'

'PC Pearce.' He looked over his shoulder and pointed. 'He's by the first tent, with the kids who found the body.'

Karen thanked him, stepped through the gate and walked towards the floodlights, carefully picking her way through the mud. It would be difficult to get the evidence out of here without disturbing any remaining footprints or vehicle tracks. The ground was saturated.

PC Pearce spotted Karen and began to walk towards her. He was a tall man with a broad frame that had likely seen many hours in the gym.

'DS Hart. You're in charge?' he asked after Karen had shown him her ID.

'For now. What can you tell me?' Karen asked.

'Victim is female. Not been here long. She was found in one of the trenches. It's strange actually . . .' He trailed off, his baby face puckering in a frown.

'What's odd?'

'The trench she was found in is really deep. One of the teenagers that found her fell in and couldn't get out because he'd injured his ankle. I checked the other trenches, and none of the others are that deep.'

Karen nodded, filing the information away for later. 'Do we have an ID?'

Pearce shook his head. 'No. I checked for signs of life, but when it was clear she had passed, I didn't want to disturb the scene further. I thought it better to wait for the SOCOs to arrive.'

'Good call. You've spoken to the teens who found her?'

'I've taken initial statements. All attend college in Lincoln. Two girls. Two lads. All seventeen.'

'What were they doing out here?'

'Making their way home. Got chucked off the bus and decided to take a shortcut across the fields.'

'Does that check out?'

'I haven't spoken with the bus company, but one of the girls lives in Stow. Three of the teenagers are still here. Mia Palmer, Leo Redmond and Christie Stark.' He pointed to each of them in turn. 'The other kid, Mason Wright, was taken to hospital with a suspected broken ankle. Christie's father, Professor Thomas Stark, just arrived to take them home. I take it you'll want to have a word with them before they leave?'

'Yes, I'll do that now,' Karen said.

'I thought you would,' the officer said, looking pleased he'd made the right call. 'Especially as Professor Stark is in charge of this dig site.'

'He is? That *is* interesting.'

The teenagers were shivering when Karen approached them. It was a cold night, and they'd had a nasty shock and wouldn't want to hang around any longer than necessary.

'I know you're all going to want to get home, but I need to ask you a few quick questions before you do.'

The three teenagers kept their eyes on the ground, shuffling nervously. The professor was wrapping his long black coat over his daughter's shoulders. She hadn't even been wearing a coat – no wonder she was shivering.

'I know you've already spoken to PC Pearce,' Karen said, 'but I need to know if you saw anyone else while you were walking across the fields?'

Mia rubbed at her smudged eyeliner. 'We've already told the officer everything we know. We didn't see anything unusual until we got to the dig site. I didn't even know Christie's dad worked here. We were just taking a shortcut to my house.'

Karen looked over at Christie's father.

'Professor Tom Stark,' he said with a quick, brisk smile. He was a tall man in his late forties, with salt-and-pepper hair poking out from under a grey wool hat. 'I had no idea they were out here. Christie told me she was at Mia's, studying.'

His tone was disapproving, but gentle, and Christie ducked her head, looking sheepish, but didn't say anything.

Karen pressed for more details – were they sure they hadn't seen anyone else out here? Any vehicles in the fields or on the roads? Or a light from a torch? But the teens just shook their heads, seemingly eager to go home and forget about the incident.

'I was told the other young man who was with you when you found the body was hurt, and he's been taken to hospital—'

Before Karen could continue, the professor cut in. 'Yes, it looked nasty. But it's not our fault. This is private farmland with no public right of way. We have full permission for the archaeological dig, all above board. The area was secured, as it should be. Yet, despite these precautions, the lad was drunk and chose to trespass on restricted grounds. It's hard to safeguard against such recklessness. We can't be held accountable for his stupidity.'

'I'm not assigning blame,' Karen said. 'Just trying to understand what happened. Did you recognise the victim, Professor?'

Stark shook his head, exhaling a misty breath. 'No. I arrived after the police and haven't seen the body, but her description doesn't match any of our team or sound familiar.'

Stark's dismissive, almost hostile tone raised Karen's hackles. His transparent attempt to distance himself from the incident suggested an underlying agenda that went beyond being a worried parent who was concerned for his daughter.

'The trench the victim was found in is much deeper than any of the others—' Karen began, only to be quickly cut off by Stark.

'Yes, much deeper than usual. We found what looked like a communal stove or oven and went further down to make sure we didn't miss anything.'

'Did Christie call you?' Karen asked.

'No. One of your colleagues contacted me to collect her. A bit of a shock, I can tell you.'

'I can imagine. You got here quickly.'

'Of course. I left immediately when I got the call. I was understandably worried about my daughter.'

His manner struck Karen as a tad too assertive, and he was too eager to deflect any potential blame. Was this down to his

21

personality? The behaviour of an academic used to being in charge? Or did he have another reason for being so defensive?

Karen nodded, and then looked at Mia, Leo and Christie. 'You all look very cold – I won't delay you much longer. I just need to ask if any of you recognised the woman?'

The teens shuffled nervously but shook their heads.

'Never seen her before,' Mia said through chattering teeth.

'No idea who she was,' Leo added with a shrug.

'Christie?'

The young woman kept her eyes on the ground and shook her head. She leaned into her father, who put his arm around her. The poor girl looked shaken – understandably so after finding a body like that, but Karen wondered if there was more to it.

She noted the girl's body language – downcast eyes, the slight trembling – which could suggest more than just shock at finding a body. Perhaps Christie had seen or heard something else, something she wasn't sharing. Karen would need to speak to her again.

Karen handed out her card. 'We'll need full statements from you all tomorrow. But for now, you can go and get warm.'

'All right, come on, Christie, let's get you home,' Professor Stark said.

He ushered his daughter away, his arm still around her shoulders. There was something overbearing about his actions that gave Karen pause. Was he simply being a concerned parent, or was he worried about what Christie might say?

'Are you taking them all home?' Karen called after him, gesturing to Mia and Leo. She would need to organise a lift for them if he wasn't.

The professor gave a brisk nod. 'Of course. Not a problem.'

Karen and PC Pearce watched them walk off, then Pearce said, 'The professor was quite quick to deny responsibility for the kid's broken ankle, wasn't he? He'd be at the top of my suspect list.'

'I'm reserving judgement for now,' Karen said, 'but I agree he seemed defensive. Though that doesn't necessarily make him a murderer.'

Both the professor and his daughter had seemed uneasy, almost as though they were hiding something. But then again, maybe Karen was just reading too much into their reactions. The trauma of finding a body could account for their behaviour.

Pearce clapped his hands together. 'Right, so what's next?'

'Next,' Karen said, looking beyond him to the crime scene, 'is getting an ID for our lady in the trench.'

Chapter Two

'Who's the crime scene officer in charge?' Karen asked, but before Pearce could answer, she spotted him near the white incident tent.

Tim Farthing.

Tim was brash, irritating, and one of the most annoying people she'd ever worked with, but over the past year or so she'd found herself reluctantly warming to him. Not that she'd ever admit it.

Despite his sarcastic flippancy, he was a hard worker. She was secretly pleased it was him.

Karen suited up in light blue overalls and used the shoe covers provided by PC Pearce before she joined Tim, who was busy checking off a list.

'Evening, Tim.'

Tim glanced up at her dismissively before returning his attention to the list. 'Oh, it's you.'

'It is indeed. Expecting someone else?'

'I was hoping for a detective who appreciates me.'

'What makes you think I don't appreciate you? Anyway, it doesn't matter who you were hoping for. You're stuck with me, I'm afraid.'

The SOCO made a big show of sighing heavily.

'So, what can you tell me?' Karen asked.

'I think it's best I show you.' Tim led the way. 'She's in a trench. We've got the tent up to protect her from the worst of the weather.'

They stopped beside a long, deep trench. The earth was a mixture of reddish soil and small stones. Despite the tarpaulin folded on one side of the trench, the ground was wet and muddy. The tent erected to shield the body was open at the front, and Karen could just make out the legs of the victim from where she stood. Yellow markers, set out by the SOCOs, were dotted around the trench.

'We've already done a sweep for evidence,' Tim said. 'And my team photographed everything in situ.' He turned to Karen and then pointed to the ladder that lay against the side of the trench. 'Ready?'

It looked slippery, but Karen nodded. She needed to see the body. Tim started to descend the ladder, and Karen followed him down.

She could see why the teenager who'd fallen in the trench had struggled to get out with an injured ankle and no ladder. The sides were steep and slick, and Karen had to take it slowly to keep her footing.

When she reached the bottom, she headed to the forensic tent. The door flap was open, letting in the bright light from the floodlamps.

'All right to go straight in?' Karen asked. She didn't want to stand anywhere she shouldn't, especially as the pathologist hadn't seen the body yet.

'Unless you want to stand there admiring the tent.'

She let her steely stare do the talking. Tim knew what she meant; he was being purposefully difficult. But then that was Tim Farthing all over. She shouldn't have expected anything less.

He smirked.

'You are hard work,' Karen said as she ducked inside.

The temperature seemed to drop by a few degrees.

In the centre of the tent lay the woman's body. She was on her right side, her face half-hidden by blonde hair that had come loose from its ponytail. She wore a dark green waterproof jacket, indigo jeans and walking boots.

There was no smell of decay, so the victim couldn't have been dead for long. Karen moved closer to the body. The skin on the woman's face and hands looked grey and mottled in the harsh lights from the portable lamps.

Her eyes were drawn to a strange contraption locked around the victim's neck and wrists. It was made of wood and metal and resembled a violin in size and shape. The metal band around the neck squeezed against the skin, and there was evidence of bleeding – or was that rust? The bands around her wrists were also close-fitting, and the device forced the victim's head down towards her chest. The edge of the metal dug into the soft flesh under her chin.

'What *is* that?' Karen muttered.

'A shrew's fiddle,' Tim said, as though the item were common. 'It was used for punishment and torture centuries ago, usually on women, hence the name. The neck and wrist restraints kept victims locked in that hunched position for hours or even days at a time. It must cause excruciating pain in the back and neck.'

Karen turned to look at him, eyebrows raised.

'I've never seen one in real life, but I've seen pictures of them. They were designed to cause maximum discomfort. Totally barbaric.'

Karen continued to look at Tim.

'Okay. I googled it.'

'Do you think this is how she died?'

'No idea. The pathologist will have to determine the cause of death.' Tim's flippant tone was a contrast to his solemn expression.

'So, this was a murder then?' Karen said quietly. 'Not an accident or a suicide. She didn't put herself in that contraption?'

'No, and the fact that this is an archaeology site – well, the shrew's fiddle seems significant.'

'Why? Do you think it was found here? It was a discovery?' Karen repressed a wave of repulsion as she stared at the device.

It didn't look that old. Surely wood would have rotted away after centuries, wouldn't it? Although, maybe not. She'd read somewhere that Lincoln Cathedral still contained some of its original wood in the doors. So, under the right conditions, a wooden artefact could last a long time.

'Finding out *why* is your job, not mine,' Tim said, angling the light he was holding so Karen could see better.

'Did you find any ID on her?'

'We haven't touched the body. Photographs only until the pathologist gets here.'

As if on cue, the pathologist – Raj – appeared at the top of the trench, carrying a medical bag and a large umbrella. It looked like he was wearing black tie beneath his forensic suit, as though dressed for the opera, not a muddy field.

He peered down at them and then looked at the ladder with a sigh of disappointment. 'I was at a dinner. I suppose you need me down there?'

'I'm afraid so,' Karen said.

He gave another sigh, put his bag and umbrella at the edge of the trench and slowly climbed down, taking care not to slip on the ladder. Once at the bottom, he nodded at them both as Tim went back up and passed him his bag. 'This wasn't what I had planned for this evening. But we're short-staffed. There's a nasty tummy bug floating around; people have been dropping like flies. Professor Lawrence lost seven pounds in a week!' Raj patted his ample stomach. 'Luckily, I've avoided it so far.'

'Glad to hear it,' Karen said.

Raj was a professional with many years of experience, but Karen saw him flinch at the sight of the shrew's fiddle around the victim's neck.

'What is that?'

Karen looked at Tim. 'You're the expert.'

'Hardly. I told you – I googled it.' He huffed, but then gave Raj the same explanation he'd just given Karen.

Raj nodded, his face grim. 'Well, we can remove it once we get her back to the morgue.' He bent down and began examining the woman with gloved fingers.

They stepped back and watched the pathologist work. Karen wanted answers. She needed to know who this woman was as quickly as possible, and why the killer had chosen to place her here. And more to the point, how had her killer got hold of a device like that?

'She could be one of the archaeologists,' Karen said, thinking aloud. 'We need to identify her as soon as possible so we can start interviewing people.'

Raj was too invested in his work to reply, and Tim only shrugged.

She glanced at the SOCO. 'Any thoughts, Mr Google?'

He scowled. 'If we find ID on her, your job will be almost done for you.'

Raj had finished his initial exam and began to search through the pockets of the victim's coat. He pulled out a wallet, which he passed to Karen. She opened the wallet, pulled out a driver's licence and read the name. 'Alison Poulson.'

As Karen searched through the other cards in the victim's purse, she asked Raj, 'Can you estimate how long she's been dead?'

Raj frowned. 'No more than a couple of hours, I'd say.'

'How did she die? Was it that fiddle thing around her neck?' Karen asked.

'I don't think so,' Raj said slowly. 'She has a head wound. I think that's more likely the cause of death.'

'So, the shrew's fiddle is just decoration?' Karen asked.

'I don't like your idea of decoration,' Tim said.

Karen ignored him. 'Do you think the device was put on the victim post-mortem?'

Raj shook his head solemnly. 'I'm afraid not. The shrew's fiddle was put on the victim before her death.' He gestured towards the device. 'The bleeding and extensive bruising around her neck indicate she was alive when it was locked into place. It was a cruel death. She would have been trapped in that agonising position as she died.'

A wave of nausea washed over Karen. She put a hand to her throat. She could almost feel the metal biting into her own flesh. Imagining Alison Poulson's final terrified moments made her stomach churn. This wasn't just murder – it was a calculated act of sadism.

The killer had taken pleasure in Alison's suffering. The realisation made Karen's skin crawl. This hadn't been a momentary loss of control, but the product of a twisted and cruel mind.

'Whoever did this wanted to cause her maximum pain and humiliation,' Karen said, trying to clear her head and focus on what she could do to catch whoever had done this. 'The use of this shrew's fiddle must have been deliberate. It could be a message? A symbol? What do you think?'

Raj turned to her and smiled. 'I admire your enthusiasm, Karen, but the answer to that is beyond me. The autopsy might provide more answers.'

Karen nodded. 'Fair enough.' She couldn't expect Raj to speculate on motives in a soggy trench in the middle of a windswept field.

She climbed the ladder, feeling relieved to get out of the muddy hole.

Tim followed her a few moments later. 'Happy now? You've got an ID. The hard part is done, isn't it?'

Karen watched as the victim was lifted from the trench. The real work was just beginning. The identification of Alison Poulson was the starting point. They still had to discover the motive behind her murder. And why her body had been found at the dig site.

She wondered about the shrew's fiddle. Was it a genuine arte-fact that had been buried in the field for centuries? Or had someone brought it to the site? Karen felt a surge of anger. The sheer brutal-ity of the way the shrew's fiddle had been used to humiliate and torment Alison Poulson made her blood boil. This went beyond a simple murder – there was an undercurrent of contempt. Had the killer been driven by a personal hatred of Alison, or a deep-seated loathing of women in general?

She turned to Tim, expecting to see her disgust mirrored in his expression. His features remained frustratingly impassive, as if this was nothing more than another day at the office for him. That only added to her simmering fury. But then she caught the slight furrow in his brow, the tightness around his eyes. He felt the cruelty of this crime, too, even if he was hiding it behind his usual flippant manner.

Karen began to walk back to her car. Now, they had the unen-viable task of tracking down Alison's loved ones to tell them she wouldn't be coming home. That was the worst part of the job.

So Tim was mistaken. The hard bit was definitely still to come.

Karen spotted the uniformed officer at the gate waving a woman through. Just what they didn't need – another person to disturb the scene.

She walked towards the woman to head her off. They could do without more footprints to eliminate. The crime scene officers were going to have a difficult enough time as it was.

'Hello!' the woman called when she was a few feet away. Karen guessed she was in her early fifties. A petite, attractive woman, her hair scooped back into a messy up-do. She wore a long navy coat, jeans and expensive-looking green wellington boots. At least she was dressed for the muddy field.

'I'm Detective Sergeant Karen Hart . . . and you are?' Karen asked.

'Sylvie Broadbent.' She had a posh voice – Home Counties.

'Are you involved with the dig?'

'Sort of,' she said. 'I'm actually the producer of the television show that's filming here. *Britain's Biggest Treasure Hunt*. I don't suppose you've heard of us?'

Karen nodded. 'I have.'

'Well, as the producer, I'm in charge of production schedules and—'

Karen put a hand up. 'I'm sorry, Sylvie, but there will be a delay, and there's nothing I can do about that. Preservation of the crime scene takes precedence over filming.'

'Of course. I didn't mean to imply our TV show was more important than a murder investigation. I just wanted to introduce myself in case I can be of any help. And also – if I'm honest – get the lie of the land before my bosses are on my back tomorrow.' She smiled. 'I like to get ahead of problems. Do you know who the victim is yet?'

'Enquiries are ongoing,' Karen replied – a stock answer – but then hesitated, weighing the potential benefits of questioning Sylvie

31

now, against the normal protocol of waiting for the next of kin to be informed. The last thing she wanted was for Alison Poulson's family to find out about her murder from someone else. But if Sylvie knew the victim, it could prove to be a valuable opportunity to gather information while it was fresh in her mind.

'Do you know an Alison Poulson?' Karen asked.

Sylvie's eyes widened. She instinctively took a step back, as if the news had physically jolted her. 'Alison? She's the victim?' After a pause she added, 'I'm sorry to hear that.' But her expression didn't quite match her words. She didn't look sorry; she looked confused. 'How did it happen?'

But Karen wasn't here to answer Sylvie's questions, especially as she hadn't spoken to Alison's family yet. 'What was Alison like?' Karen asked.

'I'd only known her a couple of weeks. Alison worked for the council as the development projects officer. I had to deal with her for the shoot, to get permission to film here. She wasn't exactly popular,' Sylvie explained. 'Alison could be . . . difficult.' She air-quoted the word *difficult*. 'She was always finding fault with everything and everyone. Even when she came down to watch the first day of filming, she had an opinion on how we worked – the lighting, the dialogue, even the way Trevor and Molly presented their catchphrases to the camera. I think she thought she could do a better job herself.'

'Was there anyone in particular who held a grudge against her?'

'Where do I start? The list of people who didn't like Alison is longer than those who did.' Sylvie then rattled off a list of names: the cameraman Alison had yelled at for getting in her way; the runner whose coffee she'd emptied on the ground because it was too cold; and Sylvie herself, with whom Alison had had countless arguments about filming times and access to certain areas of the dig site. The list went on and on.

Sylvie sighed. 'I know I shouldn't speak ill of the dead, but she wasn't a particularly pleasant woman. She treated people badly. And, well, she just made everything more difficult than it needed to be.'

'So, what do you think happened?'

'I think she probably pushed someone a bit too far, and they snapped. She had a run-in with Benjamin Price, the farmer who owns these fields. We thought everything was fine because Alison had told us she'd sorted all the necessary permissions. But a few days ago, the farmer turned up, gun in hand, shouting the odds, telling everyone he was going to blast Alison to kingdom come when he next saw her.'

'So, he threatened Alison?'

'Well, he was shouting threats all right, but Alison wasn't here at the time.' Sylvie paused and looked thoughtful. 'I'm not sure. Maybe it was all bluster. But it was pretty scary. I'm a country girl myself. I grew up around guns . . . and well, it's just not safe to wave them around like that.'

Karen nodded. 'You've been very helpful. We'll be having a word with Mr Price.'

Sylvie pointed to a collection of farm buildings. They were just visible in the distance, two fields over. There were no lights on. 'He lives over there, I think. Turned up with his dogs, too – snarling and snapping at everyone. Not the dogs' fault. They'd obviously picked up on his bad energy.'

Karen was glad she'd taken the time to talk to Sylvie. The farmer was definitely a person of interest.

'I'd like to speak to everyone involved with the dig,' Karen said. 'I know it's late, and they'll be in bed now, so perhaps tomorrow morning, first thing?'

Sylvie nodded. 'We're due on site at seven a.m.'

'The site will be off-limits until the SOCOs are done with the scene. Can you let them know not to come to the site tomorrow morning? We'll set up a temporary incident room locally and talk to them there.' Karen paused for a moment before adding, 'And please, don't mention the victim's identity to anyone just yet. We need to inform the family first.'

'Of course,' Sylvie replied.

'I'll text you the incident room location tomorrow morning if you give me your mobile number.'

Sylvie recited her number for Karen, then asked, 'Any idea how long this sort of thing normally takes?'

'It's difficult to say, but the crime scene officers are going to need to thoroughly examine the area. My guess is that it will be at least a couple of days.'

Sylvie looked disappointed but nodded. 'You have to do your job. It's a shame for the show, but I do understand this takes priority.'

Karen glanced at her watch. It was very late. 'How did you hear about what happened here tonight?'

'I'm staying at the Cross Keys pub just down the road, with some of the crew,' Sylvie explained. 'The others had already gone up to bed, but I'm a bit of an insomniac, so I was working on some paperwork in the lounge bar area, and the landlord mentioned there was some sort of commotion going on in the field. I wasn't sure of the details – I just knew that the police had turned up. It's all over the local social media groups.'

Karen wasn't surprised. There was bound to be plenty of chatter and speculation swirling around an event like this. News travelled fast in small villages. The local residents were probably already speculating about what had happened. Once the press got wind of a murder in their sleepy backwater, things would really heat up.

34

'Well, I appreciate you letting me know about the situation with Mr Price,' Karen said. 'Here's my card. Give me a call if you think of anything else that might be relevant.'

Sylvie took the card and glanced at it. 'Of course. And please let me know when you have an update on how long the site might be closed off.'

'Will do,' Karen replied, already mentally compiling a list of tasks for the next day. Interviewing the dig team was now a priority, as was paying the farmer a visit.

The crunch of tyres on the gravel lane caught Karen's attention, and she turned to see a car pulling up by the gate. DC Rick Cooper got out of the car and gave his details to the uniformed officer, who waved him through.

Karen and Sylvie made their way across the muddy field towards him.

'Evening, Sarge,' Rick called out, his voice muffled slightly by the scarf wrapped around his neck. 'What can I do to help?'

Normally Karen would have quickly filled him in, but she didn't want to reveal too many details in front of Sylvie. Instead, she introduced Rick to Sylvie, then said, 'Miss Broadbent is staying at the Cross Keys pub, can you take her back there? We can't have people wandering around the scene.' She shot a meaningful glance towards the television producer, making it clear this wasn't a request.

As they all turned to head back towards the gate and Rick's car, the sudden sweep of headlights across the field made them squint.

The vehicle looked vaguely familiar, and Karen's heart sank as Cindy Connor emerged, a photographer close behind her.

Great. Just what they didn't need – the press.

How had Cindy got wind of this so quickly?

Sylvie had said the news was already all over the local social media groups. Did Cindy stay up all night scrolling through the village gossip forums for potential stories? Or had someone tipped her off?

'Detective Hart,' Cindy said as she rushed over. 'I heard there's been an incident. A murder? Can you confirm the victim's identity?'

Karen tensed, her jaw tightening. Cindy Connor was like a dog with a bone once she got the scent of a story. Karen could already see the gears turning in the reporter's mind, sizing up potential angles and sound bites.

Sylvie opened her mouth, no doubt about to give Cindy the details she wanted, but Karen fixed her with a stern look. 'Under no circumstances are you to speak to the press.'

Cindy's eyes narrowed. Every strand of her perfectly styled blonde hair was still, despite the breeze. 'The public has a right to know what's going on here, Detective. They deserve the truth.'

Karen felt the familiar spark of irritation she always experienced when dealing with the media's insatiable hunger for information. Cindy and her ilk didn't care about the truth. They cared about clicks and copies sold. 'You'll get your information once we've notified the next of kin. Have some respect.'

Cindy glared at Karen. 'I'm just doing my job.'

'And I'm doing mine. I'd prefer to do it without a media circus getting in the way.' Karen knew Cindy wouldn't back off easily, but she wasn't about to let the pushy reporter compromise the case.

'So you're not going to tell me anything?'

'There'll be a press release.'

'When?'

'When we're ready.'

Cindy huffed, and the photographer started taking shots, the invasive telescopic lens focused on the flood-lit crime scene.

'Can you not just wait?'

'No,' Cindy said simply. 'It's a story.'

'No, it's a *crime*, one that has taken a human life.'

Karen watched as the photographer continued to snap away and Cindy began to type on her phone. They were vultures. How could they have so little respect for a woman who had just lost her life? They were using that zoom lens to capture every grisly detail they could. It was a violation, stripping away any last shred of dignity Alison Poulson had left.

DCI Churchill would be outraged if news about the shrew's fiddle got out before they were ready. He was meticulous about public image. And Cindy would delight in making them look bad.

Rick seemed to sense her frustration and placed a hand on her shoulder. Karen took a deep breath. They were on public property. Cindy and the photographer weren't breaking any laws. She had to let this go.

'Under no circumstances are you to let them through that gate,' Karen said to the uniformed officer.

'Right you are,' he said, standing a little straighter and looking less morose. He seemed glad to be doing something useful.

He firmly waved Cindy and her photographer back a few feet from the boundary line, putting some much needed distance between them and the crime scene. Cindy started to protest, but was abruptly silenced as one of her impractically high heels sank into a deep muddy puddle.

She let out a little yelp of disgust, and the grimace that twisted her perfectly made-up face was almost comical.

Cindy gingerly lifted her muck-covered foot.

It might have been childish, but Karen found it satisfying to witness Cindy getting a taste of the indignity she often inflicted on others.

After Rick and Sylvie had left, Karen walked along the lane to her own car. Her eyes were drawn to the distant farm buildings. The darkness seemed to cling to Benjamin Price's property. The disgruntled farmer was their first potential suspect. His threatening behaviour was a big red flag. One of the team would need to pay Mr Price a visit.

Chapter Three

The drive to Scothern in the morning took Karen along quiet roads. The streetlights faded away, and the blackness seemed to close in as she drove through villages where every house was still – the curtains shut and windows dark.

It was nearly six a.m. when she turned on to Sudbrooke Road. Her headlights cut through the fog that had descended over the fields surrounding the village, making the countryside appear eerie and ghost-like. She drove past a copse of trees, their thin branches jagged and already shedding orange leaves.

Karen felt her eyelids drooping and she yawned. Lack of sleep was catching up with her.

She followed the satnav's navigation, proceeding on to Church Street and then turning into Vicarage Lane at the junction next to the church and graveyard.

Officers had tried to deliver the death message to Alison's husband, but they hadn't been able to get an answer when they called at the Poulson residence in the early hours of the morning. Karen hoped she'd catch David Poulson now, before he went to work.

Before getting out of the car, Karen steeled herself for what lay ahead. She had delivered this kind of tragic news to families many times before, and been on the receiving end after the deaths of her husband and daughter. But it never got any easier. She took a deep breath, then stepped out into the chilly, pre-dawn air.

It was a pretty area, filled with detached homes and small, neat gardens. The house opposite had been decorated for Halloween. A large pumpkin sat by the front door, spiders' webs had been drawn in white on the windows, and a floppy inflatable ghost slouched in the middle of the front lawn.

Karen glanced up at the Poulsons' house, which was similar in style to the others along the lane. Red-brick construction, two storeys, bay windows on either side of a red door. The curtains were drawn.

After another steadying breath, Karen walked up the short path, past the blue Subaru parked on the driveway, and rang the doorbell. The faint chime echoed inside the house. She saw a light come on through the frosted glass pane above the door number. After a moment, she made out the silhouette of a man approaching.

The door opened, revealing a tired-looking man with thinning dark brown hair and a thick, untrimmed beard. His eyes were bloodshot, and his skin was pale. He was dressed and looked ready for the day. Clearly, she hadn't woken him up.

His clothes were clean. No mud. No blood.

'Mr David Poulson?' Karen asked.

He nodded slowly. 'Who are you?'

'Detective Sergeant Hart of the Lincolnshire Police,' Karen explained, showing her ID. 'I'm very sorry to disturb you this early. May I come in? I'm afraid I have some difficult news.'

David stared at her, a flicker of fear passing over his face. 'The police? Has something happened?'

'Why don't we discuss this inside, sir?' Karen said gently.

David stepped aside to let her enter. She followed him down a short hallway lined with bright prints of flowers and into a small living room.

'Have a seat.' He gestured to a teal velvet sofa. Karen sat down while he took the armchair, leaning forward with his elbows on his knees. 'What's happened? Is it Alison?'

'Mr Poulson, I regret to inform you that Alison's body was discovered last night in a field near Stow. I'm very sorry for your loss.'

David stared at her, the colour draining from his already pale face. 'What? No, that . . . that can't be right. *Alison?*' He put a hand over his mouth as the reality sunk in, his eyes filling with tears.

Karen remained quiet, letting him have a moment to grapple with the devastating news. She knew the shock and horror he must be experiencing. She waited as he dropped his head into his hands and began to cry.

After some time, David lifted his head, wiping his eyes on the sleeve of his shirt. 'I don't understand,' he managed eventually. 'What happened?'

Karen hesitated, uncertain how much to reveal right now. She didn't want to overwhelm David with the horrific details just yet.

'We're still investigating the circumstances,' she replied carefully. 'We're treating her death as suspicious at this time.'

'Suspicious?' David's eyes widened. 'You mean she was murdered . . .'

'We'll do everything in our power to find out what happened to your wife,' Karen assured him. 'Right now, my colleagues are gathering information. I'll need to ask you some questions, too.'

He nodded, his shoulders slumping. 'Anything you need.'

'Can you tell me where Alison worked?'

'At the council. She's worked there for years. Started straight out of school, then got promotion after promotion. She's quite high up . . . I mean, she *was* quite high up.' David shook his head, his eyes welling up again.

'I know this is difficult. I'm sorry I have to ask these questions now, but it is important.'

He sniffed and nodded.

'Did Alison mention any problems or issues at work lately?' Karen asked. 'Any disputes or altercations with anyone?'

'No.' David's voice wavered as he struggled to keep his emotions under control. 'She was happy there. She was always friendly with her co-workers. Never had any problem with them. But you'd have to check with them to be sure.'

'Thank you. We will. Were there any changes in her behaviour lately? Any signs of trouble?'

'She seemed like her usual self. She was always busy, always rushing here and there, but that was normal. Alison has been under a lot of pressure at work lately.'

'Did Alison travel for work at all? Maybe for meetings or conferences?'

'Not often. Only when she had to.'

'Recently?'

'No.'

'What about personal relationships?'

Karen noted David's brief hesitation and the way his gaze darted to the window before returning to her.

'No problems that I know of,' he finally replied. 'Like I said, she seemed fine. Busy, but nothing unusual about that.'

Karen watched him closely. His eyes flickered with something that might have been anxiety or panic. She noted his nervous fidgeting, the tension in his jaw, and the way he avoided eye contact. She wasn't certain, but she had a strong sense that David wasn't telling her everything he knew. She decided to push a little harder.

'Officers came by the house earlier, but you weren't home?'

David rubbed the back of his neck, clearly struggling to collect himself. 'Oh, right. I, uh . . . I work a night shift now. At a warehouse. I lost my IT consultancy job a few months ago, so I've been doing night shifts to make ends meet.' He gave a hollow laugh. 'Finally get some work, and now this . . .' He trailed off.

'The car on the driveway . . . is that yours?'

'The Subaru?' David nodded. 'Yes, it's mine.'

'And your wife's car? Where's that?'

'I don't know,' he said. 'I assumed she went to work early.'

'Did she often go to work before you got back from your night shift?'

'Not often, no. But sometimes, if there was a big project or deadline, she would get up early and leave before I got home.' He sniffed and rubbed his nose. 'It's not that unusual for her to leave early, so I didn't think anything of it.'

They needed to find Alison's car. Karen made a mental note to prioritise that. She would also need to check if David had access to any other vehicles.

'What car does your wife drive? Do you have the registration?'

David nodded again. 'She drives a white Mercedes C-Class.' He reeled off the registration number. 'Why?'

'We'd like to locate it.'

A Mercedes C-Class wasn't the ideal car for driving across muddy fields. It was possible the killer had used Alison's car to transport her body to the excavation site, but it wouldn't have been the most efficient option and would indicate a lack of planning.

'Do you or your wife own any other vehicles, Mr Poulson?'

'No, just the Subaru and the Mercedes.'

Karen tried to keep an open mind. He seemed genuinely upset. Perhaps the body language she was picking up on was down to grief. She gave him another moment before asking gently, 'Mr Poulson, did you know Alison was involved with the archaeology site near Stow?'

'Archaeology?' David echoed, clearly confused. 'No, she never mentioned anything about it. Why do you ask?'

'We found her body near the excavation.'

He shook his head, looking more bewildered by the minute. 'She didn't tell me about it. Her assistant, Lucas, might be able to tell you more.'

Karen found it odd that Alison hadn't spoken to her husband about the archaeology site, especially since the TV producer – Sylvie – had implied Alison had spent a considerable amount of time there. It made Karen wonder if the couple were even on speaking terms.

David got up and walked to a chest of drawers set into a recess in the opposite wall, opening a drawer to rummage around inside. He pulled out a stack of small cards and handed one to Karen.

It was Alison's business card. Karen took a moment to study it. *Alison Poulson. Director of Operations for Sustainable Development.* The lettering was embossed gold, in curly script. Her office address was listed, and a phone number and email for her assistant, Lucas Black, was underneath.

David sat down and rubbed a hand over his jaw, glancing around the room as if seeking comfort among the cluttered shelves and photos.

His gaze then drifted past Karen to the window. She turned to see what had caught his attention, but there was nothing out of the ordinary. The driveway lay empty save for the Subaru, and her car was parked on the road. The house opposite, with its Halloween decorations, seemed just as it had been when she'd arrived. She refocused on David Poulson. His face was etched with grief, but there was something else in his eyes. Fear? Guilt? It was hard to tell.

'Mr Poulson, I'm sorry to ask this now, but it's important we establish where you were last night,' Karen said gently. 'Can you account for your whereabouts between nine and eleven p.m.?'

David's Adam's apple bobbed as he swallowed hard. 'I told you . . . I was at work. I start my shift at nine p.m., so I left here around eight thirty.'

'Do you have any colleagues who can corroborate that?' she asked gently, trying not to pressure him too much.

'You sound like you're asking for an alibi.'

'I have to ask. It's just procedure.'

His jaw tightened, and Karen thought he might refuse to cooperate, but eventually he said, 'Yes, the warehouse has cameras, and my shift supervisor can vouch for me.' He reached for his phone and scrolled through his contacts.

A heavy silence fell between them as David found the contact details. His fingers trembled slightly on the screen of his phone. 'Here,' he said after what felt like ages. The slight edge in his voice was new, likely fuelled by resentment at being viewed as a potential suspect so soon after losing his wife.

His knuckles turned white as he gripped the arm of the chair tightly. Though understandable given the circumstances, his defensive behaviour only made Karen more suspicious.

After giving her the number of his shift supervisor, David cleared his throat. 'My relationship with my wife has been strained for a while. I should tell you now before someone else does.'

Karen kept quiet and waited for him to continue.

'Money troubles didn't help. I lost my job and got behind on bills. Alison had to pick up the slack. We kept separate bank accounts, you see. She was always the strong one. The successful one.' His voice caught, and he looked out of the window again. 'She deserved more than I could give her. She was doing great, getting promoted and winning awards. I felt like I was dragging her down.' David wiped his eyes, overcome with emotion again.

Karen stayed silent, letting him take his time. She glanced at a family photo on the wall – the Poulsons smiling on holiday. Alison looked tanned and relaxed, in a sundress and floppy hat.

'I think we were turning a corner, though,' David said. 'Alison had been happier lately. She had been trying to finish work earlier, taking fewer calls in the evenings. I think we were finally putting our problems behind us.' Tears ran down his face again. 'And now this . . .'

'Can I get you some water, or a cup of tea?' Karen asked.

But David waved her away. 'Something stronger is what I need right now.' He went to a cabinet and poured a large measure of whiskey into a short glass. After a long swallow, some colour returned to his cheeks. 'I don't usually drink at this time. But it's the shock.' He sat back in his chair and closed his eyes briefly.

'Is there anybody you'd like me to call? Someone who could come and keep you company?'

'No, thank you. I'll be fine.'

Karen wasn't so sure, but she let it go. It was a fine line to walk. He was a suspect, but she had to be sensitive to his bereavement.

'What happens now?'

'A family liaison officer will be in touch later today. They'll be able to answer any questions you have and keep you updated on the police investigation. In the meantime, we'll try to find out what happened last night. We would also like you to formally identify Alison later today, if you feel up to it.'

David nodded, his eyes distant.

After a few words of condolence, Karen stood and gave David her card in case he remembered anything that might help the investigation.

'Please don't hesitate to call me or my colleagues if you think of anything else. We'll do our best to get some answers for you.'

45

They walked out of the living room and into the hall. David opened the front door.

Karen noticed him again glancing over her shoulder, his eyes narrowed with hostility. She turned to see who had caught his attention – but there was no one there. Just the house across the street.

'Who lives there?'

'Oh, uh, I don't know,' David said with a shrug.

Karen studied his tense expression. 'You don't know your neighbours?'

'Not really. Just to nod hello to.'

'It's just you keep looking over at that house.'

David blinked in surprise. 'Do I? Must be a nervous habit then – no reason for it.'

'Did they know Alison?'

'No,' he replied quickly. Maybe a little too quickly.

She was sure there was something David didn't want her to know. Possibly something about his neighbours.

Karen thought about pushing for more information, but she decided against it. She didn't want to labour the point, especially after delivering such devasting news.

'I just can't believe she's . . . gone.'

'I'm so sorry, Mr Poulson.'

David nodded numbly as Karen zipped up her jacket. His face was pale again and grief-stricken.

Karen felt a rush of pity for him, even as questions swirled in her mind. Her professional instincts forced her to entertain the unsettling possibility that David himself could have murdered Alison. The gruesome nature of the shrew's fiddle found around Alison's neck suggested a killer consumed by raw hatred, driven by a desire to degrade and torture – could David really have harboured that much rage towards his wife?

Karen studied his face. Tears still glistened on his cheeks. The niggling instinct at the back of her mind told her that David Poulson was concealing something, but she found it hard to imagine this man inflicting such sadistic horror on his wife.

Karen's gut told her David was unlikely to be the man behind such a murder, but she knew better than to fully trust her first impressions.

But now wasn't the time for an interrogation. She stepped out into the still morning air, glancing back briefly to see David standing forlornly in the doorway. Then she walked back to her car.

David Poulson's explanation for why he hadn't reported his wife missing and hadn't been at home when the officers came to report her death earlier was satisfactory. They'd need to speak with his shift supervisor and check his alibi, but her instincts told her David was telling the truth about being at work last night. But she couldn't shake the sense that David had been holding something back.

She made a mental note to look into the Poulsons' neighbours back at the station. David had kept looking at the home opposite for some reason, despite his claims otherwise. She didn't buy the 'nervous habit' explanation at all. There had to be a connection he wasn't disclosing, and it was her job to find out what that was.

Chapter Four

A chill mist hung low over the Nettleham police station car park as the early morning sun battled to pierce through. Karen shivered as she got out of the car. Her eyes felt gritty and sore, as they always did when she hadn't got enough sleep.

Across the tarmac, she spotted DS Arnie Hodgson's old Vauxhall grinding to a halt in its usual spot. The car was as unkempt as its owner – rust nibbling at the edges, paint peeling in patches.

'Morning, Arnie,' she said as he opened the driver's door.

Arnie grunted in response, extracting himself from his vehicle with all the grace of a man twice his age. 'I heard about the body found at the archaeology dig site,' he said, slamming the car door. 'DCI Churchill's probably chuffed to bits.'

Karen raised an eyebrow. 'Oh? Why do you say that?'

'There's a TV show about that dig.' There was a touch of humour in his gruff voice. 'Churchill might get his mug on telly.'

Karen groaned; Churchill preening for the cameras was a sight she'd rather not see.

As they approached the station entrance, DC Rick Cooper limped into view. His dark hair was neatly styled, but his face was tense with pain. 'Morning, Karen, Arnie.'

'What's up with you?' Arnie asked, coming to a stop beside him.

'It happened during my cardio workout this morning. I did a full circuit session followed by a run.' Rick grimaced, flexing his foot.

Arnie shook his head, lips pursed in disapproval. 'I told you, lad – too much exercise is a bad thing. Jogging's bad for your health.'

'That's not true.' Rick leaned against the wall and gingerly tested his weight on his foot. 'It's good for you.'

Arnie snorted. 'Looks like it.'

'It's just a temporary setback.'

'Good for you, my backside. It's murder on your joints. I've seen it time and time again. People start running and end up with all sorts of injuries.' He reeled off some statistics: 'One in four runners gets injured every year. Half of those injuries are to the knees. And a quarter of them are serious enough to require medical attention.'

Rick looked at Karen, his expression a mixture of surprise and disbelief. 'You're making that up! Is it true, Sarge?'

Karen shrugged. Knowing Arnie, he'd just made the statistics up on the spot. 'I don't know. Running injuries aren't really my area. Walking is enough for me.'

'Walking is the sensible, safe option,' Arnie said, then he seized the opportunity to list some other common runner's injuries.

'You should think about taking up jogging,' Rick said, looking pointedly at Arnie's stomach. 'Might do you some good. You need to look after your body at your age.'

Arnie snorted, patting his generous belly. 'This body is a temple. I take good care of it.'

Rick raised an eyebrow. 'Really? And what's your idea of self-care?'

'Buying myself a sausage sandwich from the canteen.' Arnie grinned. 'Which I'll be doing after this morning's briefing.'

As Rick crouched down to loosen his laces, Karen leaned in closer to Arnie and whispered, 'You're trying to scare him.'

Arnie grinned wickedly in response before continuing with his list of exercise-related injuries: stretched ligaments, torn muscles . . . The list went on and on until Rick finally interrupted him. 'All right, all right. I'll take it easy for a bit.'

Arnie nodded sagely as the three of them walked into the station. 'That's the spirit. Now, let me tell you about this bloke I knew who used to run marathons and had a very unfortunate accident . . .'

The briefing room was already close to full when Karen, Arnie and Rick entered. At the front of the room, DC Sophie Jones was deftly organising stacks of notes. Her movements were quick and precise. There was none of the hesitance or fumbling that had plagued her in the months since her injury.

Karen scanned the room, noting the tense energy that charged the air. Her gaze settled on DCI Churchill, who stood at a raised desk at the front of the room, his arms crossed as he studied the large screen mounted on the wall behind him.

Karen slid into an empty seat beside DI Scott Morgan.

His sharp eyes flicked to meet hers briefly before returning to the paperwork in front of him. 'Sounds like you had a busy night.'

'I did. An interesting one. I think we already have some strong leads.'

Before she could tell Morgan more, Churchill clapped his hands together. 'All right, listen up.'

The chatter died down immediately. 'Thanks to DC Jones's thorough organisation of the briefing notes, we have plenty to go over this morning.'

Sophie gave a small smile at the praise.

Churchill launched into the briefing, outlining the grim details of Alison Poulson's murder. Some of the crime scene photos were included in the briefing notes and projected on the screen. The images of Alison were graphic, some of them close-up shots of the shrew's fiddle tightly gripping her throat, the torture device biting cruelly into the skin. Her face was white and frozen in a blank expression, eyes open and mouth agape.

The photos of the torture device turned Karen's stomach. The more Karen learned about the shrew's fiddle, the more disturbed she became. She'd discovered that there were replicas available for purchase online, marketed as novelty items for historical re-enactments or BDSM enthusiasts. She wondered if the person who had killed Alison had bought one of these replicas to use on her, indicating that this was a premeditated murder. It was a chilling thought.

Karen had seen many crime scenes over the years, but the brutality of what had been done to this woman's body still shocked her. Around the table, she noticed similar looks of disgust and sadness on her colleagues' faces. They were all professionals, but no one could remain unaffected by the images.

Churchill's voice was as crisp and businesslike as ever as he continued providing details on the investigation so far, but Karen detected a subtle undercurrent of anger in his tone. He was as upset by this crime as the rest of them.

He then moved on to the preliminary crime scene report and pathologist's notes, but Karen was already familiar with the details. She stifled a yawn, the long night beginning to catch up with her. She straightened in her seat as Churchill's gaze settled on her.

'Now,' Churchill said, 'DS Hart has arranged for us to set up an incident room at the village hall in Sturton by Stow, near the dig site.' He gave her an approving nod. 'Let's divide up tasks. DS Hodgson and DS Hart, you two can handle the archaeologists and dig volunteers' interviews.' Churchill paused. 'On second thoughts, let's make that DS Hodgson and DI Morgan.'

'I'm happy to do the interviews. I'm not too tired to help,' Karen said, even as images of Alison Poulson's body in the muddy trench flashed through her mind. She could still picture every agonising detail with haunting clarity. The victim's contorted face and the vicious bite of the shrew's fiddle embedded in her flesh.

This case had already struck a nerve. But she wouldn't let it show – she had to stay focused and professional. Alison's life had ended in unimaginable torment and pain. She deserved justice, and Karen was going to make sure she got it.

Churchill eyed Karen doubtfully. 'If you're certain . . .'

'I am, sir.'

'Right. DS Hart, you're with DS Hodgson then. And DC Cooper and DI Morgan, you can speak with the victim's colleagues at the council offices. And . . .' Churchill nonchalantly rearranged some papers on the desk in front of him and then straightened his tie. 'You've already spoken to the television producer, Karen?'

Arnie caught Karen's eye and winked.

'I did. Sylvie Broadbent. She told me Alison Poulson had a difficult temperament, and mentioned she and a few others witnessed Benjamin Price, the farmer who owns the land, making threats against Alison just a few days ago, though Alison wasn't present at the time. I'd like to speak with him asap to find out more.'

Churchill nodded. 'It's essential we follow up on that – but only after the interviews with the archaeologists on site, the TV crew and Alison's co-workers.'

'It might be worth prioritising the farmer,' Karen suggested. 'He made threats while waving a shotgun and certainly sounds like he has a short fuse.'

Churchill looked thoughtful.

'I'll go,' Sophie offered. 'I can handle it. It's about time I got back out there.'

Churchill's gaze moved to Sophie. 'DC Jones, I know you're eager to get more involved, but let's not rush things. I want you here at the station coordinating interviews and running background for now.'

Sophie's jaw tightened, but she nodded. 'There's something else. We should consider that whoever committed this crime might kill again. Soon.'

A tense silence fell over the room as all eyes turned to Sophie. Karen noted the young detective's hands trembling slightly before she hid them out of sight under the table.

'What leads you to that conclusion, DC Jones?' Churchill asked, his tone sceptical.

'The shrew's fiddle, sir. It's not a common item, so it's likely been carefully selected by the killer.'

'It could be an old object found at the dig site. Maybe the killer took advantage of what was to hand,' Morgan suggested.

'It's not only that,' Sophie said. 'It's the staging of the body, so Alison would be discovered with the device. There's a theatricality to it . . .'

Sophie could be right . . . Karen hated the thought of another victim enduring what Alison Poulson had gone through.

Sophie had a fascination with serial killers, studying their psychology and methods with an intensity that sometimes unnerved her colleagues. If she believed they were dealing with a murderer who might kill more than once, Karen was inclined to take her seriously.

Sophie continued, 'The fact the device was applied while Alison was still alive suggests the killer took pleasure in Alison's suffering. It feels like this murderer will do this again.'

Karen's heart sank at Sophie's choice of words, because talking about a feeling was a sure way to make Churchill and Morgan reject a theory. She had learned that the hard way. She trusted her gut and believed that intuition about a suspect or crime could be invaluable. But Morgan was all about cold, hard facts, and Churchill was nearly as dismissive. Hunches and feelings held no weight for either of them.

But to Karen, Sophie's theory sounded scarily plausible. *Probable*, even.

'Let's not get ahead of ourselves,' Arnie cautioned. 'We don't have any evidence yet to suggest this is anything more than an isolated incident.'

'But we can't rule it out,' Karen said. 'It's a valid point. The killer went to great lengths to get our attention with Alison's murder. That kind of sadism and provocative staging could indicate a worrying pattern of behaviour.'

Sophie shot Karen a grateful look, then said, 'It's just an idea we should consider.'

Churchill held up a hand. 'Noted. We'll keep the possibility in mind as we move forward with the investigation. But let's focus on the facts we have in front of us for now.'

Sophie nodded, eyes on her notes. Before the attack, she would have pushed the point harder, perhaps even taking matters into her own hands and doing some research on the side, but now she accepted Churchill's decision with a nod.

They could be making a mistake by not pursuing Sophie's theory more aggressively. The thought of another innocent person falling victim to this killer was horrifying. They couldn't afford to be wrong about this.

'I understand your concern, DC Jones,' Churchill said, his tone softening. 'But we need to proceed carefully. We can't let speculation drive our investigation. We have no evidence we are dealing with anything more than a single murder. Have any similar previous cases been discovered?'

'No, I did check, but nothing suggests this perpetrator has killed before – at least not in the same way.'

'Well, that's reassuring. And good initiative on your part. But let's focus on the murder we have on our plates right now.'

Sophie looked like she wanted to argue further but fell silent.

Karen watched their exchange, feeling a mixture of relief and concern. She was glad Churchill had said no to Sophie dealing with Benjamin Price. Sophie was capable, and determination had always been one of her strengths. But Karen did not like the idea of Sophie questioning Price, who sounded like a very violent man.

When Sophie had been attacked so viciously almost a year ago, the young detective had been out trying to investigate a lead on her own – a serious mistake that had almost cost her life. Alone and unarmed, Sophie had been assaulted with an iron bar outside a workshop in a deserted area of Lincoln. The assailant had left her for dead.

In the days and weeks that followed, Karen and the rest of the team had tried desperately to catch the person responsible. It had been an awful time. And the image of Sophie barely clinging to life in an ICU bed with a fractured skull still haunted Karen.

It was a miracle she'd survived.

Sophie's recovery had been slow – both physically and mentally. The attack had taken a toll on her, leaving her depressed and fragile. Even now, as she insisted on returning to full duties, Karen worried that it might be too soon. She knew that Sophie was eager to get back to work, but the emotional scars from the assault ran deeper than the physical ones.

'Now, the husband . . .' Churchill prompted, noticing Karen was distracted.

'Right, David Poulson,' Karen said, focusing on her notes. 'He seemed genuinely shocked and upset when I told him about his wife's death. But there were a few things that felt off. He admitted they hadn't been getting on lately and that he felt he'd been dragging her down after he lost his job. He also kept glancing out his window at the house opposite. I looked into the neighbours, but nothing stood out. Still, there's something there, something he was hiding. I'm not sure if it has anything to do with Alison's murder though.'

Churchill nodded thoughtfully. 'Perhaps a chat with the neighbours is in order at some point. But for now, let's focus on the interviews with the people working on the dig site, and with the victim's colleagues. We need more basic information before we start to go off on tangents.'

Karen nodded and didn't push the point further. 'I've no solid evidence anyway. It was instinct more than anything else – just the way he kept looking at that neighbour's house.'

Arnie spoke up. 'Instinct can be a copper's best tool. Important not to ignore it.'

'When we're questioning people, should we mention the shrew's fiddle or how we think she died?' Rick asked. 'Or should we keep that quiet?'

'Be nice if we could stop the press from getting wind of it,' Arnie said.

'I'll leave it to your discretion,' Churchill said. 'Ideally, I'd want to keep it out of the press – we don't want the public to panic. But we need to know more about this device and where it came from, so I think we at least need to tell the archaeology group what we've found. We'll need their input.'

Karen agreed. Public panic would only make the situation worse. But the archaeology group's expertise would be important in working out where the device had come from. She hesitated for a moment before speaking up, because she knew Churchill wouldn't really want to hear this. 'Sir, there's a slight chance the press might already know about the shrew's fiddle.'

Churchill frowned. 'How?'

Karen didn't think they could have got a clear picture of the victim or the shrew's fiddle, but she felt compelled to warn Churchill just in case. She'd seen photographers go to great lengths to get the perfect shot of a crime scene before, like climbing on top of their cars or even scaling trees. 'Cindy Connor was at the crime scene along with her photographer. They didn't get beyond the tape, but the photographer had a camera with a pretty powerful zoom lens.'

His jaw clenched. 'Why didn't you clear them out of there immediately?'

'We made sure they didn't enter the field, but there wasn't much else we could do. We couldn't stop them from taking pictures from a distance.'

'Their behaviour doesn't surprise me. Always looking for a sensational story.' Churchill paused for a moment. 'If they got a clear shot of the shrew's fiddle, it could complicate things. We'll have to be prepared for the possibility of leaks and speculation.'

'The victim was in a deep trench and was placed in a body bag before being lifted out. Even with their fancy camera lens, it's unlikely they would have managed to get a picture of the shrew's fiddle. Unless they managed to get a high vantage point in the vicinity. But I didn't see them climbing any trees.'

Churchill looked slightly relieved. 'Let's hope so. Still, we need to be cautious. The last thing we need is the media running wild with this.'

As the meeting ended and everyone started filing out of the room to start their assigned tasks, Karen shuffled her notes into a pile.

Morgan snapped his laptop shut and rose from his seat beside Karen. He had been quietly tapping away during the briefing, and Karen had a feeling he'd been looking into something.

'Have you got a minute?' Morgan asked Churchill as he walked by.

Churchill stopped and waited.

'I've dealt with Benjamin Price before,' Morgan said, his voice low and serious. 'I thought I recognised the name. A few months back, a couple of young lads were poaching on his land. Price caught them and chased them with a shotgun. He's definitely got a temper. Gave them a right scare. He's hot-headed. It wouldn't take much to set him off.'

'But the shrew's fiddle around Alison's neck . . . that sends a very personal message,' Karen said. 'The way she was left, locked in that contraption . . . it was a death designed to punish her.'

Churchill considered Karen's words. 'Price *was* heard making threats against the victim.'

'I agree we should still talk to him,' Karen said. 'But this wasn't just a crime of sudden anger. The use of that medieval torture device suggests someone whose hatred has been festering for a long time.' She shook her head slowly. 'It doesn't fit with what we know of Price's hot-headed temper. It points to something much darker – a deeply ingrained resentment that has been building over years. Do you really think that sounds like Price?'

'Maybe not,' Morgan said. 'This is a particularly gruesome crime. But there's a chance Price would be savvy enough to try to cover his tracks, maybe using the shrew's fiddle to confuse the investigation. Perhaps he wants us to be looking for a killer with a completely different motivation, so we won't look too closely at him.'

Karen had to admit there was logic to Morgan's theory.

'All right, you both make fair points,' Churchill said. 'Let's prioritise speaking to Price based on the threats he made.'

Karen nodded. 'I agree.'

Churchill turned to Morgan. 'If only we had someone who could speak to Price . . . someone who's had dealings with him before, perhaps.'

Morgan's eyebrows rose. 'You want me to speak with him?'

Churchill smiled. 'How nice of you to volunteer.'

Chapter Five

Sophie sat at her desk rummaging through the bottom drawer, which contained some of her books on serial killers. She selected a hardback titled *Chaotic Minds: Inside the Psyche of Serial Killers* by Dr Ash Stoughton.

Sophie knew she had struggled to put her point across properly during the briefing. She'd wanted to make the team see they were dealing with a perpetrator who'd had a taste of killing and torturing, and would likely yearn for another hit. She'd known what she *wanted* to say – and was sure she was right – but for some reason, her words had lacked conviction. And then her hands had started to shake.

She didn't think anyone had noticed. Except Karen.

Karen always noticed.

When Sophie had been recuperating, Karen had been there for her. She'd even put up with Sophie's outbursts when Sophie had taken out her frustrations on her during the lowest moments. Karen had made it clear she was concerned Sophie had come back to work too soon, but Sophie was determined to prove that she could handle it.

Karen stopped by Sophie's desk. 'Are you okay?'

Sophie forced a bright smile. 'I'm fine, just wanted to check something.' She held up the book. 'Trying to get a better understanding of this killer.'

Karen nodded, her eyes scanning the title. 'I don't want you to be right about the killer striking again, but I think you might be.'

Sophie opened the book and began reading aloud from a chapter titled 'The Misogynistic Murderer: A Chilling Exploration of Hate-Driven Murder'.

> *In many cases, serial killers who target women are men who harbour a deep hatred for the opposite sex. These killers view their victims as objects beneath them, to be controlled and destroyed.*
>
> *The crimes are often characterised by extreme cruelty and the use of torture. They may employ methods to prolong their victim's suffering, deriving pleasure from inflicting pain. The use of restraints or drugs are common as it allows the killer to exert complete control over their victim.*
>
> *It is important to note that this type of perpetrator is rarely satisfied with one victim. Their hatred and need for control are insatiable, driving them to seek out new targets. They may have long rest periods between kills, but the urge to torment and destroy eventually resurfaces, leading them to strike again.*

Karen was quiet for a moment, letting the words sink in. 'Do you think that description fits the killer?'

'I really do.'

'Then we need to catch whoever did this before they target someone else.'

Sophie closed the book. The brutal nature of the crime, the use of the shrew's fiddle, and the evident enjoyment the killer had taken in their victim's suffering all pointed to someone who would likely kill again. She just hoped they were caught before they got the chance.

Christie sits on the sofa, restless and nervous, unable to sleep despite being up nearly all night. Her fleece pyjamas are soft and cosy, but she feels brittle and cold. She hasn't wanted to close her eyes again after a nightmare woke her at two a.m.

She stares out at the grey autumn morning, the trees stripped of leaves, the driveway wet from last night's rain.

When she hears a floorboard creak behind her, she nearly jumps out of her skin. She clutches the arm of the sofa. But it's just her mum, standing in the doorway with a concerned look on her face.

'Couldn't sleep, love?' she asks gently.

Christie shakes her head, rubbing her eyes with her fists.

Her mum looks at her closely, and a small frown creases her forehead. 'It's still playing on your mind?'

Christie shrugs. If her mother knew she'd recognised the dead woman they found last night, she'd understand why Christie barely got a wink of sleep. If she tells the police, this could destroy her family.

But she can't tell her mum. She can't tell anyone.

Her mum sinks into the cushions beside Christie on the sofa and puts an arm around her shoulders. Christie wishes she were a little kid again so she could curl up in her mother's lap. She doesn't want to keep secrets from her.

Why did she ever agree to go out last night with Leo, Mason and Mia? This should never have happened. She should have stayed home and finished her homework. Her eyes prick with tears. Yesterday, homework was all she had to worry about, but today she is terrified one of her parents might be sent to prison.

'I know finding that body must have been horrible, darling,' her mum says gently, stroking Christie's hair.

If only that was all. An image of the woman's lifeless body flashes into Christie's mind. That horrible thing wrapped around her neck. Christie shudders at the memory. But she can't tell her mum that she knows her, that their family will be in trouble if anyone finds out.

'I had a horrible dream. I keep thinking about her . . . wondering why anyone would do that to another person.'

Her mother says gently, 'I wish I could tell you why, but I don't understand it either. There are some nasty people in this world. But you're safe here.' She touches Christie's cheek. 'I remember the first time I saw a dead body. I had trouble sleeping too.'

Her mother doesn't talk much about her work. She's a freelance journalist now. But before having Christie, she reported from war zones. She gave it all up when she fell pregnant.

Christie knows the brutal things her mother saw took a toll. She's never told Christie exactly what happened, but it was bad enough that she warned Christie to steer well clear of journalism as a career.

Bringing it up now is her way of trying to comfort her daughter, to make her feel less alone, but all Christie feels is fear twisting her insides. Their family could be torn apart, and she doesn't know how to stop that from happening.

Her mother gently clasps Christie's chin and turns her head until their gazes lock.

'It's going to be all right,' she says softly. 'I'll make us some toast. Do you want strawberry jam?'

Christie always has toast and jam when she's upset or under the weather. Usually, it's comforting, but today she's not sure she can swallow anything.

As her mother walks to the kitchen, Christie calls out hesitantly, 'Where's Dad?'

She heard him leave an hour ago. He didn't say goodbye.

'Work. He wanted an early start because he has to go down to Sturton by Stow village hall to speak with the police at some point this morning.'

Christie's heart pounds. The police. What do they know?

She scrambles to her feet and races to the kitchen. But her mum continues airily as she slots the bread in the toaster, 'Just routine questions. Your dad's not in any trouble. They're talking to everyone who's been working on the dig site. They'll want to find out who the poor woman is and inform her family, I expect.'

Christie wishes she could believe her.

As her mother continues to talk about the police investigation, Christie's stomach twists into knots. She wants to tell her mother everything, but if the truth comes out, it won't be just routine questions that the police will be asking.

Her mother is so calm. Christie wonders if she's aware of the dead woman's identity and how it implicates their family. Christie searches her mother's face for any sign of recognition or concern, but her expression remains inscrutable. Maybe she really doesn't know the identity of the woman in the trench yet.

For a fleeting moment, Christie considers confessing everything to her mother. But the words stick in her throat. No, it's better to keep quiet, to pretend she's just shaken from finding a body, nothing more.

'After you saw the dead body,' Christie says, with her back to her mother, 'how long before the bad dreams went away?'

'Not long. Sometimes I'd have a bad night when I least expected it, but you'll get through it. Tonight will be better – you'll see.'

Her mum spreads jam on the thick, warm toast, oblivious to the danger of the situation.

Christie's chest feels tight as she imagines the worst-case scenario: her family torn apart, one of her parents taken away in handcuffs. She can't bear the thought of losing them, of their lives being shattered. She has to keep this secret, no matter how much it eats away at her. She has to hope the police will never find out why Christie recognised the murdered woman.

Christie is terrified, and feels very much alone.

Word had spread that Sturton by Stow village hall had been commandeered by the police, so everyone who walked, cycled or drove past was rubbernecking, their eyes following Karen's Honda as she pulled into the car park.

After parking, she looked up at the grey October sky that threatened more rain. Then checked the time on the dashboard clock. The briefing had gone on longer than expected. They'd need to start the interviews soon.

She glanced over at DS Arnie Hodgson in the passenger seat as he stuffed the last bite of his sausage sandwich into his mouth.

'You've got a bit of grease on your shirt there,' Karen said, nodding towards the small stain on Arnie's chest.

He glanced down and grunted. 'Not to worry. I'll just do my jacket up. That will cover it.' He crumpled up the sandwich bag and shoved it in his pocket as they got out of the car.

As Arnie fumbled to close his suit jacket, the fabric strained tightly across his belly. No matter how much he yanked and tugged, the buttons refused to fasten.

He grumbled, muttering, 'Must be the new dry-cleaners. They've shrunk it!'

Karen hid a smile and said nothing as they walked towards the entrance. She'd been known to blame a tight waistband on the washing machine from time to time.

The hall was a seventies-style building at the heart of the small village, just over a mile away from the archaeology site in Stow. The windows were large and rectangular, set in the central part of the building. A section of the glass seemed to be covered with a red, translucent film, creating a bright contrast with the rest of the clear panes.

On a typical day, the hall would host festivals or parties, but today it was being used for something a lot less cheerful.

Ahead of them, officers were unloading equipment from police vans parked haphazardly by the entrance. Boxes of stationery, printers and cables were being carried inside their makeshift incident room.

Arnie held open the glass-panelled wooden door. 'Allow me,' he said politely, gesturing for Karen to go first. He shuffled in behind her, his ill-fitting jacket still gaping open.

Inside, the hall had already been divided into two sections. On one side, officers were setting up desks in rows, unpacking printers and computers. Whiteboards on stands were positioned at the back, near a large projector screen.

In the centre of the hall, a huge red curtain sectioned off a couple of tables and chairs. This would act as their interview space, although the flimsy barrier wouldn't provide much soundproofing or privacy.

Karen and Arnie weaved through the officers and made their way to a quiet corner, where they put their laptop bags on a wobbly trestle table that would be their base for a few hours at least.

A young officer was heaving a bulky coffee machine on to another table, cursing under his breath when the plug refused to reach the nearest socket. The machine would be indispensable over the next few days. Karen would have to make sure they had a decent supply of ground coffee. They were going to need it.

For now, though, it was time to get to work. They had five minutes until the first of the interviewees was due to turn up. She'd asked Sylvie Broadbent to arrange it so that the people who'd been working at the archaeology site arrived at ten-minute intervals to minimise the number of people hanging around waiting.

Karen made her way towards the whiteboards, determined to angle them so they couldn't be seen by a curious interviewee. They were currently blank, but would soon be covered with notes and photographs. Out of the corner of her eye, Karen saw Arnie head straight for the coffee machine to get a pot brewing. Some things never changed.

She was glad to have him here, she realised. Over the past couple of years, Karen had grown increasingly fond of her gruff, cynical but dependable colleague. He had a way of speaking without filters and could be rough around the edges, but Arnie brought a sense of stability to the sometimes unpredictable nature of their work. He might be bullish and messy, but he could also be kind and genuine.

Karen's phone buzzed and she glanced at the screen. An email from Churchill. Subject: *PRESS*. Her heart sank. *Please don't let this be a leak.*

She glanced at Arnie, who'd wandered back over to the desk and was pulling his laptop out of his bag. Then she opened the email, her eyes scanning the contents. It was a link to an article Cindy had written about the crime. Soon the national press would pick up on the incident and have a field day. Public interest would be intense thanks to the TV show connection.

Karen clicked the link, her stomach churning as the page loaded.

She scanned the photos, remembering the zoom lens on the photographer's camera, praying there were no shots of the shrew's fiddle or Alison's body. Churchill would have her head if those details got out. And more than that, Alison deserved dignity in death. Everyone did.

When she reached the end of the article, Karen let out a sigh of relief. No mention of the torture device; no gruesome crime scene photos. Small mercies.

But they wouldn't be able to hold back the press interest for long when news about the shrew's fiddle got out.

'Hello, hello!' a woman called out, her voice echoing around the hall. 'Am I early?'

Sylvie Broadbent swept into the hall with an air of confident elegance. Karen knew the woman was in her early fifties, but today she looked at least a decade younger. She had her hair up like last night, but now it shone under the overhead lights.

'DS Hart! There you are,' she called out as she spotted Karen near the whiteboards. She strode over, her high-heeled boots clicking on the floor. 'I'm your first interview for the day. I hope that's okay.'

'Of course. Good to see you again,' Karen replied.

Sylvie smiled. 'I've organised everyone from the site, both the TV crew and the archaeologists. They'll be turning up every ten minutes or so, just as you requested.'

'That's perfect, Sylvie,' Karen said. 'I really appreciate your help with this.'

'No problem at all. I'm glad I can be of assistance.'

Arnie, who had been engrossed in setting up his laptop, suddenly looked up.

'Arnie,' Karen said, introducing them. 'This is Sylvie Broadbent, the producer of *Britain's Biggest Treasure Hunt*, the TV show that's been filming at the dig site.'

'Pleased to meet you, Arnie,' Sylvie said in a sultry voice, extending her hand.

Arnie shook her hand with a hint of awkwardness. 'You too. Are you ready?' he asked, gesturing over to the table that had been set up for the interview.

'Only if you promise you'll be gentle with me.' Sylvie batted her eyelashes at him.

Arnie blinked at her in surprise and then shot a confused look at Karen. His face flushed a deep red, and he stumbled over his words. 'Uh . . . well . . . I . . .'

Karen watched as Arnie spluttered his response. He glanced at Karen again helplessly before managing to regain some composure.

'Maybe,' he said, his eyes darting to Sylvie and then back to Karen, 'I should get us all some coffee? Must be brewed by now.'

Sylvie gave a flirtatious laugh. 'That would be lovely.'

As Arnie hurried off to get the coffee, she winked at Karen. 'This should be fun.'

There was an undeniable change in Sylvie. The wellies and practical clothing she'd been wearing at the muddy archaeology site the previous night had been replaced by a form-fitting red dress and high-heeled boots. Sylvie seemed to have switched into a completely different personality type in front of Arnie, too – from warm and friendly to flirtatious femme fatale.

Arnie might come across as gruff and thick-skinned, but he could still be made uncomfortable. Some people assumed that men were somehow unbothered by unwelcome advances, but the truth was that anyone could feel uneasy in such situations. Karen decided to nip it in the bud. 'We're not here for fun. We're investigating a murder. The heavy-handed flirting isn't okay.'

Sylvie looked taken aback. 'Oh,' she said, her voice softening. 'I didn't mean . . . I'm sorry if I made you both uncomfortable.'

'It's not fair on him,' Karen continued. 'DS Hodgson is here to do his job.'

'Of course,' Sylvie said, her tone apologetic. 'I understand. But . . .' She looked across at Arnie. 'He's surely used to attention from women. They must be throwing themselves at him all the time.'

'Why do you say that?'

Sylvie gestured to Arnie, who was standing by the coffee machine looking puzzled as he jabbed at random buttons. 'Well, look at him,' she said. 'He's just like one of those detectives you see on TV, all tough and rugged. He's got a bit of Paul Newman about him, too.'

Karen followed Sylvie's gaze. Arnie's hair was dishevelled. His shirt was stained with grease from his sausage sandwich, and his too-small jacket refused to button up over his belly. She tried to understand what Sylvie was seeing but couldn't manage it.

'Anyway,' she said, turning back to face Sylvie. 'Cut back on the flirting, all right?'

Sylvie smiled at Karen. 'I'll be on my best behaviour,' she promised. 'You have my word.'

Karen led her over to the interview area, and gestured for her to take a seat. Then she pulled across the red curtain, attempting to give them some privacy for the interview.

She smiled at Sylvie. 'Let's make a start.'

Chapter Six

The biting wind sent flurries of leaves dancing as Morgan's car turned on to the gravel path leading to the farm.

'Right,' Morgan said to Rick, who gripped the armrest as they bounced over a particularly large pothole. 'Benjamin Price. The farm has been in his family for years. He's notorious for his bad temper and colourful language. Lost his wife to cancer a year ago, and by all accounts, he's become even more volatile. Got into a row with some ramblers last week for trespassing on his property. The man has a short fuse.'

Rick nodded, absorbing the information.

'I'll let you lead the questioning on this one, Rick,' Morgan continued, glancing at his younger colleague. 'But if things go south, I'm stepping in.'

They pulled up outside a farmhouse that had seen better days; the external white paint was stained in patches and weather-worn. Price was out front, his sandy hair ruffled by the wind. He was barking orders at a thin man in blue overalls.

Morgan's gaze followed the farmhand as he hurried away, head down, trying to avoid eye contact.

Rick raised his eyebrows and looked at Morgan. 'Not exactly a charmer.'

'No, and I can't imagine old Price is an easy boss to work for.'

They got out of the car, the bitter wind whipping around them. Rick was trying hard not to limp as they cautiously approached Price, who was now glaring at them. They could hear dogs barking from inside the farmhouse as they got closer.

'Mr Price, Detective Constable Cooper and Detective Inspector Morgan,' Rick said briskly, showing his ID and looking Price straight in the eye, determined not to be intimidated. 'We need to ask you some questions.'

Price's eyes narrowed as he looked at Morgan. 'I know you. You're the one who let those poachers off with a slap on the wrist.'

Morgan held back a sigh. 'The courts decided a caution was appropriate, not me.'

Price's ruddy face contorted with anger. 'Appropriate? They're vermin, those poachers. Should be locked up for good. You lot don't do your job properly.'

'We do our jobs to the best of our ability, Mr Price,' Morgan replied, his voice neutral.

Rick stepped in, attempting to steer the conversation back on track. 'Mr Price,' he began cautiously. 'We're here about Alison Poulson. Her body was found on your land last night.'

Price stiffened, and he looked beyond them to the fields in the distance. 'Haven't heard anything about that.'

Morgan studied the farmer closely. He didn't believe for a second that Price didn't know about the discovery of the body. It was a silly lie. Pointless. An officer had spoken to Price about the murder last night when they were cordoning off his land. He clearly wanted to distance himself from the crime.

'She was found in one of the trenches on the archaeology site,' Rick said.

Price straightened, folding his arms across his chest. 'So, what's that got to do with me?'

'Can you account for your whereabouts last night?' Rick asked.

Price's face reddened. 'Account for my whereabouts? No, I won't! That's none of your business. I don't have to tell you anything.'

He turned abruptly and stomped towards the house. Exchanging a look with Rick, Morgan followed.

The inside of the farmhouse kitchen was chaos – crumbs and dust on all the counters. Open bills and crumpled envelopes were scattered across the scrubbed pine table, and dog-eared farming magazines and newspapers were stacked in piles on the floor.

The dogs, shut in another room, were barking furiously. The window was filthy. On the windowsill sat a photo of a smiling woman, presumably Benjamin Price's late wife, in a shiny silver frame. It was the only clean thing in the kitchen.

Price was still grumbling under his breath about how useless the police were as he filled the kettle.

'You lot did nothing when my tools got nicked last year,' he erupted suddenly, jabbing a finger at Rick. 'And now you want me to answer your questions?'

'Did you know Alison?' Rick asked.

'Unfortunately.'

'She got your permission for the archaeologists to dig on your land and the TV crew to film?'

'No.' He put the kettle down with a thud. 'She asked me about the archaeologists but didn't mention anything about the TV show. I've had people trespassing all over my fields this week.'

'That caused a disagreement between you and Alison?'

'Of course it did. She was taking advantage. No one offered to pay me anything for it. When I confronted her, she threatened to cause trouble for me. Said she'd report me to Environmental Health for misuse of pesticides. All lies. But that wouldn't stop someone like her. She was a horrible woman.'

'So, you threatened to' – Rick looked down at his notes – '"blow her to kingdom come"?'

Price scowled. 'Don't you lot try to pin this on me. You're looking for an easy collar.'

'Did you see or hear anything unusual last night?'

'No, I was in bed by nine p.m. I have to get up early.'

Morgan watched as Rick asked Price more questions, but the farmer remained stubbornly tight-lipped, refusing to provide any meaningful information. The atmosphere grew tense as Rick pressed on, trying to get Price to cooperate.

'Do you know what a shrew's fiddle is?'

'A shrew's what?' Price's face crumpled in confusion.

'So you've never seen one?'

'I've no idea what you're going on about.'

'I see. We do need to establish your movements last night, sir,' Rick said. 'It's routine in a murder investigation.'

At the word *murder*, Price swiped two mugs from the counter into the sink, smashing them both and making Rick jump.

'I've had enough of this,' he growled. 'I had nothing to do with that awful woman's death. But she got what was coming to her if you ask me. Now, if you don't mind, I've work to do.'

He barged past them and disappeared outside, heading towards the barn.

Through the window, they watched him stomp angrily across the yard and hoist himself up on to a tractor. The engine roared to life.

Morgan met Rick's eye. 'Let's go. There's nothing else we can do here.'

'Sorry, boss. I could have handled it better.'

'You did a good job. Wouldn't have handled it any differently myself.'

As they turned to leave the kitchen, a timid voice spoke up behind them.

'He's lying, you know. About last night.'

They turned to see the young farmhand hovering anxiously. He must have been listening in to their conversation with Price.

'Go on,' Morgan prompted.

'I was in the barn late last night, trying to repair one of the machines. Mr Price said if I don't fix it, it's coming out of my wages,' the lad continued, words tumbling out in a rush. 'Anyway, it must've been about ten when I saw Mr Price leave by foot over the fields. He was gone for over an hour.'

Morgan frowned as Rick asked the farmhand further questions. This shed a different light on things. He hadn't seriously considered Price as a suspect because he seemed prone to explosive bursts of temper, and that didn't fit with a killer who'd used a torture device – giving the victim a long, drawn-out death. But you couldn't always tell. And if he'd lied about going to bed early . . .

The way Alison was left after her murder seemed very out of character for Price. He was known for fiery outbursts, not calculated acts of violence, and Morgan wouldn't have pegged him as the type to use objects like the shrew's fiddle for symbolism. Then again, impressions could be deceiving. They needed to keep an open mind.

'Thank you, Eddie,' Rick said after taking down the farmhand's name and contact details. 'We'll be in touch if we need anything else.'

The young man hurried away towards the barn after they'd exited the farmhouse.

Morgan stared after him thoughtfully as they walked to the car, then turned to Rick. 'Why does it always have to be so complicated? Can't people just tell the truth for once?'

75

Christie's hands tremble as she quietly turns the handle to the study. She slips inside and gently closes the door. The room is dim, with heavy wooden furniture and shelves crammed with boxes and old books. She moves slowly, holding her breath, afraid to make any noise.

Is it still here? She starts with the desk drawers, sliding them open one by one. Notebooks, crumpled receipts, paper clips – but no, the file is not here.

Her heart pounds as she rummages through the clutter on the desktop, through the stacks of research papers her father has been reading for his new book on the Jacobite rebellion. The file has to be here somewhere. She saw it last week. It was on the desk.

It has Alison's photograph inside. It's incriminating. If the police find it . . .

She must find it and get rid of it.

Unless it's been destroyed already. That would have been the sensible thing to do.

She finds herself hoping that it's gone – burned, or ripped into tiny pieces. Her nerves are frayed, thoughts racing. Her father still isn't back from talking to the police. What if he's been arrested?

She wishes she never recognised that woman. A bead of sweat trickles down her neck as she searches the room. *Come on, come on, where is it?*

Christie's gaze falls on the small black filing cabinet covered with books under the window. *Is it in there?* She tugs on the drawers, but the cabinet is locked and there is no sign of the key.

The door to the study creaks open, and Christie spins around, knocking over a book.

Her mother walks in, looking at her curiously.

'Oh, I . . . I was just looking for a pen,' Christie stammers, grabbing a random pen from the desk, her cheeks burning at the lie.

Her mum frowns. 'Don't mess up your father's research. You know how fussy he is about his notes when he's writing a book.'

'I know, I'm sorry.'

Her mum sighs and sets her laptop on the desk, plugging it in to charge. 'It was a long night. You've got the day off college to catch up on sleep.'

Christie nods numbly. Sleep. She can't imagine ever sleeping again after what happened last night.

'You don't want to get behind. Haven't you got a test on Friday? You'll need to be well rested for that.'

Christie nods and leaves the study. Her mother is talking about college as if everything is normal, but nothing will ever be normal again.

Chapter Seven

Karen sat across from Sylvie Broadbent in the makeshift interview room at the village hall. Arnie – sitting next to Karen – took a sip of his coffee.

'Ms Broadbent,' Arnie began, 'can you tell us more about your relationship with the victim, Alison Poulson?'

'Oh please, call me Sylvie. Ms Broadbent makes me sound so old.' She shot a flirtatious glance at Arnie.

He cleared his throat gruffly. 'Right then, Sylvie. How well did you know Alison?'

'Well, as I told Karen here last night, I hadn't known her long. Alison was the council representative I needed to arrange the filming location with. She was . . . a bit prickly,' Sylvie said carefully. 'Not the easiest person to get along with.' She suddenly turned to Karen. 'Have you spoken to that farmer chap yet? Benjamin Price? I told you how he turned up on set the other day waving his shotgun around.'

Karen nodded. 'Our colleagues are dealing with Mr Price.'

'Oh good,' Sylvie said, leaning forward eagerly, as if anticipating a juicy plot twist. 'So, do you think he did it? Has he been arrested?'

Karen was bemused by Sylvie's casual attitude, unsure if the producer was truly aware that this was not a scripted drama but a real-life crime with serious consequences.

'Sylvie, this might seem like an exciting plot from one of your shows, but this is a real investigation into a serious crime. Someone has lost their life, and the consequences for those involved are very real.'

Sylvie sat back in her chair, a mixture of understanding and embarrassment on her face. 'I'm so sorry. You're absolutely right. I got a bit carried away there. It's just . . . I've never been this close to a *real* crime before.'

Karen offered a reassuring smile. She couldn't help warming to the eccentric TV producer. This was an unusual situation, and everyone had their own way of handling the shock. 'You're being really helpful. We appreciate it. But I'm afraid we can't comment on arrests.'

'I understand.' As Sylvie spoke, she subtly angled her body towards Arnie.

He leaned forward, elbows on the table. 'Any idea who else might have wanted to harm her? Have you heard any rumours or whispers?'

Sylvie hesitated before replying coyly, 'I wouldn't want to point fingers. I'm not a gossip.'

Karen frowned. She'd been quick enough to point the finger at Benjamin Price. 'We're not asking for gossip. If you have information, no matter how trivial you think it is, you should share it with us.'

Sylvie's gaze flickered to Karen, then drifted back to Arnie. It seemed she couldn't resist.

'It could be vital to the case, but we won't know unless you tell us,' Arnie said.

Sylvie's eyes lingered on him as he spoke. It was clear she was still very taken with him. Her lips curved into a small smile. 'You're right. I can see why you're a successful detective. I'd tell you anything.' She leaned back in her chair. 'You know, DS Hodgson, you have a very photogenic face. Have you ever been on TV?'

Arnie looked surprised by the question, then pleased. He rubbed the back of his neck self-consciously. 'No.'

Sylvie raised an eyebrow. 'Really? You'd make a great lead detective on a crime show.'

Arnie blushed and looked down at his notes, avoiding Sylvie's gaze.

Karen watched the exchange with amusement. Arnie was a good detective, but he didn't need compliments to boost his ego. She cleared her throat to redirect the conversation back to the case at hand. 'We're short on time.'

Sylvie hesitated for a moment before speaking. 'Well, I did overhear Alison arguing with her husband on the phone a few days ago. They seemed pretty heated.'

'Do you remember what they were arguing about?'

Sylvie shook her head. 'I couldn't make out all of it, but Alison definitely said something about betrayal.'

'Betrayal?' Arnie rubbed his chin thoughtfully. 'Meaning the husband betrayed Alison, or the other way around?'

Sylvie leaned in. 'Now, that is a very good question. But I'm not sure. It could have been either. You're really good at this, aren't you?'

'This argument,' Karen said. 'When did it take place?'

Sylvie turned to Karen, blinking as if she'd forgotten she and Arnie weren't alone. 'Oh, let me think . . . it was last Friday, in the afternoon.'

Karen jotted a note. 'And you said you heard Alison mention betrayal?'

'Yes, she definitely used that word. Sounded very angry.' Sylvie smoothed a hand over her hair.

'Right.' Karen glanced at the oversized clock on the wall. Their ten minutes was up. 'I think that's all for now. Thanks for all your help. We'll be in touch if we have any other questions.'

Sylvie smiled, her attention firmly on Arnie. 'Please, call *anytime* if you need me. I'm *always* happy to help.'

Karen resisted the urge to roll her eyes.

After Sylvie left the hall, Karen glanced at Arnie. 'So, what did you think of Ms Broadbent?'

Arnie grinned. 'She's a bit of a character, isn't she?'

'A bit of a character? She was practically throwing herself at you.'

'She was just having a bit of fun. No harm in that.'

'You know, if we need to speak to Sylvie again, I can always swap you out with someone else.'

Arnie looked at her in surprise. 'Why would you do that?'

'Just thought you might be more comfortable.'

Arnie's brow furrowed. 'Why wouldn't I be comfortable?'

'Oh, I don't know . . . maybe because she's got you in her sights?'

Arnie chuckled. 'Is that what you think? That I'm uncomfortable?'

'Well, aren't you?' Karen asked.

'Actually,' Arnie said, grinning widely, 'I'm rather enjoying the attention. There's life in the old dog yet.'

Karen narrowed her eyes. 'Don't let her distract you.'

'I'm not. It's not my fault I'm irresistible to certain women.' He straightened his tie.

Karen shook her head, but a small smile tugged at her lips.

Arnie raised his hands in mock surrender. 'All right. I'll be on my guard. But I reckon she's harmless. Some women just fall for my charms. Nothing I can do to stop it.'

'Poor you. Must be a tough cross to bear.'

Arnie smirked. 'I think she wants me to be her next leading man.'

Karen laughed. 'I'm sure you'd be a huge hit on TV, Arnie.'

'Why, thank you. I'm glad you appreciate my talents.'

◆ ◆ ◆

Professor Stark strode into the village hall, his salt-and-pepper hair slicked back and his jacket buttoned up to the neck.

'Detectives,' he said, his voice clipped and posh. 'I hope you won't keep me long. I have a great deal to organise and a meeting with my head of department at the university in an hour.'

Karen glanced up from her notes. 'We understand you're a busy man, Professor Stark, but we believe you might be able to help us with our investigation.'

She should have known he'd be annoying. She'd got that impression last night. It was often said that making judgements based on first impressions was a bad idea, but Karen found her first impressions were often accurate. She remembered how defensive Stark had been the night before, and how shaken Christie had been. Of course, that was to be expected after just stumbling across a gruesome murder scene, but Karen had to wonder if there was anything else there. Christie hadn't seemed scared of her father; if anything, she'd leaned into him, needing his support. But there could be something Karen was missing. She would need to check on Christie later.

Arnie cut in, his gruff voice contrasting sharply with Stark's polished one. 'I'm sure you can spare ten minutes of your time. This is a murder investigation, after all.'

'Yes, sorry. I didn't mean to sound so brusque,' he said, reluctantly taking a seat at the table.

Karen kicked things off, her voice calm and measured. 'How's Christie doing?'

'Fine.'

'Really? She seemed very upset last night.'

'Of course she was upset. She *had* just found a dead body.'

'That's why I'm asking how she is today.'

Stark straightened the crease in his trousers. 'I'm sure she's fine. She's staying home today. But I didn't actually see her before I left for work this morning.'

'You didn't check on her?' Arnie asked with a lift of his bushy eyebrows.

'What is this? You're supposed to be asking me questions about the case, not judging my parenting skills. Christie is fine. She's with her mother.'

Professor Stark wasn't winning the Father of the Year award anytime soon. He didn't seem to have much parental concern, considering the traumatic event his daughter had experienced. But at least he'd cared enough to come and collect his daughter last night. Karen had dealt with far worse parents in her time.

'How well did you know Alison Poulson?' Karen asked.

Stark hesitated for a moment before answering. 'We were merely acquaintances,' he said. 'I knew her through my work at the university and occasionally saw her at social events. She was the development projects officer at the council and worked with the university on a lot of different schemes.'

Karen pressed on. 'So, you knew Alison, but last night you told me that the victim didn't sound like anyone you'd worked with.'

Stark shifted uncomfortably in his seat, his face flushing slightly. 'I . . . I was mistaken,' he stammered. 'But it was hardly my fault. I didn't actually see the victim.'

Arnie leaned forward, his eyes narrowing as he studied Stark closely. 'How long have you been working at the university?'

'I started my role at the university two months ago,' he said smoothly. 'We moved to the area when I took up the position.'

'And what is your role, sir? Your official job title?' Arnie asked.

'Professor of Archaeology. Chair of the department, in fact. I've written a few books too. General history subjects, written at a level the general public can understand. Of course, I have to greatly simplify the complexity for the layperson.' Stark's smile was patronising, as if he were doing the world a great service by deigning to share his knowledge with the masses.

'Very impressive,' Arnie said drily.

Although she'd warmed to Sylvie almost instantly, Karen couldn't say the same for Stark. He came across as arrogant and cold. His superior attitude grated on her nerves. She wondered if his ego was a result of his academic success or if he'd always been this way, even before becoming a professor.

Karen took a printout from the file in front of her and slid it across the table for Professor Stark. It was an image of Alison Poulson's body, a close-up of the shrew's fiddle around her neck.

Stark looked taken aback but recovered quickly. 'Good grief. Is that what I think it is?'

'That all depends on what you think it is,' Arnie said.

'A shrew's fiddle.' Professor Stark's eyes widened as he took in the gruesome detail of the device clutching Alison Poulson's neck. 'It was used as a brutal and humiliating form of punishment, reserved for women who were considered to be nags or too outspoken.'

Karen watched him closely, noting the flicker of horror had retreated and been replaced by something else. *Excitement?* 'Is it a replica?' he asked, not taking his eyes off the photograph. 'Or an original?'

'We were hoping you'd be able to answer that question,' Karen said.

Stark hesitated for a moment before replying. 'If it's a replica, it's a very good one,' he said finally. 'But I can't say for sure from this photograph. I would need to see the original to make a definitive assessment.'

His tone was matter-of-fact, as though discussing a routine archaeological find. Karen supposed that was exactly what this was to him. He seemed to be able to disconnect from the knowledge the artefact was attached to the dead body of his female colleague.

Karen found Stark's detachment unsettling. It seemed as though he couldn't grasp how serious this was. And it was the same with his daughter. He had appeared distant, unable to fully understand or react to Christie's distress. It was almost as though he lacked the emotional intelligence to behave in the way most people would expect of him.

He was clearly a man who struggled with empathy and understanding people. In some ways, he reminded Karen of Tim Farthing. Much like the professor, Tim was an expert in his field, but he struggled with social interactions. He tended to say the wrong thing at the wrong time, often coming across as insensitive or even rude without meaning to be. Perhaps for both men it had something to do with being so wrapped up in their work. Karen wondered if Professor Stark's focus on his academic research had led to him neglecting his personal life, or if there was something deeper going on here.

'Was it found at the archaeology site?' Arnie asked.

Stark shook his head firmly. 'No,' he said, then he paused. 'I don't think so. It would have been catalogued if it had, and I'd have spotted it on the lists if it was recorded. Plus, the people on the TV show would have been over the moon. They love stuff like this. But it's not unheard of to find something like this in old settlements. I've uncovered some interesting medieval weapons and torture devices in previous digs. Never a shrew's fiddle, though.

This is a first.' Stark sounded almost gleeful. He leaned back in his chair, becoming more animated as he described the various torture devices they had uncovered during earlier digs – iron maidens, racks, thumbscrews . . .

As Karen listened to the professor speak about these ancient instruments of pain and suffering, she suppressed a shudder. It was clear that Stark knew a great deal about them. He was incriminating himself. But he wasn't stupid. If he'd killed Alison and used this torture device on her, would he really be telling them about it so enthusiastically?

'Do you think I could see it?' Stark asked. 'I'd be able to tell you whether it's a replica or not.'

Karen shook her head. 'Not just yet, Professor Stark. We need to analyse it in our labs first.'

She saw the condescension in his eyes as he replied, 'I hardly think the scientists employed by the police will be up to the task. I'm the expert here, after all.'

Karen and Arnie said nothing, letting the professor's words hang in the air.

The silence seemed to make Stark feel silly. He snapped: 'Fine. I was just offering to help.'

Karen ignored the outburst. 'Do you know anyone who might have wanted to hurt Alison?'

'No. She wasn't exactly popular, but I can't see why anyone would want to kill her, especially not with a shrew's fiddle around her neck.'

'Why wasn't she popular?' Arnie asked.

'Well, she was . . . difficult to get along with, shall we say? She had a sharp tongue and wasn't afraid to use it. Personally, I couldn't abide the woman, but still, that's a horrible way to go. Was the neck violin put on before she died or after?'

'Neck violin?' Arnie grimaced.

'Sorry, shrew's fiddle. It's called a neck violin by some.'

'We're not releasing those details yet, sir. I'm sure you understand,' Karen said. She tapped her pen on her notepad as she considered her next question. 'Did Alison get along with anyone involved in the dig or the TV show?'

If Alison had at least one friend, that could make their investigation a whole lot easier. She might have confided in them.

Professor Stark leaned back in his chair and looked up at the high ceiling, thinking. After a moment, he nodded. 'Yes, now that you mention it, she did seem to get on quite well with Tilda Goring.'

'Tilda Goring?' Arnie repeated. 'The show's director?'

'That's right. I needed to speak with Tilda last weekend about their filming access to the dig site. I popped into the Cross Keys on Saturday evening and found Alison and Tilda sharing a bottle of wine. They seemed to be getting along famously.'

This was promising. 'So Tilda and Alison were friends?'

'Friendly, at least. Tilda's been staying at the Cross Keys while they film the show, and they saw quite a bit of each other.'

Karen shared a knowing look with Arnie. They'd need to speak to Tilda as a priority.

'That's very helpful,' Arnie said. 'Did she get on with anyone else on the show?'

Stark smiled for the first time in the interview. 'Actually, yes. She seemed to be a bit starstruck by Trevor Barker, one of the presenters for the show. Heaven knows what she saw in him. He's a washed-up old DJ, but yes, she seemed to have a soft spot for him. That's according to Trevor anyway. He said she asked for his autograph.'

'Great,' Arnie said. 'We'll hopefully get some information from Trevor when we speak to him later.'

'I wouldn't hold out much hope for that,' Professor Stark said. 'They've both gone into Lincoln for the day.'

Arnie frowned. 'Both? Who's with him?'

'Molly Moreland, the other presenter. They've gone shopping.'

Karen felt a surge of annoyance. She'd specifically asked Sylvie to get everyone from the archaeology team and the TV crew to come to the village hall today to be interviewed. Either not everyone had got the message, or if they had, they'd ignored it.

'That's showbiz types for you,' Professor Stark said with a shrug. 'Always swanning about. Personally, I think they've gone into the city in the hope of being recognised. They think they're more famous than they are.'

Karen wasn't happy. They really needed to speak to Trevor Barker. If Alison had confided in him, she wanted to know what they'd talked about.

Stark pushed his chair back, adjusting the cuffs of his jacket. 'I should get going,' he said. 'I have a meeting at the university.'

'Yes, you did mention it,' Karen said. 'Thank you for your time.'

Stark nodded curtly and left the village hall.

Karen turned to Arnie, shaking her head. 'Can you believe it? Imagine going off to Lincoln shopping when you've been asked to answer questions about a murder. I don't know what's between the ears of those presenters.'

'According to the gossip columns, not a lot,' Arnie joked. 'Don't worry about it. We'll catch up with them eventually. What did you think of Stark?'

'Very suspicious,' Karen said. 'You?'

'Almost too suspicious. Would he really share all that stuff about expertise on torture devices if he killed her? I don't think so.' Arnie held up a piece of paper with their schedule printed on it. 'Ms Tilda Goring is next on our list. Let's see what she can tell us about Alison.'

Chapter Eight

Morgan and Rick arrived at the West Lindsey District Council offices in Gainsborough after half an hour's drive. The council offices were in a light-coloured, modern building with large windows and a curved frontage. Morgan parked near the restaurant next door, and they made their way inside. Rick trailed behind, walking slower than usual with a slight limp. When Morgan glanced back, Rick quickly straightened up and clearly tried to hide the pain.

The reception area was modern and practical. A tall woman with long wavy hair, wearing a name badge with *Beth Cousins* printed on it, stood behind a long counter. 'How can I help you gentlemen today?' she asked.

They showed their ID, and Morgan explained they were there to speak to Alison Poulson's work colleagues, starting with her assistant, Lucas Black.

The receptionist's smile faded. 'It's awful what happened. I can't believe it. I didn't know her well, just to say good morning to when she came into the office. She preferred working from home.'

After Morgan and Rick signed the guest register, Beth escorted them upstairs and through the building. Stopping beside the office at the end of the hall, she knocked on the door and waited for a moment before opening it.

She entered the room, then stopped suddenly and gasped, a hand flying to her mouth. 'Lucas!'

Stepping inside, Morgan's gaze followed hers to a man precariously perched on one of the sash window ledges. His left hand clutched the window frame, his knuckles white with tension. He was crouched low and leaning out dangerously far.

Lucas Black seemed ready to jump.

Rick lunged forward. He wrapped his arms around Black's waist and yanked him safely back inside.

'What are you doing?' Black yelled, flailing his arms and trying to shake Rick off. 'Have you lost your mind?'

'You were about to jump!' Rick said.

'No, I wasn't.' Black brushed himself down, looking offended.

Rick leaned against the edge of the desk next to him, wincing as he flexed his injured foot. 'Great,' he muttered under his breath. 'I've made it worse now.' He glanced at Black, who was glaring at him. 'You could have killed yourself, leaning out the window like that.'

A soft meow drew Morgan's attention to the window. He looked outside. On a narrow ledge, clinging on precariously, was a small tabby cat. Further along the ledge was a fat pigeon, who ruffled its feathers as it watched the cat curiously.

'You were trying to save the cat?' Morgan said.

'Nearly had it, too,' Lucas grumbled, giving Rick a pointed look as he adjusted his frameless glasses. 'It's done it before. Never learns. Always gets stuck. It wants to get the pigeons.'

Morgan leaned through the window, resting his elbows on the ledge. He wasn't prepared to risk a fall like Black. The trick was to let the cat come to him. To make the cat think it was all its idea.

Morgan spoke softly, extending his hand slowly. The tabby eyed him warily at first, but when Morgan didn't make any sudden movements, it seemed to relax. Inching closer, the cat eventually allowed him to scoop it up in his arms. He cradled the cat gently and set it down on a nearby desk.

The cat immediately began to explore its new surroundings, batting at a pen holder and knocking over a stapler.

Black watched in amazement. 'How did you do that? It seems to like you. I always get a scratch for my troubles when I manage to grab it.'

Morgan shrugged. An ex-girlfriend had once told him cats liked him because he was as stand-offish as they were. He was sure she hadn't meant it as a compliment.

The receptionist picked up the cat, cooing over it affectionately. 'I'll take him downstairs, the little tyke.'

She left Rick and Morgan alone in the office with Black.

Black gestured to two chairs facing his desk. 'Please, have a seat.'

The office was small and cluttered. A filing cabinet overflowed with bulging folders and loose papers. Documents covered every flat surface, leaving little room on the desk for Black's computer monitor, keyboard, and a small, framed photo of a young blonde woman.

Black was tall and slim, with unruly brown hair that kept flopping over his forehead. He brushed it back impatiently as he sat down. 'You're here about Alison?'

'Yes. I'm Detective Inspector Morgan, and this is Detective Constable Cooper,' Morgan said. 'We'd like to ask you some questions about your relationship with Mrs Poulson.'

'Alison could be a tough taskmaster at times, but we worked well together. She was very driven and expected a lot from the people around her. But she respected my contributions.'

'You're Alison's PA?' Rick asked.

Black bristled. 'I'm the assistant development projects officer, not a personal assistant.'

'I see,' Rick said. 'And what work did you and Alison do here?'

'Alison liaised with external companies who want to set up projects in the area. We work with lots of different businesses and charities. Every day is something different. My role was to support Alison with the projects. I helped with research, coordination, budgeting – anything she needed me to do. We made a good team.'

'Had Alison seemed upset or worried about anything recently?' Morgan asked.

'No, she didn't really get upset. More angry sometimes. She could be a bit of a ball-breaker.' He blushed. 'Excuse my language.'

'Would she have confided in you if something was bothering her?'

Black thought for a moment. 'Probably not. We had a purely professional relationship. But I always admired her. It was rewarding working for someone so driven and talented.'

Something about Black's description and tone felt false to Morgan, as though he was trying too hard to make Alison sound good.

Morgan's gaze landed on the framed photo on Black's desk. The blonde woman was grinning at the camera with the Forth Bridge in the background. 'Your girlfriend?'

Black shifted uncomfortably. 'We're, uh, on a bit of a break at the moment.' He picked up the frame and stared at it. 'She lives in Scotland now.' He set the photo back down, angling it away from Morgan and Rick. 'Do you have any leads yet on who killed Alison? Is it true she was found in a trench?'

Morgan nodded, his gaze fixed on Black's face. 'Yes, she was found in a trench at the archaeological dig site in Stow. Have you visited the site?'

Morgan saw a flicker of surprise in Black's eyes, but he quickly recovered. 'Yes, a few times. Once with Alison and a couple of times on my own, just to check things were progressing well.'

'This is purely routine,' Rick said. 'But can you tell us where you were last night?'

'An alibi you mean?' Apprehension passed over Black's features.

'Yes, just for the paperwork.'

'Um, I was at a pub until about ten. Then I went home.'

'Alone?'

'Yes.'

Rick pulled out his tablet. 'You'd better give me the name of the pub. Then we can get this all signed off today.'

'Is that really necessary?'

'I'm afraid so.'

Black provided the details. As Rick continued the questioning, Morgan sat back in his chair, thinking. He had the feeling that there was more to Black's relationship with Alison than he was letting on. The way he spoke about her seemed rehearsed, as though he was trying to either make himself look good or Alison seem less difficult than she really was.

He decided not to mention the shrew's fiddle, or any leads they had at this point.

As the interview came to an end, Morgan thanked Black for his time and said they'd find their own way back to reception. When they got there, they found Beth Cousins playing with the tabby cat.

She looked up guiltily. 'Sorry. I'm not supposed to keep him in here, but it's cold today . . .'

Rick grinned. 'Your secret is safe with us.'

'Is there anyone here at the council who Alison was particularly close to?' Morgan asked as the cat wound around his legs.

Beth shrugged. 'Not really. If I'm being honest, most people avoided her. When she came in, she was usually on the warpath about something or other. Poor Lucas. He bore the brunt of it.'

'Yes, sounds like they had a difficult relationship,' Morgan said, going along with it and making it sound like Black had already confided in them.

'Yes, but it wasn't Lucas's fault. He was a saint to put up with her as a boss. She bullied him constantly. Did he tell you about his girlfriend?'

'He mentioned her.'

'Well, I think that was the worst thing Alison ever did to him. It was unbelievably cruel.'

'You mean . . .' Morgan began, letting his words hang there, hoping Beth would finish the sentence.

'Yes . . .' Beth's eyes darted around the reception area to make sure no one was close enough to overhear. Then she leaned in and lowered her voice. 'When Alison went out of her way to sabotage poor Lucas's relationship with his girlfriend at the office summer party. Alison suggested all kinds of things about Lucas cheating on her and not being committed. Complete rubbish, of course, but the damage was done. His girlfriend believed the lies and left for Scotland without him.'

Beth shook her head and continued, 'And that wasn't even the worst of it. Lucas applied for a new job that would have let him transfer up to Scotland so he could win her back. But Alison gave him a terrible reference so he wouldn't get the job. She wanted to keep him under her thumb at the Development Projects Office.'

The picture Beth painted of Alison and Black's relationship was very different to the one Black had presented. Morgan could imagine a controlling personality like Alison wanting to keep a competent employee close by. It sounded like her sabotage had probably cost Black both his relationship and a new job.

'That's really low,' Rick said. 'Poor bloke.'

'But Lucas told you all this already, right? I'm not telling tales?'

'Mm,' Rick said non-committally.

'Lucas is a lovely young man, and he didn't deserve any of that.'

Morgan nodded slowly, thinking over the implications. Black certainly had motive if he had wanted to take revenge on Alison. Her manipulative scheming had cost him dearly. And Black had opportunity too; he'd been to the dig site. They'd need to confirm his alibi to make sure he hadn't acted on his motive.

Beth might think Lucas Black was a lovely young man, but Morgan knew everyone had a limit to how far they could be pushed before they snapped.

Chapter Nine

Karen and Arnie had a few minutes before Tilda Goring was due at the village hall for her police interview, so while Arnie was checking his email, Karen used her mobile to call Sophie. She knew how frustrated Sophie was at being relegated to desk duty while she recovered. Sophie had many virtues, but patience wasn't one of them. She was growing restless with the restrictions placed on her duties, and Karen worried she might try to take on too much before she was truly ready. The young woman was a talented officer, but stubbornly impatient with obstacles. Karen didn't want her setting herself back by overdoing it. The slow return to full duty was for her own good.

She leaned back in her chair while waiting for the call to be answered.

'Karen?'

'Sophie, how's it looking from your end?'

'Nothing exciting. No, the Poulsons' neighbours are just that – neighbours. No skeletons in their closets that I can dig up.'

Karen frowned. 'That's odd. David Poulson was really glaring at that house.'

'Well, I've done an exhaustive search. I'm not sure where else to look. Unless . . . I could go and speak to the neighbours?'

'Sophie . . .' Karen's voice held a warning tone.

'I'm drowning in paperwork. It's not fair I'm cooped up here while everyone else is doing proper police work.'

'But you *like* paperwork.'

Sophie's voice rose with frustration. 'Even *I* don't like it this much!'

Karen caught the resentment. She knew how badly Sophie wanted to be back in the job, and working at full capacity. But Karen also recognised that the single-minded drive in Sophie could become reckless. They'd seen that before, when she'd decided to investigate alone. 'You're still doing an important job, Sophie. I understand your frustration. But you need to let yourself properly recuperate first.'

'Feels like I've been sidelined.'

'Well, technically, you have been, but you'll be back to full capacity soon enough.'

'I'm fine now.' Sophie sighed. 'I should be out there, knocking on doors, talking to people, not pushing paper.'

Karen paused – an idea was forming in her mind. Talking to the Poulsons' neighbours didn't seem like it would be a high-risk situation. It might be the ideal way to ease Sophie back into public-facing work gradually. It was certainly less risky than talking to someone volatile like Benjamin Price. 'Maybe we *should* have someone chat with the Poulsons' neighbours . . .'

'Exactly! I can go there now.'

'Not so fast.' Karen held firm. 'You need to run it by Churchill first.'

Sophie's tone turned cajoling. 'Oh, come on, Karen—'

'No,' Karen said sharply. 'I'm not going against Churchill's orders. And don't even think of just going off on your own. You remember what happened last time.'

The line grew quiet.

'Sorry. I shouldn't have brought that up. Just . . . don't do anything rash.' Karen's voice softened. She'd been so worried about Sophie after the assault. The idea the younger officer hadn't learned her lesson and would go waltzing off chasing leads on her own again was a terrifying thought.

'Fine,' Sophie huffed, clearly fed up.

The call ended with a click, and Karen slid her phone into her pocket.

'Sophie not happy?' Arnie asked, looking up from his own phone.

'She's tetchy. Bored with being stuck at the station all the time.'

'Ah, it looks like our next interviewee has arrived,' Arnie said as a short woman with orange and blue hair walked in. 'What an *interesting* hairstyle.'

Tilda entered the village hall briskly, wearing a long khaki skirt and a white blouse. Mirrored sunglasses were perched on top of her head, even though the sky outside was overcast. Around her neck, a chunky pendant dangled from a silver chain, which she touched absently as she made her way to where Karen and Arnie sat.

Karen studied Tilda closely as she approached. The director had a strong presence – her brightly coloured hair and no-nonsense demeanour commanded attention.

'Ms Goring,' Karen said, her voice firm but polite. 'Thank you for coming in to speak with us.'

Tilda nodded, sitting down. 'Of course. I want to help in any way I can.'

Arnie crossed his arms over his broad chest. 'We appreciate that,' he said. 'Can you tell us about your relationship with Alison Poulson?'

Tilda's phone rang before she had a chance to answer Arnie's question. She fished it out of her bag. 'Sorry. I'll switch it off. I hate mobiles – so invasive.' She frowned at the screen and then tutted.

'Press. They'll be crawling all over this place later.' She shoved the phone back in her bag. 'Sorry, what was the question again?'

'Your relationship with Alison Poulson.'

'We only met a few weeks ago,' she said slowly. 'But we hit it off right away. Alison was a strong woman, just like me – she knew what she wanted out of life.'

Karen raised an eyebrow, intrigued by Tilda's words. 'What do you mean by that?'

'I mean that Alison was determined and motivated in her career. She was adventurous, not afraid to go after what she wanted. Some people thought she was hard as nails, but I knew she was just ambitious.' Tilda sighed, her eyes filling with tears for a moment before she blinked them away.

Arnie leaned forward, interested in Tilda's emotional response. 'Did you two have anything more than a friendship?' he asked bluntly.

Tilda shook her head, wiping away tears. 'No, nothing like that.' She paused briefly before adding softly, 'But we did have a special connection. Kindred spirits, I suppose.'

'Any reason someone might want to harm her?'

'Some people had their noses put out of joint because she could be forceful, but I can't think of anyone who would actually want to hurt her, except maybe that awful farmer.'

'Benjamin Price?' Karen asked. 'Did you see him causing a ruckus at the archaeology site a few days ago?'

Tilda nodded, her expression grim. 'Yes, it was terrifying. He was pointing a gun at people and shouting about how he'd been ripped off by Alison.'

'What do you think he meant by that?'

'I think he believed he was owed a payment for having the TV show filmed on his land,' she said. 'And when he found out that he wasn't going to get one, he lost his temper.'

If Price had been so angry about not being paid for letting *Britain's Biggest Treasure Hunt* film on one of his fields, why hadn't he threatened Tilda or Sylvie or one of the other crew members at the dig? Had Alison done something in particular that had set him off?

Karen leaned forward, her eyes fixed on Tilda's face. 'Why do you think Benjamin Price was only angry at Alison?'

Tilda blinked and hesitated, as though she hadn't considered that. 'I think it must be because Alison was the one who arranged it. She was the one who convinced him to let us film on his land. It seemed like he thought she'd tricked him into allowing us to film there for free.'

'Do you remember what Price said specifically?' Karen asked.

'He was shouting about not letting Alison pull the wool over his eyes.' Tilda shook her head and lifted her shoulders in a defeated shrug. 'But I'm not sure what he meant. He's utterly deranged.'

Karen exchanged a glance with Arnie. Benjamin Price was looking more suspicious by the minute.

From what they'd heard he was a volatile individual – one who might snap under pressure. And if he believed that he'd been cheated out of something by Alison Poulson and the TV crew, it wasn't hard to imagine how that could have led to violent consequences . . .

But the shrew's fiddle . . . that really didn't seem like it would be Price's MO.

The shrew's fiddle pointed to a darker motive, and a careful, vindictive killer.

Arnie asked a few more questions before turning to Tilda Goring's alibi. 'Can you tell us where you were last night? We need to ask everyone their whereabouts.'

'I'm staying at the Cross Keys pub,' Tilda said. 'Last night, I had a few drinks with dinner, then went to bed early.'

Arnie hesitated, glancing over at Karen with an uneasy expression. He put a photograph face down against the table. 'Ms Goring,' he began gently, 'I'm afraid I have to show you something that may be . . . upsetting.'

'Go on then,' she said briskly, though her fingers went to the odd-looking pendant at her neck, touching it like a talisman.

Arnie took a deep breath and slowly turned the photo over, sliding it across the table to Tilda. It showed the shrew's fiddle that had been found clasped around Alison's neck, though not in as much graphic detail as the crime scene photo they had shown Professor Stark.

Tilda went very still as she stared down at the image. Her face drained of colour, and her lips tightened into a thin line. When she finally spoke, her voice was a horrified whisper. 'Is that . . . a shrew's fiddle?'

Arnie nodded grimly. 'I'm afraid so. It was found on the victim's body. Do you recognise it? Have you seen one before?'

A shudder went through Tilda's body. She shoved the photo away with a choked cry. 'That evil thing was around Alison's neck? Why would someone do something so vile?'

Karen reached out and gently took the photo as Tilda put her head in her hands, shoulders shaking with sobs.

Arnie looked helplessly at Karen, clearly out of his depth. 'There, there,' he said, patting Tilda's shoulder.

'I know this is very distressing,' Karen said gently. 'But can you tell us what you know about the device?'

Tilda took a few gulping breaths, struggling to regain her composure. 'I don't understand. Who would be so twisted . . . so cruel . . .' She broke down into sobs again.

Arnie continued to pat Tilda's shoulder gingerly. 'There now, it's okay,' he said awkwardly. 'We're going to find who did this to your friend, don't you worry.'

Karen waited until Tilda's sobs had receded and tried again. 'You've seen a shrew's fiddle before?'

'Only pictures of one,' Tilda sniffed. 'One of the historians we used on an episode last year showed me. He thought it might be an interesting thing to have on the show. He was probably right. Viewers seem to love the gory stuff. Our episode about excavating the settlement wiped out by the Black Death got our highest figures last year.'

'You've no idea why the device was used on Alison, or who might have a reason to use it?'

Tilda's face crumpled as she shook her head.

'It sounds like you were a good friend to Alison, even though you'd only known her a short time,' Karen said.

'I'd like to think so. Alison didn't open up easily, but over a bottle of wine, she'd start to relax and chat.'

Karen asked, 'Was anything worrying her or on her mind?'

'As a matter of fact, she did mention a few things that were concerning her. For one, that oaf of a husband was giving her grief again. He hated her career. Hated that she was doing better than him.'

Arnie nodded. 'Anything else?'

'There was some issue with her assistant Lucas making mistakes on important documents, which reflected poorly on her. And she suspected he was angling for her job.' Tilda sighed. 'Poor Alison.'

'Did she give any indication that she felt threatened or in danger?' Karen asked.

Tilda pursed her lips, thinking. 'No, I don't think she felt physically threatened. Just stressed by her job and home life. The only time she seemed really frightened was when I told her about that mad farmer pointing a gun at us at the dig when Alison wasn't there.'

'Did she confide in you often?'

'Oh, yes, she trusted me. She told me all sorts of things.'

'Like what?'

'Well, for a start, she told me she was going to dump her husband. Good thing, too. He just held her back.'

'Alison and David weren't giving things another chance?' Karen asked, surprised because that was what David Poulson had said.

'Ha! In his dreams.'

Arnie said, 'You seem very sure of that, Tilda.'

'I am.'

'Why?'

'Because Alison had fallen for someone else.'

Chapter Ten

Sophie practically bounced down the stairs from Churchill's office. The DCI had a knack for turning what should have been a simple yes or no into an interrogation of his own officers, but she didn't care. In the end, he'd given her the green light.

After weeks of desk duty, she was finally going to conduct an interview. Okay, so it probably wouldn't be the most exciting interview she'd ever participated in. James and Laura MacGregor were the middle-aged couple who lived opposite the Poulsons' home in Scothern. Her questioning them was hardly likely to crack the case. In fact, Sophie thought it was quite likely that David Poulson's animosity towards his neighbours amounted to an argument over bins or something equally boring.

Still, at least she was getting back out there and doing some proper police work again.

She picked up the file containing everything she'd found out about James and Laura MacGregor. James was a web designer while Laura ran a popular YouTube channel and blogged about baking, and as luck would have it, both were working from home today.

Sophie grabbed her phone and quickly sent a text to Karen.

Great news! Churchill said I can go and talk to the Poulsons' neighbours in Scothern. Heading over there now. Can't wait to get out of the station.

As she headed out to her car, Sophie flipped through the file, reviewing the background info and list of questions she had compiled. She was determined to nail this interview. She was back in the thick of it at last.

By the time Sophie pulled up outside the MacGregors' house in Scothern and switched off the engine, her stomach was fluttering with nerves.

The front of the house was covered with Halloween decorations. A large inflatable ghost in the middle of the lawn wobbled in the breeze.

Maybe it was the decorations that had irritated David Poulson. They were a bit garish, especially compared to the Poulsons' neat and tidy front garden and driveway.

She noticed a patrol car parked in the driveway opposite and realised that the family liaison officer, PC Jim Willson, was likely inside, giving David Poulson an update on the investigation.

Jim was a friendly face; he was one of those police officers everyone liked. Knowing he was just across the lane made Sophie feel a bit better.

Sophie walked up the drive to the MacGregors' front door, eyeing the plastic skeletons hanging from hooks on either side of the window. She paused for a moment, taking a deep breath. It was just a routine interview to gather information, nothing to be nervous about.

She pressed the doorbell, hearing it ring inside the house. After a few moments, the door opened a crack, and a woman's face appeared. She had been crying, her eyes red-rimmed and puffy.

'Mrs MacGregor? I'm Detective Constable Sophie Jones; we spoke on the phone about me asking you and your husband a few questions.'

The woman nodded, opening the door wider. Behind her, Sophie saw a man banging cupboard doors loudly in the kitchen. His face was like thunder. Laura MacGregor glanced at him before turning back to Sophie. 'Yes, of course, please come in.'

Sophie stepped inside. The atmosphere was tense. James MacGregor glowered as he made a pot of tea, slamming down mugs on the counter. He nodded an acknowledgement as Sophie entered the kitchen with his wife, but he said nothing.

Sophie cleared her throat. 'I'm very sorry to intrude, but I need to ask you both a few questions about your neighbours – the Poulsons. Sadly, Mrs Poulson was found deceased yesterday.'

Laura glared at her husband. 'We saw it on the Scothern Facebook group this morning.' She pulled out a stool for Sophie at the breakfast bar. 'Tea?'

'Please. Milk, no sugar.' Sophie sat down and pulled out her notepad, pen poised to take notes. 'How long have you lived opposite the Poulsons?'

'Oh, I don't know. Six years, maybe?' James scratched his stubbly chin.

'I think you'll find it's eight years, actually,' Laura said sharply.

Mr MacGregor's expression tightened. He waited a few seconds before turning back to Sophie. 'That's probably right. Hard to keep track of time nowadays.'

'And in all those years living opposite, how well would you say you knew Alison and David?'

The MacGregors exchanged a glance. 'Not very well at all really,' Laura said after a moment. 'We'd say hello if we saw each other on the drive, comment on the weather and stuff like that. But that was about it.'

James placed a mug of tea in front of Sophie. 'They kept themselves to themselves.'

Sophie's pen hesitated over her notebook. Their answers didn't seem to line up with years of living opposite the other couple. She decided to push further. 'You never socialised with the Poulsons at all? Never had them over for dinner or drinks?'

'No, never,' James said firmly. Laura shook her head.

'Did you ever have arguments or disagreements with them? Over parking or bins or noise?' Sophie asked.

Again, the couple both shook their heads. 'Nope, can't recall any arguments,' James said.

Sophie frowned, tapping her pen on her notebook. Something didn't feel right. She noticed Laura glaring at her husband again. There was definitely tension between them.

'I could be wrong, but I'm sensing you know more about the Poulsons than you're letting on,' Sophie said. 'I need you both to be completely honest with me. This is a murder investigation.'

The MacGregors squirmed under her gaze. Finally, Laura broke the silence. 'I had my suspicions for some time . . .'

'Laura . . .' James's voice held a warning tone.

'She's from the police,' Laura snapped back, waving a hand towards Sophie. 'They'll find out eventually, and it will be worse for us if we don't tell the truth now.'

Sophie raised an eyebrow. Now they were finally getting somewhere. 'That's very true. If you're withholding information—'

'Keep quiet!' James exploded.

'Excuse me?' Sophie's eyes widened.

'I was talking to her, not you,' James said hurriedly, nodding at his wife.

'Well, I'm not talking to *you*!' Laura turned her back on her husband.

Sophie stared at them both. This wasn't going quite the way she'd planned.

Laura's eyes narrowed, and she turned to Sophie. 'I found out my husband was having an affair with our neighbour,' she spat, jabbing a finger in the direction of the Poulsons' house.

James held up his hands defensively. 'Sweetheart, it was just a brief fling, nothing serious—'

'Nothing serious?' Laura cut him off, her voice rising. 'I found love letters, and texts on your phone! How long did you think you could keep up your sordid little affair before I found out?'

Sophie watched the argument with fascination.

'It was just a bit of fun,' James pleaded, his face pale. 'I've apologised. You know you're the only one for me.'

'Only one for you?' Laura shouted. 'You made a fool out of me, carrying on right under my nose.'

Sophie cleared her throat. 'So, let me get this straight – you were having an affair with *Alison* Poulson?' She didn't want to assume. It could have been David, or even one of their other neighbours.

James nodded, shoulders slumped. 'It was never serious though, just a brief flirtation.'

Laura screwed up a tea towel and threw it at James. 'And now she's dead!'

'And did David Poulson discover the affair?' Sophie asked.

James shook his head. 'No, we were very discreet.'

'Not discreet enough. I found out,' Laura muttered bitterly.

'When did you find out?' Sophie asked Laura.

'Yesterday.'

Sophie felt guilty at the rush of excitement she was experiencing. The situation was obviously very traumatic for Laura, but this was a huge break in the case. She turned to James. 'I'll need to see any evidence you still have of the affair – letters, texts, emails.'

Sophie wanted all the information she could get to prove motive.

James shifted uncomfortably. 'I don't have anything anymore. I got rid of it all when Laura found out.'

Sophie frowned. That was convenient. 'You destroyed potential evidence in a murder investigation?'

'When I got rid of it, I didn't know there was a murder investigation,' James said. 'But I swear I didn't hurt Alison.'

Laura let out a derisive snort. 'Oh please, like you expect us to believe that? You were obsessed with her!' She turned back to Sophie. 'Mark my words, if you want to find out who killed that woman, you need look no further than my cheating husband!'

'Laura! You don't mean that.'

'I do.'

'You can't really believe I'd kill anyone.'

Sophie watched James splutter his denials as Laura continued her tirade. This interview had been far more productive than she could have imagined. Karen would be very pleased when she heard how Sophie had uncovered the secret affair, and potentially a motive for someone to hurt Alison.

Sophie was scribbling down notes when a loud crash from outside made her jump. She glanced up, pen frozen over her notepad.

'What on earth was that?' Laura asked, moving towards the hallway.

Sophie followed Laura and James into the sitting room.

Another bang echoed down the quiet lane, followed by a man's raised voice. Sophie felt her heart rate increase.

James pulled the curtain back from the large bay window overlooking the drive.

'It's Poulson,' he said, peeking out the window and then stepping back. 'He's gone completely mad.'

Sophie hurried over to the window. Outside on the driveway, David Poulson was kicking the panels of the MacGregors' blue Audi. He then grabbed one of the wheelie bins and hurled it on to the middle of the drive. It hit the stones with a loud crunch, spilling recycling waste everywhere.

Poulson looked like a man possessed; his face tight with fury. He snarled at them through the window.

Sophie recoiled, feeling a tightness in her chest as though a giant hand were crushing her ribs.

Poulson stomped back to the MacGregors' car and slammed his fists on the bonnet. 'Come out here, you coward!' he yelled towards the house. 'I know what you did. I'm going to kill you!'

Sophie took an involuntary step back from the window.

The raw anger and violence were stirring up terrifying memories. Memories she'd tried hard to suppress.

The night she was attacked came flooding back in horrifying clarity. The distant rush of a train. The eerie creak of the roller door on the mechanic's workshop, rocking in the wind. The haunting face of a clown mask, grinning at her from the party shop window. Footsteps behind her, growing louder, closer. Then, a blinding pain exploding in her skull.

Jim Willson rushed across the lane. He was saying something to Poulson, trying to calm him down, but it wasn't working.

She struggled to catch her breath, pulse pounding in her ears. Fragments of that night continued to assault her senses. The leaves swirling in the deserted car park. The taste of blood in her mouth. The rough tarmac against her cheek. Then the sterile smell of the hospital, the incessant beep of machines. She couldn't move, couldn't speak, effects of the brain injury and the drugs. Trapped in her own mind, unable to communicate the terror she felt. Her body wouldn't cooperate, just like now.

Poulson's yelling continued, and he rushed to the window again, screaming. To Sophie, his face changed into that of the man who'd left her for dead. The sound of Poulson's fists hitting the window was terrifying. Each thud sent a jolt of fear through her body. But she couldn't even flinch. Her muscles felt like lead, refusing to respond to signals from her brain.

'He's lost it!' James shouted, turning to look at Sophie. 'That lunatic is going to wreck my car! Get out there and stop him.'

'No, I don't think it's safe,' Laura muttered.

'She's a police officer,' James shouted back. 'It's her job!'

Sophie blinked hard, trying to force the vivid flashbacks from her mind. But they kept coming – disjointed and terrifying. The grinning clown. The footsteps. The pain. The hospital. She couldn't escape them, couldn't break free from the panic that held her in its grip.

She focused on steadying her breathing. She was here in the MacGregors' warm living room, not outside a workshop on the cold ground.

'Well, don't just stand there; go and stop him!' James shouted again.

She knew she should intervene and help Jim, but she couldn't make her legs move. The panic flooding her system kept her rigid. Her body felt disconnected, just like it had in the ICU all those months earlier. She willed herself to move – to do something, anything – but she remained frozen.

'Are you okay?' Laura asked.

Sophie couldn't speak. The room spun around her. The walls seemed to close in, the air thick and suffocating. The memories kept coming, faster and more vivid. The clown. The footsteps. The pain. The hospital. Over and over, like a never-ending nightmare she couldn't wake up from. She gripped the back of the sofa, trying to hold on to reality, but the panic was too strong, pulling her under.

'It's okay,' Laura said, rubbing Sophie's back. 'I think he's calming down.'

Laura's hand on Sophie's back seemed to break the spell. She was in the MacGregors' living room. She was safe.

They watched as Jim defused the situation. Finally, his measured words seemed to be having an effect. The shouting stopped, and after another minute or so, David allowed himself to be led away.

'Can I get you a glass of water?' Laura asked. 'You look very pale.'

Sophie murmured her thanks, wishing her heart rate would slow down. She was mortified by her reaction. Yes, Jim had handled it, but what if he hadn't been there?

Sophie sipped her water slowly. The panic attack had shaken her, leaving her feeling vulnerable and unsettled. Maybe she wasn't cut out for this job anymore.

Why wasn't she over it yet? It was so frustrating – she kept telling herself she *should* be past all this, but she wasn't. The nagging feeling that she should have moved on by now just wouldn't go away – and somehow only made the panic worse. It was a vicious cycle, and Sophie didn't know how to break free.

A moment later, there was a knock at the front door. It was Jim.

'Everything all right in here?' he asked, stepping inside. 'Poulson's calmed down now. I'm not sure what happened. He just totally flipped. His GP is going to call by later.'

Sophie's hand trembled as she lifted the glass to her lips.

'You okay there, Sophie?' Jim asked gently.

'Fine, thanks.' Embarrassment burned her cheeks.

The flashback had been so real; she could still taste the fear.

'I'll leave you to it then?'

Sophie nodded.

'If you need anything, I'm just across the street. I'll stay with Poulson for a while.'

'I think that's probably best.'

After Jim left, Sophie felt the weight of the MacGregors' gazes on her. She hated that they were looking at her differently now. Laura's eyes were filled with concern while James was looking at her with a mix of speculation and wariness.

Laura, who had been so angry before, now just seemed drained and defeated.

'Do you want to press charges?' Sophie asked James. She glanced out at the car with its dented bonnet, and the scattered rubbish on the drive.

He looked out at the mess, then shook his head. 'Probably best to leave it. Poulson's got enough on his plate.' His voice held an edge of guilt that hadn't been there before.

Sophie tried to press him for more details about his relationship with Alison, but he shut down completely, refusing to say another word on the matter.

Realising she wasn't going to get anything else useful from the MacGregors, Sophie gathered her things.

'Well, I think I've got everything I need for now,' she said, trying to force confidence into her voice. 'I'd advise you not to contact Mr Poulson for the time being, and if he comes around again, call the police straightaway.'

Laura nodded. James stared at the floor.

'I'd better clear up.' He headed outside and started clearing away the spilled recycling.

Laura watched him from the doorway, arms crossed over her chest. The fiery indignation from earlier had left her. She seemed more sad than angry now.

Just as Sophie was about to leave, Laura pressed a bundle of papers into her hand. 'Here, you should take these. They're the love letters and notes Alison wrote to James. I don't owe that cheating scumbag a thing. He can deal with the consequences of what he did.'

Sophie thanked her. 'This is very helpful.'

Laura just nodded, her lips pressed in a firm line.

Despite the nerves and the horrendous panic attack, the interview had been more successful than Sophie could have imagined.

She walked down the garden path. Her head was buzzing. The affair didn't just put James MacGregor in the hot seat. It also gave David Poulson a clear motive if he'd found out about his wife's infidelity. It even gave Laura MacGregor a motive – jealousy towards a love rival – although Sophie found it hard to imagine her killing someone.

Laura seemed too ordinary to be capable of such a violent act. Her life revolved around baking and blogging. Sophie couldn't picture her as a cold-blooded killer, meticulously planning and executing a murder involving a torture device. It just didn't fit the profile of a woman who spent her days baking cookies and cakes.

As the letters belonged to James, she couldn't just take them without his permission or a warrant. Legally, she should get his consent before going through them. She stopped beside him as he bent down, scooping up scattered plastic bottles and crumpled paper from his driveway.

'Your wife gave me some letters that Alison wrote to you.' Sophie held them up. 'I wanted to ask your permission to go through them as part of the investigation.'

James straightened up, his jaw clenching. He shoved the rubbish into the recycling bin. 'I don't know if that's a good idea.'

'You're under no obligation, but refusing does make it seem like you have something to hide.'

James's eyes darted between Sophie and the letters. He reached for an empty tonic can at his feet and crushed it in his hand. 'Fine. Take them. There's nothing incriminating in there.'

'Thank you. I'll return them once we've finished with them.'

'Don't bother. I never want to see those letters again.'

He bent down and aggressively grabbed a crushed cardboard box, tearing it into smaller pieces before shoving it into the bin.

'Are you sure?' Sophie asked. 'They might hold sentimental value.'

James paused, a handful of cardboard clenched in his fist. 'Sentimental?' He let out a bitter laugh. 'Those letters are nothing but trouble. Do what you want with them, then burn them for all I care.'

He turned away and began dragging the bin back towards the house.

As Sophie walked towards her car, she noticed Jim jogging across the road towards her.

'Just wanted to check you're okay before you head off.'

Sophie's cheeks flushed. 'I'm okay. Just a bit shaken up. Thanks for de-escalating Poulson.'

'No problem.' Jim's gaze lingered on her for a moment before he nodded and added, 'Well, I'd better get back.'

'Thanks again.'

Sophie watched him go. She hated that he'd seen her at her weakest and that he knew about the panic attack. Would he tell others at the station about it? Churchill would confine her to office work for the rest of her career. She hated the thought of people talking about her behind her back. Who'd want to work with her if they thought she'd bottle it when things got tough?

Sophie slid into the driver's seat, resting her forehead against the steering wheel as she let out a shaky breath. The image of Poulson's enraged face still lingered in her mind, his fists pounding against the window as he yelled threats. The paralysing fear that had gripped her in that moment had been all-consuming.

Her hands shook as she started the ignition. She had dreamed of being a police officer for as long as she could remember. And now that dream was slipping away.

Ever since the attack, she hadn't felt like the same person. Her confidence was gone. She was now someone plagued with fear and self-doubt. Someone who froze when things got tough.

What if Poulson had been armed with a knife instead of just his fists? Would she have been able to act? Or would the panic have paralysed her just the same, leaving Jim vulnerable . . . at risk of being seriously injured or worse? She couldn't trust herself anymore, and a police officer who couldn't be relied on was a liability.

Tears welled in Sophie's eyes as the realisation sunk in. As much as it devastated her, she knew that she couldn't continue like this.

The attack had left her with more than the scars on her scalp. It had given her anxiety and taken away the capable officer she used to be. Being part of the police service was Sophie's identity. It was more than just a career – it was her purpose. Letting go of that felt unthinkable.

But she couldn't endanger others because she couldn't hack it.

Sophie now had some tough decisions to make. The thought of walking away from everything she had worked so hard for was devastating. But if she couldn't cope, she couldn't do the job. It was as simple as that.

Chapter Eleven

Karen left the village hall and stepped out into the cold October afternoon. Arnie had already left, getting a lift back to the station with one of the other officers. They'd heard that the two TV presenters were back from Lincoln and having lunch in the pub, so Karen was heading there to speak to them.

It didn't take long to drive to the Cross Keys, where most of the crew from the TV show were staying. The car park was packed, thanks to the press who seemed to be using it as a base. Karen had to park a short distance away, across the village green. As she approached the pub, a gaggle of photographers turned her way, before someone muttered, 'Don't bother, she's no one famous.'

Inside the warm pub, she spotted Molly and Trevor sitting at a table by the window. The curtains had been drawn, no doubt to stop the intrusive photographers getting snaps of the celebrities. Molly wore an off-the-shoulder floral dress that showed off her tan and cleavage. Trevor was sporting an overly tight polo shirt. His obvious hairpiece was too low, hiding most of his forehead.

Molly was jabbing a finger in Trevor's direction. His face was distorted in a scowl. It looked like the beginning of an argument between the co-hosts. Not something unusual; they had quite the reputation for their off-screen bickering.

Steeling herself for the encounter, Karen approached Trevor and Molly. Half-eaten plates of food and full wine glasses were on the table in front of them.

'If you hadn't insisted on stopping at every shop in the city, we could've been back an hour ago!' Trevor was saying.

'Oh please, the only reason you wanted to rush back was so you could have a nap. You're such an old fart these days,' Molly shot back, before delicately dabbing her mouth with a napkin.

Karen cleared her throat. 'Afternoon, Mr Barker, Miss Moreland. I'm DS Karen Hart with the Lincolnshire Police. Mind if I have a quick word?'

'Please join us,' Trevor said, gesturing to the empty chair at their table. 'Let me get you a drink. What's your poison? Wine? G&T?'

'I'm on duty, but thank you,' Karen replied as she slid into the seat.

'Thought you were low-carb, Trev?' Molly asked as she grabbed a crusty slice of bread off Trevor's plate and took a bite.

'Oi, you've got your own!' Trevor snapped, smacking her hand away. 'You'll be needing the gym after this, porky.'

Molly gave him an icy stare. Then she turned to Karen with a smile. 'Sorry. You must think we're awful. But he did tell me to stop him if I ever saw him eating carbs.'

Their flippancy grated on Karen's nerves. A woman had died, horribly, and all they seemed to care about was food and petty squabbles. She wasn't interested in their dietary habits. She tried to direct the conversation back on course. 'I'd like to ask you both a few questions about Alison Poulson.'

'Ah, Alison. Awful business,' Trevor said through a mouthful of cheese and pickle, crumbs falling down his shirt.

'Just terrible,' Molly added. 'I do hope you catch whoever did it.'

'Yes,' Trevor agreed with a nod. 'It's completely messed up our shooting schedule.'

Karen gritted her teeth. Alison's death wasn't just 'awful' or 'terrible' – it was a brutal, senseless tragedy. And if Sophie's instincts were right, this killer could just be getting started. They needed to catch them, fast, before someone else suffered Alison's fate.

Karen tried to push down her frustration and stay focused. 'You both knew the victim then?'

'Oh, I wouldn't say *knew* her,' Trevor answered, waving a hand. 'Crossed paths once or twice. She was with the local council, wasn't she?'

'That's right, she worked in a department focused on development projects. Did you have much to do with her during filming?'

'Not really.' Trevor shrugged. 'Though she did ask me for an autograph. Always nice to meet one of my fans.'

Molly rolled her eyes. 'She wasn't a fan, you muppet.'

He pushed some more cheese in his mouth, looking somewhat embarrassed.

'Tell the detective what happened, Trevor,' Molly said with a grin. 'It was so funny.'

Trevor shot her a scornful look before turning back to Karen. 'It was nothing, really. Alison simply asked for my autograph one day, that's all.'

Molly let out a shrill laugh. 'Oh, come on, that's not how it happened, and you know it!' She turned gleefully to Karen. 'The silly fool thought Alison was asking for an autograph when she just wanted him to sign some paperwork.'

'Yes, all right, you've had your fun, Molly. It was an innocent mistake.'

'Should have seen his face when she asked what he was doing!' Molly laughed. 'Priceless!'

'Yes, hilarious,' muttered Trevor, thickly buttering a slice of bread.

As they chattered on, oblivious to the gravity of it all, a cold weight settled in Karen's stomach. They didn't grasp the seriousness of the situation at all. More lives could be on the line, and every second wasted on their nonsense was a second the killer remained free. 'So, just to clarify, there was some confusion because you thought Mrs Poulson wanted an autograph when, in fact, she needed you to sign something work-related?'

'Exactly,' Trevor huffed. 'An easy mistake, but this one here won't let me live it down.'

'Oh, lighten up,' Molly said, still grinning as she lifted her wine glass. 'It was funny. Although . . .' She lowered her voice and leaned forward. 'Perhaps that gives Trevor a motive!'

Karen hid her impatience and irritation. She was determined to extract every potentially useful scrap of information. For Alison's sake. Even if she had to endure Trevor and Molly's complete lack of respect to do it.

'Shut up, Molly. The detective won't know you're joking.' He gave Karen an awkward smile. 'Molly knows I wouldn't hurt a fly.'

'Oh, do I?' Molly lifted her eyebrows and took a sip of wine.

'Yes, you do!' Trevor said, then shoved his plate away. A slow smile stretched across his face. 'Although now I think of it, you have a pretty big motive yourself.'

Molly's smug grin disappeared. 'What do you mean?'

'Come now Molly, darling – no need to be coy. Why don't you tell the detective about how Alison tried to get you sacked?'

It was Molly's turn to scowl now. 'I haven't the faintest idea what you're going on about, Trevor.'

But Trevor was grinning, clearly enjoying having the upper hand. 'Oh, I think you do. Didn't she file some formal complaint against you?'

Molly's glossy lips pressed together in a thin line. When she spoke, her tone was clipped. 'She tried to. It was a minor misunderstanding, nothing more. Alison overreacted.'

'What was the complaint about?' Karen asked, intrigued. They might finally be getting somewhere.

'Oh, it was nothing really,' Molly said airily. 'It was just a little dent. I didn't know she'd parked behind me. Alison's car was in my blind spot, so it was her fault, but she made such a fuss.'

'What happened *exactly*?' Karen asked. They hadn't yet located Alison's car, and they'd been looking for it.

Molly sighed. 'I reversed into Alison's car in the pub car park. Hardly touched it really. Just a teensy scratch. I said I'd pay to fix the damage. Got her car towed to a garage, who promised to get it back in a day or two, good as new. But that wasn't enough for Alison. She tried to get me fired!'

'It *was* an overreaction,' Trevor said sympathetically.

'She reported it to Tilda, our director,' Molly continued after another gulp of wine. 'Obviously, Tilda ignored her – I'm the star of the show.'

'*One* of the stars,' Trevor said pointedly.

Molly rolled her eyes.

'If I'm understanding correctly,' Karen said, getting the conversation back on track, 'Alison tried to get you fired after you reversed into her car, but you barely knew her otherwise? That seems strange. Did you have any other interactions?'

'Our paths rarely crossed. We'd only seen her a couple of times at the dig site before that. I'm not sure why she decided to be such a bitch.'

'She was intimidated by you, pet,' Trevor said, patting Molly's hand.

Molly sniffed and nodded. 'I don't like to speak ill of the dead, but she was a difficult woman.'

'Which garage took Alison's car in for repair?'

Molly provided the details, and Karen made a note before asking, 'And did Alison get a temporary courtesy car?'

'I assume so,' Molly said. 'But I don't know for sure.'

Karen looked at Trevor, who shrugged. 'Haven't the faintest idea. Sorry.'

Trevor stood up from the table. 'I need to visit the little boys' room.'

As soon as he was out of earshot, Molly leaned forward conspiratorially. 'He's gone to fix his toupee. But don't mention it. He's very sensitive about it. I don't know why he doesn't splash out on a better one. He can afford it.' She drained her wine glass. 'He's a sweetheart really. It was a poor joke on my part. Trevor's all bluster. Wouldn't hurt a fly.'

'He seemed genuinely annoyed about the autograph. You're saying there was no real animosity between them?'

Molly let out a dismissive laugh. 'He was just embarrassed. But he's harmless, trust me.'

'We shouldn't consider him a suspect, then?' Karen said.

Molly smirked. 'Darling, the only thing Trevor's guilty of is hanging on to my coattails. He doesn't have the brains or the backbone to hurt anyone. He's about as dangerous as a used teabag.'

Karen studied Molly closely, but her bright smile seemed genuine.

Trevor returned, his hairpiece now straightened. 'Did I miss anything?'

Karen stood up. 'No, I think we're done here for now. Thank you both for your time. Here's my card if you remember anything else useful.'

Molly took the card between two fingers, glancing at it briefly before dropping it in her pink Michael Kors handbag.

Karen left the pub and typed a message to Arnie, asking him to check out the garage and giving him the details she'd been given by Molly.

They'd been looking for Alison's Mercedes C-Class, but it must have been in the garage this whole time. If Alison had driven herself to Stow last night, she must have been using a different car. Finding that was now a priority.

The first fat drops of rain hit the pavement, soon becoming a steady downpour. Karen hurried across the village green. Glancing up, she noticed the old whipping post standing tall near the centre of the small green. Karen paused beside it, reading the plaque. She studied the weathered wooden post and its shackles, imagining the cruelty that had played out there centuries ago.

Karen ran her fingers over the ancient iron, which felt cold and rough with age. People had been chained here, lashed for some petty crime while a jeering crowd looked on. The thought sent a chill through her.

It reminded her eerily of the torture device found clasped around Alison Poulson's throat. That awful shrew's fiddle, designed to humiliate and cause pain. Someone had decided to use it on Alison Poulson for a reason. To punish her for speaking out of turn? For not knowing her place? The idea filled Karen with a slow, simmering rage.

She pushed her wet hair back from her face. This case was a reminder that darkness still lurked in people's hearts, no matter how modern and enlightened the world pretended to be.

She thought of Alison, lying cold and stiff in the muddy trench, the iron clenched ruthlessly around her neck. What did it mean? Alison had been a shrew? A nag?

Alison had been described as hard, difficult and unlikeable by almost everyone. Had someone decided she was too outspoken? Too abrasive?

Karen reflected on some of the awful names women had been called over the centuries – *shrew, nag, harpy, witch*. Spiteful labels meant to demean and control.

The rain was letting up. Karen took one last look at the whipping post and then continued on. She had work to do.

First things first. They needed to find the car Alison had been driving last night. With luck, it might give them some much-needed answers.

◆　◆　◆

Detective Constable Farzana Shah sat at her desk, a cup of rapidly cooling hibiscus tea by her elbow. Morgan had asked her to verify the various alibis they had collected so far.

Farzana had been staring at CCTV footage playing at 2.5x speed for over an hour. It wasn't the best part of the job, but it was important. Especially as Lucas Black had said he'd been at the Red Lion pub when Alison Poulson was murdered. But when Farzana had attempted to verify his alibi, the landlord had told her he hadn't seen Lucas last night.

That meant either Lucas had been in the pub, but the landlord had been too busy to notice, or Lucas had lied about his alibi.

So now Farzana had the unenviable task of combing through CCTV from last night trying to spot Lucas Black. She kept her keen gaze on the footage, looking for any sign of a man with floppy brown hair and frameless glasses.

On the monitor in front of her, two middle-aged women walked towards the entrance, laughing. A young couple holding hands followed them inside. But still no Lucas.

As the footage continued to play, Farzana picked up her desk phone and rang the supervisor at the warehouse where David Poulson worked. She needed to verify Poulson's alibi, too.

The call was answered by a gruff-sounding man.

'Hello, is this Mr Andrews?'

The man grunted in affirmation.

'This is DC Farzana Shah from Lincolnshire Police. I'm calling about an employee of yours, David Poulson.'

'Yeah, I heard the news about his wife. Terrible. What do you need from me?'

'I'd like to verify the hours David worked last night. Would you be able to confirm he was on shift that entire evening, from nine p.m. to five a.m.?'

'That sounds about right. Hang on, let me pull up the records to double-check.' Farzana heard the tapping of computer keys as she kept her gaze fixed on her monitor.

'Yeah, he clocked in at 8.53 p.m. and finished at 5.09 a.m.,' the supervisor finally said. 'I can send you a copy of his time sheet if you need it.'

'That would be very helpful; thank you, Mr Andrews,' Farzana replied, still watching the CCTV footage. She gave him her email address so he could send the time sheet and then added, 'I'll also need you to sign a statement confirming David Poulson's hours for our records. Are you able to come into the station later today, or tomorrow?'

The supervisor grunted again. 'Suppose I can pop in this afternoon.'

'Excellent. I'll prepare the statement for you to review, and then you can sign it this afternoon. Thanks for your help.'

The supervisor muttered a goodbye and hung up.

Farzana put the phone down, feeling pleased. That corroborated Poulson's alibi nicely. That was one suspect off their list.

Sadly, she wasn't having the same luck with the recorded footage from outside the Red Lion. The recording was nearing 9.30

p.m. now. She watched a large, bald man entering the pub. Nope, definitely not Lucas. Where *was* he?

After a few more minutes, she leaned forward. She froze the frame, noticing a figure lingering outside the pub. Was that him? She studied the screen. Zooming in, she huffed in frustration. No, definitely not Lucas. She set the footage playing again.

After minimising the viewing window so she could use the computer without missing any comings or goings at the pub, Farzana looked up the number Professor Stark had given for his colleague, Professor Ross Mackenzie. She needed to verify Stark's claim that he'd been working late with Mackenzie at the university on the night of the murder. Pulling up the Lincoln University staff page, she found Mackenzie's photo and bio. He appeared to be in his sixties, with a halo of puffy white hair and ruddy cheeks. His credentials were impressive.

Farzana dialled the number, and the call rang three times before a man answered. 'Hello?'

'Hello, is that Professor Mackenzie?'

'It is.'

'Good afternoon, Professor. This is Detective Constable Farzana Shah from Lincolnshire Police. I'm calling to ask you about last night. I believe you were working with Professor Thomas Stark?'

'Yes, that's right. Tom and I stayed at the university, working late finalising a research grant proposal.' Mackenzie spoke with a mild Scottish lilt.

'Could you confirm what time you were both there until? And whether Professor Stark left before or after you?'

'Let me think . . . Yes, Tom came to my office around half six, and we worked together until almost eleven. He left just before me. I'd say he was there until around 10.45 p.m. or so,' Mackenzie replied.

'Thank you, Professor, that's very helpful. I'll get a statement typed up for you to review and sign when you have a moment.'

Professor Mackenzie hesitated on the other end of the line. 'Oh dear, that won't be possible just now. I'm actually about to leave for Scotland. My elderly mother has had a bad fall, so I'm afraid I'll be away for a few days.'

'I'm so sorry to hear that,' Farzana said. 'Any chance you could pop into the station before you leave?'

'I wish I could, but I'm already cutting it close time-wise. Perhaps when I return? I should only be away for a few days.'

'Of course. Just give me a call when you're back.' Farzana gave him her direct number. 'I hope your mother recovers quickly.'

'Thank you, my dear, much appreciated.'

After saying goodbye, Farzana set the phone down. Professor Mackenzie had corroborated Stark's alibi. But it would have been good to get a signed statement before he left Lincoln. Still keeping one eye on the pub footage, she made a note to follow up when he returned.

There was no one outside the pub, and it would be closing soon. She frowned. Where was Lucas?

Just then, a figure walked into the frame wearing a dark jacket and a baseball cap. Farzana leaned in closer to the screen and slowed the playback speed. The camera angle wasn't great, but it *could* be him. The height and build looked right. She watched the figure walk along the street towards the pub, hands in pockets. Right before reaching the pub entrance, he half turned, glancing back over his shoulder.

It wasn't Lucas, after all. She slumped back in her chair.

The timestamp now read 11.15 p.m. Lucas had claimed he'd left the pub at ten p.m., heading home alone. But so far, after going through nearly five hours of footage, Farzana had found no sign of him entering or exiting the pub last night.

Farzana stared at the screen and sat back. Why would Lucas have lied about being at the pub if he had nothing to hide?

The landlord hadn't seen him, and there was no sign of him on the external security footage. There was only one explanation: Lucas Black had not been at the Red Lion last night. He had deliberately fabricated an alibi for the night of Alison Poulson's murder. The question was – why? And what was he trying to cover up?

Chapter Twelve

Arnie ambled into the station, munching on a Twix bar.

He headed to the open-plan office and spotted Farzana at her desk. 'Afternoon,' he said through a mouthful of chocolate.

She glanced up at him, pushing her hair back from her face. 'I've just been looking into Lucas Black's alibi. He lied. No sign of him at the Red Lion last night.'

'Well, well, well, lying to the police. That's not a good look for Mr Black,' Arnie said, swallowing the last of his chocolate bar. 'Does DI Morgan know?'

'Yes, I informed Morgan straightaway. He's gone to speak to Lucas now.'

'Good job,' Arnie said. He crumpled up his Twix wrapper and tossed it towards the bin, missing by a mile.

He scooped it up and deposited it in the bin, successfully this time. 'Keep me updated if you hear back from Morgan before me.'

'Will do,' Farzana said, turning her attention back to her computer screen.

Arnie headed over to his own desk, which was overflowing with files, scraps of paper and dirty mugs. He really needed to tidy up. But what was the point? It would only be messy again a few minutes later.

As he shuffled some papers around the desk, he noticed Rick sitting with Sophie at her desk. His arm was around her shoulders. Arnie walked over to them.

'What's up?'

Rick looked up. 'Sophie's a bit upset.'

Arnie's gaze shifted to Sophie, his expression softening when he saw her red eyes. 'What's the matter, kiddo?'

She kept her eyes downcast and fumbled with a pen on the desk. 'I'm fine.'

'You don't look it.'

Sophie took a deep breath. 'I didn't handle things well at the MacGregors' house earlier. David Poulson came over and started shouting abuse and throwing things. I panicked and froze up.' She looked at Arnie, her eyes swimming with tears. 'I had flashbacks to the night I was assaulted, and my heart started racing . . .' She sniffed. 'I feel so useless. I'm no good if I can't cope.'

'Hey now, don't be so hard on yourself,' Arnie said gently. 'You took a nasty knock on the bonce. It's going to take time to get back to full strength.'

'But I've been recovering for ages, Arnie. I should be back to normal by now. If Jim hadn't been there today, anything could have happened. And it would have been my fault.' Sophie shook her head. 'I'm useless. Maybe I'm not cut out for this job anymore.'

'That's not true,' Rick said, shooting a look at Arnie that said *help me out here.*

Arnie's heart sank. He wasn't good at this sort of thing. They needed Karen. She always seemed to know the right words to say. He'd seen this type of reaction before, the self-doubt and uncertainty. He'd been there himself, once upon a time.

Arnie patted Sophie's shoulder. 'The point is, don't be so tough on yourself. There's more to life than police work.'

Rick shot him daggers, and Arnie guessed he'd said the wrong thing. Again.

Sophie sniffed. 'Not for me there isn't. This job is everything; it's all I've ever wanted.'

Arnie pulled up a chair. Time to bring out the big guns. Open up and show a bit of sensitivity. That was all the rage these days, wasn't it? Rick still had an expression like he'd just sucked a lemon. But what did he expect? Arnie wasn't a therapist, for pity's sake. His life was hardly a model one.

Arnie cleared his throat. 'I was doing a job about fifteen years back.' His voice sounded weird. Hoarse. He hadn't spoken about this in so long. Found it easier not to. But he knew it might help Sophie, so he continued. 'I went into a house, thought it was empty.' He paused, taking a deep breath. 'Turned out there was a bloke inside, hiding. Off his head on drugs. Thought I was a demon or some such nonsense. Anyway, he took a swing at me. I thought it was just his fist at first, but then I saw the blade. Caught me in the shoulder and then . . .' Arnie patted the top of his chest. 'He got me here a few times. I tried to fight him off, but I fell and hit my head. Concussion, fractured skull, the works. Left to bleed out on the floor. Nearly died.'

Rick and Sophie listened in silence, hanging on his every word.

'I was out of action for months,' Arnie continued. 'When I came back, I didn't feel right. Constantly on the lookout for concealed weapons, even during the most mundane situations. Couldn't shake the feeling that I was one step behind everyone else.'

'You never mentioned that before,' Sophie said.

Arnie shrugged. 'Well, we don't really talk about that stuff, do we? You just pick yourself up and carry on. One foot after the other and all that.' He leaned back in his chair. 'A bloke I know from the pub was telling me his office gives them mental health days. Sounds like a nice idea . . . although if I took a day off every time I needed one, I'd never be at work!'

Rick chuckled, but Sophie couldn't even manage a smile.

Arnie looked at her. 'I know how you feel. But you'll get through this, kiddo. It just takes time.'

Sophie nodded. 'All right. I'll give it a bit longer.'

'Until then, we'll help you out. Won't we, Rick?'

'Course we will,' Rick said. 'We're a team, aren't we? Always got each other's backs.'

Sophie's lips curved into a faint smile. 'Thanks,' she said, her voice still shaky. 'I appreciate it.'

Arnie left them to their paperwork and walked back to his own desk. He hoped Sophie would regain her confidence soon. She was a good copper; she just needed time.

Sophie was sorting through the stack of letters that Laura MacGregor had given her. They were love letters from Alison to James – steamy stuff that made Sophie blush just to scan over them.

They were filled with passionate declarations and vivid descriptions of desire, and were far raunchier than Sophie had expected. The letters made it clear that Alison and James had been intimately involved, but there was no mention of them leaving their spouses or being in love.

DC Farzana Shah came over, a slip of paper in her hand. 'There you are. Laura MacGregor called. She wanted to let you know that she recorded a YouTube livestream on Tuesday evening. She said it might help prove she and her husband were both at home.'

Sophie blinked. She should have already checked that. Why hadn't she thought of it? 'Thanks, Farzana,' she said, trying to keep the annoyance out of her voice.

She found a surprising number of videos on Laura's YouTube channel, each one boasting an impressive viewer count. The most recent video, titled 'Baking with Laura: Autumn Treats!' was right at the top.

The livestream went on for a staggering two and a half hours. *Who in their right mind would watch someone else baking for that long?*

But she dutifully pressed play, watching as Laura chatted to the camera, assembling her baking equipment. She increased the playback speed to the highest level. An ad break came on abruptly – for an obscenely expensive mixer – and went on . . . and on. Sophie found herself tapping her foot impatiently until finally, mercifully, it ended and Laura returned to dolloping cake batter into tins.

Then James strolled past in the background and flashed an easy smile at the camera before vanishing off-screen again. Laura looked up from her work and shot him an adoring glance before continuing with her demonstration.

They were picture-perfect: Laura in a pretty dress looking every inch the domestic goddess; handsome James passing by like he'd just stepped out of an aftershave advert – all smiles and charm. This was all for show, a carefully crafted image for their audience. No glowering, arguing, or slamming cupboards on YouTube. They looked like the ideal couple – no one would know the truth about them from this video. James fleetingly appeared several more times, each time smiling at his wife, playing his role to perfection.

As the stream came to an end, Sophie leaned back in her chair, deflated. The MacGregors' alibi seemed pretty solid if the YouTube timestamps were anything to go by.

She felt a pang of disappointment. So much for this being an exciting break in the case. Working on this investigation was like trying to solve a Rubik's cube blindfolded, Sophie thought, dropping her pen on the desk. It was time to go back to the drawing board.

The MacGregors were a dead end.

◆ ◆ ◆

Karen had experienced doors being closed in her face many times on the job, and it always left her seething. But this time, with Christie Stark on the other side, it was particularly frustrating. She needed to talk to the teen. Karen was afraid the girl might be holding back some crucial information about Alison's murder, something she was afraid to tell them.

Melissa Stark had turned her away, saying Christie was finally getting some much needed sleep. Christie's mother's protectiveness was understandable, but it left Karen infuriated because she was sure Christie knew more than she was letting on. But pushing too forcefully now might lead to Christie retreating further into her shell. Cooperation was key, and alienating the family would only make her job harder.

Karen kicked at a pile of leaves. How could she coax the full story from Christie if she couldn't even speak to her?

Sophie's theory about the killer striking again had burrowed into her mind. If she was right, and Christie had seen something or knew something that incriminated the murderer, then she could be in danger. The sadistic killer who had killed Alison wouldn't hesitate to silence Christie.

Karen's steps slowed as an image of Christie, murdered in the same brutal way as Alison, flashed in her mind. The shy, quiet girl, her body in the trench, the cruel metal of the shrew's fiddle biting into her neck . . .

Anger surged through Karen, hot and fierce. She wouldn't let that happen. Christie wasn't even eighteen yet, a child caught up in this nightmare.

She would keep trying to talk to Christie. She had to do it soon, before the killer made their next move.

◆ ◆ ◆

Morgan strode into a cafe nestled between a shoe shop and a hairdresser's on the busy high street. He was here to confront Lucas Black about his false alibi. The receptionist at the council offices had told him that this cafe was where Lucas had lunch.

The aroma and drone from the coffee machines hit him immediately. The walls were lined with framed black-and-white photos of coffee mugs and beans. A counter displayed pastries and cakes. Light jazz music played softly in the background. Morgan glanced around the seating area until his eyes landed on Lucas. He was alone at a table near the back, picking at a sandwich with one hand while scrolling on his phone with the other.

Morgan approached Lucas's table, and the young man looked up, eyes widening in surprise as he recognised the detective. His face paled.

Morgan slid into the seat opposite him.

'I was just finishing up,' Lucas muttered, shifting in his seat.

Morgan settled into the chair, resting his forearms on the table. 'I think you should stay a bit longer. We need to talk.'

Lucas's jaw tightened. He set his phone on the table and sat back, swallowing nervously. 'What about?'

'Let's start with why you lied to me,' Morgan said. 'Because I've learned you weren't entirely truthful about your whereabouts when Alison was murdered.'

Lucas looked even paler now. He swallowed before saying, 'I don't know what you mean.'

'Let's not play games,' Morgan said. 'We both know you lied. I want to know why. You claimed you were at the pub, but we've confirmed you weren't there at all last night. So why lie?'

Lucas sighed heavily and took off his glasses to rub his eyes. 'I thought it would look bad if I said I was home alone.'

Morgan studied the other man closely. 'You made up an alibi because you thought it would make you look guilty if we knew you had no one to corroborate your whereabouts?'

Lucas shifted again, breaking eye contact. 'It seemed like a good idea at the time.'

Morgan leaned forward, keeping his voice low but firm. 'Let me make this clear, Mr Black. Lying to the police during a murder investigation is serious business. Rather than helping your case, you've only managed to incriminate yourself further.'

Lucas held up his hands defensively, eyes wide with alarm. 'But you can't think I had something to do with this.'

Morgan said nothing and watched Lucas squirm.

'I was home, watching telly,' Lucas said miserably. 'Not exactly a rock-solid alibi, is it?'

'No, it isn't. I also have reason to believe you were misleading us when you described your relationship with Alison.'

'What? She was my boss. We didn't have a *relationship*.' Lucas seemed to shudder at the thought.

'I don't mean that kind of relationship. But you implied you got on well.'

'Perhaps it isn't fair to say *well* exactly, but . . .' Lucas trailed off.

'In fact, she was horrible to you, wasn't she? Tried to ruin your life? Set your girlfriend against you and then ruined your job prospects.'

Lucas stared at him. 'How did you find out?'

'I'm a detective. It's my job to find out.'

Sighing, Lucas pushed his floppy brown hair back from his forehead. 'I didn't like Alison. She was a terrible boss, and she was horrible to me. I resented her, but I didn't want her dead. I only lied because I didn't want to get dragged into this mess. I knew it would look bad if I didn't have an alibi.'

Morgan studied the young man's face, searching for any hint of deception. But Lucas just looked shaken. Morgan decided to give him the benefit of the doubt, for now.

'All right,' he said. 'I'm going to need you to account for your actual whereabouts last night. The truth this time.'

Lucas nodded. 'Yes, of course. After work, I just went straight home. Made a stir-fry for dinner and watched TV all night. I never even left my flat after getting home from the office.'

Morgan studied Lucas's open, earnest expression. His story sounded believable enough. Still, Morgan wasn't ready to fully clear him yet. 'I've got an officer reviewing camera footage from the street outside your building. If you're lying again, we'll know soon enough.'

Lucas leaned forward urgently. 'Wait, really? I didn't know there were cameras outside . . .' He trailed off, frowning. After a beat, he met Morgan's gaze again. 'But it doesn't matter. I'm telling you the truth this time. I was at home all night. I should've just told the truth from the start.'

'All right, we'll leave it there for now. But we may have more questions in due course.'

'I'm happy to do anything I can to help.'

Morgan left the cafe and turned up his collar as the wind picked up. As he walked back to his car, he mulled over his conversation with Lucas Black. The man had seemed rattled to learn about the CCTV footage outside his building. Was it simply genuine surprise to learn there were cameras nearby? Or was it the fear of being caught out in a lie again? Morgan wasn't sure, but the footage would give them the answers they needed.

At the hospital, Karen signed in, clipped on her visitor badge, and took the lift down to the basement. The sterile hallway was quiet except for the buzzing of fluorescent lights overhead. Karen followed the familiar route until she reached the autopsy suite.

Raj was waiting in the anteroom, wearing light blue scrubs. His kind eyes crinkled as he smiled. 'Right on time. I've just finished. Would you like me to talk you through what we've got?'

'Please. I'm keen to know what you've learned about our victim.'

Raj grabbed a plastic apron and a pair of gloves and pushed open the swing doors with his elbow. Karen followed him inside.

His expression turned serious as he turned to the body lying on the examination table. Alison Poulson seemed small and fragile under the harsh lights. Karen steeled herself. Autopsies were always difficult.

Raj showed her the nasty head wound behind Alison's temple. 'This was the fatal blow. Made by a thin, metal object, perhaps one of those pegs used to hold down the tarpaulin.'

If a metal peg from the dig was the weapon, it suggested Alison was killed at the scene rather than her body being dumped there after her murder. Karen was impressed by his keen observation skills. 'I remember seeing those metal pegs at the crime scene, too. You've got a sharp eye for detail, Raj. Hopefully, Forensics will be able to find the one the killer used.'

'You need to notice the little details in my line of work,' Raj said, carefully lifting one of Alison's hands. 'See here? These cuts and abrasions on her knuckles indicate she put up a struggle. I've taken scrapings and samples.'

'With any luck, she might have scratched her killer and got some DNA under her fingernails,' Karen said, mentally filing away the information. 'Anything else?'

'Yes,' Raj said, moving away from Alison's body to a selection of 6x9 photographs on the stainless-steel lab bench. He pointed to one, which was a close-up of the bottom of Alison's jeans. 'There were mud and grass stains on her jeans and shoes, consistent with the victim having been dragged at least a short distance.'

'Perhaps from a car to the trench,' Karen said, studying the photo. 'What about the time of death?'

'About an hour before her body was found. So around ten p.m. on Tuesday night.'

That made sense. The teens had stumbled on the body around eleven, so Alison hadn't been dead long. In fact, the teenagers had probably narrowly missed the killer dumping Alison's body. 'Anything else? Any signs of sexual assault?'

'No, and no sign her clothing had been removed.'

They both turned back to Alison's body. 'She has some minor cuts and bruises on her arms and legs, possibly from stumbling through the dig site, or they may have been inflicted soon after death.'

Karen's gaze moved to Alison's neck, where angry red welts circled the pale skin. 'These marks are from the shrew's fiddle?'

Her gut twisted, imagining Alison's last terrified moments.

'Yes, poor lass – no one deserves that,' Raj said.

'No, they don't,' Karen murmured.

Raj gestured to another photograph on the bench. Karen recognised it as the same object she had seen locked around Alison's throat when they discovered her body.

'Dreadful thing,' Raj said.

Karen stepped closer to examine the photo. As she remembered, the wood was old and weathered, with rusting metal brackets at the joints. The two smaller holes at one end had encircled Alison's wrists. The larger hole in the centre had forced her neck into an agonizing arch.

'That can't have been easy to get off her,' Karen said.

Raj shook his head, his expression grim. 'It was on tight. Caused significant bruising. I'm afraid I had to cut it off.'

Karen looked back at the angry red marks on Alison's skin. The cruelty of it turned her stomach. What had the poor woman endured in her final moments?

'Any fingerprints or DNA on the device?' she asked.

'Forensics is still processing it,' Raj replied. 'We should know if there's anything useful to identify the killer soon.'

Karen nodded, considering their next steps. 'When Forensics is finished, I'd like Professor Tom Stark to examine it. He might recognise the time period or its origin. Determine if it's a replica or an actual medieval artefact.'

'Good idea,' Raj agreed. 'Was it uncovered at the dig site?'

'No one from the archaeology team or the show admitted to finding the device there. So it might have been brought there by the killer.'

Karen's gaze returned to Alison's body. No one deserved such a cruel end to their life.

Chapter Thirteen

Karen walked into the office and spotted Arnie, hunched over his desk and scribbling notes, his scruffy hair sticking up at odd angles.

She stopped beside his desk and pulled over a chair. 'I spoke to Sophie.'

Arnie looked up, eyebrows raised. 'Oh?'

'She seemed surprisingly upbeat considering everything that happened at the MacGregors'. Whatever you said to her must have worked.'

Arnie leaned back in his chair, a grin spreading across his face. He looked pleased with himself. 'I didn't say all that much.'

'Well, it seems to have done the trick.' Karen rubbed her temples, trying to ease the headache she could feel building.

'You look wiped out,' Arnie said, his face creasing with concern. 'Did you get any kip at all last night?'

'Not yet.'

He shook his head. 'You need to look after yourself. You'll be no good to anyone if you're asleep on your feet.' He rummaged through his desk drawer before pulling out a slightly squashed chocolate bar. 'Here, get that down you. A nice bit of sugar will perk you up.'

'Thanks,' Karen said gratefully, unwrapping it. She bit into the sweet chocolate and felt a tiny bit better.

Karen's mobile buzzed in her pocket. Pulling it out, she saw a message from Mike. He was home tonight after his few days away, and she was looking forward to seeing him.

Mum has invited us for dinner tonight. Fancy it? X

Karen stifled a groan. The last thing she wanted after an exhausting day was an evening with Mike's mother. But she knew he'd been trying to get them together more and wanted them to get along. She felt a pang of guilt at the thought of letting him down.

That would be nice. But I can't tonight. Work is manic. X, she typed back, hoping Mike would understand.

'Everything all right?' Arnie asked.

'Yes, everything's fine.' Karen gave a tired smile. 'Did you manage to track down Alison Poulson's car?'

'Yes, Molly Moreland was right. It's been at a garage in Saxilby getting repaired after Molly reversed into it on Sunday.'

'That explains why we weren't able to find it.'

'I also have the details for the car she would've been driving last night. A silver Lexus. The details are in the case database.'

'Hopefully, we'll make some progress now that we're looking for the *right* vehicle. I thought it was odd how it seemed to have vanished, because Alison would have driven to the dig site in Stow if she met the killer there. The car she used must be nearby.'

'Or she was killed elsewhere, and her body was taken to the dig site,' Arnie said. 'What did Forensics have to say about where she was killed?'

'Forensics are still working on it. Raj said she was killed with a blow to the head by a thin metal object. He suggested the murder weapon could be one of the pegs holding down the tarpaulin. Which implies she was killed at the scene. There was a significant amount of blood found underneath her body too, so it's likely that she was killed nearby and then dumped into the trench shortly after – while still bleeding.'

Arnie nodded thoughtfully. 'Maybe she got a lift to the dig site with someone. Even her killer, potentially.'

'That's possible,' Karen said. 'Or maybe the killer drove off in her car after doing the deed?'

'The sooner we locate the Lexus, the better.'

DCI Churchill walked into the office, looking impeccable as always. He did a double take when he saw Karen. 'DS Hart, you're still here? Please don't tell me you haven't had any rest yet.'

'I just need to coordinate the search for Alison Poulson's car,' Karen said. 'You see, we've found out she wasn't driving her own car last night—'

Churchill put up a hand. 'I'm aware. I read the case database updates. But you must go home and get some sleep. DS Hodgson can handle the search for the Lexus.'

Karen opened her mouth to protest, but Churchill cut her off. 'No arguments. A good detective knows when to take a step back. Go home and get some sleep; that's an order.'

Realising Churchill wasn't going to take no for an answer, Karen reluctantly gathered her things. 'Yes, sir.'

After Churchill left, Arnie's mobile pinged with an incoming text. The tips of his ears pinkened as he read it.

'Something important?' Karen asked.

'Oh, erm . . . it's Sylvie, the producer from *Britain's Biggest Treasure Hunt* . . . She asked me to dinner.'

Karen raised an eyebrow. 'And will you be accepting?'

Arnie shook his head, looking slightly embarrassed. 'No, it wouldn't be right while the investigation's ongoing.'

'Probably for the best,' Karen agreed, stifling another yawn. 'Right, I'm off home to get some sleep. Let me know if you find anything on the car.'

As Karen walked to her car, she mulled over Sylvie's advances on Arnie again. Was the woman truly just smitten?

She had certainly seemed very keen, though Karen wasn't totally convinced. Something about the producer's behaviour struck her as odd. Was she romantically interested in the gruff detective sergeant, or did she have some other reason for cosying up to the police? Maybe she wanted to pick Arnie's brains for one of her TV show ideas.

Karen and Mike had met when he was a suspect on a case. But nothing had happened between them until the investigation was over. Arnie understood why it was a bad idea to get involved with Sylvie while the case was ongoing, but would he be able to resist the flirtatious TV producer?

Karen decided to keep an eye on Sylvie Broadbent.

The laptop finishes loading, and Christie quickly opens up an internet browser. She types *Stow murder investigation* into the search bar, bracing herself for what she might find.

The first few articles recap the basic details – the location, the estimated time of death, a vague description of the victim. They're still not naming Alison in the articles, but the police must know who she is by now.

One article catches her eye: 'Police Pursue New Leads in Stow Murder Case'. With a shaking hand, she clicks the link. The article is sparse on details, but it mentions that investigators have identified several persons of interest and are currently following up on potential evidence. Christie's blood runs cold.

Christie couldn't find the file on Alison Poulson in the study when she looked earlier. Someone has moved it.

She digs deeper, scouring local news sites and online forums for any scraps of information. Some posts speculate about the identity of the victim and the killer's motive, but nobody seems to have inside knowledge. Christie can't decide if the lack of solid information is a relief, or a ticking time bomb.

As she scrolls, Christie stumbles across a leaked crime scene photo. It's just a shot of the field cordoned off with police tape and lit with floodlights, but her stomach churns as it brings back memories of Alison's body, that thing still locked around her neck. Christie squeezes her eyes shut, trying to block out the gruesome image. But it's seared into her mind.

There's no way this crime has anything to do with her parents. It can't. It's all a horrible coincidence. She imagines telling them about it. Maybe they'll laugh and call Christie daft, then give her a hug.

She should have told her dad straightaway.

But she was in shock, her mind reeling as she tried to process what she'd seen and what it meant. She knows she should have spoken to her dad at the time, when the horror was still fresh. But the words stuck in her throat – confusion and fear holding her tongue.

Christie pretended to be asleep when the detective called by earlier, kept her eyes shut tight when her mum looked in on her.

She knows her dad has been questioned by the police about Alison's murder. Maybe he can give her some insight into the investigation, help her gauge how close they are to the truth.

But the thought of asking him sends a cold prickle over her skin. If she reveals that she recognised Alison at the crime scene, her dad will know she's been keeping secrets. He won't understand.

Christie doesn't have a close relationship with her dad. He's a quiet, bookish man, more comfortable in his study than chatting with his teenage daughter. They don't have the kind of bond where they chat about their feelings or confide in each other. Most of the time, Christie's lucky to get more than a distracted *hmm?* when she tries to talk to him.

He isn't much more communicative with Christie's mother. They seem to live separate lives under the same roof, orbiting each other but never actually connecting.

As she grows older, Christie is realising more and more that her parents aren't perfect. They have flaws and secrets of their own. The thought makes her feel distant from them, like they're two strangers wearing familiar faces.

Even so, she's sure she must have blown this all out of proportion. Her mother has always said Christie has an overactive imagination. Besides, maybe the police will never discover the connection to Alison Poulson. She's read countless stories about incompetent police work and unsolved crimes. Maybe the detectives will never uncover the truth. Maybe, by some stroke of luck, they'll all escape the consequences.

As soon as the thought crosses her mind, a wave of guilt crashes over Christie, making her cheeks burn with shame. How can she wish for that? Alison died with that horrible thing wrapped around her throat. She didn't get lucky.

Footsteps sound along the hallway, growing louder. Christie quickly snaps the laptop shut and tries to look casual as her bedroom door opens and her mum pokes her head in.

'How's the homework going?' her mum asks.

'Fine,' Christie says, hoping her face doesn't betray her as she slides the laptop to the side. 'All finished, actually.'

Her mum smiles. 'You got it *all* done?'

Christie nods, hating the deception but not wanting to reveal the true reason for her wanting to use the laptop.

'I'm impressed. Has there been any news on the dead woman?' her mother asks. 'I haven't been able to find much online. It's not even on the local TV news.'

Christie shakes her head, guilt gnawing at her insides. 'I don't think the police know who she is yet.'

'I thought about writing a piece about it for the—'

'No!' Christie blurts out, more forcefully than she intended.

Her mother's eyebrows lift in surprise.

'Sorry,' Christie backtracks, cheeks flushing hot. 'It's just . . . It really upset me. I . . . I don't want to think about it anymore.'

Her mother nods. 'You're right. That was tactless of me. It must have been horrible for you to find her like that.' She steps across the room and rubs Christie's back soothingly. 'Do you want to talk about it?'

Christie shakes her head, tears pricking at her eyes. 'No, I just want to try and forget about it.'

'All right. But if you change your mind—'

'I won't. Please, Mum. I just want to be left alone to relax and stop thinking about it.'

Her mum gives Christie's shoulder a gentle squeeze. 'If you're sure . . .'

'I am.'

As her mum leaves, Christie flops back on her bed.

Alison was a real person – with a life, a career, a family – and now she's gone. Christie wants to tell her mum . . . but the fear still claws at her, holding her tongue.

The irony is not lost on Christie that one of the people she trusts most is also the person she suspects was involved in Alison's murder.

It was almost nine p.m. and Karen still hadn't drifted off. She sighed and turned over in bed, the duvet a tangled mess around her legs. She was annoyed she hadn't managed to speak to Christie again yet.

She was sure the teen was holding something back. The details of the case kept playing on a loop in her head. Like a broken record she couldn't switch off.

Mike was out having dinner with his mum and stepdad. She felt bad not going with him, but she really needed to get some sleep.

The front door slammed shut. Karen sat up. She hadn't expected Mike for another hour at least. She threw back the covers and went downstairs.

Mike stood in the hallway, his coat half-off, shoulders slumped. Sandy stayed close to him, picking up on his tension.

'You're back early.'

He turned to face her, his expression a mix of frustration and guilt. 'I screwed up, Karen.'

'What happened?'

'I asked Mum about my biological father again.'

Karen raised an eyebrow. So much for letting it go.

'Lorraine and James left halfway through dinner. James told me off for upsetting her. I was this close to telling him to mind his own business.'

She could see the pain in Mike's eyes. This mystery surrounding his father was weighing him down.

'I was out of order,' he said, shaking his head. 'James has been a father to me since I was a toddler. He is my dad. I just . . . I need to know my origins, where I come from.'

'Your origin story?' Karen smiled. 'Sounds like you're a superhero.'

Mike's lips curved, but the smile didn't reach his eyes.

'I'll put the kettle on,' she said, heading to the kitchen. Tea always helped in difficult situations.

Mike followed, Sandy glued to his heels. As Karen busied herself with filling the kettle, she felt Mike come up behind her. His arms encircled her waist, and he rested his chin on her shoulder. 'I just don't understand her refusal to talk about it. It makes me think the worst.'

Karen suspected Lorraine was hiding something about Mike's paternity too. What mother would refuse to tell their child about their biological father unless there was a dark secret? Or something Lorraine was ashamed of, perhaps? But speculating wouldn't help Mike right now. He needed support, not suspicion.

Karen wasn't unsympathetic. The woman must have her reasons for keeping it secret, but her behaviour towards Mike was cruel. Lorraine laid the guilt on thick, turning things around to make Mike feel bad for wanting to know who his father was when it was only natural for him to have questions.

She wished there was some way to make Lorraine see sense, but Mike's mother hadn't warmed to Karen, and she couldn't picture them sitting down for a heart-to-heart anytime soon.

The kettle clicked off. Karen poured the steaming water into the mugs and finished making the tea. 'Come on, let's take these inside.'

Mike took his mug with a quiet 'Thanks'. He blew on the surface before taking a sip.

Karen curled up on the sofa beside him, the mug warming her hands. 'I'm sorry about what happened tonight,' she said gently.

Sandy settled at Mike's feet as if sensing he needed comfort.

'I shouldn't have ruined the evening by pushing her about my dad again. I should have just left it alone.' Mike stared down into his tea. 'She's not ready to talk about it. I thought I could handle not knowing, focus on the relationship I have with her, and forget about the father I've never known. But lately, I can't stop thinking about it. I have a right to know where I come from. Who I am.'

Karen nodded. She wished there was an easy fix she could offer him. 'I'm always here if you need someone to talk to. And we

149

can keep looking for answers. There might be another way. DNA, maybe?'

Mike managed a small smile and lifted her hand, pressing it to his cheek. 'I'm lucky to have you.'

They sat in comfortable silence for a few minutes, sipping their tea. The only sound was Sandy's gentle snores. Karen could feel her eyelids growing heavy. It had been such an exhausting day.

Mike seemed to notice. 'You should get to bed.'

'Are you sure? I can stay up if you want company.'

'Thanks, but I'm going to take Sandy out for a walk. You go and get some rest.'

'Oh. I thought Sandy already had her evening walk?'

'She has, but this walk's more for me. I need to clear my head.'

Karen studied his face. She could see the lingering tension from the argument with his mum. Maybe the fresh air would do him good.

'Do you want me to come with you?' she offered.

Mike kissed her forehead. 'No, you need sleep. I won't be long.'

'All right, if you're sure.'

'Positive. Get some rest.' Mike stood, and Sandy jumped up, instantly alert.

Karen watched them head out, wishing there was more she could do. But sometimes people just needed space to wrestle their demons alone.

She washed up the mugs in the kitchen and then headed upstairs. Karen thought she'd toss and turn for a while, worrying about Mike and fretting over the case, but this time she was asleep almost as soon as her head touched the pillow.

Chapter Fourteen

Arnie had received another text message from Sylvie, half an hour ago. This time, there was no option of politely declining her advances. She'd offered him something no detective could refuse. Information.

He was early, as usual. He stood outside the Cross Keys pub, hands shoved in his coat pockets, shoulders hunched against the chill autumn night. Sylvie's text message replayed in his mind:

> *I've got something important to tell you about the case.*
> *Meet me at the Cross Keys pub at 9 p.m.*

It was 8.50 p.m. Still ten minutes to go, but Arnie thought there was no harm in being early. The other officers at the station liked to joke about his messiness and his haphazard style, but they could always count on him to be on time.

He checked his phone again, though he already had the message memorised. Sylvie wanted to see him, and he had to admit that made him feel good. He knew he shouldn't get involved with someone connected to an ongoing case, but he couldn't help being flattered. Sylvie was a good-looking woman. And it was a nice boost to his ego.

Arnie headed into the pub. Warm air and the smell of strong bitter washed over him. He scanned the room and spotted Sylvie sitting at a table, nursing a glass of red wine.

When she saw him, her face lit up. Another ego boost. If she kept that up, he might actually believe she was interested in him rather than the case.

'You're early!' Sylvie said. 'I like that in a man.'

Arnie felt his cheeks flush. 'Well, I don't like to keep a woman waiting.'

Sylvie grinned. 'Can I get you a drink?' She stood up, gesturing towards the bar.

'Oh, I can get these,' Arnie offered, reaching for his wallet.

'Nonsense,' Sylvie said. 'I invited you – it's my treat.'

Arnie hesitated for a moment, then shrugged. He was all for equal opportunities. 'I'll have a pint, thanks. Whatever bitter's on tap.'

They made their way to the bar, where Sylvie ordered another glass of red wine for herself and a pint for Arnie.

'So, tell me, DS Hodgson, any breaks in the case yet?' Sylvie asked as they waited for their drinks.

'I can't discuss the details of an ongoing investigation.'

'Oh, come on,' Sylvie said with a coy smile. 'Just a hint?'

Arnie hesitated. He probably shouldn't say anything at all, but Sylvie made it hard to resist. She had a way of looking at him that made him feel like the most impressive person she'd ever met. 'We're pursuing some promising leads,' he finally said. That was all right. It wasn't really saying much at all. Nothing that could get him into any trouble.

'I knew you'd get to the bottom of it,' Sylvie said, leaning forward. 'I could just tell. You have intelligent eyes.'

The bartender placed their drinks in front of them. Sylvie thanked him and asked him to put them on her tab.

As they picked up their drinks and returned to their table, Arnie said, 'So, go on then, what's this important thing you need to tell me?'

Sylvie glanced around furtively, then lowered her voice. 'I forgot to mention it earlier. But I think I know where Alison's car might be. You're looking for it, aren't you?'

Arnie tensed. 'Yes. Where is it?'

'Let me back up a bit,' Sylvie said. 'Every time Alison came to the site, she'd moan about the mud splattering her car. She told me she'd taken to parking it on one of the farmer's tracks – apparently, they're tarmacked. I'm not sure if she told the farmer about it, though. Especially after their . . . er . . . disagreement.'

'Where is this track? Near the excavation site?' Arnie asked.

Sylvie shrugged as they sat down. 'I presume so, although I don't know exactly. Is that helpful?'

Arnie nodded slowly. 'Yes, that could be very helpful.'

Sylvie beamed. 'Oh, I am glad. It's quite exciting. I know I shouldn't say this, but it's almost like being in an Agatha Christie story! Speaking of which, have you given any more thought to what I said?'

Arnie frowned. He was still thinking about Alison's car. They hadn't found the Lexus yet, despite searching the area around the dig site and her home. If she had hidden it on one of the farm tracks as Sylvie suggested, it could have easily been overlooked. Karen would want to know about this. But she'd looked wiped out earlier, and Arnie wasn't about to disturb her sleep.

'What's that?' he asked, distracted.

'About the TV show. I'm sure I could get you attached to the project.'

Arnie flushed. 'I'm not really the Poirot type.'

'Of course not. You're far more manly – any show with you as the lead detective would be much grittier than that.'

153

'Acting isn't really my cup of tea,' Arnie said, taking another swallow of bitter.

'More a behind-the-scenes man?'

'Exactly.'

'Well, we could get you attached to the project as a consultant. Wouldn't you like that?'

'Sorry, just need to make a call,' Arnie said, setting his glass down. 'Back in a sec.'

Arnie stepped outside the pub, phone already in hand, oblivious to the cold. He dialled Morgan's number and lifted the phone to his ear, watching Sylvie through the pub window as he listened to it ring.

She sat alone now, sipping her wine, oblivious to his gaze. He admired the graceful curve of her neck as she tilted her head back.

'Morgan,' the DI answered abruptly.

'It's Arnie. I've got a lead on the victim's car.'

'Go on.'

'The TV producer, Sylvie Broadbent, seems to think Alison Poulson had been parking her car on one of the local farm tracks, trying to keep the mud off it.'

'Any idea which track?' Morgan asked.

'No, she doesn't know exactly. Seems odd the farmer hasn't reported it, if he's come across the vehicle on his land.'

'Not necessarily,' Morgan said. 'Most of the farmland in the area belongs to Benjamin Price.'

'Well, considering Price's row with Alison shortly before she died, he should have connected the dots.'

'He knows he's a suspect. If he found her car on his land, he might not be too eager to come forward.'

Arnie nodded absently – though, of course, Morgan couldn't see him. Someone had stopped by Sylvie's table for a chat. Tilda Goring. With that blue hair, it couldn't be anyone else. Sylvie was shaking her head in response to whatever it was the other woman was saying.

'Right. So, the car . . .' Arnie asked, dragging his attention back to the call.

'I'll see if I can get the resources for a warrant to search Price's land, including outbuildings, in case he's decided to hide it.'

Arnie grunted. 'You won't manage that tonight.'

'No, and we're spread a bit thin at the moment, but this could be a solid lead. I'll head over to the farm tonight, have a look around, and have a word with Price.'

'You want me to come along?'

'No, you deserve a few hours off. Stay at the pub in case your TV producer has anything else useful to share.'

Arnie felt his face heat up, even in the cold. Was he that obvious?

'Will do,' he said, hoping he sounded neutral.

'Keep me posted if you get anything else.'

'Likewise,' Arnie said.

Morgan ended the call without another word.

Arnie slipped the phone back into his coat pocket and stood there for another moment, watching Sylvie. She really was incredibly attractive. Was she really interested in him? He caught a glimpse of his reflection and tried to smooth down his hair. *Who are you kidding*, he thought to himself. *She's well out of your league, mate.*

He could be a fool at times. With a shake of his head, he went inside.

Sylvie looked up as he slid into the seat opposite her once more.

'Sorry about that,' he said. 'Just had to make a quick call to follow up on what you told me.'

Her eyes lit up. 'Ooh, so I really have helped?'

155

'Could be a big help, yes. We're going to check out those farm tracks and see if we can locate the car.'

'How exciting!' Sylvie said, then quickly added, 'Well, not exciting obviously. Terrible thing, Alison being killed. But still thrilling to be part of a real police investigation. You must find it thrilling sometimes, too.'

Arnie considered the question. *Thrilling* wasn't the word he would use, especially not with a case like this where a woman had met a violent end. But there was a certain satisfaction in following leads, unravelling knots, trying to make sense of crimes.

'Has its moments, I suppose,' he said. 'But mainly just a lot of hard work.'

Sylvie nodded, looking thoughtful. 'That's what makes it a noble profession. I can see you're dedicated.'

She reached across the table and gave his hand a squeeze. Arnie liked the feel of her soft hand on his. He knew he should pull away and keep things professional, but he let her slender fingers linger on his rough palm for just a moment longer.

This woman was going to be trouble. He could feel it. He should leave. And yet he stayed where he was.

'I have a question for you,' Arnie said. 'It sounds like Alison often came to the dig site, but she was employed by the council. I wouldn't have thought she'd have much to do with the TV show after the initial permits and such were organised.'

Sylvie took a sip of her wine and then set the glass down carefully. 'You know, there really wasn't any good reason for Alison to keep coming by. Not officially, anyway. I just presumed she had some interest in archaeology or wanted to rub shoulders with Trevor and Molly. Although I think Alison spent more time chatting with Tilda than anyone.'

'We heard they got on well.'

'Like a house on fire,' Sylvie said. 'Tilda's a friendly sort. She does have a penchant for the dramatic, but then I've found that to be the case with most directors.' Sylvie tilted her head and gave him a flirtatious look. 'Producers are far more down to earth.'

Arnie chuckled. 'Is that so?'

'Oh yes. We have to rein in the creative types. Make sure they don't get too carried away. So, tell me,' Sylvie said, keeping her gaze fixed on him. 'What made you want to be a detective?'

Arnie took a sip of his bitter. His reasons were private, not something he shared lightly. He'd been asked this question loads, in interviews, performance reviews and the like, and he'd always made up a joke about the decent pension and the possibility of early retirement. Not that the pension was as good these days, more's the pity. But Sylvie's expectant gaze coaxed more than the usual flippant answer out of him.

'Had a mate who went missing at a fairground when we were teenagers,' he said. 'His body was found a year later. Police were useless. Or at least it appeared that way to me at the time. They probably did the best they could with the resources they had. I wanted to be the kind of officer who could get justice for people like him.'

'That's so sad,' Sylvie said, her eyes glistening. 'I'm sure you do get justice for a lot of victims.'

Arnie's throat felt tight. He didn't usually talk about this, not even with people he was close to. Though he wasn't really close to anyone these days. His parents had passed years back. He had a sister living not far from Glasgow, but he didn't see her much. As for friends . . . well, they were acquaintances really, people to chat with at the pub. His work colleagues were probably the closest thing he had to friends. Was that a bit pathetic? Probably.

Sylvie lifted her almost empty wine glass. 'Fancy another?'

Arnie smiled but shook his head. He didn't need any more drink inside him. There was something about this woman that made him open up. He hoped he wouldn't end up regretting it. Knowing his luck, though, he probably would.

He reached for his pint. Why had he suddenly turned into such a chatterbox? He was supposed to be finding stuff out about Sylvie, not the other way around.

Chapter Fifteen

The night air was crisp as Morgan walked along the narrow lane that led to Benjamin Price's farm. Above him, the sky was clear and seemed to stretch for miles in all directions. A crescent moon gave the surrounding fields a pale glow, and there were so many stars. The big skies were one of the many things he loved about Lincolnshire.

Morgan had left his car near a copse of trees a quarter of a mile down the track. He didn't want to announce his presence – not yet. Instinct told him a quiet approach would get more answers from a man like Price, who showed contempt for the police. They hadn't had much luck with direct questioning, so Morgan thought a different strategy was called for.

He turned off the lane and into the large parking area, his shoes crunching on the gravel. Ahead, Morgan could make out the barn. To the right stood the farmhouse, lights glowing in the windows on the ground floor. Instead of going directly to the house, Morgan moved towards the trees lining the drive.

From this vantage point, he could see into the farmhouse kitchen. Morgan watched as Benjamin Price came into view, stopping by the kitchen table to light his pipe. Inside, the overhead lights cast the farmer's craggy features and heavy jowls in a harsh, artificial glare.

Price seemed relaxed, unhurried, maybe stopping for an evening smoke before turning in for the night.

The farmer had admitted to arguing with Alison Poulson, and they had witnesses to confirm he'd been waving around his shotgun that day. But he had seemed defiant rather than distraught when Morgan and Rick had asked him about the nature of that confrontation.

The farmer's rebellious attitude suggested he felt no remorse for threatening Alison, but his hot temper didn't match her calculated, deliberately torturous murder. A heated argument followed by Price lashing out was one thing . . . but would Price have used an item like the shrew's fiddle before leaving Alison's body in his own field, where she could be easily discovered? That didn't seem likely to Morgan.

Since the farmer was still up, Morgan decided he might as well have a word and ask him if he'd seen Alison's Lexus, even though he doubted he'd get a straight answer. Morgan stepped out from the shadows, but then paused.

Price was shrugging on his coat. Why would the farmer be leaving his house at this time of night? The timing of Price's departure struck Morgan as suspicious. Was he simply going for a late-night walk, or was there something more sinister at play? Maybe Price was heading out to cover his tracks or dispose of evidence related to Alison's disappearance.

Morgan hesitated, weighing his options. He could confront Price now, or follow him and see where he was going. Challenging Price might lead to a dead end, with the farmer likely to deny any wrongdoing. On the other hand, following him could reveal what Price was up to on his late-night excursions.

Price exited the farmhouse, buttoning up his heavy waxed jacket. The dogs whined as he shut the front door on them, then locked it. Then he set off towards the barn. Intrigued, Morgan decided to follow.

As Price approached the barn, Morgan tensed, wondering if this was a good idea. The farmer was known for his short temper. He'd expected Price to go into the barn, but the farmer walked right past the entrance, pulled a torch from his pocket, and carried on along the side of the huge building.

What was he up to?

Morgan paused, watching the bobbing light of the farmer's torch growing fainter as he moved further away and entered the field. After a moment's hesitation, Morgan pursued, his shoes slipping on the wet grass. He kept his distance, not wanting to draw Price's attention.

As he drew parallel with the barn, Morgan nearly tripped on a hidden dip in the darkness, only just catching himself in time. He inhaled sharply, glancing forward to see if Price had noticed his presence. But the farmer's hulking figure continued to lumber steadily away.

Moving as fast as he dared, Morgan followed Price through the field. The earth was pitted and uneven, churned by the passage of cows. As he walked, he smelled the damp vegetation and freshly turned earth. Morgan picked his way carefully in the gloom. Price, with the help of the torch and a lifetime's knowledge of the land, made quicker progress.

Trying to keep up, Morgan increased his pace, but felt his foot sink into something mushy, slimy . . . a soft bit of mud, or . . . ? He sniffed the air. Ugh, definitely a cowpat. Cursing under his breath, he wiped the offending muck from his shoe in the long grass.

Nearing the far side of the pasture, Morgan hesitated. The field ended in a long gate, with an old wooden stile allowing passage over it. Price had already climbed up and paused on top of the stile, sweeping his torchlight behind him.

Morgan ducked down beside the hedge, barely daring to breathe. After a tense moment, the farmer continued onward. As Price disappeared on the other side of the gate, Morgan clambered up the stile as stealthily as possible. He cringed as the old wood creaked under his weight.

Beyond the gate, Morgan could make out a narrow lane winding away into the trees ahead. Price's torch bobbed along it, casting flickering shadows on to the high hedgerows lining the path.

After five minutes of brisk walking, Morgan noticed the hedgerows beginning to thin up ahead. The lane was widening out, allowing glimpses of open fields on either side.

And then Morgan saw a church spire rising above the tree canopy, dramatic against the night sky. As understanding dawned, Morgan slowed his pace.

Price made his way along a narrow path leading through the graveyard. Even in the darkness, Morgan could make out the hunched set of the farmer's shoulders. Up ahead, the pale stones marking the graves were visible in the faint moonlight.

Price slowed as he reached a grave beneath a towering yew tree. Morgan hung back, not wanting to intrude. Then Price sank to his knees on the damp earth, head bowed.

Morgan averted his eyes, feeling like he was spying on an intimate moment. But he couldn't bring himself to leave, so he waited in the shadows.

After some minutes had passed, Morgan chanced a glance back towards the farmer. Price was still kneeling, one hand resting on top of the headstone. His shoulders shook slightly, and Morgan realised that the man was crying.

At last, Price straightened, wiping his coat sleeve roughly across his face. He patted the headstone once more, then got to his feet. As he turned to go, his gaze landed on Morgan lingering at the cemetery's edge.

Price froze. Even in the gloom, Morgan could see the farmer's eyes widen in shock. Then, in the next instant, his expression contorted with rage.

'What are you doing here?' he shouted, barrelling towards Morgan.

Morgan stood his ground. 'I'm sorry for intruding.'

'Can't a man visit his wife's grave in peace?' Price spat, face mottled with fury. His hands were clenched into fists by his sides.

There was a nervy moment when Morgan thought the farmer might lash out, but then the fight seemed to drain from Price all at once. His shoulders slumped, and he turned away with a sigh.

'This is where you were last night, isn't it?' Morgan asked gently. 'When Alison was killed?'

Price gave a curt nod, not meeting Morgan's eyes. 'I come here every night, around this time. Have done ever since . . .' His voice trailed off.

'You lost your wife.'

Price nodded. 'Yes. Daft as it sounds, I like to talk to her. Tell her about my day.' He scuffed at the earth with his boot. 'I know she can't hear me. But it helps somehow.'

'It's not daft at all,' Morgan said quietly. The pieces fell into place. Morgan got the sense the farmer was telling the truth. While Price was clearly a man eaten up by anger and grief, Morgan couldn't imagine him channelling those emotions into the kind of vicious act that had ended Alison's life.

Price drew in a shuddering breath and straightened his shoulders. 'Reckon I'd best be getting back. You coming, or are you planning to hang around the graveyard all night?'

They fell into step together along the narrow path, their breath fogging in front of them.

'Have you found out who killed her yet?' Price asked after a while.

Morgan shook his head. 'Not yet. But we will.'

The farmer just grunted in reply.

'We're still looking for Alison's car,' Morgan said. 'We think she was using a courtesy car, a silver Lexus. Have you seen it?'

Price gave him a long, assessing look. 'I have,' he said finally. 'Would have told you about it earlier if you and that other bloke hadn't come along, making your unfounded accusations.'

'No one was making *unfounded* accusations,' Morgan replied evenly. 'We asked you about the time you threatened Alison with a shotgun. That was not an unfounded accusation – because it happened. There were witnesses.'

Price's expression remained stony.

'So, where is it, then?' Morgan asked, struggling to keep his frustration in check. Price had withheld crucial information, and while Morgan empathised with the farmer's grief, he couldn't ignore the fact that this omission had held back the investigation. He took a deep breath, knowing that any sign of anger would likely cause Price to shut down again.

'In the barn, where she left it,' Price said with a shrug.

'She had your permission to use the barn?'

'Yes, I'm not an ogre.'

Morgan studied the farmer carefully. 'So why did you threaten her?'

Price's jaw tightened. 'I didn't.'

'*Again*, there were witnesses,' Morgan said.

Price was silent for a moment. 'I was just putting her in her place,' he finally admitted gruffly. 'She was taking advantage.'

'By?' Morgan prompted.

'By digging up my field and not giving me anything for it. They were all getting money from the project except me.'

Morgan frowned. 'Even Alison? Where did you hear that from?'

Price shrugged. 'Told me so herself. She was gloating. Practically admitted she was taking bribes in exchange for giving projects the go-ahead.'

'She got a bribe to sign off on the archaeology site?'

'Maybe not that one. But plenty of other projects got green-lighted after they greased her palm, I reckon.'

When they reached the barn, Price removed the padlock and yanked on the handle. The huge doors squealed as they opened. He disappeared into the dark interior, then a moment later the lights flickered on.

Sitting between a huge tractor and an even bigger digger was a silver Lexus. The car that Alison Poulson had been driving the night she was murdered.

Chapter Sixteen

Karen woke early the following morning. The spot next to her in bed was empty, the sheets cool to the touch. Mike must have slipped out, unable to sleep. Maybe he'd been kept awake by her tossing and turning. She'd had an awful nightmare – back in that muddy trench at the crime scene, staring down at a body. But this time, it hadn't been Alison Poulson's lifeless eyes gazing up at her. It had been Christie Stark's.

The teen's face had been ashen, her youthful features contorted in agony. And around her slender neck, biting viciously into the delicate skin, was the shrew's fiddle.

The dream had felt so real. Too real. Because Karen knew that the possibility of a second victim could become reality if they didn't find this sadistic killer in time.

Karen glanced at the clock as she headed to the shower. It was only 6.30 a.m., but she wanted to get an early start. A couple of hours at the office, then she'd head over to the Starks' and speak to Christie.

She went to the kitchen and made herself a strong coffee, then reached to grab a banana to save making breakfast. Next to the fruit bowl was a scrap of paper. Mike's hurried scrawl read:

Couldn't sleep. Went to work early to catch up on paperwork.

The incident with his mother was clearly still playing on his mind. Karen wished she could help, but honestly wasn't sure how, especially now she was so tied up with this case. She hated the idea of not being there for him, but she couldn't take her focus off the investigation at this crucial stage.

She checked her mobile as she walked to the front door. She had an email from Arnie telling her Morgan had found Alison's courtesy car last night. Karen smiled. Maybe things were finally moving in the right direction.

Her mobile buzzed with an incoming call. Cindy Connor's name flashed up on the screen. Karen groaned. It was too early for this. But there was a chance the journalist could be calling with information . . .

'DS Hart.'

'Karen, listen, I need more information about the murder at the archaeology site. My readers are clamouring for details. What is the victim's connection to *Britain's Biggest Treasure Hunt*?'

The fact that Cindy was asking Karen for information made it clear she didn't have any new leads herself. If she had something, she would've led with that, to entice Karen into a quid pro quo exchange. 'Cindy, you know I can't release anything until we're ready. There will be a press release in due course. Farzana's working on it.'

Karen rubbed her forehead, feeling a headache coming on. Cindy was relentless, always pushing for more.

'Come on, Karen. Just a few titbits. I'll make it worth your while.'

Karen wondered what Cindy could possibly offer her. The journalist didn't have any new information, or she would have mentioned it by now. 'And how exactly would you do that?'

'Well, I don't have anything specific yet, but you know I'll come through for you in the future. We've helped each other out before.'

Karen scoffed.

There was a pause on the other end of the line. 'Come on. We've been through a lot together. I helped you with Chapman.'

Cindy had *helped* by publishing an article publicising Chapman's dodgy dealings, meaning a large contract he'd been angling for fell through. But Cindy had got something out of it too. It had been a big story for her. She wouldn't have done it otherwise. Cindy was definitely an *I'll scratch your back if you'll scratch mine* character. But right now, Cindy didn't have a backscratcher to offer. She was just wasting Karen's time.

'Look, I've got to go. Like I said, there will be a press release when we're ready. Until then, my hands are tied.'

She hung up before Cindy could argue.

Christie sits at the kitchen table, staring blankly at her untouched bowl of Shreddies. She wouldn't be able to eat a bite even if she wanted to, with the knot of anxiety sitting in her stomach. The events of Tuesday night keep replaying in her mind like a nightmare she can't wake up from.

Christie's phone chimes, a new text lighting up the screen. She's expecting another notification from the group chat with Mia, Leo and Mason. They've been sending messages – mostly silly jokes and memes from Mason, who's been going stir-crazy because the doctors say he has to rest.

But this is a private message from Mia: *Mason's home from the hospital today. Foot in a cast. Going to bring a card round later for you to sign. x*

Christie smiles and quickly types back: *Glad he's doing ok. See you later x*

She's grateful to have this new group of friends, even though she doesn't feel she can tell them everything. How could she possibly explain she's worried one of her own parents might be involved in Alison's murder?

The doorbell ringing makes Christie jump. Her mother rises from her seat to answer it, giving Christie's shoulder a gentle squeeze as she passes. Christie hears the door open, followed by the sound of a female voice.

'Good morning, Mrs Stark. I'm Detective Sergeant Karen Hart. I was hoping to speak with Christie before she heads off to college, if that's all right?'

'Of course, Detective, come on in. I'll put the kettle on.'

Christie's heart pounds as she listens to the detective's footsteps approaching. This is it. She has to keep it together and not let anything slip. She still hasn't found the file – the one with Alison Poulson's photograph in it.

The detective enters the kitchen with a kind smile. 'Morning, Christie. How are you?'

'I'm fine,' Christie lies, forcing herself to meet the detective's gaze and act normally.

The detective takes a seat at the table across from Christie. 'I know the other night was traumatic for you. Are you holding up okay?'

Christie shrugs and says again that she's fine. She can tell the detective doesn't believe her.

Christie's mother returns with three mugs of tea. 'Here you are.'

'Thank you, Mrs Stark.' The detective takes a sip of her tea. 'If you need someone to talk to, Christie, there are counsellors who specialise in helping people process traumatic events.'

The detective keeps talking. Her sharp eyes seem to capture everything. So many questions. Christie wishes her mother would leave the room. Her presence is making Christie even more nervous. But instead, her mother moves over to the sink and starts washing up.

The detective slides a leaflet across the table. Christie takes it without looking at it, clutching it tightly under the table.

'I know this is difficult,' Karen says gently, 'but I need you to think back to that night again. Try and remember every detail you can.'

Christie shakes her head. 'I've already told you everything. I didn't see anyone else around that night.'

The detective studies her closely. 'And you didn't recognise Alison Poulson at all?'

Hearing the name said aloud makes Christie flinch involuntarily. From the corner of her eye, she sees her mother turn slowly from the sink, suds dripping from her hands, her face pale.

'No, I didn't know who she was,' Christie says quickly. Too quickly. The detective's eyes narrow, and Christie's pulse skyrockets.

But at that moment, the front door bangs open. They all turn. Christie sags with relief as her father appears in the doorway, a welcome distraction.

'Detective Sergeant, what a surprise,' Professor Stark says, looking between Karen and Christie with concern. He tosses his tweed jacket over the back of a chair and puts the jar of instant coffee he's holding on to the counter. 'Were you looking for me? I just had to visit the corner shop. We can't survive the morning without coffee.'

'I'm the same,' the detective says, rising to her feet. 'I was passing, so I thought I'd pop in and see how Christie was doing. Now I'm here, though, I wonder if you have time for a quick chat?'

'Of course. We can talk in my office.' He ushers her towards his study down the hall.

Christie hesitates, then follows them. She hovers in the doorway as the detective wanders round the room, studying the paintings and prints on the walls. Her father leans casually against his large desk, arms folded across his chest.

'Quite a collection you have here,' the detective remarks, pausing before an ornate portrait of Bonnie Prince Charlie. 'Scottish history fan, are you?'

'Indeed. A fascinating period. I'm writing a book on the Jacobite rebellion, exploring how history might have unfolded differently if the gold sent to aid the Jacobite cause had arrived in time,' her father explains. He's got that look in his eyes again. The same look he always has when he talks about his work. It's like he's not quite in the real world. 'This financial support was intended to bolster Charles Edward Stuart's campaign to reclaim the British throne for the Stuart dynasty. Unfortunately for the Jacobites, it only reached its destination after their defeat at the Battle of Culloden.'

Christie bites back a groan. Why won't he stop talking? He's always ready to lecture anyone who'll listen. If the detective doesn't stop him, he'll ramble on for hours.

The detective's gaze lands on a print of a brooding Caravaggio painting. It's weird. Just a young man lounging about with some fruit. Christie has never liked it.

'Are you familiar with Caravaggio?' her father asks, delighted at the detective's apparent interest.

'I'm afraid not.'

'A true master of the art world, but also a man shrouded in mystery and scandal,' her father says with enthusiasm. 'Did you know he was once involved in a deadly brawl over a tennis match? The incident forced him to flee Rome with a death sentence hanging over his head. Despite his tumultuous life, Caravaggio's influence on artists like Rembrandt and Vermeer is undeniable.' He nods at the picture. 'This is not his most famous work. But it is a favourite of mine. I love how he hides things in plain sight. I'm drawn to the details lurking beneath the surface.' Christie's father steps closer to the detective. 'See there, in the shadows?'

The detective peers at the print, then shakes her head. 'I'm afraid I don't. What am I missing?'

'Ah, most people miss it. It's a tiny reflection of the artist in the wine, a subtle self-portrait. Easy to overlook at first glance.' Christie's father grins.

Christie shifts impatiently in the doorway. She just wants this to be over. She's worried the detective will find something that connects her family to Alison Poulson's murder.

That file she saw last week – the one with the murder victim's photo in it – is still on her mind. How will they explain that without looking guilty if the police find it? She's pretty sure one of her parents will have got rid of it by now; they're not stupid, after all. But they don't know Christie saw it. She shouldn't have been so curious. There's a reason people say curiosity killed the cat, after all.

Both her parents *must* know what was in the file, because it's been lying around in the study for the past two weeks. Christie shouldn't have looked. If she hadn't looked, she would be in blissful ignorance right now. Well, maybe not blissful exactly.

Not after finding Alison's body. She'll never forget the sight of the woman with that awful thing clasped around her throat.

But at least she wouldn't be scared that one of her own parents was responsible. That one of them . . . No. She can't even let herself think it. She feels like she might throw up.

The detective turns back to Christie's father. 'Professor, I was hoping for your assistance. We'd like you to take a look at the shrew's fiddle found on the victim.'

Her father's eyes light up. 'Absolutely. I would be delighted to help.'

'I know you have your tools and equipment here.' The detective gestures at the magnifying glasses and other instruments lining his desk. 'I could bring it here this afternoon. Around two o'clock?'

'Perfect. I look forward—'

'No!' The word is out before Christie can stop it. Both adults turn to stare at her. 'I . . . I mean . . .' she stammers. 'Do you have to bring that thing here? It was on a murdered woman. I don't want it in our house.'

Her father blinks in surprise, but the detective is first to respond. 'Of course. You're right, Christie. I'm sorry, that was thoughtless of me.' She turns back to Christie's father. 'How about at the village hall then? We're using that as an incident room. We could find you a desk. Or at the forensic lab?'

Christie's father is still giving his daughter a bewildered look. 'The village hall will be fine.'

An awkward silence settles over the room. The detective glances at her watch. 'Well, I should be off. Thank you for your time, Professor, Christie.'

Her father sees the detective to the door. After she leaves, he turns to Christie with concern. 'What's wrong, darling?' he asks gently. 'It's just an old relic. Nothing to be frightened of.'

Christie looks away, unable to meet his eye. 'I don't know. I just don't want it here. It gives me the creeps.'

He pulls her into a hug. She tries to relax, but her body is too tense.

'You've been through an ordeal. Try not to dwell on it too much.' He kisses the top of her head. 'Now, you'd better get ready for college, or you'll miss the bus.'

'I'm not going today. I don't feel well.'

He frowns. 'You do look a little peaky. Perhaps a duvet day will help.'

He smiles, and Christie nods before running up the stairs, eager to escape. She hates not knowing what will happen next. How can her parents be so relaxed? That detective suspects something. Christie knows it. She'll be back again, and who knows what questions she might ask next time. All Christie can do is hope she can keep her nerve.

Chapter Seventeen

Karen parked outside the village hall in Sturton by Stow. She was a few minutes early for the briefing that was going to be held in the makeshift incident room.

She saw Arnie pacing back and forth in front of the hall. His usual slouched posture had been replaced with tense shoulders, and his hands were buried deep in his pockets against the morning chill. His face was red, and he looked . . . irritated.

He strode over to Karen as she stepped out of her car.

'What's up?' she asked. 'Why aren't you inside already?'

Arnie gave an exasperated huff. 'Churchill turned up early. He wanted to be introduced to the "TV people".'

'But we've already interviewed them,' Karen said. 'He wants to talk to them again?'

'Yes, but he's not questioning them about the case . . . It's like he's auditioning for his own detective show or something. He sees himself as the new Morse. He's in there, schmoozing.' Arnie nodded towards the hall with a grimace. 'I had to come outside, or I'd have died of second-hand embarrassment.'

'I'm sure it can't be that bad.'

Arnie gestured for her to hurry up. 'Sylvie's there, and he made her bring Molly, Trevor and Tilda too. You've got to get in there and stop him before he makes fools of us all.'

Karen raised an eyebrow at Arnie's dramatics but said nothing. Instead, she started towards the hall's entrance. She couldn't believe Churchill would be unprofessional. He loved positive press coverage and was very image-conscious. But he wouldn't compromise an investigation just for a bit of fame.

She pushed open the doors to the hall and took in the scene. DCI Churchill was holding court at the centre of a small group of people. The red curtain was still drawn across the interview room, creating a makeshift divider.

Churchill's voice carried across the large open space. '. . . and that's when I knew the murder weapon had been swapped out to frame an innocent man. We cracked the case wide open after that.'

Karen saw Sylvie standing near Churchill, looking bored as he regaled Molly, Trevor and Tilda with a past case. Sylvie caught Karen's eye and gave her a desperate look.

'Ah, Karen,' Churchill said when he noticed her arrival. 'Come in; we were just getting to know each other a bit better. Ms Broadbent here was kind enough to bring down the presenters from the television programme.'

He gestured grandly at Molly and Trevor, who were slouched on folding chairs, looking irritated at having their time wasted. Tilda stood off to the side, leaning against the wall, absent-mindedly twirling her pendant.

'Yes, well, we should get started with the briefing, sir,' Karen said evenly. 'We have a lot of ground to cover.'

Churchill waved a hand. 'Not everyone is here yet, and I was just about to announce that the archaeology site is open to them again. We've finished with the scene. You can resume filming.'

'Finally,' Trevor said, getting to his feet. 'We'd better start work straightaway. A pleasure to meet you, but we should get going.' He offered Molly his arm.

Churchill looked crestfallen at having his time with the TV crew come to an end. 'Thank you for your help,' he called to Molly and Trevor's departing backs.

They didn't bother to respond.

Sophie and Rick arrived, passing Molly and Trevor at the door.

'Morning,' Rick said cheerfully when he saw Karen and Arnie.

Sophie gave a small smile but said nothing. There were dark circles under her eyes that make-up couldn't fully conceal.

Karen noted Sophie's tired appearance with concern. The young detective had seemed to rally after Arnie's pep talk, but she hadn't slept well by the looks of things. Karen decided to check in with her after the briefing.

Churchill was still standing with Sylvie and Tilda over by the curtained divider. 'Tell me more about your upcoming television project, Ms Broadbent. I hear your production company is putting together a new series.'

Sylvie shifted on her feet, looking uncomfortable at being put on the spot.

'Oh, yes?' Rick asked as he pulled out a folding chair for Sophie before taking a seat himself. 'What's it about?'

'A detective series,' Churchill answered eagerly before Sylvie could respond. 'I'd like to offer my assistance, given my expertise.'

Karen noticed Arnie rolling his eyes.

'It's still in the very early concept stages,' Sylvie said carefully. 'We're exploring different ideas for the central detective figure.'

'I'm happy to sit for some interviews and provide insights into the life of a detective,' Churchill offered. 'Maybe even consult on scripts once you have them.'

'Give me strength,' Arnie muttered.

Sylvie gave Churchill a polite smile. 'I'll keep that in mind, thank you. But we're still working out the basics.'

Churchill nodded, not deterred in the slightest by Sylvie's luke-warm response. 'I think viewers are looking for something exciting these days,' he said. 'Not the usual clichéd detective with a drink-ing problem . . . What do you think, Ms Goring?' As he spoke, he turned to include Tilda in the conversation, but she merely shrugged. Churchill barrelled on, unbothered. 'No, they want someone dynamic. Successful and smart.' He straightened his tie.

Arnie stifled a laugh. 'The man doesn't know when to take a hint,' he said under his breath to Karen.

'Actually, Detective Chief Inspector,' Sylvie said. 'We were thinking of going for more of a gritty, street-smart detective. Not so polished around the edges.' She glanced at Arnie. 'More his type than yours. The viewers love a flawed hero.'

Churchill was taken aback. He glanced between Sylvie and Arnie uncertainly.

Karen watched Arnie stand a little straighter, not even trying to hide his smug smile.

'Like *Arnie*?' Churchill frowned. 'Are you sure?'

'Oh yes,' Sylvie said. 'The camera would love him.'

'I see . . .' Churchill said, clearly put out. 'I think it's time to start the briefing. We've wasted enough time already.'

He ushered Sylvie and Tilda towards the door. 'Thank you again for your insights, but we really must get down to business.'

Sylvie gave them an apologetic look as she left. Karen noticed Arnie's eyes following her out.

Churchill turned to Arnie first. 'Let's start with suspects. What have you got for us?'

Arnie pulled over a chair and sat down, pulling some crumpled notes from his jacket pocket. 'Well, boss, to put it simply, we have quite a few. Though most have alibis, which cuts down the list considerably.'

'Well, let's have a recap of them all,' Churchill said. 'We need to make sure we haven't missed anything.'

Arnie counted the suspects on his fingers. 'First, there's the husband – David Poulson. He admits they were having marital problems, rows over money and the like. But he has an alibi for the time of death. He was at work. Farzana checked out his alibi. So I think we can safely take him off the suspect list.'

Arnie held up a second finger. 'Then there's the Poulsons' neighbours, the MacGregors. Sophie paid them a visit. Turns out Alison was having an affair with James MacGregor, giving both husband and wife a pretty good motive. Maybe the wife wanted revenge, or the husband didn't want news of his affair to get out.'

'Their whereabouts on Tuesday night?' Churchill asked, directing his question at Sophie.

'They were at home together,' Sophie said. 'Laura was doing a YouTube live around the time of the murder. Her husband appeared in the background a couple of times, and Laura was so angry with him, I don't think she'd cover for him if he'd snuck out.'

'And then we've also got Alison's co-workers,' Arnie added. 'Her deputy, Lucas Black, has a pretty strong motive. He thinks Alison ruined his relationship and career prospects. Caught him in a lie over his alibi, too. Though, when Morgan spoke to him again, he said he was home alone all night. There are cameras outside his building, and Farzana checked them. Seems he was telling the truth this time.'

Churchill's gaze swept the room. 'Where is Morgan, anyway? He's not usually late.'

'He had an early meeting about another case,' Arnie said. 'But Sophie sent him a copy of the briefing notes.'

'All right, keep going,' Churchill said.

Arnie smoothed out a crinkled sheet of paper. 'Benjamin Price, the farmer who threatened Alison. Morgan spoke with him again last night. Alison's Lexus was found in Price's barn. Looks fishy if you ask me, but Morgan thinks Price is telling the truth when he said he was visiting his wife's grave around the time Alison was killed.'

Churchill nodded. 'Anything else?'

'Well, like I said, Morgan doesn't believe Price is involved. He did say that Price suspected Alison of taking bribes, though.'

Churchill raised an eyebrow. 'Interesting. We'll need to investigate that. What about the archaeology crew and the people from the TV show?'

'We've spoken with all of them,' Karen said. 'No red flags so far. Molly had a run-in with Alison quite literally when she reversed into Alison's car, and Trevor was humiliated when he mistakenly thought Alison was asking for his autograph. Neither has a strong motive for wanting Alison out of the way. Nothing you'd expect someone to kill for.'

'And the producer and director?' Churchill asked.

'Sylvie's sound,' Arnie said, then cleared his throat when everyone turned to look at him.

'Is she now?' Rick said with a grin.

'What I mean is . . . she's been very helpful, that's all. She told us we might find Alison's Lexus on the farmer's land.'

'I see,' Churchill said. 'And the director?'

'Tilda Goring was at the Cross Keys on Tuesday night,' Karen said. 'Like most of the TV crew, she's been staying there, and they were all drinking in the bar until gone eleven. Security footage confirms it. The archaeologists, the ones who do the actual excavation, are employed by the production company. They were also at the pub.'

Churchill nodded slowly. 'And the academics?'

'They're locals,' Karen said. 'Apparently, the crew use different specialists for each episode. They've brought in Professor Tom

Stark for this one. He has an alibi, working late at the university with a colleague; Farzana checked that out. His daughter, Christie, was one of the teens who found the body, though, which is an odd coincidence.'

Churchill paused for a moment. 'I don't like coincidences. Anything crop up when you investigated the background of the four teenagers who found the body?'

Sophie replied, 'Nothing out of the ordinary. I've checked out their backgrounds. Only Christie seems to have a link to the victim, through her father working at the dig.'

'Christie was very upset when I spoke to her again this morning,' Karen said. 'But that's only to be expected. Must have been traumatic for the four of them, especially as Alison had been locked into the shrew's fiddle.'

'Yes, it must have been a horrible shock for them. What about the forensics report? Rick, have you got anything for us?'

Rick opened his laptop. 'Yes, sir. The report is back. The crime scene officers detected blood traces throughout the trailer on site, where the film crew store their equipment. It's possible that the killer met with Alison there, killed her with a blow to the head, put the shrew's fiddle on her, then dragged her body over to dump it in the trench.' He paused for a moment, scrolling on the screen before continuing. 'The killer tried cleaning the scene, but luminol showed blood spatters in hard-to-reach areas, like the crevices of the equipment and the corners of the trailer. The blood is human, and the type matches with Alison, although the DNA results aren't back yet.'

Churchill nodded approvingly. 'Anything else?'

'They haven't found the murder weapon but are still analysing objects gathered from the scene. I've asked them to move the tarpaulin pegs to the front of the queue.' Rick glanced at Karen.

'With some luck, the lab might find blood traces left on the metal or the killer's fingerprints.'

'Keep me updated on any forensics developments,' Churchill said. He glanced around at the team. 'Now, let's assign today's tasks.'

Before Churchill could continue, Sophie spoke up. 'Sir, I've got something else to add. I've just received an email from Farzana.'

'Go on.'

'As you know, we haven't located Alison's mobile. Harinder suspects because there's no signal; it's likely the battery and SIM card have been removed. But Farzana reached out to the phone company for access to Alison's messages and voicemails, and she's sent over an audio clip from one of the voicemails. She says the caller was Clive Rothwell, a wealthy property developer. Shall I play it now?'

Churchill nodded. Sophie clicked play on an audio file, and the room was filled with a man's voice, low and menacing. '*Who do you think you are? You're going to regret this! No one crosses me, Alison. No one! Just you wait.*'

The team exchanged glances as the message ended. Churchill leaned on the back of a chair, his eyes narrowed. 'That was from Clive Rothwell?'

Sophie nodded. 'The call was placed from a phone registered to Rothwell, and it sounds like he was very unhappy with Alison Poulson.'

'*Unhappy* is an understatement,' Arnie said. 'That sounded like a threat to me.'

Chapter Eighteen

Arnie fumbled in his pocket for his car keys. 'We'll take mine,' he said to Karen as they headed out of the village hall.

'We could get a pool car . . .'

'No, this will be quicker.'

Karen eyed Arnie's Vauxhall dubiously as she climbed into the passenger seat. The car smelled of stale coffee, and old fast-food wrappers littered the floor. She tried to find a clean spot to put her bag but ended up keeping it on her lap.

Arnie slid behind the wheel and turned the key in the ignition. 'Sorry about the mess,' he said, even though he didn't sound very apologetic.

'We could have taken my car,' Karen said.

'We *always* take your car.'

'For good reason. I clean it occasionally.'

Arnie huffed. 'It's clean *underneath*. It's just a bit cluttered.'

He pulled out of the car park, and they were soon cruising along the open roads heading towards Louth. Karen lowered the window a fraction, letting the brisk autumn air blow away the stale smell.

'So, Clive Rothwell,' Arnie said. 'What do we know about him?'

'Property developer,' Karen replied, scrolling through some background on her phone that Sophie had sent over. 'Made a fortune building fancy hotels, golf courses and the like. Started off as a bricklayer's assistant working on building sites, and now he's rubbing shoulders with the cream of society.'

Arnie grunted. 'Sounds like we'll have our work cut out. He'll be one of those "new money" snobs. Can't stand them.'

'His projects probably bring a lot of jobs and money into local communities,' Karen said.

'Trust me,' Arnie said. 'His sort only part with money when they're forced to. He's not going to be regularly donating money to food banks.'

'You sound like you've made up your mind about him already.'

'I have. The message he left Alison told me all I need to know to form an opinion on his character. Leaving threatening messages for a woman – does that sound like a nice bloke to you?'

'No,' Karen agreed. 'And you're right, the message was unnerving. Rothwell was furious about something.'

'Alison might've blocked approval for one of his big development projects,' Arnie said. 'That would have upset him big-time.'

'Yes, and maybe he lost his temper.'

Arnie nodded slowly. 'We could be looking at a bribery situation too. Rothwell slips Alison some cash to get his plans approved. She takes the money but then gets a guilty conscience and blocks the project.'

'Leading to a very angry wealthy man who feels he's been betrayed,' Karen said. 'I'm surprised he's willing to talk to us today. He's got money, which means he can afford a big legal team who'd enjoy tying us up in red tape to stop us getting close to him.'

They drove on, fields and hedgerows rushing past in a blur. The landscape began to change, becoming hillier and the roads steeper as they entered the Lincolnshire Wolds. Arnie shifted down a gear as the road started to wind and curve through the rolling terrain.

'Nearly there,' Karen said, checking their progress on Google Maps. 'Rothwell's estate should be just up ahead.'

Arnie slowed the car as they approached an imposing set of gates. Two grand pillars were topped with a pair of stone lions. The gates, made of ornate black metalwork, were closed, blocking entry to the sweeping drive that led through manicured grounds up to a sprawling manor house.

'Would you look at that,' Arnie muttered. 'That's some progress from a bricklayer's lackey.'

He stopped the car beside an intercom, and they both gazed up at Masthorpe Hall. This wouldn't be easy. Rothwell had power and influence.

Arnie pressed the button. 'Detective Sergeant Hodgson and Detective Sergeant Hart from Lincolnshire Police,' he said after the intercom's light flashed green. 'We're here to speak with Mr Clive Rothwell.'

There was a pause.

Silence.

'Try again,' Karen said.

But before Arnie could press the button a second time, the gates began to open slowly. Arnie raised his eyebrows at Karen.

They'd called ahead and spoken to Rothwell's assistant, so their visit wasn't unexpected. But the silence on the intercom unnerved Karen more than she'd like to admit. Why hadn't anyone replied before opening the gates?

'Into the lion's den we go,' Arnie said as he accelerated slowly up the sweeping drive towards Masthorpe Hall.

Arnie parked directly in front of the entrance. He and Karen got out and walked up the stone steps to the grand oak double doors. Karen rang the discreet doorbell. But there was no answer.

Arnie grasped the large brass door knocker and rapped it firmly three times.

They waited. No one came.

There was a small camera by the door; its light was flashing. Karen had a feeling they were being watched. They were right on time for their scheduled appointment. She glanced over at Arnie and saw irritation written all over his face.

'I think he's playing games with us,' Karen said in a low voice.

Arnie's jaw tightened. He reached out and knocked again, harder this time. The sound seemed to reverberate around the courtyard. Still nothing.

'This is ridiculous,' Arnie muttered. 'We arranged this visit with his assistant. So where is he?'

Karen stepped back and scanned the front of the house. The windows were dark. No sign of movement inside.

She understood the rich developer probably wasn't thrilled to have the police arriving on his doorstep, but they had made it clear they needed to ask him some questions relating to a murder investigation. Obstructing the police never made you look innocent. But maybe he didn't care about that.

'Shall we take a walk around the back?' Arnie suggested. 'See if we can find someone to let us in?'

Karen nodded. They set off down the path that led around the side of the huge house. As they passed under an archway, the path changed from gravel to stone slabs. Karen stopped at the corner of the house where there was a sunroom. She shaded her eyes, trying to peer inside.

Suddenly, she heard Arnie cry out. It was more a yelp of surprise than pain. She rushed forward and saw him sprinting back towards her at full speed. Hot on his heels were two enormous Doberman Pinschers, teeth bared, snarling and barking.

For one awful moment, she thought the dogs might bring him down. But he put on a burst of speed, shoes slipping on the grass.

The Dobermans had nearly reached him when a voice called out, 'Baron! Cassius! Halt!'

The dogs immediately stopped their pursuit, heads snapping around to focus on their master. Karen looked over to see a tall, imposing man with silver hair walking towards them. He had a narrow, lean face and was impeccably dressed in a tailored suit and silk tie.

'Down,' the man commanded. The dogs obeyed instantly, settling on to their bellies.

Karen hurried over to Arnie. 'Are you all right?'

'Yeah, yeah, I'm fine,' he said breathlessly, loosening his collar. 'Thought I was a goner for a minute there.'

The man approached them, an insincere smile on his face. 'Sorry about that. I forgot you were coming. I'm Clive Rothwell.' He extended his hand.

Karen didn't take it, anger flaring. 'You didn't forget. You just buzzed us in to your property, and our visit was only arranged this morning.'

Rothwell dropped his hand to his side and looked unbothered by Karen's outburst.

'What kind of game are you playing here, Mr Rothwell?' she demanded. 'We've been waiting at your front door.'

Rothwell's smile didn't falter. 'And if you'd *stayed* by the front door, the dogs wouldn't have bothered you. But never mind. All's well that ends well. Please do come inside.'

He turned and headed for the house without waiting for a reply, expecting them to follow. The dogs flanked him obediently.

Karen shot Arnie a frustrated look. Rothwell was already trying to rile and intimidate them. And by losing her temper, Karen had played right into his hands. This was going to be more difficult than she'd anticipated.

They had no choice but to trail after Rothwell into the house. Karen wouldn't let him rattle her again, no matter what tricks he pulled from now on. They needed to get answers about Alison Poulson.

Rothwell led them through a hallway with chequerboard tiles into an expansive kitchen with gleaming granite countertops and stainless-steel appliances. Karen noted the Shaker-style cabinets and central island – everything looked newly renovated yet in keeping with the period grandeur of the old house.

'Please, have a seat.' Rothwell gestured to some stools at the island. 'I'll make some coffee.'

Karen and Arnie sat at the island, while Rothwell busied himself making coffee at an elaborate espresso machine.

'Just you rattling around this big old place, is it?' Arnie asked, looking around the large kitchen.

'My housekeeper has her own private quarters,' Rothwell replied without turning around. 'And my assistant, Miss Wells, has an office in the east wing. But yes, I live here alone.'

He carried over the cups of coffee and set them down on the counter beside a small milk jug and a bowl of brown sugar cubes.

Karen and Arnie thanked him and moved their cups towards them.

Rothwell glanced at the two Dobermans still hovering in the doorway, watching the scene intently. 'Baron, Cassius – go to your beds.'

The dogs immediately turned and trotted off down the hall.

'I'm glad they're well trained,' Arnie said. 'For a minute back there, I thought they'd mistaken me for a bowl of Pedigree Chum!'

Rothwell gave a thin smile. 'They are extremely well trained.'

Karen decided it was time to get to the point. 'Mr Rothwell, you know why we're here.'

'Yes. Alison Poulson,' he said, nodding. 'Very sad business. But I'm afraid I won't be much help to you.'

'And why's that?' Karen asked.

Rothwell sipped his coffee calmly. 'Because I didn't know Alison.'

'Is that so?' Karen said. 'You've never worked together?'

'Not that I can remember. She worked for the council, didn't she?' He waved a hand dismissively. 'My assistant handles that side of things.'

'What side of things?' Arnie asked.

'Permits, forms . . . things like that.'

'Did you ever speak to Alison directly?' Karen asked.

'Not that I can remember.'

'Then maybe we can jog your memory.'

Rothwell gave a cold laugh. 'Please do.'

Karen set her cup down and leaned forward, her forearms on the cold granite worktop. 'You say you didn't have much to do with Alison, but we have a recording that suggests otherwise.'

Rothwell's expression didn't change. 'A recording? How . . . *interesting.*'

'From Alison Poulson's voicemail,' Arnie clarified. 'A rather angry-sounding message was left a few days before she died. We'd like you to listen to it.'

'By all means,' Rothwell said, sounding polite and calm, though his jaw had tightened.

Karen took out her phone and played the short clip. Rothwell's unmistakable voice filled the large kitchen.

'*Who do you think you are? You're going to regret this! No one crosses me, Alison. No one! Just you wait.*'

Rothwell was silent for a moment after the message ended. Finally, he said, 'Yes, that's me. I admit I left a strongly worded message for Alison.'

'Any particular reason you were threatening her?' Karen asked.

Rothwell sighed. 'In my business, sometimes you need to issue a few stern words, or people will walk all over you.'

'What were you so angry about?'

'Nothing very important.'

'Do you often issue threats over inconsequential matters?' Karen asked.

Rothwell's eyes narrowed. 'It was about a new development I have in the works. A golf club near Stow. Still at the very early stages. Unfortunately, Alison let me down.'

'How?' Arnie asked.

Rothwell looked him up and down. 'I don't think you'd understand.'

Arnie stared at Rothwell. 'Try me.'

'She said we'd have no trouble getting the relevant permissions. Turns out, she was wrong.'

'That must have made you very angry,' Karen said.

'I certainly wasn't overjoyed at the news. I'd already invested considerable time and money into the project. But I've moved on to bigger and better things. A new golf resort in Scotland. Twice the size of the one planned in Stow.'

Arnie took a sip of coffee and then turned to Karen. 'You know, I was wondering if his threat against Alison went beyond words.'

'Me too,' Karen said. 'Did it, Mr Rothwell? Because she ended up dead a short time later.'

'I hope you aren't suggesting I had something to do with her murder?' Rothwell asked sharply. 'Perhaps I need to call my solicitor.'

190

Karen was surprised he'd agreed to see them without one, but that was typical of people like Rothwell; they thought they were untouchable.

She held his gaze. 'Where were you on the night of Tuesday 22nd October?'

Rothwell took his time replying, taking a long, slow sip of his coffee first. 'I was at a function at my golf club that evening. You can check with my assistant and the many people in attendance. I had nothing to do with Alison Poulson's death.'

'We will be checking your alibi,' Karen said.

'I'd expect nothing less from Lincolnshire's finest.' Rothwell's tone was mocking. He drained his coffee and then stood abruptly. 'I've given you all the information I can. So, if there's nothing else . . .'

He was dismissing them. Karen stayed seated. There were still more questions she wanted to ask, but Rothwell was shutting down on them fast. This wasn't the first time they'd been up against a wealthy 'businessman' who enjoyed threatening people and abusing his power, and it wouldn't be the last.

She waited a few beats, long enough to get under Rothwell's skin. She noticed the tension in his face. Then Karen gave Arnie a nod and stood up. 'That will be all for now, Mr Rothwell. We'll be in touch if we need anything more.'

'I'm sure you will,' Rothwell said curtly.

He led them out through the front door, past the Dobermans lying on their beds.

Once outside, Karen let out a frustrated breath.

'Did you notice?' Arnie asked as they walked to the car. 'When I played that voicemail, Rothwell's eye twitched like crazy. I bet he's lying about where he was Tuesday night.'

'I'm not so sure,' Karen said. 'He knows we're going to check.'

'Well, it doesn't mean much even if he *was* at his fancy golf club. He could have got someone else to do his dirty work,' Arnie said, looking back at the imposing house. 'I bet we'd find plenty of incriminating material if we could go through his office and personal records. Men like Rothwell don't make their fortunes by staying on the right side of the law.'

'We know he wanted approval for this new project near Stow,' Karen said. 'Let's look into that. See who else is involved. If he was paying Alison off, we might find the money trail.'

'Don't like our chances. I don't think he's stupid enough to make direct deposits into Alison's bank account. But I know his type,' Arnie said as he started the engine. 'He thinks flashing cash makes him untouchable.'

Karen knew his type too. In fact, Rothwell reminded her of a local gangster she'd tried and failed to bring down in the past. Quentin Chapman. She wondered about approaching Chapman for information but then immediately dismissed the idea. That would only complicate matters, and they had to do this by the book if they were to have any chance of a conviction.

They drove back along the winding drive, Masthorpe Hall growing smaller in the rear-view mirror until it disappeared. Karen listened as Arnie gave her his opinion on Rothwell: smug, self-satisfied and ruthless.

Karen agreed with most of his analysis. When cornered, men like Rothwell, with their endless money and resources, were very dangerous indeed.

Christie steps tentatively into the kitchen. Her mother is loading the washing machine. She doesn't turn around when Christie enters.

'Mum?' Christie's voice sounds smaller than usual.

Her mother throws the last of the washing in the machine. 'Yes, love?'

Christie takes a deep breath. *It's now or never.* 'Last week . . . I looked inside a folder. In the study.'

Her mother straightens and closes the washing machine door. Slowly, she turns to face Christie. 'What?'

'I wasn't snooping, I swear. I just needed some paper. I couldn't find the notepad on Dad's desk, so I looked in the file and . . .' Christie can't meet her mother's eyes. She stares at the floor. 'I saw a picture. Of the murdered woman. Alison Poulson.'

'You looked in the file?'

Christie nods, tears welling in her eyes. 'I'm sorry, Mum. I didn't mean to . . .'

Her mother's voice softens, seeing Christie's distress. She comes over, pulling Christie into a hug. 'Oh, sweetheart.'

Christie buries her face against her mother's shoulder, letting the tears fall. 'I recognised her. When we found the body. I knew it was Alison.'

Her mother tilts her head back, searching Christie's face. 'Why didn't you tell the police?'

'I was scared,' Christie says in a quiet voice. 'I didn't want you or Dad to get in trouble. I'm sorry.'

'It's going to be okay, love. I'll sort it.'

Sort it? What does that mean? Another knot of worry forms in Christie's stomach. She's started down a path she's not sure she's ready to follow, unsure of what lies ahead.

Chapter Nineteen

Karen and Arnie sat side by side at a table in the village hall, case files and notes spread out in front of them. The temporary incident room had been tidied up since the morning briefing, with the whiteboards now pushed back to the far end of the hall and the excess chairs stacked neatly against the wall. Arnie was on the phone to Churchill, letting him know how their chat with Rothwell had gone.

On the table next to Karen was the shrew's fiddle, secured in an evidence bag. The medieval torture device looked sinister even in its transparent wrapping, the metallic edges still hinting at the pain it had been created to inflict. Karen checked her phone for what felt like the hundredth time.

'He's late,' she muttered when Arnie ended his call.

Arnie leaned back in his chair, loosening his tie. 'Only ten minutes.'

Karen frowned. Talking to Rothwell had left her in a bad mood. 'I just want to know more about the shrew's fiddle. Was our killer trying to send a message using a torture device from hundreds of years ago, or was it planted to throw us off?'

'You think Stark will be able to tell us that?'

'I hope he'll at least be able to tell us if it's genuine.'

She glanced up at the sound of the main door opening. Professor Tom Stark entered the village hall, looking slightly dishevelled with his long coat open and his scarf slipping down more on one side than the other.

'Apologies,' he said, grabbing his scarf as it fell off. 'The lecture ran long, and traffic was awful.'

'No problem,' Karen said, rising from her seat. 'We're just glad you could help. I've prepared this table for you by the window. The light's better over here.'

The professor set his leather satchel on the table and began removing his toolkit – various brushes, sharp implements, and magnifying glasses. 'It's my pleasure. This isn't an opportunity that arises every day.'

As the professor pulled on a pair of gloves, Karen carefully lifted the shrew's fiddle out of the evidence bag and placed it on the disposable liner she had laid out. Stark leaned in, peering at the object.

'Fascinating,' he murmured. 'A classic example. This one appears to be from the late-medieval period.'

'Not Roman, then?' Karen said, and then wished she'd kept her mouth shut when Stark gave her a condescending smile.

'Oh no, very clearly *not* Roman.'

'But the excavation, isn't that a Roman site?'

'Mm,' Stark said. He wasn't listening. He picked up a magnifying glass and slowly moved it over the device, scrutinising every inch. 'Remarkable condition, given its age. Being buried may have helped its preservation.'

Karen leaned back against the table as Professor Stark continued examining the shrew's fiddle. She watched him work, making the occasional note or murmuring to himself as he peered through magnifying glasses at different parts of the torture device.

She was just about to ask him if he'd found anything useful when the village hall door banged open. Sylvie came rushing in, slightly out of breath.

'Oh, thank goodness you're here!' she said, hurrying straight to Arnie.

'I'm afraid I'm quite busy at the moment,' Arnie said gently. 'We've got the professor here examining some key evidence for us. I don't have time for a chat just now.'

But Sylvie didn't seem deterred. 'I'm not here for a chat.' She looked around the hall. 'Has Tilda spoken to you yet?'

Karen tried to focus on Stark's work, but Sylvie's presence was distracting. She went over to join them just as Arnie guided the distraught Sylvie into a chair.

'What's all this about Tilda?'

'She's got a theory. Thinks she knows who the killer is.'

'Who?'

'She wouldn't tell me. She was being very cryptic about it all. Tilda has always had a flair for the dramatic. But she did mention one thing.' Sylvie paused and looked at them both in turn. 'Apparently, she thinks it's all to do with Scotland.'

Karen and Arnie exchanged a puzzled look. 'Scotland?' Karen asked. 'Did she explain what she meant by that?'

Sylvie shook her head. 'No, that's all she said. It's connected to Scotland somehow.'

Arnie pulled out his mobile and tried ringing Tilda, but it went straight to voicemail.

'Why didn't Tilda come to us directly with this information?' Karen asked.

'She said she was going for a walk to clear her head. Then she was going to come here and tell you her theory.'

Stark came over. 'I'm so sorry to interrupt, but I'd like to show you—'

Karen cut him off. 'Let's go back over here,' she said, guiding Stark back to the table where he'd been examining the shrew's fiddle. The large, open village hall wasn't ideal for private discussions.

'I'm afraid I have some bad news,' he said. 'This isn't an authentic shrew's fiddle. It's a replica. Very well made, but definitely not genuine.'

He picked up a magnifying glass and slowly turned over the device. 'See here,' he said, peering closely at the underside of the neck hole. 'There's something engraved.'

Karen leaned closer, and he handed her the magnifying lens. 'What is it?'

'A very small inscription, barely visible to the naked eye. *B. V.*' Stark straightened up, removing his gloves. 'That confirms it. This shrew's fiddle is not medieval at all. It's a much more modern replica.'

'You're sure?'

'Positive,' Stark said. 'The simplicity of design and metal composition should have tipped me off. The initials clinch it.'

'Why would someone want a replica torture device?' Karen wondered aloud. And what on earth would possess them to use it on Alison Poulson?

Stark shrugged. 'I can't answer that, but I might have some useful information.'

Karen was intrigued. 'Oh?'

'I can tell you who made the replica,' Stark said. 'I've worked with him before.' He reached into his wallet and pulled out a business card. 'Basil Vexley,' he said, handing it to Karen. 'He's quite a talent. He specialises in making reproductions of torture devices. I used him once to create some for a display when I worked at the Museum of Oxford.'

Karen took the card and examined it.

Basil Vexley

Historical Craftsman

Horncastle, Lincolnshire

'Very helpful,' she said.

Stark nodded. 'I'm sure he'd be happy to help. He's a bit of an eccentric, but he's very knowledgeable.'

As Stark began packing away his toolkit, Karen asked, 'How is Christie doing? She seemed upset this morning.'

Stark glanced up, looking troubled. 'I think this whole affair is playing on her mind. She's always been rather sensitive and sheltered, so I was surprised she went out drinking on Tuesday. I suppose it's par for the course with teenagers. I wish she hadn't been the one to find poor Alison. A gruesome sight for anyone, let alone a teenage girl.'

Karen offered her sympathy, and when he'd finished packing his bag, Stark said, 'I'll leave you to it then. I have another lecture to give this afternoon. Good luck with the investigation.'

Karen watched Stark leave the village hall, feeling slightly more optimistic than before. At least they now had a new lead to follow, even if it was a strange one.

She wandered back to Arnie and held out Basil Vexley's business card. 'It looks like we'll be making a trip to Horncastle in the near future.'

Arnie took Vexley's card. 'A craftsman? What's he got to do with the case?'

'Professor Stark thinks he made the shrew's fiddle.' Karen looked around the village hall. 'Where's Sylvie?'

'I persuaded her to go back to the Cross Keys.' He frowned, looking at his mobile phone. 'But I can't get in contact with Tilda Goring.'

'Have you left a message?'

'Yes, but I have to admit, what Sylvie said has got me worried.'

Karen nodded slowly. They were all concerned Alison was just the first victim of a sadistic killer. If the killer was aware Tilda knew their identity, there was a chance she could be targeted to silence her. 'Do you think she really knows who the killer is?'

Arnie shook his head. 'I honestly have no idea. Maybe someone confided in her. Or, more likely, she's made a wild guess.'

'What do you think she was referring to when she said it was all about Scotland?'

'No idea. Sylvie did tell me Tilda has a dramatic side. Likes to be the centre of attention. Perhaps this is just a storm in a teacup.'

'Maybe, but I'd feel better if we could speak to her directly about it.'

'Me too,' Arnie admitted. He glanced again at Vexley's card. 'So, you're thinking this Vexley chap made the shrew's fiddle to order? Maybe for the killer?'

'I'd say there's a good chance. I'd like to speak to him as soon as possible.'

Karen's mobile rang. She pulled it from her pocket, frowning when she didn't recognise the number flashing on the screen.

'Detective Sergeant Hart,' she answered.

'This is Melissa Stark.' The woman's voice was tentative and quiet.

'If you're calling for your husband, I'm afraid you've just missed him.'

There was silence on the other end of the call. 'Mrs Stark? Are you still there?'

'Yes, I um . . . It's you I wanted to speak to.'

'How can I help you, Mrs Stark?'

There was another long pause before she replied. 'Please, call me Melissa. I was wondering if . . . that is, if you have a moment, I'd like to speak with you.'

Karen glanced at her watch. She needed to get going if she wanted to follow up on the lead about the replica torture device. And they needed to find out exactly what Tilda knew. But something in Melissa's hesitant tone gave her pause. She cast her mind back to her conversation with Christie that morning.

'Has something happened with Christie?' she asked gently. 'If you'd like me to recommend a counselling service, I'm happy to—'

'It's about the murder of Alison Poulson. I have some information.'

Karen tensed, immediately alert. She motioned for Arnie to pass her a pen. 'What kind of information?'

'It's . . . it's difficult to explain over the phone. I'd feel better speaking in person if you have time.'

Karen glanced at Arnie. He raised his eyebrows questioningly.

'Of course,' Karen said. 'I can come to your house right away if that suits you?'

'Yes, thank you.'

'I'll be there as soon as I can,' Karen said before ending the call.

She quickly relayed the conversation to Arnie.

'Melissa Stark? The professor's wife?' He looked puzzled. 'What's she got to tell you about Alison Poulson's murder?'

'No idea.' Karen grabbed her coat and bag. 'But she specifically asked to speak to me in person and said she has information related to the case. It sounded important.'

Arnie nodded thoughtfully. 'Well, you'd better go and see what she has to say. I'll stay here, and hopefully Tilda Goring will be along shortly to solve the case for us.' He waved Vexley's business card. 'And then we can take a trip to Horncastle and have a chat with our medieval craftsman friend.'

Chapter Twenty

Karen approached the Starks' front door. Before she could even knock, it swung open.

'Detective, please come in,' Melissa said.

Karen stepped into the living room, where Christie was standing by the fireplace, her body language tense and her eyes downcast. Her hair was pulled back into a low ponytail, and she wore leggings and a hoodie, nervously playing with the hood's drawstrings.

Melissa gestured for Karen to take a seat before sitting down herself. She took a deep breath, twisting her hands in her lap. 'I need to tell you something about Alison Poulson.'

Karen waited for Melissa to continue.

'I'm afraid I haven't been entirely truthful with you,' Melissa began, looking down at her hands. 'When you mentioned her name, I recognised it – but I was too shocked to say anything.'

Karen leaned forward. 'So, you did know her?'

Melissa nodded. 'Not personally. But I had been . . . investigating her.'

'Investigating?' Karen raised her eyebrows. 'In what capacity?'

'For a story. You see, I'm a freelance journalist. I've been working on a piece about Alison Poulson and her involvement in alleged corruption,' Melissa said. 'Specifically, her association with a man called Clive Rothwell.'

'Clive Rothwell? The property developer?' Karen sat up straighter. *Rothwell.* His threatening voicemail, coupled with his behaviour when they'd paid him a visit, had put him on their suspect list already.

'Yes.'

'I see. And what exactly did this alleged corruption involve?'

Melissa sighed. 'I hadn't uncovered anything solid yet. I was still in the early stages of researching Rothwell and Alison's history. Trying to connect the dots. I'm afraid I don't have any smoking-gun evidence.'

'You're quite new to the area, aren't you? How did you learn about the connection between Alison Poulson and Clive Rothwell?'

'A friend from college tipped me off,' Melissa explained. 'She thought I'd enjoy getting my teeth stuck into the story. In fact, I think you know her – Cindy Connor. She said you two were friends.'

Karen almost laughed at the word *friends* being used to describe her relationship with Cindy Connor. They certainly weren't best buddies; more like wary adversaries.

'I know Cindy,' Karen said. 'Do you have any notes or sources I could look at to get an idea of the direction of your investigation?'

'Of course, I've got all my research files on my laptop and some information in a folder. Let me go and grab it.'

As Melissa left the room, Karen leaned back in the armchair, her mind spinning. She had assumed the Starks were newcomers to the area with no links to the victim other than through Professor Stark's connection to the archaeology site. But Melissa's journalism work tied her directly to Alison.

Christie was watching Karen warily, but ducked her head to avoid eye contact when Karen looked her way.

Melissa returned with a silver laptop and a blue foolscap folder. 'I've compiled everything here – articles about Alison and Rothwell, timelines, meetings. It's not much yet, but please feel free to review it all.'

Karen took the laptop and folder. 'Thank you. Would you mind if I kept it for a few days?'

'Not at all.'

Melissa shifted in her seat, looking uncomfortable. 'There's something else. On Monday morning, I had a phone call from Alison. She'd found out I was investigating her.'

'How?'

'I don't know. She asked to meet, and I agreed. She showed up here on Monday afternoon, asking to talk. I reluctantly agreed, mostly out of curiosity over how she knew about the story. Anyway, she tried hard to convince me to drop the piece on her.' Melissa glanced at her daughter. 'Christie, love, would you mind putting the kettle on? I think we could all use a cup of tea.'

Christie seemed reluctant to leave the room. But she headed to the kitchen while Karen considered this new information.

When her daughter was in the kitchen and out of earshot, Melissa said, 'Christie's been terrified. She knew I was working on the story. She saw the file. There was a photograph of Alison. I think that's why she's been so worried. She's afraid my connection to Alison will get me hauled off to the police station for question-ing.' Melissa gave a nervous laugh.

Karen filed away this new piece of information. Christie had lied when she'd said she didn't recognise the victim.

Karen's first reaction was relief. She'd been so scared that this killer would strike again. She'd been worried Christie knew some-thing about the murder that might put her life in danger, but Christie had actually been trying to hide Alison's connection to her mother.

Karen had known Christie was holding back. This confirmed it. And the girl's lie made sense now. A silly move, but it was understandable. She was just a kid trying to protect her mum. Finding Alison's body like that, with the horrific torture device around her neck, would have been a terrible shock. It must have sent Christie into a panic. Even some adults would've reacted the same.

But as the pieces fell into place, Karen's suspicions turned to Melissa. Had her confrontation over this exposé on Alison turned violent? Could Alison's death have been an accident? Maybe enlisting her husband's help to dispose of the body? Maybe they used the shrew's fiddle to throw off the investigation? He was certainly arrogant enough to try. And what about Melissa? She didn't seem arrogant, or the type to lash out. But what if Alison had attacked first? What if Melissa had been defending herself?

'And your husband didn't know that you were working on this story?' Karen asked.

'No.'

'I find that strange. Because he *worked* with Alison,' Karen said. 'Did you purposefully keep it from him?'

Melissa hesitated. 'I gave up journalism when Christie was born. I wasn't sure if I wanted to go back to it. I was just testing the water with this story. So I didn't bother Tom about it. And Tom never mentioned that he knew Alison. We don't really talk about work.' She offered a small smile. 'That makes him sound awful. But he's not. It's just that he's often in his own little world, surrounded by his books. Sometimes, I think he prefers the past to the real world.'

Karen's gaze shifted to the window as a black car pulled up outside the Starks' house. The driver's door swung open, and Cindy Connor emerged, her platinum-blonde hair styled in its usual helmet-like bob that didn't dare so much as flutter in the breeze.

Karen watched Cindy stride towards the front door. The journalist's make-up was flawless. She wore a fitted trouser suit and a crisp white shirt.

Melissa gave Karen an uneasy smile. 'I hope you don't mind. I asked her to come for moral support.'

The doorbell rang, and Melissa rushed to let Cindy inside.

'Thanks for coming,' Melissa said. 'We're in the living room.'

Cindy stepped inside, her sharp eyes immediately landing on Karen.

'Detective Sergeant Hart,' she said coolly.

Karen nodded in return. 'Cindy.'

There was a moment of awkward silence as the two women sized each other up.

Christie appeared, holding a tray with a teapot and cups, which she set on the coffee table.

'Thank you, love,' Melissa said, gesturing for everyone to sit, then she turned to her daughter. 'I think you should leave us to it.'

Frowning, Christie reluctantly walked back towards the kitchen.

As they settled on to the sofa and armchairs, Cindy crossed one slender leg over the other and turned to Karen. 'I assume Melissa's told you about the investigation she's been working on regarding Alison Poulson and Clive Rothwell?'

'She has,' Karen replied. 'And she told me you were the one who brought the story to her attention in the first place.'

Cindy smiled tightly. 'I have good sources. And I believe there could even be a connection to our . . . mutual friend, Quentin Chapman. Via Rothwell's projects.'

Karen's eyes narrowed. Chapman was a ruthless character. There was no doubt he was a criminal up to his neck in dodgy dealings. But he'd also saved Karen's life once, and that made her feelings towards him . . . complicated. She remained silent, allowing Cindy to continue.

'I'm still working to bring Chapman down,' Cindy said, her eyes glinting. 'He has tentacles everywhere, but he covers his tracks well. It's not easy getting dirt on him. Don't suppose you have any information you could pass my way?'

Karen leaned forward, speaking quietly but firmly. 'Be careful, Cindy. I know you're chasing your next big headline, but Chapman is dangerous.'

Cindy lifted her chin. 'I can handle it.'

Famous last words, Karen thought.

Melissa poured the tea and passed the cups around.

'Forget about Chapman then,' Cindy said. 'Back to Alison Poulson and Clive Rothwell. I believe there's a connection between them that goes beyond the latest golf club project Rothwell is planning.'

'What sort of connection?'

'Well, Rothwell's been involved in suspect developments for years, and Poulson smoothed the way for most of them. But about a month ago, it all went sour, and they had a falling-out. There was even talk of legal action.' Cindy paused. 'But Poulson supposedly had some incriminating evidence against Rothwell. Files containing details of crooked dealings and shady business practices. Poulson was using them as leverage to keep Rothwell in line.'

Karen's mind raced. A firm connection between Alison Poulson and Clive Rothwell was just what they needed. 'How did you find out about this?'

Cindy only smirked. She picked up her cup and took a sip.

Karen thought hard for a moment. Then smiled. 'Lucas Black. Alison Poulson's assistant? He would have known about this, right? Maybe he was even involved?'

Cindy tilted her head to the side. 'I can't reveal my sources.'

It was Black. It had to be. 'Is this evidence in Black's possession?' Karen asked.

'That's the weird thing. The files have disappeared. Unless Alison was keeping them at home.'

They'd need to search Alison's house and her office. But they'd need to tread delicately, too, getting a warrant and the appropriate permissions. The files could be the key to understanding Alison's murder.

Melissa gave another nervous little laugh. 'I guess you're not locking *me* up today, then?'

Karen didn't smile. 'No, but I still have some questions for you.'

Melissa's face fell. 'Oh. Of course.'

'Where were you on the night Alison Poulson was murdered?'

Melissa blinked, clearly taken aback. 'I . . . I was here. At home.'

'Can anyone confirm that?'

'Mum?' Christie stood in the living-room doorway, clutching a tea towel in her hands and looking terrified.

'Everything is okay, sweetheart,' Melissa said gently, getting up and walking over to her.

'I just . . . I don't understand why the detective is asking where you were that night.' Her voice trembled. 'You didn't have anything to do with . . . with what happened.'

Melissa stroked Christie's hair. 'No, of course not. The detective knows that, but she's just doing her job and needs to ask these kinds of questions. It's all going to be fine. But I need you to go to your room now.'

'But Mum . . .'

'I mean it, Christie.' Melissa closed the door, took a deep breath, and returned to her seat.

'On Tuesday,' Melissa said. 'I was here, at home. My husband was working late at the university that night, and as you know, Christie was out with friends in Lincoln.'

'So, do you have anyone who can verify your whereabouts?'

Cindy made a scoffing noise. 'Surely you don't think Melissa could be involved? Don't be ridiculous.'

Karen kept her focus on Melissa. 'Well, do you?'

Melissa bit her bottom lip, then said, 'No . . . I don't suppose I do.'

Cindy put her teacup down so hard it clattered against the saucer. 'This is absurd. Melissa is one of the gentlest, most ethical people I know. The idea that she could be involved in something like this is preposterous.'

Karen turned her cool gaze on the journalist. 'I'm simply following procedure and exploring all possibilities. I can't rule anyone out at this stage of the investigation.'

Cindy opened her mouth to reply, but Karen held up a hand. 'I'm being incredibly patient allowing you to be here while we talk. Don't push it.'

She turned back to Melissa, who was fiddling with a loose thread on the cuff of her cardigan.

But Cindy wasn't done. 'I thought you were more intelligent than this. What does your instinct tell you?'

'I rely on facts and evidence, not instinct,' Karen said, cringing as the words left her mouth. She sounded exactly like Morgan.

Cindy rolled her eyes. 'Sometimes instincts can lead you to the truth. You, of all people, should know that.'

Karen studied the journalist. Cindy had been quick off the mark, arriving at the crime scene before any other reporter. It was suspicious, to say the least. Had Melissa tipped her off? Called her friend the moment her daughter found Alison's body?

'I've been thinking about how quickly you got to the crime scene,' Karen said.

Cindy's lips curled into a smirk. 'Just good at my job.'

'Right. And I'm sure it had nothing to do with Melissa giving you a heads-up.'

Melissa's eyes darted between the two women. 'I don't know what you're suggesting, but—'

'I'm suggesting after your daughter stumbled across a body, the first thing you did was call Cindy.'

Melissa's eyes widened. 'What? No, I didn't. I was focused on Christie, on making sure she was all right.'

'I saw a post about the police at the archaeological site in a Facebook group,' Cindy said. 'That's why the photographer and I turned up.'

Karen studied Cindy's face, searching for any hint of a lie. It was possible, Karen supposed. These local groups were always buzzing with gossip. Sylvie said she'd found out about the police being at the dig site from social media, too. They'd checked it out, and there had been posts within minutes of the first police vehicle arriving. She let the matter drop for now.

Karen grabbed Melissa's laptop and folder to take with her. 'Thank you for your time. I'll be in touch if I have any further questions.'

As she made her way to the car, she could sense Cindy's eyes boring into her back. She slid into the driver's seat and pulled out her mobile to update Morgan. There could be a link between Alison's murder and the missing files, and Lucas Black might have the answers.

As she waited for Morgan to pick up, she thought about Arnie, wondering if he'd managed to track down Tilda Goring yet.

She glanced in the rear-view mirror, half expecting to see Cindy glaring at her from the window, but there was no one there. She wondered just how deep Cindy Connor's interest was in the case. She didn't know the answer to that.

But the one thing she did know was that Cindy would be pursuing her own agenda. Cindy always did.

Chapter Twenty-One

Arnie stood in the main bar at the Cross Keys pub, his phone pressed to his ear, as he tried to call Morgan. He needed to get hold of his colleague, and he needed to do it fast. But the DI wasn't picking up.

Arnie had been trying to track down Tilda Goring. He needed to speak to her urgently to find out if she really did know the reason for Alison's murder. But he'd had no luck finding the TV show's director. The woman had disappeared. Sylvie had said that Tilda had wanted to go for a walk to clear her head, before coming to speak to them, but that was over an hour ago now.

The TV crew were all staying at the Cross Keys, and Arnie had been hoping Tilda was still there. Sylvie was hovering nearby, seemingly not wanting to let Arnie out of her sight.

'I'm sure Tilda will be fine,' he said to Sylvie, trying to sound reassuring. 'But I'm going outside to call a colleague. We need to find Tilda. I'm sure you'll be safe here in the pub.'

Sylvie bit her lip and looked around the bar nervously. 'I don't know, Arnie. I think I'd feel better if I stayed with you.'

'Look, Sylvie, I know you're feeling a bit jumpy. But I do need to work right now.'

'I'm annoying you, aren't I? Sorry.' She looked crestfallen, which made Arnie feel like a cold, heartless so-and-so.

He just needed to make this call and track down Tilda Goring. And Sylvie following him around like a lost puppy was making things a hundred times harder. He needed to focus.

Arnie put a hand on Sylvie's shoulder. 'You're not annoying. I just need to make this call.'

She sniffed. 'Of course, it's fine. I understand.'

The phone continued to ring. *Where was Morgan?*

'I didn't mean to hurt your feelings, Sylvie.'

She hesitated for a moment, then nodded. 'Okay. Maybe we could get a drink together tonight. To make it up to me?' Sylvie beamed, suddenly back to her normally sunny self, and Arnie got the distinct impression he'd been played.

Since Morgan wasn't answering, Arnie ended the call and slipped his phone back into his pocket. He diplomatically – in his opinion anyway – ignored Sylvie's question about a drink later. He glanced around the room. The lunchtime rush was over, and the pub was nearly empty. The only people still lingering were the TV crew, who were sitting at a long table in the corner, sipping their drinks and chatting.

Arnie spotted the landlord, a tall, thin man with a bushy beard, behind the bar. He made his way over to him. 'Any sign of Tilda?' he asked, showing his ID.

The landlord shook his head. 'Afraid not, mate. I haven't seen her since lunch.'

Arnie let out a frustrated sigh. 'I need to speak with her. It's important. Do you mind if I look at her room? Just to make sure everything's all right.'

The landlord hesitated. 'I don't know. I can't just go letting anyone up to the guests' rooms.'

Arnie showed his ID. 'I'm a police officer. Not just anyone.' He leaned closer. 'Look, I'm worried about her. She's not answering her phone, and she's been saying odd things. I just want to make sure she's okay.'

'We are really concerned,' Sylvie chipped in. She nodded at Arnie. 'You can trust him. He's the real deal.'

The landlord studied Arnie's face for a moment, then let out a resigned sigh. 'Fine. But just a quick look, all right? And if she kicks off about it, you take the blame.'

Arnie nodded. 'Thank you.'

The landlord set down the cloth he'd been cleaning the bar with and led the way to the staircase at the back of the pub. Arnie followed, with Sylvie on his heels.

The landlord led them up to the first floor and stopped in front of a door at the end of the hallway. 'This is it,' he said, producing a bunch of keys from his pocket. 'But I'll need you to make it quick. I've got work to do.'

'No problem.'

As the landlord went through the keys, trying to find the right one, Sylvie whispered to Arnie, 'Look at us – just like Bonnie and Clyde.'

'Bonnie and Clyde were the *criminals*, Sylvie.'

'Oh, yes . . . Morse and Lewis then.'

The landlord unlocked the door and pushed it open. Arnie walked inside. Sylvie went to follow him, but Arnie held up a hand. 'Best you stay out there, just in case, eh?'

Sylvie stepped back promptly. 'Oh yes, of course. I don't want to contaminate any evidence, do I? Good thinking.'

The room was small and sparsely furnished, with a single bed, a wardrobe, a small desk, and an armchair. The curtains were drawn, casting the room in shadow.

Arnie slipped on a pair of gloves he had in his pocket, crossed to the desk, and pulled open the top drawer. It was empty. He moved to the small wardrobe next – nothing inside except a few hangers. He checked the en-suite shower room, but that was empty, too.

He turned back to the landlord. 'Has she left?'

The landlord shook his head. 'Not as far as I'm aware. She didn't check out.'

Arnie snapped off his gloves and strode out of the room. 'I don't like it. Something doesn't feel right.'

The landlord shifted uncomfortably. 'Well, I've let you look around. Can I get back to work now?'

'Yes,' Arnie said. 'Thanks for your help. If you see Tilda, could you let her know I'm looking for her? Tell her to call Nettleham station and ask to speak to DS Hodgson.'

The landlord nodded, and they left the room, the landlord locking the door behind them.

As they descended the stairs, Arnie turned back to Sylvie. 'Did Tilda drive here?'

'Yes, she did. Gave me a lift, too. I thought of that, and I checked. Her car is gone.' Sylvie added proudly, 'See, being around you has made all this detective stuff rub off on me.'

Arnie stopped in his tracks. 'Gone? You didn't think to mention that earlier?'

Sylvie's face fell. 'Well, I did tell you I couldn't find her.'

Maybe Tilda had left on her own accord. If she'd taken her car surely that was a good sign.

They exited the pub and walked through the beer garden. It was a cold, overcast afternoon. The garden was deserted, the tables and chairs empty. A few leaves blew across the uneven patio.

'Oh, that's funny,' Sylvie said, squinting towards the car park.

'What is?' Arnie asked.

Sylvie pointed to a small silver hatchback parked at the far end of the car park. 'Her car. It's there after all. Tilda must have come back again.'

Arnie headed towards the car, Sylvie following. He peered through the windows. The car was empty, but he could see a blue suitcase in the boot.

'She must still be here somewhere,' Arnie said. 'But where is she? And why isn't she answering her mobile?'

Sylvie shrugged. 'Tilda's not really a phone person. She hardly ever has it charged, and even when it is, she often turns it off. I wouldn't be surprised if she's either turned it off or put it on silent today because we keep getting calls from the press. It's very irritating.'

Give me strength, Arnie thought. Why could this job never be easy?

It was now over an hour since Tilda Goring had disappeared. Arnie wasn't one for walks unless it was to get him from A to B. He certainly wouldn't take a walk for enjoyment, so he was no expert. Should a leisurely stroll take this long? Tilda was an adult and could take care of herself – so in most cases, her absence for an hour wouldn't be a cause for concern. But, given the circumstances, Arnie was definitely concerned. Tilda had told Sylvie she knew who was behind the murder. Had Tilda told anyone else? Had the killer found out? If so, Tilda could be in serious trouble.

Arnie's phone buzzed in his pocket. He pulled it out and saw Morgan's name on the screen. He stepped away from Sylvie before answering. 'Morgan, where are you?'

'I'm heading to Gainsborough,' Morgan said. 'Going to bring in Lucas Black personally. I've just had an enlightening conversation with Karen. Lucas may well be the key to solving Alison's murder. What do you need from me?'

'A miracle,' Arnie muttered. 'I'm trying to find Tilda Goring – the woman who claims to know the killer's identity. But she seems to have vanished off the face of the earth.'

◆ ◆ ◆

When Karen returned to the village hall, she spotted Arnie sitting on a folding chair, staring at his phone, face creased with worry.

She made her way over to him. 'What's wrong?'

'I can't find Tilda Goring,' he said. 'I've been trying to call her, but she's not answering. I tried the pub. Drove around the village and checked the dig site. I even tried calling the TV production office, but no one there has seen her either. They told me she missed an important call earlier.'

'That doesn't sound good.' Karen thought through the possibilities. Tilda's disappearance was concerning; the woman claimed to have information about Alison's murder, so the timing was suspicious. But did she really know anything? Or would her testimony only prove to be the wild imaginings of a TV director?

Working with the television crowd had taught Karen that some of them could be a bit flighty, their thoughts often taking fanciful detours. Like Sylvie, Tilda's background wasn't limited to factual programming – she'd also worked on thrillers and a detective series. It wouldn't be a stretch for her to concoct a dramatic scenario, although presumably unintentionally.

But if Tilda's claims were true, if she really did know something . . . Karen's stomach knotted at the thought. The killer might try to silence her, to keep their secrets buried. Especially the type of killer they seemed to be dealing with here – one that enjoyed torture and drawing out the death of the victim.

Two hours had passed since Tilda had set out on her walk. She was supposed to have been coming to speak to them. So where was she? She could be perfectly fine, sidetracked by something mundane. But Karen's unease persisted, a nagging presence at the back of her thoughts.

'Her car is still in the pub car park, and her suitcase is in the back,' Arnie said.

'Then maybe she hasn't gone far.'

'Maybe. But then why isn't she answering her phone?'

'Perhaps she has it on silent?'

'That's what Sylvie said.'

Karen raised an eyebrow. 'You two are getting close.'

Arnie blushed. 'I told her about Tilda's disappearance,' he admitted. 'I had to. She was at the pub when I went looking for Tilda.'

Just then, his phone rang. He pulled a face at Karen before answering. 'Hodgson,' he said gruffly.

From the tone of the conversation, Karen guessed it was DCI Churchill calling. Her mobile buzzed with a new message. It was from Mike. He was just checking in to see how her day was going. Karen felt a pang of guilt. She'd intended to send Mike a message earlier, to see how he was doing after last night, but had forgotten all about it. Mike was always so understanding about her work, but she'd been neglecting him. Karen quickly typed a reply, telling him she was looking forward to seeing him later.

She slipped her phone back into her pocket and watched Arnie. His face grew more and more pinched. He glanced at Karen, and she could see the frustration in his eyes.

Arnie began to pace back and forth, running a hand through his hair, which made it stick up in all directions. 'Yes, sir,' he said, his voice tight. 'Of course, sir. Understood. We'll head there straightaway.'

He ended the call and let out a long breath. 'He wants us to prioritise the replica maker. He thinks talking to the bloke who made the shrew's fiddle is the most important lead we have right now.'

Karen nodded. 'He's probably right. If Basil Vexley can tell us who got him to make the replica, we might have the name of our killer.'

Arnie grimaced. 'I know. But I was hoping we'd be able to find Tilda first and get some answers out of her. Churchill has assigned Rick to get a proper search underway, and he's putting Sophie to work digging into Melissa Stark's background. He thinks she might have more to do with Alison Poulson than she's letting on.'

Karen agreed, even though she also believed their priority should be tracking down Tilda. Karen wanted them all out looking for her, but Churchill had to weigh up the benefit-cost risk, and she didn't envy him that task. No one really wanted to hold back resources due to funding, but they had a limited amount, and if they threw everything at finding Tilda, they might miss something else. She hoped Churchill had made the right call. Because Karen's mind kept returning to the worst-case scenario. What if Tilda *did* know something that meant her life was in danger? 'Churchill's probably right there as well. If Melissa was working on a story on the murder victim, it's a lead we need to follow up.'

Arnie grabbed his coat. 'Come on then. We'd better get moving. Churchill wants us to head over to Horncastle and find this Basil Vexley.'

'All right. But this time, we're taking my car.'

Chapter Twenty-Two

Karen took the A158 to Horncastle. The in-car satnav was on the blink, which meant she'd need to rely on Arnie's ability to use Google Maps. And as Arnie had mentioned on many previous occasions, he didn't like a little voice bossing him about. Luckily, Karen knew the way roughly. She estimated the journey would take about three-quarters of an hour from Sturton by Stow.

The shrew's fiddle was in an evidence bag in the boot. Just knowing it was there made Karen's skin crawl.

She drove in silence for a while, the only sounds the hum of the engine and the occasional swish of the windscreen wipers. The rain was coming down hard, and the sky was a dull, leaden grey.

Arnie scrolled through his phone.

Karen glanced at him. 'You're quiet.'

He shrugged. 'Just thinking.'

'About the case?'

'Yeah.'

'Any strikes of inspiration?'

'No.' He was quiet for a bit, then added, 'About Sylvie . . .'

Karen raised her eyebrows. 'Yes?'

Arnie shifted in his seat. 'She's . . . persistent.'

'She does seem very . . . determined.'

'I'm not encouraging her.'

'Of course not.'

Arnie grunted. 'I'm too old for that nonsense.'

Karen hid a smile. 'I don't think she sees it that way.'

Arnie's cheeks flushed, and he tried to hide his embarrassment by moaning about Google Maps again. 'This thing is useless. We don't want to go that way. We'll get caught up in the after-school traffic.'

They fell silent again, and Karen's thoughts drifted back to the case. She was eager to speak with Basil Vexley, although she wondered what he would be like. A craftsman who made replica torture devices. How had he fallen into that job? She didn't remember that being suggested as an option on school career day.

As they approached Horncastle, the rain began to ease off. Karen glanced at Arnie, who was now turning his phone upside down and scowling at the map. 'We're nearly there.'

Horncastle was a small market town with a mix of old and new buildings. The town centre was a collection of shops, pubs and cafes, with a few historic buildings dotted among them.

Vexley's workshop was located on a narrow side street. Karen parked the car, and they got out, pulling up their collars against the chilly drizzle.

The workshop was in an old, stone three-storey building. The windows were small and dark, and there were steps leading up to the entrance.

Karen and Arnie walked up to the front door. An intercom was fixed to the wall beside it. Karen studied it for a moment. There was a bat symbol and the name *Vexley* next to the button.

Weird.

She pressed it, and there was a crackle of static, then a voice said, 'Yes?'

'Detective Sergeant Hart and Detective Sergeant Hodgson from Lincolnshire Police. We're here to see Mr Vexley.'

There was a pause, then the voice replied, 'Come in.'

The door buzzed and clicked, and they pushed it open. The interior was dimly lit, and the only source of light was a few flickering candles. Had there been a power cut?

A young woman was standing by the door, her arms crossed. She wore all black, with heavy eyeliner and dark lipstick. Her hair was dyed a deep shade of purple, and she had multiple piercings in her ears and nose.

'Hello,' Arnie said cheerfully. 'What's with all the candles?'

The woman studied the candles. 'What do you mean? What's wrong with them?'

'Er, nothing. But why are you using them? Is the power out? Did you forget to pay the bill this month?' Arnie chuckled.

'Mr Vexley likes candles,' she said, her tone flat. 'Follow me.'

She led them through a small reception area and down a narrow staircase. The walls were stone, and the air was damp and cold.

At the bottom of the stairs, the woman stopped and gestured towards a black door. 'In there.'

Karen and Arnie exchanged a glance, and then Karen reached for the handle. The door creaked open, and they stepped inside.

The first thing Karen noticed was the smell. It was a mixture of sawdust, varnish and incense. The room was poorly lit, and the air was so heavy with the smoky fragrance that it made her cough.

She glanced around the workshop. It was filled with all manner of strange objects. A large wooden workbench was covered in tools, and shelves were lined with jars of pigment, brushes and various other bits and bobs. The walls were adorned with macabre paintings and sketches of medieval torture devices. A large, wrought-iron chandelier hung from the ceiling, and its flickering candles cast eerie, dancing shadows on the walls.

But it was the items displayed on the tables and hanging from the walls that made Karen's skin crawl. There were all manner of

221

gruesome-looking contraptions. She recognised the rack and the thumbscrews. But there were others she'd never seen before, and she didn't want to know what they were used for.

Karen shivered and pulled her coat tighter around her. She could sense Arnie tensing up beside her.

Where was Vexley? The workshop appeared empty.

'Helloooo,' Arnie called out.

A man stepped out from behind a tall set of shelves. 'Good afternoon, Officers,' he said. His voice was soft and slightly nasal. 'I'm Basil Vexley.'

Vexley was a thin, wiry man with a long, angular face. Karen guessed he was in his mid-fifties. He had wild, untamed hair and was wearing a stained apron and holding a small chisel. One of his eyes was hidden behind a large jeweller's loupe that he wore attached to a headband.

'Thank you for seeing us, Mr Vexley,' Karen said. 'We spoke on the phone. I'm DS Karen Hart, and this is my colleague DS Hodgson.'

'Of course,' Vexley said. 'I'm always happy to assist the police in any way I can.'

'We were hoping you could help us with this item,' Karen said. She held out the evidence bag containing the shrew's fiddle. 'We believe this is one of your creations.'

Vexley's eyes lit up as he took the bag from Karen. He took it over to his workbench, switching on a powerful lamp.

'Ah, so you do have electricity!' Arnie said.

Vexley looked up, distracted. 'Sorry?'

'Never mind.'

He examined the shrew's fiddle closely. 'Ah, yes. This is one of mine. A true work of art, if I do say so myself.' Vexley continued to examine the device, lovingly turning it over in his hands. 'Exquisite, don't you think? The way the wood has been carved and shaped to fit the contours of the human body. And the metalwork – simple but ruthlessly effective.'

Karen felt a surge of revulsion. This man was admiring the device that had been found on Alison Poulson's body, possibly used to torture her before her death.

Vexley finally tore his gaze away from the shrew's fiddle and looked up at them. He must have seen the discomfort on their faces, because his smile faltered.

'I always make sure that my creations are historically accurate,' Vexley said. 'I pride myself on attention to detail. I spend hours poring over historical texts and illustrations, ensuring every piece I create is as authentic as possible. I'm impressed you realised it was a replica. I'd aged the wood and treated the metal with chemicals to emulate the passage of time.'

'We relied on the expertise of Professor Tom Stark,' Karen said. 'He spotted a stamp on it and suggested it was one of yours.'

'Ah, Tom! How is he these days? I've not seen him for a while.'

'He's fine,' Arnie said. 'We'd like to know who you made this item for. Do you keep records of your sales?'

Vexley smiled apologetically. 'Oh, I'm afraid I can't help you there. Client confidentiality, you understand. I'm an artist. I can't go around revealing my patrons.'

Karen crossed her arms over her chest. 'Mr Vexley, this is a murder investigation. A woman was killed, and this contraption was found on her body. You need to tell us who you sold it to.'

Vexley's smile faded. 'I'm sorry, but I can't do that. It would be highly unethical.'

Karen took a deep breath, trying to keep her temper in check. 'Mr Vexley, I don't think you understand the seriousness of this situation. A woman is dead. We believe she was killed by someone who purchased one of your devices. You need to help us find out who that person is.'

Vexley shoved the shrew's fiddle back across the bench towards them and looked at Karen and Arnie, his eyes hard. 'I'm afraid I can't help you. Now, if there's nothing else, I'm a very busy man. I have work to do.'

Karen gritted her teeth. She couldn't believe this. She'd been so sure that Vexley would be able to help them. She'd been counting on it. They'd get access to his records one way or another, even if they had to get a warrant, but that would take time. Time they didn't have.

Vexley turned away from them and began tidying up his workbench, dismissing them with a flick of his hand.

She forced herself to speak calmly. 'Mr Vexley, if we have to, we'll come back with a warrant. But if we do that, it won't just be your order records we'll be looking through. We'll need to go through your whole workshop.' She turned to Arnie. 'What do you think, DS Hodgson?'

Arnie sniffed and looked around at the shelves. 'Seems a shame. That'll cause such a mess. It will take Mr Vexley days to get the place in order again. But . . .' Arnie shrugged. 'If he won't cooperate, I suppose it's our only option.'

Vexley straightened up and glared at them. 'This is outrageous.'

Karen and Arnie said nothing, just looked at him expectantly.

He let out an exasperated huff, then turned and stalked over to a large, leather-bound ledger sitting on a shelf. He snatched it up and marched back over to them, the book clutched to his chest.

He flipped it open and began to turn the pages. 'This is highly irregular,' he muttered. 'I've never been treated in such a manner in all my years as a craftsman.'

Karen and Arnie exchanged a glance.

Vexley jabbed a finger at the page. 'There. That's the woman who ordered it. There are her contact details.'

Karen leaned in to peer at the page. It was filled with neat, tiny handwriting. She read the name. Then read the name again, gobsmacked. It made no sense.

'You're sure about this?' she asked.

'Of course I'm sure. I never make mistakes.'

Karen looked at the page again. 'She paid you for this? She placed the order?'

Vexley nodded. 'Yes. She placed the order over the phone and then picked it up in person.'

Karen felt like her head was spinning. 'Take a look,' she said to Arnie.

Arnie looked at the ledger, then did a double take. 'What the . . . ?'

Karen saw her own confusion reflected in Arnie's eyes.

Vexley was irritated. 'What?' He inspected the ledger again. 'It's all there in black and white. Perfectly clear. Mrs Alison Poulson ordered the shrew's fiddle as a priority job. I worked day and night. She paid extra.'

Alison Poulson.

Karen was speechless. Why on earth had Alison Poulson ordered the shrew's fiddle?

She took a deep breath and tried to think. She couldn't get her head around it. Alison Poulson, the ambitious career woman, had ordered a medieval torture device. It made no sense.

Maybe someone had been impersonating her? She pulled out her phone and found a photo of Alison. She held it out to Vexley. 'Was this the woman?'

He took the phone and studied the photo. 'Yes, that's her. She came here to collect the shrew's fiddle last Saturday.'

Karen's mind raced. Alison had ordered the device and then come to collect it in person. What had she been planning to do with it? And how had it ended up on her dead body?

She took the phone back from Vexley and slipped it into her pocket. 'Thank you, Mr Vexley. You've been very helpful.'

Vexley gave a curt nod. 'Yes, well, I believe we're done here.'

Karen and Arnie made their way back up the stairs and out of the workshop. Once outside, Karen took a deep breath of fresh air. After the gloom of the workshop, even the dull grey sky seemed pleasant.

She glanced at Arnie. 'Well, that was unexpected.'

He grunted. 'You can say that again. What on earth did Alison Poulson want with a shrew's fiddle – and how did it end up clamped around her neck?'

Chapter Twenty-Three

Lucas Black sat at the table in the interview room at the station, his hands clasped together so tightly that his fingers were turning white. The walls were painted a dull shade of beige, and the only decoration was a small, framed poster opposite Lucas's chair, reminding people of their right to have a solicitor present during questioning. Lucas had declined that right.

DI Morgan and DC Rick Cooper sat across from Lucas.

Morgan studied Lucas as the young man took his glasses off to clean them. His hands were trembling. Morgan took his time, letting the silence stretch out. He knew from experience that sometimes it was the best way to get someone to talk.

Finally, he said, 'I'd like to ask you about a file Alison Poulson had – supposedly containing incriminating information against Clive Rothwell.'

Lucas swallowed hard. 'I . . . I don't know what you're talking about.'

Morgan raised an eyebrow. 'Are you sure you don't know? Only, it seems to have gone missing.'

Lucas shifted in his seat, avoiding eye contact. Morgan guessed he was trying to understand how they'd found out about the file, but Morgan wouldn't be mentioning who'd told them about it.

Cindy Connor could be a thorn in the police's side, but he'd never reveal her name.

'No idea. Sorry.'

Morgan leaned back in his chair, tapping his pen against the notepaper in front of him. 'You see, the thing is, Mr Black, we've already caught you in one lie. You told me you were at the pub the night Alison was killed, but it turns out that wasn't true. So, you'll forgive me if I'm a bit sceptical when you tell us you know nothing about this file.'

Lucas looked down at the table, his fingers twisting together. 'Alison didn't talk to me about that stuff. I know nothing about a file on Rothwell.'

Morgan leaned forward, his voice low and steady. 'I think you do know, Mr Black. And I think you're scared. Scared because you know that if this file is what got Alison killed, then you could be in danger, too.'

Lucas's eyes widened, and he looked between Morgan and Rick, his mouth opening and closing like he was a fish out of water. 'I . . . I never thought . . . I mean, I didn't know that . . .' He trailed off, looking terrified.

Morgan watched him carefully. He knew he was close to getting the truth. Maybe he needed to try a different angle.

'All right,' Morgan said. 'Let's try something else. What can you tell me about Scotland?'

Lucas looked puzzled by the sudden change of subject.

Morgan tried again. 'We believe Alison's murder might be related to Scotland.'

He felt ridiculous even saying it out loud – they had no real evidence to suggest any connection – but Tilda Goring had apparently said that Alison's murder was *all to do with Scotland*. She couldn't have been any more cryptic if she'd tried. And of course, no one could find Tilda now to ask what she'd meant.

Lucas just blinked at him.

'You were planning to move to Scotland to win your girlfriend back – but Alison ruined that for you, too, didn't she?' Morgan pressed.

Lucas's expression darkened. 'Yes, she did. She cost me my relationship. I resented her for that, but I didn't kill her.'

Morgan considered this. Lucas had a clear motive. If Alison had confided in Tilda about Lucas's resentment, Tilda might have realised that was his motive for killing her. And if Lucas had discovered that Tilda was on to him, it put a worrying spin on her disappearance. But Morgan found it hard to imagine Lucas killing Alison. His money was still on Rothwell.

Then Lucas seemed to have a brainwave. 'Actually, *Alison* was planning a trip to Scotland herself.'

'When?' asked Rick.

'Next week.'

'You didn't tell us that,' Rick said.

'I didn't think it was important.'

'What was she going for?' asked Morgan.

'I don't know,' Lucas replied quickly. 'Probably a holiday. She'd booked annual leave.'

'Did she tell you where in Scotland?'

'No.'

'Who she was going with?'

'No.'

They weren't getting anywhere with the Scotland questions, so Morgan moved the interview back on track.

He leaned forward a bit more. 'You were close to Alison, weren't you? Even if you resented her, you worked with her every day. You must have known her well. You know how important it is to find this file. It could be the key to solving her murder.'

Lucas looked up at Morgan, his eyes pleading. 'Please, I swear, I know nothing about this file. Alison didn't tell me anything.'

Morgan held Lucas's gaze for a moment longer. The young man was lying. He knew about the file, and he was justifiably afraid. Morgan glanced at Rick, who gave a small, disappointed shake of his head.

Rick's tone was friendly as he said, 'Lucas, you need to understand something. If you know anything about this file, you're in danger. If Rothwell thinks you have evidence against him, you're a liability. But if you trust us, we can protect you.' He locked eyes with Lucas. 'We can keep you safe, but we need your help.'

Lucas's eyes darted between Morgan and Rick. His hands were still shaking. The young man was clearly under immense stress.

'It's so hot in here,' Lucas said, tugging at the collar of his shirt. 'Why aren't there any windows?'

Rick ignored the question and said, 'We need to learn everything you know about this file. Anything Alison told you about it.'

'I can't talk about this. I just can't.' He looked at Morgan in desperation. 'Please, I don't know anything about Alison's murder or the file. I've already told you everything I know. I just want to go home.'

'You're lying again, Lucas,' Morgan said, his tone hard. 'I think you're scared, and I think you're trying to protect yourself. But you must understand that we're your best chance at staying safe. We can't protect you without your cooperation.'

Lucas covered his face with his hands. 'I can't. I can't do this. I can't tell you anything.'

'Lucas, listen to me. We already know about the file. You wouldn't be telling tales on anyone, but you could be very vulnerable if you have evidence against Rothwell. You need to trust us.'

He looked close to tears. 'You can't do anything – not against Rothwell. You don't understand. He's dangerous. He's ruthless. If he thinks I've told you anything, he'll come after me.'

'We *can* protect you,' Rick said. 'But we need your cooperation. Tell us what you know, and we can get you somewhere secure tonight.'

'You can't help me. No one can. Rothwell has too much power.'

'If he can't find you, he can't hurt you,' Rick said. 'And with enough evidence, we can put him away.'

Lucas met Rick's gaze. 'Really?'

Rick nodded.

There was a long pause, and then Lucas finally spoke quietly. 'Alison never told me the specifics of what she had on Rothwell, just that it was something big. Something that could ruin him. She kept the file in the locked cabinet in her office.'

Good. Now, they were finally making some progress. Morgan asked, 'Did you ever see the documents inside the file?'

'No, Alison didn't let me look at it. I knew where she kept the key, though . . .'

'Okay.' Morgan turned to Rick. 'Let's get someone down to the council offices straight away.'

Rick stood, but before he reached the door, Lucas said, 'It's too late.'

Morgan frowned. 'What do you mean?'

Lucas covered his face with his hands again. 'I've already given Rothwell the file. I don't have it anymore.'

Morgan's stomach sank. So much for that lead. They'd been so close to getting their hands on the evidence that could potentially lead to Alison's killer and put Rothwell away for his seedy business practices. But now it seemed they were back to square one.

'I did the right thing,' Lucas said in a small voice. 'I had to. Now Rothwell knows I'm not a threat. He won't hurt me now, will he?'

The chance to nail Rothwell was slipping through Morgan's fingers. He kept his voice low and steady. 'Lucas, you need to tell us everything you know about Rothwell. The more we know, the better we can protect you. But you need to be honest with us.'

Lucas shook his head, his eyes filled with fear. 'I can't. I want to speak to the duty solicitor now, please. I think I need them after all.'

Morgan sighed and paused the interview. He nodded to Rick, who went to speak to the officer standing outside the door, asking them to organise the solicitor.

As they waited, Morgan studied Lucas. The young man's eyes were fixed on the door as though he expected Rothwell to burst in at any moment. Morgan knew he was scared stiff. And he couldn't blame him.

They'd lost the opportunity to get their hands on the file. Now, they'd have to find another way to get to the truth. Morgan just hoped they hadn't lost their only chance.

Lucas Black stepped out of the police station, his heart still pounding from the interview. He was relieved to be free to go, but the detective's parting words echoed in his mind. *Don't leave the area, Mr Black. We may need to speak with you again.*

The rain had stopped, but the sky was still a dull grey. Lucas hesitated at the front of the building, wondering if he should call a taxi and wait inside. But he couldn't stand the thought of being near the police station any longer than necessary. He needed fresh air, even if it was damp and cold. He needed space to think and to figure out what to do next.

He started down the road, flanked by fields on either side. In the distance, he could just make out the dark outline of the woods.

He'd never been so scared. First, handing over the file to Rothwell, then trapped in that interview room with the detectives' hard eyes fixed on him. The suspicion in the air had been thick and suffocating. Caught between Rothwell's wrath and the police, he'd done the best he could.

The road stretched out before him, and he pulled his phone from his pocket and checked the time. It was getting dark.

He glanced over his shoulder, half expecting to see the detectives or Rothwell following him. But the road was empty. He kept walking. He'd feel better once he put some distance between himself and the police station.

It had been a good call to opt for the duty solicitor in the end. She'd been kind and reassuring. She'd told him the police had nothing on him, and the next thing he knew, he was free to go.

The younger detective – DC Cooper – had wanted him to stick around and said he could help, maybe find Lucas somewhere safe to stay. He'd seemed genuine. But Lucas had just wanted to get out of there. Fast.

He'd been an idiot. Lying to the police about his alibi had only made things worse. But he'd given the file full of evidence to Rothwell. And the police had let him go. He could start living his life again.

It was time for a new beginning. A new job, definitely. Maybe he'd go up to Scotland like he'd planned months ago. There was no Alison around to sabotage his prospects anymore.

He'd found a job and a place to rent – a small cottage on the outskirts of Inverness. It had been perfect. But then Alison had found out and done everything she could to ruin it for him. He'd never forgiven her for that. But she was gone. His girlfriend had moved on, although Lucas was now free to move to Scotland if he wanted.

He looked up at the sky and felt a sudden gratitude for life. For the simple act of breathing. He'd been so close to losing it all.

He paused by the side of the road, listening to the birdsong at dusk. He'd never been much of a nature lover, but now he found himself thankful for the beauty around him. Lucas thought that it wasn't until your life was in danger that you started to appreciate it.

He took a deep breath, the air cool and clean, and felt a sense of calm settle over him. He'd been given a second chance. And he was going to make the most of it.

Lucas was so lost in his thoughts that he didn't hear the car approaching until it was almost on top of him. He stepped on to the grass verge to let it pass, but the car slowed to a stop beside him.

He turned, frowning. It was a black Range Rover. The driver's door opened, and a man Lucas didn't recognise got out. He wore a dark suit and had long hair in a slicked-back ponytail. His eyes were hidden behind mirrored sunglasses.

Lucas's heart began to race. He stepped back, but the man spoke before he could turn and run.

'Mr Black.' The man's voice was gravelly. He didn't smile. 'We've been looking for you.'

His expression was unreadable. Who was he? What did he want?

Did he work for Rothwell?

Oh no. This wasn't fair. Lucas had given Rothwell the file. He hadn't told the police anything.

His stomach clenched with fear. He should have stayed at the police station. He should have waited for a taxi. 'I didn't tell them anything . . . I swear.'

The man didn't answer. Instead, he moved towards Lucas.

Lucas took another step back, his hand fumbling for his phone.

But before he could even think about calling for help, the man lunged forward, grabbing him by his coat and pulling him towards the car. Lucas struggled, but the man was too strong. He felt himself being dragged towards the open door of the car, the darkness inside gaping like a mouth ready to swallow him whole.

This was it. This was how it ended. He would be bundled into Rothwell's car and never seen again.

Chapter Twenty-Four

As Lucas was shoved into the car, his glasses slipped off. He fumbled for them, then realised he wasn't alone in the back seat. Lucas turned slowly, cringing, expecting to see Rothwell.

But it wasn't the property developer.

The man sitting beside him was older, with salt-and-pepper hair. He wore an expensive overcoat and a mustard cashmere scarf. Lucas had no idea who he was.

The man turned to look at Lucas, his piercing eyes locking on to Lucas's with an unnerving intensity. 'Hello,' he said in a smooth, cultured voice. 'My name is Quentin Chapman. I'm a friend of Clive Rothwell's.' Chapman smiled, but it didn't reach his eyes. 'I'm afraid my friend has a bit of a temper. Rothwell can be . . . impulsive. He's quite upset about Alison's murder. But I'm sure you are, too.'

Lucas's mouth was dry. He tried to swallow but found he couldn't. He managed to nod. He'd never heard of Chapman, but this man was clearly the real power. He didn't work for Rothwell; Rothwell worked for him. Lucas was in over his head. Why had he ever accepted the job working with Alison Poulson?

'Rothwell is a valuable business partner,' Chapman continued. 'He's been working on a very exciting project. A project that would bring a great deal of prosperity to the region. But Alison – well, she decided to turn against him. It's a shame, really. She didn't understand the benefit of loyalty.'

Chapman's gaze searched Lucas's face. 'But I think you do, don't you? You're a bright young man. You see the potential. The economic growth. The jobs.'

Lucas shrank back against the seat. The man with the ponytail was right outside. Lucas glanced at the door handle. Maybe he could open the door and make a run for it.

He reached for the handle, but his hand froze when Chapman spoke again. 'I wouldn't do that if I were you. The door is locked.' He nodded at the huge bloke standing guard. 'From his size, you might guess he's slow, but he's surprisingly swift. You wouldn't stand a chance.'

Lucas's heart was pounding so hard he thought it might burst. He turned to Chapman, his eyes wild with panic. 'Please,' he said, his voice shaking. 'Please, I won't say anything. I'll keep my mouth shut. I promise. I won't tell anyone about any of this. Please, just let me go.'

'The wisest men are those who say the least. Are you familiar with the Stoics, Lucas?'

Lucas's eyes filled with tears, and his nose started to run. He sniffed. 'Please don't kill me. I'll do anything you ask.' He clutched his hands together and tried to kneel in the footwell. 'I'm begging you.'

Chapman raised an eyebrow. 'Such behaviour is unbecoming, Lucas. I thought you would be better than this. I'm disappointed.'

Lucas's breath was coming in short, ragged gasps.

'I'm not going to kill you, Lucas.'

'No?' Lucas wiped his nose with the back of his sleeve.

'No, and neither is Rothwell. However . . . I think it's time you took a little holiday.'

'I . . . I was thinking of going to Scotland.'

237

Chapman laughed. 'Not Scotland, but I have a place in mind for you. A beautiful, peaceful spot. You'll be able to relax. And best of all, no police will bother you there.'

◆ ◆ ◆

David Poulson sat at the kitchen table, staring at the cup of tea he'd made for himself but hadn't touched. The family liaison officer, Jim Willson, was sitting across from him, talking about football. David had made the mistake of mentioning he was a West Ham fan, and now Jim seemed to think they were best mates. He'd been there for over an hour, and David was finding it increasingly difficult to keep up the act of the grieving husband.

The officer had already had two cups of tea and was showing no signs of leaving. It was exhausting.

Jim seemed to notice David's distraction and cleared his throat. 'I'm sure they'll catch the person who did this, Mr Poulson. The team is working around the clock.'

David nodded in response. He knew it was just a platitude. The police had no leads and no suspects. They were no closer to solving Alison's murder than they had been on the day she was killed.

Jim took another slurp of his tea. David's hands tightened around his mug, remembering the night Alison had died. He'd felt a surge of shock and disbelief, followed by a wave of nausea. But then . . . then he'd felt something else. A strange mixture of emotions. Regret, of course. And anger. But also . . . relief. A terrible, guilty relief.

He'd loved Alison very much once. But that had been a long time ago. Before the arguments, the accusations, the affairs. Before the constant feeling of walking on eggshells in his own home.

Before he'd started to hate her.

It wasn't his fault, he told himself. She'd pushed him. Needled him. Kept picking at him until he snapped. She'd driven him to it.

But now she was dead, and he couldn't help feeling some sadness. Regret for the way things had turned out. Regret for the way he'd let his anger consume him. He'd tried to be a good husband – he really had – but Alison was never satisfied. She'd always wanted more. More money, more excitement, more attention.

She'd been having an affair, for goodness' sake. Right under his nose.

He was jolted from his thoughts by Jim's voice. 'Mr Poulson? Are you all right?'

David forced a smile. 'I'm fine. Just tired.'

Jim nodded sympathetically. But he didn't take the hint and leave. Keeping up this act was draining.

David's gaze flicked to the window, and he spotted the postman starting to walk up the drive. A welcome distraction. 'Won't be a minute,' he said to Jim, who had started a rant about the West Ham manager. David pushed back his chair and went to get the post.

He met the postman halfway up the drive. He handed over a pile of letters and a small parcel, then hesitated. 'I heard about . . .' He gave David a sympathetic smile. 'Well, you know. I'm sorry for your loss.'

'Thank you,' he said, taking the letters and the parcel.

David tucked the letters under his arm and opened the package as he walked back to the house. The package was addressed to Alison. She must have ordered it before she died.

David ripped open the brown wrapping. The object inside was wrapped in layers of tissue paper. He carefully peeled back the layers and then stopped in surprise.

It was a small brass plaque. He turned it over in his hands, examining it. The surface was smooth and cool to the touch. He frowned as he noticed the engraving on the front.

The plaque slipped from his fingers and clattered to the ground.

David's heart seemed to stop. What did it mean? Who had sent it? And why?

He bent down and picked up the plaque. The words were still there, staring up at him. He read them again and shivered.

Chapter Twenty-Five

Karen stepped into the office, her nose wrinkling at the smell of takeaway food. Her stomach rumbled, reminding her it was dinnertime.

Before she reached her workstation, she noticed that Jim Willson, the family liaison officer, was huddled around a desk with Morgan and Rick. They were so engrossed in whatever they were looking at that they didn't notice Karen's arrival. She walked over to them.

'Have we found Tilda Goring yet?'

Morgan shook his head. 'Sadly not. Churchill's ramping up the search now. No one has seen her for a few hours.'

Karen glanced at the clock. Five hours. Tilda had been missing for five hours, and no one had seen or heard from her. Why would she vanish without a word after her earlier claims to know something about what had happened to Alison?

The unease that had been simmering in Karen's mind now boiled over into full-blown worry. What if Tilda's information about Alison's murder wasn't just speculation? What if she'd stumbled on to something real, something dangerous? The thought of the killer silencing her, of another body turning up . . .

Karen tried to stop the grim thoughts. She couldn't let her imagination run away with her. There still could be an innocent explanation for Tilda's lack of contact. Although that was looking less and less likely.

'We don't often see you up here, Jim,' Karen said.

'I was actually just about to leave. My son, Ollie, has a chess tournament tonight. But I thought I'd better let you know that David Poulson got a delivery today. It was addressed to Alison, so she likely ordered it, unless someone else placed the order in her name.' Jim pointed at what, at first glance, Karen thought was a ball of tissue paper. On closer inspection, she saw it was a small brass plaque, the sort of thing usually attached to trophies.

'It's engraved,' Morgan said.

Karen leaned in to get a better look. She read the engraved words: *For Sylvie the Shrew, Britain's Biggest Nag.*

She felt her stomach lurch as she tried to process what this meant.

'Yeah, thought it might be important,' Jim said, noticing Karen's expression as he put on his coat. 'I'll see you all tomorrow.'

'Vexley told us Alison ordered the shrew's fiddle,' Karen said after Jim had left them. 'And this plaque calls Sylvie Broadbent a *shrew*. Do you think Alison was planning to put the plaque on the shrew's fiddle and give it to Sylvie as some kind of in-joke with the TV crew? *Britain's Biggest Nag* could be a play on *Britain's Biggest Treasure Hunt.*'

Morgan looked up from the plaque, his expression serious. 'You could be right. And from what we know about Alison, this *joke* was probably not meant in a kind way.'

Rick said, 'And what if Sylvie found out about it and was angry . . . angry enough to hurt Alison?'

Karen considered that. 'I think she'd be hurt rather than angry. I can't imagine Sylvie killing anyone, let alone treating anyone in the way the killer treated Alison. I've just dropped Arnie off at Sturton on Stow. He wanted to see if Tilda Goring had returned.

Sylvie will probably be there. I'll talk to her and find out what she knows.'

'I think we should warn Arnie.' Rick's face was set in a grim expression. 'Sylvie has been cosying up to him; I reckon she just wants to pump him for information on the police investigation.'

Karen's heart sank at Rick's suggestion. They'd all noticed Sylvie Broadbent flirting with Arnie, and he'd been flattered. He would be gutted if he thought her flattery and flirtation had been intended to manipulate him. Karen winced inwardly at how much this would hurt Arnie. He came across as tough, but was a sensitive soul under that gruff exterior. He would be devastated to learn he'd been taken for a fool.

Karen may have been a little suspicious of Sylvie at first, but she now believed the woman genuinely liked Arnie. She thought it was sweet. Arnie was an honourable man and a good officer. He wouldn't take advantage of the situation while the investigation was ongoing. But he was fond of Sylvie, and Karen could see there might be something between them in the future. He'd be sad if he found out Sylvie had known about Alison's nasty intended gift and held it back.

'Well, we definitely need to tell Arnie about this right away,' Karen said firmly. 'I can't imagine Sylvie being involved in Alison's murder even if she downplayed the animosity between her and Alison.'

Morgan was quiet for a moment, then said, 'Does Sylvie have an alibi for Alison's murder?'

'She was in the pub with the rest of the TV crew,' Rick said. 'But it was busy, so any of them could have snuck out for half an hour and might not have been missed. And there are no security cameras at the pub. Not inside or in the car park either.'

'All right. I'll see what she says about the plaque and how she reacts,' Karen said.

'Do you want someone with you?' Morgan asked, but Karen could see he didn't want to be the one to break the news to Arnie.

Morgan had many talents, but he wasn't good when it came to interpersonal relationships. He'd probably slap Arnie on the back and tell him there were plenty more fish in the sea or something equally unhelpful, and Rick would likely joke about it. Rick's gentle teasing wouldn't be intended as cruel, but Karen knew it would upset Arnie.

'I'll be fine alone,' Karen said firmly.

Morgan gave her a grateful smile before they all went their separate ways – Morgan back into his office, Rick back over towards his own desk, and Karen out of the station to go and deliver the news to Arnie.

The Cross Keys was a charming pub, Arnie thought. With its dark wooden beams and roaring fire, it felt cosy and welcoming. There were worse places to have a quick break after a long day of interviews and legwork. He'd called into the pub to ask the landlord if Tilda Goring had turned up, and to chat to the TV crew, but no one had seen her, which made his copper senses tingle.

The search for Tilda had now been scaled up – it was a missing person alert. Despite the short time Tilda had been missing, the circumstances meant they had to take it seriously. Farzana was looking into Tilda's digital footprint, which would hopefully give some clues to her whereabouts, and officers were looking through surveillance footage.

Arnie had intended to have a quick bite to eat, then get back to the station to help with the search, but as usual, his plans had been hijacked by Sylvie Broadbent. The TV producer had spotted him as soon as he'd entered the pub, and before he knew it, she'd pulled up a chair at his table and was flicking through the menu and offering to buy him dinner. Arnie had tried to protest, but Sylvie wouldn't take no for an answer.

He hadn't tried *that* hard to refuse. He liked Sylvie's company, and a man had to eat.

And there were Lincolnshire sausages on the menu.

Arnie glanced over at Sylvie now. She'd gone up to the bar to order. She wore an elegant navy-blue dress that clung to her curves in all the right places, and a pair of bright red heels.

Sylvie looked over her shoulder and flashed him a dazzling smile. Arnie took a sip of his pint, feeling relaxed and well . . . happy, he supposed. He'd not felt like this for a while.

Sylvie returned, putting her handbag on the empty chair at their table. 'I can't tell you how glad I am you accepted my dinner invitation,' she said. 'I'm feeling a bit down.'

'Down?' In the short time he'd known her, Sylvie had seemed upbeat to him, but he supposed even people with sunny personalities got fed up occasionally. 'Why is that?'

'Partly the fact I'm very worried about Tilda. But it's also this whole business with the insurance company dragging their feet.' Sylvie took a sip of wine before continuing. 'The police may have given us the go-ahead to resume filming, but the insurance people haven't agreed to it yet. And we can't do anything without insurance.'

Arnie made a sympathetic noise but didn't say anything.

'And now Molly Moreland and Trevor Barker are threatening to leave, and I have to try to handle it myself because Tilda isn't here,' Sylvie said miserably. 'They're saying they don't get paid enough to sit around waiting for filming to start.'

'They sound like a right pair of divas,' Arnie muttered.

'They're not exactly known for their patience or professionalism,' Sylvie agreed. 'And they're very high-maintenance types, I'm afraid. Although I suppose you already knew that about them. There have been so many stories in the press.'

Before Arnie could respond, there was a loud commotion as Molly Moreland and Trevor Barker entered the bar, struggling with two large suitcases each. Molly's cases were bright pink and on wheels. She pulled them along, hitting nearly every chair or table she passed, much to the annoyance of the other customers.

'We should have left hours ago!' Molly snapped furiously as they got closer to Arnie and Sylvie's table.

Trevor gave an exaggerated sigh of exasperation as he put his suitcases down with a thump. 'We would have, if you didn't take so long to pack.'

Molly shot him an icy look before noticing Sylvie. 'We're leaving. As professionals, we refuse to be treated this way. Keeping us waiting is unacceptable.'

Sylvie scrambled to her feet. 'You have a contract. You can't leave.'

'Just watch us,' Molly said.

Sylvie looked close to tears. 'Please don't go.'

'Nothing personal, my dear lady,' Trevor said condescendingly as he patted Sylvie on the arm, 'but we have to leave. I didn't sign up for *Britain's Biggest Treasure Hunt* to sit around twiddling my thumbs.'

Both started towards their suitcases again but stopped dead when they saw Arnie blocking their path, arms crossed, looking deeply unimpressed. 'I wouldn't do that if I were you, Mr Barker, Miss Moreland.'

Molly narrowed her eyes. 'Why are you getting in our way?'

'Do you know what happens when people leave town during an ongoing murder investigation? It makes the police think they've got something to hide.'

Molly looked slightly less confident. 'That's ridiculous. We don't have anything to hide!'

Arnie smiled. 'Well, then there's no reason for you not to stay put, is there?'

'But we've packed,' Trevor whined. He jerked a thumb in Molly's direction. 'And it took her ages.'

'Then I suggest you unpack,' Arnie said, using his best *I'm a police officer, so don't mess with me* tone. 'There is an active murder investigation ongoing. No one should leave the area.'

That wasn't strictly true, but a little white lie wouldn't hurt.

Everyone in the pub was watching them now.

'Seriously? This is unbelievable.' Molly threw her bag on the floor. Arnie thought she might start stamping her feet next.

Molly dramatically slumped into a chair, squashing Sylvie's handbag underneath her. 'This is crazy. If we have to wait until you finish your investigation, we'll be here all year at this rate. You've not exactly made much progress!' She turned to Trevor, reaching out her hand to clasp his. 'It's all so unfair.'

'I know, pet,' Trevor said, stroking her arm. 'Let's get our cases back upstairs.'

With a sob, Molly stood up, and they both began slowly dragging their cases towards the back of the pub.

Arnie watched Molly and Trevor trudge back to the stairs, satisfied at having put them in their place. They were obviously used to getting their own way.

'Thank you,' Sylvie said, smiling widely as she sat back at the table. 'You showed them who's boss.'

'Just doing my job,' Arnie said gruffly.

That wasn't strictly true. In fact, he'd stepped a fair way out of his remit. But he had to admit it felt good to have Sylvie look at him like that.

'You were fantastic,' she insisted. 'I'm so relieved they're staying put. I don't know how I would have explained their absence to the production company.'

Arnie smiled at her. 'No need to worry now. They won't be going anywhere for a while.'

Sylvie watched him briefly before saying softly, 'You know, you're not quite how you appear at first glance.'

'What's that supposed to mean?'

'Well, you come across as this grumpy old detective who lives for the job. But there's more to you than that.' She leaned forward slightly and lowered her voice. 'I can tell you've got a good heart underneath all that bluster.'

Arnie shifted uncomfortably in his seat as a server brought their food to the table. He looked happily at his sausage, mash, gravy and peas. Food fit for a king.

Sylvie picked up her fork. 'Anyway,' she continued breezily, 'have you had any developments in the case?'

Arnie raised an eyebrow at her directness. 'We have our eye on one or two people.'

'Like who?' Sylvie's eyes widened as she set down her fork again, giving him her full attention.

'I can't tell you that.'

'Oh.' Sylvie pouted. 'Really? I wouldn't tell anyone.'

Arnie mimed a zipping motion over his lips. 'Nope.'

Sylvie sat back in her chair, disappointed. 'I can't stop thinking about poor Alison and what happened to her. And now Tilda has disappeared, and it makes me nervous.'

Arnie swallowed a delicious mouthful of sausage and mash, then said, 'I don't like it either. We're scaling up the search.'

They ate their dinner, chatting companionably.

When Arnie sighed with satisfaction and put his knife and fork together, Sylvie mirrored his actions and said, 'If you find out

248

anything about Tilda . . . you'll let me know straightaway, won't you?'

He nodded.

'Another drink?'

Arnie looked regretfully at the beer taps on the bar. 'Better make it a lemonade.' He reached for her wine glass. 'I'll get them.'

She squeezed his hand gently. 'Thank you.'

Arnie walked over to the bar and rubbed absently at his hand where Sylvie had touched him.

He wondered what her game plan was. What did she hope would come from spending time with him? She'd soon be heading back to London or some other filming location for the show, and Arnie would be out of sight and out of mind.

He sighed and leaned against the bar. It had been pleasant while it lasted.

Chapter Twenty-Six

Karen arrived at the Cross Keys pub, and saw Arnie and Sylvie through the window, sitting at a table near the open fire. Sylvie was leaning close to Arnie, her hand resting on his arm as she spoke. Arnie was laughing at something she'd said. They looked good together.

But Karen was about to ruin this moment between them.

If Sylvie knew about the plaque and Alison's intention to give her the shrew's fiddle, then she'd held it back from them. Although Karen didn't think Sylvie would have killed Alison over the incident, she had still withheld information which could have assisted with their enquiries.

Karen hated this – hated the thought of ruining Arnie's happiness. He deserved better. But the case came first. It always did.

Karen pushed open the door and walked over to their table. 'Arnie, can I have a word?'

Arnie looked up, his eyes meeting hers. He must have noticed the serious expression on her face because he immediately excused himself from the table and followed her outside into the chilly evening air.

'Has something happened?' he asked when they were standing on the pavement outside the pub.

Karen took a deep breath and tried to find the right words. 'We've had an interesting development in the case,' she began slowly. 'A package was delivered to Alison Poulson's husband this afternoon.'

'David Poulson.'

'Yes,' Karen confirmed. 'It contained a small brass plaque with an engraving on it that read: *For Sylvie the Shrew, Britain's Biggest Nag.*'

Arnie's expression changed as he processed what Karen was saying.

'I think Alison was planning on putting the plaque on the shrew's fiddle and giving it to Sylvie as some kind of macabre joke.'

Arnie shook his head. 'You think Alison was going to present it to Sylvie?'

'I do,' Karen said gently.

'That's awful. Horrible thing to do.' Arnie's face hardened, and he crossed his arms over his chest. 'Sylvie may not have known about the plaque. Could be another nasty thing Alison Poulson had planned but never got around to doing.'

'It's possible, but if she did know, she didn't tell us. You've been getting close to her and—'

Arnie seemed to deflate. 'I like her.' He shoved his hands in his pockets and looked up at the dark sky.

Karen sighed. She'd known this would be a difficult conversation, but it was harder than she'd expected. She felt like she was crushing Arnie's spirit. 'I know. But considering her connection to the case, I think it's a good idea if you create some distance. Sylvie has been taking quite an interest in you, hasn't she?'

Arnie closed his eyes. 'She has.'

'And she's been asking questions about the case?'

'Yes, but that's only natural, isn't it? Sylvie's curious because she knew the victim. And as a TV producer, she's worried about how the investigation affects the filming schedule.'

He was trying to persuade himself. Karen didn't want to take away his last shred of dignity. 'I suppose so.'

'Did she tell you that Alison had planned to present her with the shrew's fiddle?'

'No, of course not. I would have told you straightaway if I knew. Maybe she didn't even know herself.'

'There's a good chance,' Karen said. 'But I think she deliberately downplayed the bad blood between her and Alison. I just think you should consider your career and how this will look if this case gets reviewed.'

'You're right.' Arnie let out a long, slow breath, his shoulders slumping. 'What's that saying? There's no fool like an old fool.'

'You're not a fool.'

Arnie gave a humourless laugh. 'That's exactly what I am.'

Karen reached out and placed a hand on his shoulder. 'I'm not saying Sylvie is guilty of anything. You just have to be careful. I need to talk to Sylvie and ask her about this. Do you want me to tell her you've been called away?'

Arnie looked tempted but shook his head, his jaw set in determination. 'I can still do my job. I'll talk to her with you.'

Karen smiled. 'Okay. Let's go talk to her.'

Together, they headed back to the pub, but Arnie put a hand on Karen's arm as they reached the door. 'Before we go in. I need you to know . . . Sylvie might have asked questions, but I never told her anything about the case.'

'I didn't think you would have.'

As they approached the table, Sylvie looked up and smiled. 'There you are! I was starting to think you'd both gone home.'

Arnie took his seat opposite Sylvie, and Karen sat beside him.

'Sylvie, we need to talk to you about something,' Karen said, her voice steady. 'It's about Alison Poulson's murder.'

Sylvie's smile faltered, and she looked from Karen to Arnie and back again. 'What is it?'

Karen took a deep breath and began to explain. 'A package was delivered to Alison Poulson's husband earlier today.'

'What was in it?' Sylvie asked.

Karen shot Arnie a glance before she continued. 'It contained a small brass plaque with an engraving on it.'

'How odd.'

'The engraving read: *For Sylvie the Shrew, Britain's Biggest Nag.*'

'Oh.' Sylvie blinked rapidly, looking down at the table. 'I knew Alison didn't like me very much, but I hadn't expected . . . I mean, I suppose people might see me as a bit of a nag. But it's my job to make sure things run smoothly.' She looked at Arnie, her eyes shining with unshed tears. 'That was very unkind of Alison.'

'We have to ask if you knew about the plaque before it arrived?' Karen asked gently.

Sylvie shook her head emphatically. 'No! I had no idea.'

'Did Alison ever refer to you as a shrew, anything like that?' Arnie asked.

'Not to my face, no. I mean . . . we had our differences . . .' Sylvie trailed off.

Arnie fixed his gaze on Sylvie's face. He spoke quietly but firmly, as though he were coaxing out a confession from a suspect in an interview room. 'Tell us about those differences.'

'I suppose I can be . . . demanding sometimes.' Her voice wavered. 'It's just everything falls to me – the permits, dealing with the actors . . .'

Arnie nodded encouragingly.

'Alison could be quite demanding herself,' Sylvie continued. 'She rubbed nearly everyone the wrong way. No one on set liked her . . . except Tilda.'

'You didn't like Alison?' Karen asked.

'No,' Sylvie admitted after a pause.

'So, there were times when you would get frustrated with Alison because things weren't going according to plan?'

'Only once,' Sylvie said quietly. 'We had an argument. The day before she died. She turned up saying there were *more* forms to fill in. And that's not as easy as it sounds because I have to get them signed off by my bosses, who are based at our production company in London.'

'Did the argument turn physical?' Arnie asked.

'No!' The word came out forcefully, and several heads turned their way.

'I'm sorry if these questions are difficult, Sylvie, but we need to ask them,' Karen said.

'I know,' Sylvie said, in a quieter voice this time. 'I'm just upset.'

Arnie couldn't resist a dig. 'So am I. You could have told us how tense things were between you and Alison. You've made me look a right fool.'

Sylvie's eyes widened. 'I didn't think it mattered.' She put her hands flat on the table and leaned in close to Arnie. 'You actually think I killed Alison, don't you?'

The question hung heavily between them. Arnie just stared at Sylvie stubbornly without replying, so Karen answered, 'We're just trying to get all the facts straight so we can find who did kill her.'

'But do you think *I* killed her?'

'I don't know what happened, Sylvie,' Arnie said. 'I wasn't there.'

'But do you think I'm capable of murder? That I'd put that horrible thing around Alison's neck?'

'It doesn't matter what I think,' Arnie replied firmly. 'We have evidence linking your name to the shrew's fiddle.'

'I didn't kill Alison Poulson! I didn't know about that awful thing until it turned up around her neck! I would never do anything like that!' Tears started to trickle down Sylvie's cheeks, and she fumbled in her bag for a tissue. 'This is all just too much.' She blew her nose and then looked at Arnie like she was seeing him for the first time. 'Am I under arrest?'

Karen shook her head, thinking that if Sylvie was acting, her job was on the wrong side of the camera. 'No, Sylvie. We're just asking questions at this stage.'

'*At this stage?*' Sylvie reached for her bag. 'I see. Well, if I'm not under arrest, I don't need to sit here and listen to this. If you'll excuse me, I need some air.'

As she stormed out of the pub, the bar fell silent for a moment before returning to its usual buzz of conversation. Arnie rubbed a hand over his face and let out a long sigh.

'That went well,' he muttered sarcastically.

'I don't think Sylvie is guilty of anything other than underplaying her bad relationship with Alison. Take it easy on her. There's no reason for you two to keep your distance once this investigation is over.'

He grunted in response and signalled for the bill. The landlord brought it over with a sympathetic smile and discreetly left them alone.

'Looks like Sylvie isn't treating me to dinner after all,' Arnie said, pulling out his wallet. 'How did you gauge Sylvie's reaction? Was that the response of a guilty woman or an innocent one?

Because I have to be honest, Karen, I'm not sure I trust my judgement when it comes to Sylvie. Do you still think she's involved somehow?'

'No, I find it impossible to imagine Sylvie being involved. The person we're looking for is sadistic. It's likely they took pleasure in using that device on Alison. Sylvie doesn't fit the profile of our killer.'

Chapter Twenty-Seven

Sylvie rushed outside the Cross Keys pub into the cold October evening. She didn't have her jacket as she hadn't intended to go out. She shivered as the frigid air bit through the thin material of her dress. Hugging her arms around herself, she tried to warm up, but it was useless. It was freezing, but she couldn't bring herself to go back inside – not with Arnie and the other detective still there.

Sylvie felt a pang of betrayal. She'd hoped she and Arnie had a connection, that there could be something between them. She had thought he genuinely enjoyed her company and wanted to get to know her better. How utterly humiliating.

She paced back and forth in the pub's small car park, her breath coming out in little white puffs. How could they think *she* had anything to do with Alison's murder? It was true that she hadn't warmed to Alison, but that didn't mean she would have killed her. The idea was ludicrous.

Poor Alison. It had been a nasty way to go. Sylvie had always abided by the adage that you shouldn't speak ill of the dead, but it was very hard not to in Alison's case. She really had been a very difficult woman.

Hunching her shoulders against the cold, Sylvie stopped beside Tilda's empty car. The only person involved in the project that Alison had seemed to like was Tilda, and the feeling was mutual.

They'd always been scurrying off for private little chats, which was odd because Alison really shouldn't have had much to do with the project once all the permits and permissions had been sorted.

And where *was* Tilda? Sylvie was starting to get seriously worried. She had told Tilda to go to the police, so where had Tilda disappeared to? Why would she change her mind about speaking up?

This whole project had been a disaster from start to finish. And now, with Tilda swanning off, Sylvie had to deal with the fallout alone. Maybe *she* should disappear, too. Jet off to a sunny beach somewhere. The idea was very tempting.

Sylvie had believed they were in good hands with Arnie on the investigation. But now it was obvious she'd misjudged him completely. Arnie didn't know his backside from his elbow; that much was clear. She felt the sting of tears in her eyes that he, of all people, could suspect her.

How could she have got it so wrong again? Arnie had seemed different from the men she usually came in contact with in the course of her job. Over the years, she'd seen it all. The vanity, the preening, the self-obsession. She was sick and tired of the dating scene and had given up hope of finding someone she actually wanted to spend time with, someone who liked her for who she was rather than her television connections.

Arnie had been a breath of fresh air. Confident, but kind. Strong, compassionate, and a good listener. She tutted to herself. Of course he'd been a good listener. He was probably hoping she'd say something incriminating.

An icy breeze rushed by, leaving her teeth chattering. She should think about getting back. Her toes were numb. But knowing that Arnie might still be there, and she'd have to pass him to get back to her room at the pub, kept her walking on.

Sylvie reached the village green, rubbing her arms vigorously to warm herself against the biting chill of the night air. She'd better head back to the warm pub before she succumbed to hypothermia. But just as she turned to leave, a dark shape on the far side of the green caught her eye.

That's odd, she thought. There had been nothing but empty grass and the old, weathered whipping post when she had walked past earlier today. Now there was an ominous shape near the post.

As Sylvie moved closer, picking her way carefully across the muddy grass, she could make out what looked like a human body propped limply against the whipping post. No, it couldn't possibly be a real body. Surely it must be some kind of prank – an old dummy that some local kids had posed there as a gruesome joke. Yes, that must be it. Halloween wasn't far off, so it was probably something to do with that.

She looked around, expecting to see some giggling children hiding somewhere, but she was alone.

A creeping sense of dread slithered down Sylvie's spine as she drew nearer, her heels sinking into the soft earth. Something was chillingly familiar about the flash of bright blue hair on the slumped figure's head. Sylvie's mouth went dry and her hands started to tremble, not just from the icy wind.

With each step, her heels sank deeper into the mud, but she barely noticed, her eyes fixed on the pale form tied to the post. As she finally reached the middle of the green, there could be no more doubt or denial – this was no prank with a shop dummy.

It was a body. A real human body, the face a bloody, swollen mess – disfigured almost beyond recognition. But Sylvie would know that distinctive blue hair anywhere, even caked in blood and gore.

It was Tilda. And she was most definitely dead.

It was a horrific sight. Deep bruises marred her face, one eye swollen shut, the other open and glassy. Dried blood crusted her split lip and nose. Sylvie gasped in horror as she took in the rest of

Tilda's battered form. Her clothes were torn, buttons ripped off. Angry red welts covered her exposed skin. She had been viciously beaten.

Sylvie staggered back, bile rising in her throat. Sweet, eccentric Tilda, who wouldn't hurt a fly. Who could have done such a thing?

Sylvie doubled over, vomiting violently on to the grass. Then she let out a scream that echoed across the village green.

Chapter Twenty-Eight

Karen stepped out of the Cross Keys pub, the laughter and chatter from inside fading as the door swung shut behind her. She'd left Arnie inside to settle the bill, planning to give Mike a quick call to let him know she'd be home late.

The glow from the pub's windows receded, leaving her in near darkness as she pulled her mobile from her pocket and strolled towards her car.

She hadn't got far when a figure emerged from the shadows ahead. Karen tensed before recognizing Sylvie. The producer was walking slowly, unsteadily, as if in a daze.

'Sylvie?' Karen called. 'Are you all right?'

The woman didn't seem to hear. But as she drew nearer, Karen noticed Sylvie's ashen face and wide, horrified eyes. Alarm prick-led through Karen. She slid her phone back into her pocket and changed direction towards Sylvie.

'What's happened?'

'There . . .' Sylvie raised a trembling hand, pointing.

Karen looked but couldn't see anything. 'What?'

Sylvie grabbed her hand and tugged. Karen followed her to the green. When they got there, she saw what had upset Sylvie.

Tilda Goring lay slumped at the base of the whipping post. Even from a distance, Karen could see she was dead, head lolling at an unnatural angle. Rope bound her wrists to the wooden post.

Karen rushed over, pulse pounding. She crouched beside the body, quickly checking for a pulse she didn't expect to find. Tilda's skin was bloody and covered with abrasions, one eye open but unseeing. Her blue hair was matted with blood.

She swallowed hard. 'Don't look,' she said to Sylvie gently. 'Come and sit down; I'll call this in.'

She guided the shaking Sylvie to a nearby stone wall. The producer sank down, breath coming in panicked gulps. 'Try to breathe slowly. You're in shock.'

Karen stepped away and called for backup and an ambulance. Then messaged Arnie.

Arnie arrived first. He jogged across the green, face creased in concern.

He reached them, noticing Sylvie shivering on the stone wall. Breathlessly, he said, 'I got your text. What's happened?'

Karen gestured at the whipping post. Arnie's expression shifted to one of horror.

'Oh, no . . .' He raked a hand over his hair, looking between Karen and the body. 'I knew something was wrong.'

He started towards the post, but Karen stopped him. 'We'd better wait for Forensics. I checked for a pulse. She's gone.'

It wasn't easy to see in the dim light, so Karen explained to Arnie what she'd observed. 'The iron manacles weren't used. Just rope to tie her wrists.' From this distance, it was impossible to see the abrasions circling Tilda's wrists.

Arnie nodded, jaw tight.

'It looks like she was beaten and possibly whipped with something. Maybe a belt or a cane?' The vicious welts and gashes were visible on Tilda's face and through her torn shirt.

Arnie put a hand over his mouth, shaking his head. 'Evil.'

Karen continued, 'And I think her neck was broken. See how her head is at a strange angle?'

'What a horrible way to die.'

Karen's throat tightened. Seeing Tilda – or indeed anyone – treated this way was awful.

Arnie crouched down beside Sylvie. 'You found her?'

Sylvie nodded, shivering.

'Did you touch the body . . . or anything out here?'

'No . . . I just went to get help.'

Arnie slipped off his coat and put it around Sylvie's shoulders.

She shrugged it off. 'I don't need your jacket, thank you.'

'Don't be daft. It's freezing, and you're in shock. You may be angry at me, but that doesn't mean you should freeze your bits off just to prove a point.'

Reluctantly, she put the jacket back around her shoulders.

'I'm sorry,' Arnie said. 'I didn't—'

'Her pendant,' Sylvie said abruptly.

'What?'

'Tilda isn't wearing her pendant.'

Arnie raised his eyebrows and looked at Karen.

'Does she always wear it?' Karen asked.

'I don't think she's taken it off since she acquired it a month ago.'

'*Acquired* it?' Arnie asked, picking up on the fact Sylvie had used that word rather than saying Tilda had bought it or was given it as a present.

'She found it. At a potential filming site. She was scouting locations last month.'

'Where?'

Sylvie shrugged. 'I'm not sure. I didn't go on the trip.'

'That could be useful information,' Karen said. 'Thank you, Sylvie.'

At the sound of approaching sirens, Arnie straightened. Moments later, two patrol cars and an ambulance pulled up nearby, followed shortly afterwards by the SOCO van. Karen instructed the officers to cordon off the area. The paramedics moved in to check Sylvie over.

The noise and the flashing blue lights soon attracted attention in the quiet village. Karen took statements from the few residents who came out of their houses to linger around the green. Surprisingly, everyone she spoke to said they'd not seen or heard anything unusual.

The crime scene suddenly lit up, as portable floodlights were switched on. Karen blinked against the harsh glare. There were shocked gasps as the residents behind the cordon saw Tilda's body illuminated. Karen helped the uniformed officers guide people back to their houses as the SOCOs hurried to get a tent set up around Tilda's body.

Raj arrived soon after the tent was erected. The normally jovial pathologist was subdued when he saw the victim. He conducted his initial examination of Tilda's body solemnly, and Karen stayed close by, watching.

'Time of death no more than an hour ago,' Raj said finally. 'Given the visible injuries, we're likely looking at the cause of death being trauma to the spinal cord from the neck being sharply forced back.' He gestured to the marks that covered Tilda's face and body. 'Looks like she was viciously beaten.' He shook his head, sighing heavily. 'Poor woman. What sort of monster could do such a thing?'

Karen had no answer for him.

The scenes of crime officer, Tim Farthing, approached Karen. His face creased at the sight of the victim, but he remained professional.

'Another nasty one,' he said. 'I found something that might interest you.' He held up an evidence bag. Inside was a silver chain. 'It was on the ground a couple of feet away from the body.'

'The chain from Tilda's pendant,' Karen said. 'Her colleague noticed it was missing.'

'Could have been torn off in a struggle. We'll get it checked for DNA back at the lab.'

'No sign of the actual pendant that should have been attached to the chain?'

'Not so far. What did it look like?'

Karen tried to remember. She pictured Tilda talking, absently twirling the pendant as she'd answered their questions about Alison. But the details escaped her. Annoying. She could hear her old boss, Anthony, telling her that innocuous details were often crucial to solving cases, so why couldn't she recall what it looked like?

'It was . . . um . . .' She thought hard but couldn't see it in her mind's eye. 'I can't really remember. It was quite big, though.'

'Big?' Tim just looked at her. 'Well, with that detailed description, I'm sure I'll find it in no time.'

Karen glared at him, angry because he had a point. She should be able to remember. 'I'm not in the mood for your sarcasm, Tim.'

'Have you ever considered you might be in the wrong line of work? Detectives are usually more observant. Might be time for a career change.'

'Might be time for you to shut up and get on with your job,' Arnie snapped.

Karen turned. She hadn't heard him approach.

Tim lifted his hands, smirking. 'Well, aren't you both incredibly touchy tonight?'

Arnie muttered a few imaginative expletives as the scenes of crime officer walked away. 'That bloke is awful.'

'I shouldn't have risen to the bait,' Karen said. 'It only makes him worse. Do you remember what Tilda's pendant looked like?'

Arnie's forehead creased. 'It was a big chunky thing, made of glass with stuff inside it.'

'What stuff?'

'Can't remember. But Sylvie might.'

As Raj's assistants carefully moved Tilda's body into a body bag, Arnie and Karen headed back over to Sylvie, who was sitting in the back of an ambulance, wrapped in a shock blanket. Her eyes were wide and haunted as she stared at the scene unfolding before her.

'I can't believe she's gone,' Sylvie said as they reached her. 'If I'd left the pub sooner . . .'

'You can't think like that,' Arnie said. 'Besides, you might have been attacked if you'd stumbled across Tilda earlier.'

A hard lump formed in Karen's throat as she thought of Tilda's last moments. They'd been so close, too. At the pub, just metres away.

'Can you tell us what Tilda's pendant looked like, Sylvie?' Karen asked.

Sylvie spoke quietly. 'It was big, maybe two inches long. It had glass on the front, covering a lock of hair.'

'*Hair?*' Arnie grimaced. 'What colour was the hair? Whose hair was it?'

'It was dark brown, almost black,' Sylvie replied. 'I don't know whose hair it was – but next to it, on the pendant itself, there were the initials *C.R.*'

'Any idea what those initials stand for?' Karen asked.

'I don't know.'

'Did she ever mention anyone being interested in the pendant?' Arnie asked. 'Or anyone wanting to buy it from her?'

Sylvie shook her head. 'No, she never mentioned anything like that, but she was really protective of it. I did think it might be valuable.'

After Sylvie was cleared by the paramedics, Arnie escorted her back to the pub. When he returned, his face was etched with frustration, his eyes tired and his mouth turned down.

'It's been a tough evening, and it's getting late,' Karen said. 'Morgan is here now, so we can hold the fort if you want to head home.'

'I'll stay.' Arnie pressed his lips together in a firm line.

The floodlights cast deep shadows on the buildings surrounding the green. Karen gazed into the darkness, imagining the killer slinking off into those shadows, leaving Tilda's beaten body behind. The chilling ruthlessness turned her stomach.

Who could extinguish a life so cruelly? It had to be the same person who'd left Alison Poulson with her neck clamped in the shrew's fiddle.

'Tilda must have known something important,' Karen said at last. 'Or the killer believed she did.'

Arnie's shoulders slumped a little more. 'And now whatever she knew has died with her.'

Karen shook her head. 'Not necessarily. We just have to keep digging. Her mention of Scotland . . .' She buried her hands in her pockets, thinking. 'We just have to figure out what she meant.'

'Easier said than done,' Arnie grumbled.

Footsteps sounded, and Karen turned to see Morgan approaching. His sharp eyes swept over the scene. Coming to stand in front of Karen and Arnie, he crossed his arms.

'Right then,' he said briskly. 'Two deaths, both connected to the dig and the TV show. It can't be coincidence. What do we know so far?'

Karen quickly filled him in on the state of Tilda's body and the evidence, which was frustratingly scarce. She also mentioned Tilda's missing pendant. Morgan maintained a blank expression as he listened.

'The pendant bothers me,' Karen said.

'The killer likely took it deliberately,' Morgan suggested. 'As a trophy, perhaps.'

'Whatever the reason, it's another piece of potential evidence lost. Apparently, it contained a lock of hair and the initials *C. R.* And before you ask, we currently have no idea who the hair belongs to or what the initials stand for. We only know that she found the pendant when scouting future filming locations.'

'We know Tilda's said this was all to do with Scotland,' Arnie said. 'Maybe she got the pendant somewhere in Scotland.'

'It's possible,' Morgan said thoughtfully. 'I'll get Sophie to look into Tilda's recent travel. See if we can find out if she went to Scotland.'

'Or if she was planning a trip there,' Karen said. 'Perhaps she intended to go with Alison next week.'

Two uniformed officers approached them.

'Evening, sir,' one said, nodding to Morgan. 'We've finished canvassing the houses around the green. Not a single witness to the murder itself. No one saw or heard a thing out of the ordinary all night.'

Morgan thanked them for their efforts before they moved off again. Karen stifled a frustrated sigh. So much for pinning her hopes on helpful witnesses.

Chapter Twenty-Nine

It's Friday morning, and Christie Stark wishes she was still in bed. Instead, she steps out into the garden. The grass is long and wet from last night's rain, which soaks into Christie's shoes as she walks towards the old shed nestled between the camellia and lilac bushes.

She's supposed to be at college but didn't want to go.

If you're not going to college today, you can at least make yourself useful here. Moping about will make you feel worse. You need to keep yourself occupied.

Her mother's words echo in her mind. Christie sighs. Gardening is the last thing she feels like doing.

She's still worried about her mum. The police were sniffing around again yesterday, asking questions about her mum's movements on Tuesday night. They don't believe she was at home all evening. Christie wishes she never went out on Tuesday night with her new friends from college. If she'd stayed home, she could have given her mum an alibi.

Before she reaches the shed, her mobile beeps with a message. It's from Mia.

> *Last night, they found another dead body in Stow, another person associated with that archaeology dig.*
>
> *How crazy?!!*

Blood rushes in Christie's ears as she reads the message again. Another murder . . .

When did it happen? Christie opens an internet browser on her phone, searching for any news articles, but there are no further details.

She went to bed early last night but lay awake for hours, staring at the ceiling. Her parents haven't mentioned a second murder. Do they know?

Yesterday, she overheard her mum and Cindy talking. Cindy was ranting about the police, saying not to trust them, to be careful what they said and not to give anything away. Why would Cindy say that unless . . . ?

Christie shakes her head. She's letting her imagination run wild again. She shoves her mobile in the back pocket of her jeans as she reaches the shed.

The door creaks open as Christie enters, and the musty smell of old wood and potting soil fills her nose. There are tools hanging neatly along one wall – spades, forks and rakes. Bags of compost are piled up against another wall, next to some old wooden crates filled with flowerpots. A spider scuttles across a cobweb on Christie's bike leaning against some plastic storage boxes full of Christmas decorations.

A rickety potting bench with drawers underneath sits below the window. It's filled with odds and sods.

Christie rummages through the drawers, searching for the secateurs her mother mentioned. In the bottom drawer, there's a paper bag full of bulbs ready for planting and green garden string.

She pushes the bag of bulbs aside, then her hand freezes when she sees two mobile phones. They are either switched off or the batteries are flat. New models – sleek and expensive-looking. Not like anything her mum and dad would cast off and dump down here. Christie picks one up and notices a tiny SIM card underneath.

It seems weird that the SIM cards have been removed; why would they do that?

Her hand trembles as she reaches for the SIM card, a million thoughts racing through her mind. What if the phone holds information that will turn her world upside down? But the alternative – remaining in the dark – is unbearable. The not knowing is worse than facing the truth. She makes her decision and inserts a SIM card into one of the phones.

Looking through the dusty window towards the house, Christie takes a deep breath and presses the power button.

Karen sat at the back of the briefing room in Nettleham police station, sipping her coffee. She needed to focus, but her thoughts kept drifting back to Mike. Before dawn that morning, she'd found him in the garden, burning a box of photos. He'd got up while she'd still been asleep, maybe hoping she wouldn't notice.

Lorraine had given the photographs to Mike a few months ago, when he'd first started asking questions about his parentage. They were snaps of him and his biological father from when Mike was still a toddler. But someone – presumably Lorraine herself – had scratched the man's face out of all the pictures. So they hadn't exactly been useful, but Karen had still worried that Mike might regret destroying them. They might not be much, but they were a link to his biological father.

As she'd gone outside to talk to him, she'd spotted one that had been dropped on the kitchen floor. She'd picked it up and put it in a drawer instead of taking it outside to add to his burning pile.

Had she done the right thing, intervening in Mike's choice? Or should she have respected his decision and taken the photo out to

271

him, so he could burn it with the others? Maybe she shouldn't have interfered. It was his decision, after all.

She knew he was acting on impulse, purging himself of a father who had never bothered with him. But those photos were links to a past Mike knew nothing about. And what if someday he wanted that connection again?

After hiding the dropped photograph, she'd gone out to speak with him, shivering in the early morning frost. Mike had been so resolute as he'd fed each photo into the flames, watching them blacken and shrivel up before turning to ash. He had cheerily assured her that he was fine and that he just wanted a fresh start without wasting any more time on a father who clearly didn't care about him.

But Karen worried that Mike was simply burying his hurt and disappointment over the whole situation. Those kinds of feelings had a way of resurfacing when you least expected them to. She had wanted to stay, sensing he needed her, but with Tilda's murder the case had escalated to a horrible extent.

Even if she'd stayed with Mike, she didn't know how she could have helped him when he seemed intent on keeping it all bottled up inside. She knew she needed to tread lightly, giving him space but also showing her support. Mike had been there for her more times than she could count. Now it was time for her to return the favour.

Once this case was over, she'd make it up to him. They'd have time for a proper talk and could try to work out the best way for him to process all of this.

A couple of officers stood behind Karen, chatting about the press coverage. The two murders were now what everyone was talking about. It was on all the news channels, plastered across the front pages of newspapers, and trending on social media.

The media was going overboard on the pun titles. The most common one used by the tabloids was changing the name of

Britain's Biggest Treasure Hunt to 'Britain's Biggest Murder Hunt'. Other headlines were slightly splashier: 'From Treasure Hunt to Terror Hunt: Britain's Deadliest Reality Show' and 'Molly and Trevor's Deadly Dig'.

Every article Karen had read so far seemed to focus on the wrong thing. It was all drama and gossip, mainly focusing on the two TV presenters' reactions, describing how devastated Molly and Trevor were. Not much about Alison and Tilda, the *victims* – the women whose lives had been brutally cut short.

Alison might have been abrasive, and single-minded about her ambitions, but she deserved better than this. They both did. They should get sympathy, compassion. Not be reduced to a brief paragraph in sensationalist articles or fodder for arguments online.

DCI Churchill entered the briefing room and stopped beside Sophie's seat. He spoke so quietly that Karen could only just hear what he said to her. 'Before we begin, Sophie, I want to acknowledge your instincts were correct. You warned us that this killer might strike again, and sadly, you were right.'

Sophie shifted in her seat. 'Thank you, sir. I really didn't want to be right about that.'

'I know your return to work hasn't run smoothly, but I appreciate the value you add to the team.' Churchill straightened, then made his way to the front of the room.

His gaze swept over the assembled officers, his frustration seeping through. The team had been working flat out for days with little progress to show for it.

Then he outlined their current situation. 'We have alibi checks on Clive Rothwell and David Poulson,' Churchill said briskly. 'Both are watertight.' He nodded to DS Hodgson to give more details.

'Rothwell was at a party at his golf club near Louth until after midnight on Tuesday,' Arnie said, reading from his notes. 'Plenty of witnesses saw him there all night. And Poulson's nightshift manager confirmed he was working at the warehouse from nine p.m. until five a.m. So, I think we need to look elsewhere for our killer.'

'Most of the *Britain's Biggest Treasure Hunt* crew were drinking in the Cross Keys pub until late on Tuesday night,' Rick said when it was his turn to speak. 'It's possible one of them snuck out then, or last night, without people noticing, but I reckon that's unlikely.'

'It would take some balls,' Arnie said. 'Especially last night. I was in the pub, and so was Karen for a time. But it was busy, and I can't say for certain that none of them left for a short period. Even Sylvie Broadbent left, and then she found Tilda's body . . .'

'I think we can rule Sylvie out. She was with you,' Karen said. 'And she wouldn't have had long enough to inflict those injuries in the short duration between her leaving the pub and finding Tilda's body.'

Then Churchill asked, 'What about Benjamin Price – the farmer? We're sure it's not him?'

'I don't think he's a logical suspect. We know he visits his wife's grave every evening. The rector at the church confirmed that.' Morgan leaned forward slightly, resting his forearms on the table. 'Lucas Black has a tenuous link to Scotland. He was supposed to be heading there for a new job, a fresh start with his girlfriend. Alison put an end to that. He's still without a strong alibi for the first murder. He lied to us, then admitted he was home alone. CCTV shows he didn't leave from the front of his building on Tuesday night, but there are no cameras at the rear. He isn't returning our calls, so I haven't been able to ask him where he was last night. Uniform called round to his apartment, but no one answered.'

Farzana raised her hand slightly, as if asking permission to speak. 'I've left several messages, too.'

'Looks like he's gone to ground,' Arnie said.

Churchill nodded. 'It does. But let's think about this – what motive could Black have for killing Tilda Goring as well? And why take her pendant? He had a strong motive for Alison's murder, but why Tilda?'

The room was silent as everyone thought it over. Then Sophie spoke up hesitantly. 'We know Tilda and Alison had hit it off. People have told us they seemed close. Could Alison have confided in Tilda? Maybe when Tilda said she knew who the killer was, she was referring to Lucas Black, and he killed her so she couldn't expose him?'

Karen considered the theory a plausible one. Lucas had clearly resented Alison – maybe even hated her. But the violence of Tilda's death – tying her up and whipping her – suggested a killer who wanted to control, to dominate. It was hard to imagine Lucas doing such a thing, but Karen knew from experience that people could hide their darker aspects. She had seen cases where seemingly normal individuals had shocked everyone with the depths of their cruelty. As much as her instincts told her Lucas was incapable of such violence, she had to consider the possibility that he could be hiding a part of himself that was capable of terrible things.

'We searched Tilda's room, car and belongings,' Arnie said. 'Forensics isn't back yet, but we did find train tickets for travel to Banavie, this coming Wednesday.'

'Banavie?' Rick asked. 'Where's that?'

'Scotland,' Karen replied. They kept coming back to Scotland, but she had no idea why. At least now they had narrowed it down to a specific location in Scotland, even if they still had no clue why either woman had been killed.

Churchill drummed his fingers impatiently against the laptop. 'As Morgan said, we know Lucas is untrustworthy. He lied about his alibi for Tuesday evening—'

'I got the impression Lucas was scared. If he's gone to ground, I think it's because he's trying to stay out of Rothwell's way,' Rick said, then turned to Karen. 'There's Rothwell's link to Quentin Chapman to keep in mind.'

Churchill pinched the bridge of his nose and sighed.

Morgan spoke up, agreeing with Rick. 'In my opinion, we shouldn't get too fixated on Black as the only suspect. Melissa Stark also lacks an alibi confirmation for either night. Her husband was apparently working late at the university again last night.'

Arnie said, 'Professor Stark seems to be working late an awful lot recently. Unfortunate for his wife that he can't confirm her whereabouts.'

'Did we actually get confirmation that Professor Stark was at the university Tuesday night?' Karen asked. 'Didn't he say he was working on a paper with a colleague who could vouch for him?'

Farzana flipped through her notes. 'Yes, I spoke to his colleague, Professor Mackenzie, who backed up Stark's account for Tuesday night. He has no reason to lie. And besides, what's Professor Stark's motive?'

No one had an answer to that.

'I've been through Melissa Stark's laptop and the file she gave Karen,' Sophie said. 'There's lots of evidence showing Rothwell met with Alison on multiple occasions, and that she cleared a number of his projects, but no evidence of anything overtly illegal.'

Churchill sighed in frustration. 'We're getting nowhere with this.'

A gloomy silence settled over the room. Karen stared down at her notes, a hollow feeling in her stomach. She'd written a single word during the briefing. *Scotland*. But she still had no idea what Scotland had to do with Alison's murder or Tilda's. Churchill was right. They were getting nowhere.

After a long moment, Churchill clapped his hands as though suddenly remembering he was supposed to keep their motivation up, not pour cold water all over it. 'Right. Let's regroup and go over everything again from the beginning . . .'

Harinder burst into the briefing room, interrupting Churchill. He carried a laptop under his arm, and his eyes were shining with excitement. 'Sorry to disturb the briefing, but we've just had a ping from Alison Poulson's phone. It's been turned on.'

The room was silent as everyone turned to look at Harinder. He opened the laptop and showed the screen to Churchill.

'Have you managed to get a location?' Churchill asked.

'We have.'

Churchill patted him on the back. 'Very good work. Where is it?'

Harinder clicked on the map displayed on his laptop screen.

A red dot appeared in the middle of a patchwork of fields and woodland, surrounded by a circle.

'Here,' he said, pointing to the screen. 'The signal came from this area. It's not exact, but the phone is somewhere within this circle. I used basic triangulation to refine the location, cross-referencing the data with other mobile towers in the area to get a more accurate fix. But it's a rural location, which means fewer towers, leading to a wider radius.'

Churchill straightened up. 'We can work with that.'

Karen left her seat to look at the map. She stared at the screen and then felt a jolt of recognition. 'The Starks live in Spridlington, the village inside the circle.'

Churchill smiled. 'Finally, we're getting somewhere.' He looked around at the team members gathered in the room. 'Let's organise a warrant for the Starks' property immediately. We need to find that phone.'

Chapter Thirty

A few hours later, after a frustrating delay with the warrant, Karen and Morgan arrived at the Starks' house. They were accompanied by a search team, including uniformed officers and forensic search specialists.

It was a cold morning, and mist hung in the air, giving everything a ghostly appearance.

Karen and Morgan parked on the street and got out. The search team arrived just ahead of them in two vans, and the officers began unloading equipment and setting up a temporary base in the street outside the Starks' house. Faces appeared in the window of next door's property.

Karen and Morgan walked up the path to the Starks' front door. Karen didn't like this part of the job – the invasion of someone's home, the disruption and distress it caused. But it was a necessary evil. The Starks both had a connection to Alison Poulson, and Professor Stark had a connection to both Alison and Tilda. Alison's phone had pinged a signal tower near the Starks' house, and they needed to find out if the phone was here.

Melissa Stark answered the door. Her face went white when she saw Karen and Morgan on her doorstep. 'What's going on?'

Karen handed her a copy of the search warrant. 'I'm sorry, Melissa, but we need to search the premises.'

Melissa took the warrant and scanned it quickly. 'This is ridiculous. I've already given you all the information I have on Alison Poulson. I've been cooperating fully.'

'I know this is difficult,' Karen said gently, 'but we have reason to believe there may be evidence here connected to Alison Poulson's murder. We won't be long, and we'll try to cause as little disruption as possible.'

Melissa's hands were shaking as she clutched the piece of paper. 'My husband isn't here. He's at work. You can't do this without him being present.'

'We have the legal authority to carry out the search,' Karen said. 'But you're welcome to call your husband and ask him to come home if it would make you feel more comfortable. In the meantime, we need to get started.'

Melissa stepped back, allowing Karen and Morgan to enter. 'Christie, come down, darling,' she called over her shoulder.

Christie appeared at the top of the stairs a moment later, her eyes wide. 'What's happening? Why are the police here?'

Melissa gestured for her daughter to come closer, then put an arm around her shoulders. 'The police need to search the house. But there's nothing to worry about. They're just doing their job. Everything will be fine.'

Christie looked at Karen and Morgan, her eyes darting between them. 'What are you looking for?'

'We're searching for some items related to our investigation,' Karen said gently. 'We won't be long.'

Melissa led Christie into the kitchen and sat her down at the table. 'I'll make us a cup of tea,' she said.

Karen and Morgan watched as the search team began their work. Some officers went upstairs, while others started in the living room and kitchen. Two officers went out into the back garden.

Christie sat at the table, her hands clenched, her eyes fixed on the window looking out on the garden. She looked so young and vulnerable. Karen thought this whole situation must be terrifying for the poor girl. She'd already been through so much with the discovery of Alison Poulson's body at the dig site. Then worrying that her mother's involvement would get her taken away from the family. Now, her home was being turned upside down by the police.

'Why are they going into the garden?' Christie asked.

'They're just doing their job,' Melissa said again, trying to sound calm and reassuring. 'They have to search everywhere to make sure they don't miss anything.'

Melissa used her mobile to call her husband. But after waiting for a while, she gave up. 'Dad isn't answering,' she said to Christie. 'I'll try him again in a minute. He'll be able to sort all this out.'

Christie didn't respond. She just sat there, her eyes fixed on the window, her face pale and drawn. She looked so frightened, and Karen wished there was something she could do to make her feel better. But there wasn't. This was the reality of police work, and sometimes it affected the innocent.

Two officers were methodically going through the kitchen cupboards, emptying the contents on to the counters.

'Is that really necessary?' Melissa asked, glaring at Karen.

'It is. You might find this easier if you went outside, perhaps to a neighbour's house and—'

'Absolutely not! I'm not leaving you lot in here unsupervised, to rummage through our possessions.'

Melissa's phone buzzed again, and she answered it straightaway. 'Cindy, can you come over? The police are here. They're searching the house. I can't reach Tom, and I don't know what to do.'

Karen watched as the search continued. Officers moved around the back garden, their breath visible in the chilly air. They'd found nothing so far. But they'd keep looking.

The search team were moving through the house, checking every room, every cupboard, every drawer.

One of the officers called out to Karen from the hall. 'Sarge, this door's locked. We can't get in.'

Karen made her way into the hall. The officer pointed to the plain white door. She remembered it from her last visit to the Starks' house. It was Professor Stark's study. She'd been in there before, talking to the professor.

She returned to the kitchen, where Melissa sat at the table. Christie was now standing at the sink, staring out into the garden, where a couple of officers were just entering the small wooden shed at the end of the lawn. Karen saw anxiety etched on the young woman's face.

'Melissa, I need the key to your husband's study,' Karen said.

Melissa turned to look at her. 'The study? Why do you need to go in there? That's Tom's domain. He hasn't got anything to do with this. He wouldn't want people going through his things.'

'I understand, but we have reason to believe there may be evidence in there that's connected to Alison Poulson's murder. We need to search the room.'

Melissa's expression tightened. 'No, I can't give you my permission to do that.'

'We don't need your permission. We have the warrant.' Karen gestured to the paperwork on the table. 'Either you unlock it with the key, or we break the lock.'

Melissa wrung her hands together. 'Tom's going to be furious.'

'We have to search the room. Now, are you going to give me the key?'

Melissa hesitated, then stood up and went to a drawer near the oven. She fumbled around, retrieving a small silver key.

She held it out to Karen. 'This is ridiculous. You won't find anything in there. Tom barely knew Alison Poulson.'

Karen took the key and turned to leave the kitchen. As she did, she noticed Christie watching her. The young woman's eyes were filled with fear.

Karen inserted the key into the lock on the study door and turned it. The door swung open easily, and she stepped inside.

The study looked just as Karen remembered it from her last visit. The walls were lined with bookshelves, crammed with volumes on history, archaeology and art. The professor's large wooden desk dominated the centre of the room and was covered in papers and books. On the wall opposite the desk hung the large reproduction oil painting of Bonnie Prince Charlie. His eyes seemed to follow Karen as she moved around the room. Opposite that was the print of the Caravaggio painting with the hidden self-portrait.

Karen moved carefully around the room, slowly taking in the space. She scanned the titles on the top row of books: *The Fall of the Roman Empire, Roman Britain, The Roman Way of Life, History of Kings and Queens of the British Isles, Jacobean History, The Jacobite's Lost Gold, Celts vs Romans* and *Roman Crime and Punishment*.

Karen crouched to check the bottom shelves. She found cardboard file boxes labelled with dates – perhaps records from Professor Stark's excavations and research projects. She pulled one out and opened the lid. Inside lay folders stuffed with notes and photographs – a potential source of evidence, though it would take hours to go through properly. She slid the box back into place and moved on to the next box. This one contained more notes, and an OS map of the Highlands.

She opened the drawer at the base of the bookshelves and froze. Then slowly she reached inside and pulled out a small black book. On the cover, in small lettering, was the title: *The Darkest Devices: The History of Torture* by Dr Eve Fitzig.

Karen turned the pages, her stomach churning as she glimpsed illustrations of various instruments of torture.

There were more books hidden away in the drawer. She could see why the professor wouldn't want these on display. She selected another. *The Torturer's Handbook: A Comprehensive Guide to Medieval Cruelty* by Nathan Steel. The cover was a deep, blood red, with the title embossed in gold. Karen opened the book, and flipped through it, her eyes falling on a chapter titled 'The Shrew's Fiddle: A Symphony of Suffering'.

Her mouth grew dry as she began to read:

> *The Shrew's Fiddle, also known as the Neck Violin, is a particularly cruel and unusual torture device popular during the Middle Ages. It usually had a wooden frame with large hole or metal collar for the neck and two smaller holes for the wearer's wrists. The device got its name because it was often used on women with sharp tongues or those prone to nagging.*

> *The Shrew's Fiddle was also used as a means of public humiliation, with the victim's suffering serving as a warning to others. The psychological impact of this device cannot be overstated. Victims would endure not only pain but also intense emotional distress from being publicly shamed and displayed.*

> *The physical torment inflicted by the device was severe. Pain would build slowly from the unnatural position of the neck and would increase over time until the victim begged for relief or to be put out of their misery.*

> *The Shrew's Fiddle illustrates the depths of human cruelty and the lengths to which people will go to inflict suffering upon others.*

Karen snapped the book shut, her heart thudding. Stark was a historian. Could these books be merely for academic interest? He had an alibi for Alison's murder. He'd been working late at the university with a colleague. And no strong motive as far as she could see. And yet . . . her instinct told her he was involved.

She knew she had to dig deeper, to double- and triple-check his alibis. Her gut feeling wouldn't be enough. She needed evidence.

But as she stood there, staring down at his books on torture, Karen was convinced she was right. Stark had killed Alison and Tilda. And not just killed them, but tortured them, and made their last moments in life a living hell.

Behind her, she heard the tech team manoeuvring the desk to get to the plugboard so that they could remove the desktop computer. They'd need the computer and any other digital devices documented and taken for analysis.

Melissa made a small sound of protest. Karen glanced back to see her standing in the doorway. 'Standard procedure. We'll take good care of them.'

Melissa muttered something under her breath and walked away.

The computer on the desk was on. Karen nudged the mouse, and the screen illuminated. The email program was open. Harinder would be able to process the PC properly, but one email caught Karen's eye. She asked the officer to hold back as he was about to unplug the computer.

She opened the email.

It was a confirmation email from East Midlands Railway. A ticket to Banavie on Wednesday.

Banavie. That was the same destination as on Tilda's train ticket. Why was Professor Stark planning a trip there too? And why hadn't he mentioned it to them?

She closed the email and turned to the officer. 'Okay, you can start packing up now.'

As she left the study, Karen was trying to make sense of things. Professor Stark had been planning a trip to Scotland. So had Alison Poulson. And so had Tilda Goring. Were they going there together? It seemed likely, but why? She needed to speak to Professor Stark now.

She went back to the kitchen and found Melissa sitting at the table, her head in her hands. Christie was still standing at the sink, staring out into the garden. Karen went over to Melissa and sat down opposite her.

'Melissa, I need to ask you about your husband's plans for next week. Do you know if he was intending to go to Scotland?'

Melissa looked up. 'What? Oh, yes, I think he was planning a trip. Some sort of conference.'

Karen leaned forward. 'Do you remember the name of the conference? Or who he was going with?'

'I don't. He didn't give me much detail. But he had already booked his train ticket. He's been looking forward to it.'

'And where is he now?'

'At work. At the university.'

'Detective?' Christie moved away from the sink towards Karen. 'I think I know what you're looking for.'

Before Karen could reply, Christie made for the back door. 'I can show you. It's in the shed.'

The lawn was wet and muddy. Karen spotted Morgan in conversation with one of the SOCOs, and motioned for him to follow her.

Christie led them down the lawn, the wet grass soaking the hems of her jeans. They made their way to the small, wooden shed at the bottom of the garden.

As Christie opened the door, the musty smell of compost greeted them. She headed straight for a potting bench below the window.

'I was looking for the secateurs Mum wanted me to use,' Christie said, pulling open the bottom drawer. 'And I found these.'

Karen and Morgan peered inside. Nestled between a brown paper bag filled with bulbs and a tangle of green garden string were two mobile phones.

'Where did these come from?' Karen asked, taking gloves from her pocket and pulling them on.

'I don't know, and I don't know who they belong to,' Christie said, her voice quiet. 'But I turned one on earlier. It was locked.'

Before Karen could ask Christie any more questions, Melissa stepped into the shed. 'Christie, come back inside now,' she said, her tone leaving no room for argument. She turned to Karen, her eyes narrowed. 'I think you've asked my daughter enough questions.'

Christie hesitated, glancing between her mother and Karen. Then Melissa placed a protective arm around her shoulders, guiding her out of the shed.

When they had gone, Karen reached into the drawer, carefully extracting the phones. 'Alison's phone . . . *and* Tilda's?'

Morgan nodded. 'That's what I think.'

Karen straightened up. 'I want to speak to Professor Stark asap. Find out what he knows about these phones – why they were hidden in the shed.'

Morgan looked thoughtful. 'We can ask Melissa now. Do you think the professor was helping his wife? Maybe he helped her dump Alison's body in the trench.'

'No. The ways Alison and Tilda were killed were so violent, so sadistic . . . we're looking for a male killer.'

'We can't be sure. It might be more complicated than that if they were working together. Statistically it's more likely to be a male perpetrator, but let's keep an open mind.'

'I just found a drawer filled with books about the history of torture in his study. Trust me, it's him.' Karen saw the scepticism on Morgan's face. 'I know it's him.'

Morgan exhaled slowly. 'I'm not saying you're wrong . . . I'm saying we need more. He's a historian. Maybe torture is part of his field of study? He looked at the shrew's fiddle for us, didn't he? He's an expert on that sort of thing; makes sense he'd have books on the subject.'

But Karen was sure she was right. The sheer hatred, the way the killer had wanted to humiliate and punish their victims meant Karen's money was on a male killer – one with a deep loathing of women. As soon as she'd spotted the book on torture devices in Stark's study, she'd known. She should have seen it earlier.

The gall of the man to examine the shrew's fiddle in the way he had – acting like he'd never seen it before. He might hide beneath the veneer of a respectable academic, but he clearly had an unhealthy interest in torture. He'd been too quick to recognise the device, too calm in discussing its use. She'd believed he was simply awkward, in the way that academics could often be, but it had been something much deeper. And she should have seen it.

Why Alison and Tilda? She wasn't sure yet. But she was convinced Stark was the perpetrator. She also knew Morgan's opinion on gut instincts leading the way instead of evidence, so she didn't push it.

'I saw an email on Professor Stark's computer. It was a confirmation for a train ticket to Banavie for Wednesday. Melissa said he was planning to go to Scotland for a conference. But I don't believe that for a second.'

Morgan raised an eyebrow. 'You think she was lying?'

'I'm not sure. The professor might have told her that. Or she could be deliberately misleading us.'

Morgan frowned. 'So, Alison, Tilda and now Professor Stark were all planning to go up to Scotland?'

Karen nodded. 'It looks that way. The question is, why?'

Back inside the Starks' house, Karen entered the kitchen and held up the bagged phones so Melissa could see them. 'We believe one of these belongs to Alison Poulson. Do you want to tell me what the phones were doing in your shed?'

'I had no idea they were there.' Melissa peered at them. 'Maybe they're our old ones, and Tom put them in the shed. He doesn't like throwing things away.'

'They don't look like particularly old models to me.'

'No, they don't.'

'And if they were your old phones, you'd recognise them, wouldn't you?'

'I suppose so.'

Karen asked Melissa, 'Is there anything you want to tell me? Because now would be a really good time to come clean.'

There was a knock at the door. Cindy Connor appeared in the kitchen doorway, slightly out of breath. Her eyes landed on the evidence bag in Karen's hand.

'What are you doing?' Cindy burst out angrily. 'You're upsetting this family for no good reason. This is outrageous!'

Karen fixed her with a stern look. 'Ms Connor, I have to ask you to refrain from interfering. And you should not be in this house while a police search is underway.'

Cindy took a step back, eyes still burning with fury. She wrapped her arm around Melissa. 'I'm not staying. I've come to take Christie back to my house for a little while. She's just a teenager and probably scared. You should be ashamed of yourself. I thought you were better than this, Detective Hart.'

Karen should be ashamed of herself? That was rich, coming from Cindy Connor. 'So you have feelings now? Shame you didn't show a bit more compassion for Alison Poulson in your stories. Which reminds me, I'd better not see any mention of this search in your new articles.'

Melissa turned to Cindy. 'You wouldn't.'

'Of course not,' Cindy said, sending a ferocious look at Karen. 'You're my friend, Melissa. I'd never do that.'

Cindy led Melissa out of the kitchen, leaving Karen alone. She looked down at the bagged phones on the table. She was sure they were Alison and Tilda's phones. But there was only one way to be certain. Karen needed to get them back to Harinder at the station so he could work his magic.

Chapter Thirty-One

Karen was sitting at her desk back at the station. She had just given the two phones to Harinder, hoping the forensics wizard could find some useful information. The search at the Starks' house was still ongoing and would likely take at least a couple more hours.

She closed her eyes for a moment, trying to think. From what they knew so far, three people had been planning to go to Scotland next week: Alison Poulson, Tilda Goring and Professor Stark. Two of the three were now dead.

They'd left messages for him to contact them urgently, but had heard nothing back. It seemed like the professor was lying low. Karen was planning to go to the university and force him to answer her questions.

Grabbing her coat, Karen glanced over at Sophie, who was sitting with her back straight, frowning at the computer screen. She'd been reviewing hours of security footage, and it looked like it was taking its toll.

Karen made her way over to the young detective's workstation. 'How are you getting on?'

Sophie looked up, and Karen was relieved to see her smile, her cheeks dimpling. She seemed to be in good spirits. 'Okay, thanks. It's a bit tedious going through all this footage. But I'm getting there.'

'I can always take over for a while if you need a break.' Karen pulled over a chair and sat next to her.

'I'm fine, really. I'm feeling a lot more positive now.' She lowered her voice. 'Arnie was right. My full recovery will take time, and I might always have fears resurface when I'm in a challenging situation. It's just a matter of learning to deal with them.'

Sophie had been through a lot, and she was handling it with courage and determination. 'You're doing so well, Sophie. I'm proud of you.'

'Maybe we should hire Arnie out as a motivational speaker,' Sophie suggested with a grin. 'He's been giving me pep talks. They seem to be working.'

Karen laughed. 'I'm not sure the world is ready for Arnie's unique brand of wisdom just yet.' Nodding at the computer monitor, she asked, 'Have you found anything useful in the footage yet?'

Sophie's expression turned serious. 'Actually, I was just about to call you over.' She gestured to the screen. 'I've been trying to find footage of the village green, but there are no cameras in that area. But I have found something else. This is security footage from a petrol station just outside Stow. It's a bit hard to make out because the light wasn't great, and the footage is quite grainy. But take a look at this.'

Karen leaned in closer to the screen as Sophie played the clip. The footage was date-stamped from the night before. The time in the corner of the screen read 22.00.

At first, she didn't see anything out of the ordinary. But then Karen's eyes were drawn to the lower right-hand corner of the screen. A figure stood in the shadows near the edge of the frame. The figure was partially obscured, but she could make out a man with salt and-pepper hair, wearing a tweed blazer.

'I *think* that's Professor Stark,' Sophie said. 'But I'm not certain. What do you reckon? You've seen him in real life.'

He wasn't the main focus of the shot, but Karen could just about make out his features. It *was* Professor Tom Stark. He was standing near the entrance of the petrol station. Stark's behaviour was noticeably anxious. He kept looking over his shoulder, and his hands were concealed in the pockets of his blazer.

'Stark's wife told us he was working late at the university again last night and didn't get home until midnight,' Karen said. 'And yet here he is, at the petrol station, just a few minutes' drive from where Tilda was found tied to the whipping post.'

The professor turned slightly and lifted his right hand from his pocket. He seemed to be clutching something small and oval-shaped. The footage wasn't clear enough to make out the object's details, but Karen held her breath as it caught the light momentarily – a possible reflection off glass. Stark kept looking over his shoulder as if afraid of being watched. After a few moments, he slipped the object back into his pocket and hurried out of view.

Karen felt a flicker of excitement. 'This is great, Sophie. Let's get this footage sent over to Harinder right away. He can look at it and see if he can enhance the image of the object Stark was holding.'

Sophie beamed at the praise. 'I'll do that now.'

'I'm sure this is Professor Stark. I'd say we've found our prime suspect for Tilda's murder.'

Sophie saved the clip to her computer and reached for the phone on her desk. 'I'll call Harinder and tell him to expect the file.'

'Tell him I suspect the object the professor is holding is Tilda Goring's missing pendant. It's the right size and shape. The way he's clutching it and constantly checking over his shoulder . . .'

Sophie's eyes widened. 'If he is holding the pendant . . . well, it doesn't look good for him, does it?'

'No,' Karen said. 'It doesn't.'

◆ ◆ ◆

Sylvie sat at the desk in her room at the Cross Keys pub, staring blankly out of the window. She was trying desperately to remember the conversations she'd had with Tilda about her location scouting trips for *Britain's Biggest Treasure Hunt*. Tilda had brought back that pendant from one of those trips – if only Sylvie could remember which one.

She should have paid closer attention at the time. If, as Sylvie suspected, that pendant had been taken from Tilda's body by the killer, it could be an important clue as to why Tilda had been murdered. Sylvie was determined to prove herself useful to the investigation by figuring it out.

She still hadn't completely recovered from being snubbed by Arnie. It hurt. She hadn't meant to keep secrets from him. She'd been upfront about the fact she and Alison weren't great friends. All right, so she may have skimmed over the details of the arguments she'd had with Alison, but that was only because she didn't want Arnie to think badly of her.

She imagined the look on Detective Sergeant Arnie Hodgson's face when she revealed to him the origin of the pendant, solving a key piece of the mystery.

She'd enjoy that. He'd be very impressed. Maybe even impressed enough to overlook the fact she'd glossed over the specifics of her disagreements with Alison.

Sylvie sighed. Unfortunately, she wasn't making much progress.

A thought struck her – Tilda had been annoyed when Sylvie had suggested putting filming back by another week. Tilda had insisted that she absolutely could not change her plans for the coming week . . . What had her exact words been? *I've got plans, and nothing is going to stop them, especially not these continual production delays!*

At the time, Sylvie had just assumed it was Tilda letting off steam. But now . . . What had Tilda planned to do? Sylvie wracked her brains, trying to remember if Tilda had let any details of her plans slip, but she was drawing a blank.

She pulled a notepad and pen from her handbag and mentally ran through the places Tilda had scouted over the past few months. There was Sutton Hoo in Suffolk, of course. They were planning to film an episode about the famous Anglo-Saxon burial site. And Tilda had gone to Loch Arkaig in Scotland, and then Shanklin on the Isle of Wight. But none of those places triggered any specific memories about Tilda's pendant. Sylvie knew Tilda had visited other places, too . . . if only she could remember.

Then Sylvie had a brainwave. Tilda would have recorded all her location scouting trips in the *Britain's Biggest Treasure Hunt* production company database, because she always logged her expenses that way. Sylvie quickly opened the database on her laptop and eagerly scrolled through the list – Sutton Hoo, Shanklin, Wittenham Clumps, Avebury . . . yes, all of Tilda's recent trips were there . . . except . . . where was Loch Arkaig?

Sylvie carefully examined each entry again and noticed a gap from the 10th to the 13th of September. That was when Tilda had gone up to Scotland to scout out Loch Arkaig; Sylvie was sure of it. But why had that trip been deleted? *How very strange.* Why would someone have removed it from the records?

Sylvie sighed in frustration, rubbing her temples where a headache was developing. She knew there was something important connected to that scouting trip, something that might provide the vital clue that would point to Tilda's killer.

Sylvie tapped her pen on the notepad in frustration. She was certain the key to unlocking this mystery lay somewhere in the details of Tilda's scouting trips for *Britain's Biggest Treasure Hunt*. But try as she might, Sylvie couldn't dig up the information she needed from her spotty memory alone.

If only she had access to her paper files back at the production office. Sylvie liked to keep hard copies of everything – call her old-fashioned, but she didn't fully trust digital records. Sylvie distinctly remembered printing out the list of potential future episodes before leaving for Lincolnshire, complete with all of Tilda's scouting trips. That printout would be the original list, before any records had been deleted or altered.

Sylvie set down her pen decisively. She needed to get her hands on that printout, and there was no time to waste. She reached for her mobile. She would call the new secretary, Olivia, straight-away and tell her to photograph or scan the list and send it to her immediately.

Hopefully Olivia would be able to find it quickly amidst the disorganised chaos of Sylvie's office. Olivia had only been employed by the production company for a week, and Sylvie hadn't even met her face to face yet. As Sylvie scrolled through her contacts to Olivia's number, she smiled. She was going to get to the bottom of this, and perhaps even impress Arnie a little bit.

'Hello?' came the bored voice of the young secretary after a few rings.

'Olivia, it's Sylvie Broadbent here,' Sylvie said brightly. 'How are you getting on in the office?'

'Yeah, it's all right, I guess,' Olivia replied in a monotone. 'Still trying to figure out where you keep everything. I can't believe you still have paper files. Would you like me to shred them?'

'No!' Sylvie snapped, horrified; then, in a gentler tone, added, 'Yes, I know, it's very old-fashioned of me. But it's the way I work. Listen, I need you to do something. It's rather important.'

She could almost hear Olivia rolling her eyes on the other end of the line.

'I need you to check the paperwork on my desk and find the printed list of potential future filming locations,' Sylvie continued. 'It will be a few pages stapled together.'

'Don't you keep stuff like that on your computer?' Olivia asked with a put-upon sigh.

'I like to have hard copies of everything,' Sylvie explained patiently. 'It should be right on top of my desk. The locations were all the places our director, Tilda, went to scout over the past couple of months.'

'Tilda? I heard what happened. Wasn't it awful?'

Sylvie swallowed the sudden lump in her throat. 'Yes, it was.'

She heard the shuffling of papers as Olivia searched. After a minute, the secretary said, 'Okay, I think I've found it. The places listed are Sutton Hoo, Shanklin, Loch Arkaig, Wittenham Clumps and Avebury. Is that it?'

'Yes, perfect!' Sylvie said. That confirmed it – Loch Arkaig was on the original list. She hadn't been imagining things. 'Would you be able to take a photo of that sheet and email it to me straightaway, please? It's rather important.'

'Sure, no problem,' Olivia muttered. More shuffling noises followed.

Sylvie smiled to herself. She might be old-fashioned keeping paper records, but it was going to pay off.

'Got it, sending the pic to you now,' Olivia said after another minute.

'Wonderful, thank you, Olivia, you've been extremely helpful,' Sylvie said warmly.

After exchanging goodbyes, Sylvie ended the call and opened her email, refreshing it until Olivia's message appeared. She downloaded the attached image and examined it closely.

There it was – Loch Arkaig, listed clearly along with the other locations. But it had been deleted from the digital records. Very peculiar.

Sylvie sat back in her chair, puzzled. Why would Tilda have removed any mention of visiting Loch Arkaig from the database? Even if she'd decided against filming there, she still would have logged her travel expenses. Unless . . . she wanted to remove any evidence of having gone there in the first place.

But why? What had Tilda been up to on that trip? And how did it connect to her murder?

Sylvie looked through her calendar again, searching for clues. She flipped through the pages, pausing to examine each entry carefully. Then she came to the 14th of September and had a breakthrough.

That was the night they'd all gone to the senior partner's posh townhouse for drinks and canapés to celebrate the highest ratings yet, for the last series of *Britain's Biggest Treasure Hunt*. Sylvie remembered it clearly now – that was the first time she had seen Tilda wearing the pendant.

Sylvie hadn't thought much of the necklace at the time. It was rather ugly and garish – not that she'd said that to Tilda. The director had seemed quite proud of the glass bauble containing a lock of hair on a bed of velvet. Not exactly Sylvie's taste, but Tilda had been twirling it around her fingers as she chatted to Sylvie. When Sylvie asked about it, Tilda had been evasive, simply saying she'd *acquired it on a scouting trip.*

But Tilda must have picked up that pendant when she was in Scotland, Sylvie realised now. Specifically in Loch Arkaig, since that trip had been scrubbed from the records. Sylvie was certain Tilda hadn't owned it before visiting Scotland. Sylvie would have noticed such an eye-catching and hideous necklace. And after that day, Sylvie had never seen Tilda without it. Until . . .

Hot tears pricked Sylvie's eyes. How awful it had been to see poor Tilda tied to the whipping post like that. But she couldn't think about that now; it was too horrible.

Wiping her eyes, Sylvie tried to focus. Tilda must have acquired the pendant in Loch Arkaig. But what else had Tilda been up to on that mysterious trip? And how did the pendant connect to her murder? Was it a historical artefact? Perhaps it was worth a fortune?

Sylvie gathered up her handbag and room key. She needed to speak to someone who knew a lot about history. Someone who could shed some light on why Loch Arkaig might be significant.

Professor Stark was just the person. Sylvie would go and ask him – and he might have some answers about how the pendant related to all this, too.

Chapter Thirty-Two

Karen was about to head to the university to see if Professor Tom Stark was there herself. She'd been going over everything they knew about the man, who was now nowhere to be found. The petrol station footage placed Stark near the scene of Tilda's murder, making him a definite person of interest even in DCI Churchill's eyes. So she now had the go-ahead to bring him in for questioning.

Before leaving, Karen decided she first needed to check how solid Stark's alibi was for the nights Alison Poulson and Tilda Goring were killed. He claimed he'd been working late at the university, but she wanted to be sure.

Karen walked over to DC Farzana Shah's desk. 'Do you have a minute? I need to ask you about Professor Stark.'

'What do you need to know?' Farzana said, looking up from her monitor.

'You checked Stark's alibis?'

'Yes. For the night of Alison Poulson's murder his alibi checks out. But I haven't confirmed his alibi for Tilda's murder yet.'

'You're sure? Stark was definitely at the university when Alison was murdered?'

Farzana nodded. 'He was working late with a colleague, Professor Ross Mackenzie. I spoke to Professor Mackenzie myself.

He confirmed they were at the university until late on Tuesday night.'

'Did he give you a statement?'

'He did. It's right here.' Farzana dug through the papers on her desk and pulled out a sheet. 'But the statement isn't signed. Professor Mackenzie's mother was ill, so he was travelling up to Scotland to be with her. He promised to call in to sign the statement when he returned. Said it would only be a few days.'

Karen took the statement and scanned it. 'So, you spoke to Professor Mackenzie on the phone, but you haven't seen him in person?'

'No, I never met him, but I didn't think I needed to. He seemed genuine enough.'

Karen frowned, thinking this through. Professor Stark's alibi rested on the word of a colleague that Farzana hadn't even met in person. That didn't feel like a solid alibi.

And if Mackenzie was lying . . .

'Did Professor Mackenzie give you any other contact details? An email address, perhaps?'

'Yes, an email address. It should be on the statement.'

'Do we have any other way to confirm Professor Stark's whereabouts on Tuesday night?'

Farzana hesitated. 'I suppose I could check with the university again and see if anyone else could confirm his alibi.'

'I'll do that,' Karen said. 'We need to be absolutely sure he was at the university on the nights Alison Poulson and Tilda Goring were murdered. I'll ask to check the university's CCTV footage. See if I can spot Stark on the nights in question. And we need to find Professor Mackenzie, and talk to him in person as soon as he's back from visiting his mother.'

Farzana nodded. 'I'll try to track down Mackenzie to ask when he's coming home.'

Karen gathered her things. She wanted to return to the Starks' house. She trusted the search team to do a thorough job, but she wanted to go back with fresh eyes now that Stark had jumped to the top of her suspects' list.

If Professor Stark was involved in the murders, Karen knew there had to be something out there to prove it.

But first she needed to go to the university because she had a strong suspicion Stark's alibi was bogus. Professor Mackenzie's deception raised a red flag. Why would he lie about Stark's where-abouts on the night of the murder?

Unless . . . could there be two killers involved? The thought sent an icy shiver through Karen.

Could Mackenzie be Stark's accomplice?

Karen parked in the university car park and made her way to the archaeology department. The building was modern, with a glass frontage and automatic doors. Karen stepped inside and approached the reception desk. A young woman with a friendly smile looked up from her computer screen. 'Can I help you?'

'I'm a detective with Lincolnshire Police. I need to speak to someone about Professor Tom Stark. He's a member of your archaeology department. Is he in today?'

'I've not seen him.' She tapped a few keys and stared at the monitor. 'Doesn't look like he's here.'

'I was wondering if you could help me check something. I need to know if Professor Stark was working late on Tuesday evening or last night.'

'If you'd like to take a seat, I'll try to find someone who can help you.'

Moments later, a petite woman with red hair twisted into a neat bun came briskly down the stairs. 'Hello, I'm Margaret Dunn, the department administrator. How can I help?'

Karen repeated what she'd told the woman at reception.

'I see. Well, we do have an access control system and CCTV cameras. I can ask our security officer to check the logs and footage for you.'

'That would be great, thank you.'

The administrator gestured for Karen to follow her. They made their way to the security office, where a man in his forties was sitting in front of a bank of monitors. 'This is our security officer, Barry,' the administrator said. 'Barry, this is Detective Sergeant Karen Hart. She needs our help with something.'

Barry turned in his chair to face them. 'Sure, I'll do what I can. What do you need?'

'She needs to verify whether Professor Stark was on campus late on Tuesday night and last night. Can you pull up the access logs and any relevant CCTV footage for us to review?'

Barry nodded. 'I can start with Tuesday night. Give me a minute to bring up the logs.'

As Barry worked on the computer, Karen noticed the administrator watching her with a concerned expression. 'Is everything okay?'

Margaret hesitated. 'Is this about the murder?'

There was no point in hiding the truth. 'Yes. We need to confirm the professor's alibi.' When she saw the startled look on Margaret's face, she added a little white lie. 'Just routine procedure.'

Margaret nodded, but she didn't seem reassured. 'Professor Stark is relatively new to the university. He only started this term, so I haven't known him for long.'

Before Margaret could say anything else, Barry spoke up. 'I've got the Tuesday logs up now. Let's see . . .' He scanned the screen.

'Ah, here we go. Professor Stark swiped his access card to leave the building at 9.02 p.m.'

'Nine o'clock?' Karen repeated, surprised. The estimated time of Alison Poulson's murder was around ten p.m. 'Are you sure?'

'The logs don't lie. But let me pull up the car park cameras for you. We should be able to get a visual on his vehicle leaving.' He began typing on his keyboard. 'It'll take a few minutes to pull up the footage. The cameras cover the main entrance and exits, so we'll have a good view of the car park.'

'Thank you,' Karen said, then turned to Margaret. 'I'm also trying to track down another professor, who I believe worked closely with Stark. I was hoping to speak with him.'

'Who are you referring to?' Margaret asked.

'Professor Ross Mackenzie.'

Margaret frowned. 'Professor Mackenzie? I'm afraid that won't be possible. He retired last month. He doesn't even have an access card anymore.'

Karen felt a jolt of surprise. 'Retired? Are you sure? We've been in contact with him. My colleague called his direct office number and spoke to him this week.'

Margaret glanced at the phone number Karen showed her. 'Ah, that was his old office number. It's Professor Stark's now. He took over Ross Mackenzie's office when he retired,' she explained, looking puzzled. 'They didn't work together. In fact, Professor Stark was brought in as a replacement for Professor Mackenzie.'

The revelation hit Karen hard. Her theory about Mackenzie and Stark being in cahoots crumbled in light of this new information. It now seemed far more probable that Stark had fabricated an alibi to distance himself from the murders. Stark must have answered the phone when Farzana called, and pretended to be Mackenzie. He'd been covering his tracks from the start. She wondered if Mackenzie was even aware that his name had been dragged into this investigation.

She asked Margaret, 'Do you have an address for Professor Mackenzie? I really need to speak with him.'

'Of course. Let me look up his contact details for you.'

Barry called out from his desk, 'I've got the car park footage up now. Do you want to take a look?'

Karen walked over to the security officer. He gestured to the large monitor on the wall, which displayed a split-screen view of the car park. On the left, she could see the entrance, and on the right, the exit.

'Professor Stark's car is just coming into view now,' Barry said, pointing to the exit feed. 'It's the silver Audi.'

They watched the screen in silence. After a few moments, the Audi appeared, driving out of the car park. Karen checked the time-stamp on the footage. It read 21.04.

'Looks like he left right after swiping his card,' Barry said.

'Thanks for your help, Barry. I appreciate it.'

He gave her a small smile. 'No problem. Do you want me to check last night, too?'

'Please do,' Karen said. She was certain Stark hadn't been working late last night either.

Margaret came over with a slip of paper. 'Here's Professor Mackenzie's home address. I hope it's helpful.'

'Thank you. Very helpful.'

As she left the security office, Karen dialled Morgan's number.

Morgan answered after a few rings. 'Any luck at the university?'

'It looks like Professor Stark has been lying to us. He wasn't working late either on the night Alison Poulson was killed or last night, when Tilda Goring was murdered. The security logs show he left just after nine p.m. on both nights.'

'Nine o'clock?' Morgan repeated. 'That's very interesting. And what about Professor Mackenzie? Did you manage to speak with him?'

'Professor Mackenzie retired last month. It looks like Stark pretended to be Mackenzie to give himself an alibi. Ballsy move.'

Morgan swore under his breath. 'He's been one step ahead this whole time. Harinder has confirmed the mobiles found in the Starks' shed belonged to Alison and Tilda. I don't think he'll be able to wriggle out of this.'

'Have you any idea where he could be?'

'No, he's still AWOL. But we've put out an alert on his car,' Morgan said. 'He can't hide forever.'

Chapter Thirty-Three

Karen arrived back at the Starks' house an hour or so later. The search team were still there, milling around the property. From the kitchen, Karen caught a glimpse of Melissa Stark sitting on a bench in the garden, her head in her hands. She felt a pang of sympathy for the woman.

Morgan was standing near the back door, talking to one of the team. He spotted Karen and walked over to her.

'Any luck?' she asked.

Morgan shook his head. 'Not yet. No big finds since the phones.'

They both looked over at Melissa Stark, who was now staring at the upstairs windows. It couldn't be easy watching the search team go through her home.

'I feel terrible for her,' Karen said quietly.

'She's been through an awful lot,' Morgan agreed. 'But I have a feeling things are going to get worse.'

'Has she heard from Stark?'

'She says she hasn't.'

'Do you believe her?'

'It's hard to say.'

Karen nodded, then reached over to the counter to grab a pair of gloves. She'd been in Professor Stark's office earlier, but now that the search team had finished in there, it was time for her to take another look.

She left Morgan in the kitchen, and stepped into Stark's office. The room looked similar to how it had appeared when she'd left. The search team had returned items back to their original positions on shelves and in drawers. She took a moment to look around, taking it all in – the paintings, the books lining the shelves.

Karen was now sure that Professor Stark was the killer. Somewhere in this room, she knew there was a clue to understanding his motives and anticipating his next move. She had to use his personal space to get inside his head.

She made her way over to the desk and began to sift through the papers, looking for anything that might be of interest. But everything seemed to be related to Professor Stark's work at the university or his research into historical artefacts. There was a printed draft of his current work in progress: *The Hidden Jacobite Gold: Unveiling the Incredible Story Buried for Centuries*. A very commercial title. The poor professor, having to dumb down his work for the masses. Her heart bled for him.

There were notes scrawled over a research paper entitled *A Comparative Study of the Fabric Composition and Surface Treatment of Roman British Pottery Excavated at a Rural Settlement Site: Implications for Regional Ceramic Production and Distribution* – a considerably less catchy title. Stark certainly had a wide range of interests. Nothing looked out of the ordinary.

Karen's phone buzzed in her pocket. A message from Harinder. He'd sent an enhanced image of the security footage from the petrol station.

Karen opened the image and stared at the face of Professor Stark. The image was no longer grainy, and there was no mistaking the professor.

She zoomed in on the professor's hand. The focus was sharper – Harinder had made it easier to see the details. As she studied the image, she held her breath. There was no doubt about it. Professor Stark was holding Tilda Goring's pendant. She felt a rush of adrenaline. The pendant was the key to this case. Now, they had evidence that Professor Stark had been in possession of it the night Tilda was murdered.

Karen pictured Tilda tied to the whipping post, imagined Professor Stark ripping the pendant from her neck. Was he really capable of two such horrendous and callous murders? First Alison, desecrated in death with the shrew's fiddle, and then Tilda tied to the whipping post and beaten.

Sophie's reading had suggested their killer would be successful, intelligent and controlling. Karen thought back to the fact Melissa had not told her husband about her exposé on Alison Poulson. Was Stark controlling at home, trying to stop her working? Christie didn't seem afraid of her father, but she was nervous and jumpy, and a little naive for her age. Was that the result of an overbearing, controlling father?

Professor Stark had been at the petrol station with the pendant last night. But he'd come back home afterwards. Had he hidden the pendant here? Or had he taken it to work, thinking it would be safer there?

Karen's gaze took in the cluttered office. She knew she had to find that pendant. It was the key to unlocking the truth about Tilda's murder and Alison's death.

She slowly circled the room, sweeping her gaze over the bookshelves and the piles of papers. She remembered an earlier conversation with Professor Stark in this very room. They'd been discussing his paintings – reproductions of famous works.

Her eyes landed on the large print of Caravaggio's painting *Bacchus* that was hanging on the wall beside a bookcase. She remembered Stark mentioning how much he liked this particular painting because it contained hidden symbols and meanings.

Karen stepped closer to the painting. She studied the image. Professor Stark had said the painting contained a self-portrait *hidden in plain sight*.

What if? She ran her hands along the bulky wooden frame, feeling for any irregularities. Then, as her fingers reached the bottom right corner, she felt it – a small, almost imperceptible gap in the wood.

Karen carefully pried the gap open with her gloved fingers. Slowly, the frame began to come apart, revealing a small hollow space behind the print.

Sneaky.

She reached inside the cavity, her fingers brushing against something cold and hard. Then, her hand closed around the object, and she pulled it out.

The pendant.

She remembered Tilda twirling it on a chain around her fingers when Karen and Arnie had questioned her just after Alison's murder. It was large and cumbersome. The front was covered with scratched glass, and the back was made of tarnished silver, with an ornate design etched into the surface. It looked old. Very old.

Inside, beneath the glass, just as Sylvie had said, was a lock of dark hair held in place by a stitch on red velvet. The letters next to it: *C.R.* In Victorian times, it was popular to keep locks of hair from deceased loved ones in jewellery as mementos of the dead. Maybe that was what this was.

But why would Tilda want a pendant with a dead person's hair inside? It looked too old to be from a recent relative. Why had it been so important to her?

Karen studied the engraving on the reverse. A large cat – or perhaps lion – with some kind of motto encircling it.

The letters were tiny. She squinted. It looked like: *Touch not the cat bot a glove.*

What did *that* mean?

Thank goodness for Google.

She took a quick snap of both sides of the pendant, removed one of her gloves, and tapped the words into the web browser on her phone.

Google reliably informed her the words were the motto of the Clan Macpherson. But why did Tilda have this locket? Did she have some Scottish ancestry? And more importantly, why had Professor Stark taken it from her and hidden it away in his study? Had he killed her for the pendant? If he had, where did Alison fit into the picture?

Morgan stuck his head into the study. 'Karen, can you keep an eye on things here? Raj has finished Tilda's autopsy, and I want to . . .' He trailed off when Karen held out the pendant. 'Is that what I think it is?'

Karen nodded. 'He hid it in the frame of the Caravaggio picture.'

Morgan let out a low whistle. 'We really need to track Stark down. He has a lot of questions to answer.'

'He does. I'll stick around and keep an eye on things here. Say hello to Raj for me.'

'Will do.'

After Morgan left, Karen put her other glove back on and set the pendant on the desk, next to the draft of Stark's book, and then turned to look at the reproduction print again.

She decided to check if there was anything else wedged in the small hidey-hole. It was empty. With a sigh, she stepped back but then stopped abruptly, her eyes on the other large reproduction oil painting in the room. Bonnie Prince Charlie. She turned her head, her gaze landing on the pages of the book Stark was writing.

Pieces of the puzzle started to fall into place.

She reached up to the frame of the oil painting, staring into the eyes of Charles Stuart. Sliding her fingers along the frame, she felt the expected gap. It came apart with a click.

Her fingers stretched into the cavity, feeling around carefully, until this time, her fingers brushed something soft. She pulled out a small, brown velvet drawstring pouch. It felt heavy with whatever lay inside.

Karen looked at the portrait. 'What have you been hiding?'

Slowly, she undid the drawstring top . . .

Peering inside, Karen caught a glint of something shiny. Carefully, she emptied the contents on to her gloved palm. Four gold coins. They felt heavy, substantial. An archaeology find?

She turned them over in her fingers, examining the intricate designs.

Her eyes drifted to the piles of papers on Stark's desk. His book. *The Hidden Jacobite Gold: Unveiling the Incredible Story Buried for Centuries.* Could this be it? Part of the lost treasure?

Had Stark found it? Or had Tilda? A discovery like this would be huge. Life-changing. A man like Stark would want control over the discovery.

If Karen was right and Stark was obsessed with control, this could have been the trigger that had driven him to commit those horrific acts of violence against Alison and Tilda.

The gold coins felt heavy in her hand. She needed to get these to the lab and have them analysed. She had to know if they were the real deal.

Karen carefully placed the coins and the velvet pouch in an evidence bag and sealed it.

They needed to find Stark. Now.

It was dark when Raj finished updating Morgan on the autopsy results for Tilda Goring. The pathologist had determined that Tilda had been whipped and beaten before her neck was broken.

Her body had been assaulted so savagely it was swollen, raw and almost unrecognisable. Raj had found traces of fabric in her mouth and suspected a rag had been stuffed in her mouth to stop her screaming. He'd confirmed that no traces of benzodiazepines or other substances were found in her system, so Tilda would have been acutely aware of what was going on.

The thought of the suffering she must have endured, and the sheer malice and cruelty inflicted upon her, made Morgan feel physically sick.

Raj had commented that these two murders were among the worst he had seen in his career, and Morgan agreed. In all his years in the police service, he had never encountered such savage crimes. The public display, the sheer hatred and brutality were staggering.

Sophie had been proved right.

The killer hadn't stopped with one murder.

They clearly had a taste for it now, and the team had to get the monster responsible behind bars before they did it again. Now the evidence pointed strongly to Stark.

Professor Stark, the mild-mannered academic. Always so calm, so in control. But then again, Sophie had said it was all about control. Control and degradation.

Why Tilda and Alison? They had been strong women. Independent. Maybe they'd argued back, and Stark couldn't handle it. He'd needed to subdue them. Punish them. Control them.

Morgan had looked into Stark's wife, Melissa. She used to be a journalist with an incredible reputation. War zones. Interviews with dictators. But she hadn't published anything in years. Was that Stark's doing? Coercive control, maybe. No violence, but devastating all the same. Isolating her. Monitoring her every move. Taking away her purpose. Eroding her sense of self-worth.

The more Morgan thought about it, the more convinced he became.

They had to act fast to prevent more victims and gather evidence, so they could put this monster behind bars.

As he strolled across the car park, Morgan pulled his phone from his pocket, about to call Karen to update her, when it started to ring in his hand. He saw Benjamin Price's name on the screen.

Brilliant. Just what he didn't need right now. The hot-headed farmer had taken to calling Morgan daily for updates. Morgan wished he'd never given the man his mobile number.

He answered the call. 'Price,' Morgan said, trying to keep his tone level. 'What can I do for you?'

'Detective, there's a car parked on my land,' Price almost shouted down the phone. 'Right by the gate. It's blocking the way. The cheek of it! People from that TV show are using my private property like a car park!'

Morgan held the phone away from his ear as Price vented. When there was a pause, he said calmly, 'Are you sure it's someone from the TV show? I don't think they've resumed filming.'

'Course it's one of them! Who else would it be?'

Morgan rubbed his forehead wearily. 'Right, I'll have a word with them, Mr Price; ask them not to do it again, don't worry.'

Price's angry voice bellowed down the line. 'I've got a good mind to have the thing towed. It's an absolute liberty, using my land without permission. I don't care who they are. They've no right to be there.'

'I understand why you're upset, Mr Price. I'll see what I can do—'

'You'd better sort it,' Price grumbled. 'I pay my taxes!'

So do I, Morgan thought. *So do I.*

'Are you lot making any progress on finding out who killed Alison?'

'We're pursuing some strong leads,' Morgan replied vaguely.

Price gave a bark of laughter. 'Not going to give anything away, are you?'

'No,' Morgan said simply.

'This archaeology dig has been a nightmare. Wish I'd never agreed to it. I heard there was another murder, someone else associated with that TV show.'

'We're doing everything we can, Mr Price,' Morgan said neutrally.

'I'm sure you are. Now, about this car on my land – it's a silver Audi. I'll give you the number plate . . .' Price reeled off the plate details.

Morgan felt a prickle of recognition. Professor Stark had a silver Audi. 'Thank you, Mr Price. I'll get someone to look into it.'

'Make sure you do,' Price said gruffly. 'I'll call you again tomorrow in case there's an update on the murder case.'

'You really don't need to do that, Mr Price. We'll call you if there is information—'

'It's no trouble. Speak tomorrow,' Price said and hung up.

Fantastic. Morgan could hardly wait.

He immediately phoned Arnie Hodgson.

'Arnie, it's Morgan,' he said when the other detective answered. 'I need you to check out a number plate for me. Benjamin Price says there's a car parked on his land near the gate on the south side of his property. He gave a description, and I believe it could be Professor Stark's Audi.'

Morgan recited the number plate.

'Silver Audi?' Arnie said. 'That sounds like Stark's. Give me a sec to check it out.'

After a pause, he came back on the line. 'It is Stark's. The net is slowly closing in on the slippery sod. Tell you what, I'm not far from Stow. I'll swing by and check it out.'

'Good man,' Morgan said. 'Let me know what you find.'

He rang off, thinking that Stark must know they were closing in on him. If he'd killed Tilda and Alison, he was probably trying to flee. Although, abandoning his car on Price's land wasn't very sensible. He'd have to leave on foot. Unless he hadn't dumped it? Maybe he'd gone back to the dig site for some reason? To recover evidence . . . or to hide something.

Morgan scrolled through his contacts until he reached Karen's number.

Chapter Thirty-Four

The headlights cut through the inky darkness as Karen drove slowly along the Stow Road. She kept thinking about the drawstring pouch she'd found hidden in Professor Stark's office. It had been a remarkable and very unexpected discovery.

The coins were now in the hands of the forensics team, but Karen was positive they were the key to understanding the murders of Alison Poulson and Tilda Goring.

As she approached Benjamin Price's farm, Karen's mind raced with theories. The gold coins, the Jacobite history book, the painting of Bonnie Prince Charlie, the train tickets to Scotland – it all seemed to point in one direction: a motive for Stark to have committed such appalling crimes.

Skimming through a few pages of Stark's manuscript had provided Karen with a wealth of information. She didn't have it all figured out yet, but she was sure these murders were linked to the lost Jacobite gold.

Back in 1745, gold had been sent on two French ships by Louis XV to support the Jacobite rebellion against the English. But the haul arrived too late, only reaching Scotland after the Jacobites had been defeated at the Battle of Culloden.

Over the years, rumours and theories had sprung up, including one that suggested that the clansmen loyal to Bonnie Prince

Charlie had buried the gold hoard to keep it safe on the banks of Loch Arkaig, just north of Fort William.

But the gold had never been found.

Karen's working theory was that Tilda Goring had discovered the coins near Loch Arkaig, believing she'd stumbled upon the Jacobites' missing gold. It sounded far-fetched, but the coins seemed to support the idea.

If Tilda had found the coins, then perhaps she'd also stumbled upon the pendant. The initials C.R. might stand for Charles Rex, referring to his claim as the rightful king. And the Macpherson clan crest on the reverse side of the pendant linked it to a specific family line known for its role in supporting the Jacobite uprising.

It all seemed to add up.

Karen imagined Tilda stumbling upon the coins near Loch Arkaig, perhaps during her work for *Britain's Biggest Treasure Hunt*, and thinking she'd found the long-lost treasure. She might have confided in Alison and Professor Stark.

Karen thought it was possible the three of them – Alison, Tilda, and Professor Stark – had planned to excavate the gold together this coming Wednesday. But something must have gone wrong. A disagreement, or perhaps the professor had wanted all the gold and glory for himself. Greed could be a powerful motive.

Although that didn't quite fit with their earlier profile of the killer: a paranoid, controlling man who derived pleasure from inflicting pain on women. So maybe Stark's need for control *was* his primary motive, not greed. Perhaps Stark had tried to coerce Tilda and Alison into following his plan, but they'd refused to be manipulated. Maybe he'd snapped in a fit of rage, deciding to punish them for defying his authority. That scenario felt more plausible than the idea that he had killed them for financial gain or career advancement. It tied in with Karen's earlier suspicions – Stark's need for control and dominance was the driving force behind his actions.

Her musings were interrupted by the sight of a car with its hazard lights flashing in a lay-by at the side of the road. As she slowed down, she realised it was Arnie's vehicle. She pulled over and got out, approaching Arnie, who was leaning against the car, looking thoroughly miserable.

'What are you doing out here?'

Arnie let out a long-suffering sigh. 'I was on my way to Price's farm. Morgan said Stark's car is there.'

'He told me,' Karen said. 'I'm on my way there, too.' She gestured to the car. 'Broken down?'

'Stupid thing's given up on me,' Arnie grumbled, kicking a tyre in frustration. 'It started making a funny noise. Then the engine cut out completely.'

'Any idea what failed?'

Arnie shook his head. 'Haven't had it serviced in a while, I suppose.'

Karen raised an eyebrow. 'Might be a good time to remedy that, then.'

Arnie scowled. 'Thank you, Miss Hindsight. Can't say I'm looking forward to the bill, though.'

'Have you called for a tow?'

'Yes, I've got roadside assistance covered by my insurance, but they said it's going to be a couple of hours, at least.'

'If it's going to be that long, why don't we go and check out Stark's car together now,' Karen suggested.

'Right you are.' Arnie slapped the car bonnet. 'Heap of junk.'

He trudged towards Karen's car and called back over his shoulder to his: 'I'm leaving you here to think about what you've done.'

'Arnie, I'm sure the car can't actually hear you. Or do any thinking for that matter.'

Arnie shrugged. 'Makes me feel better.'

They got back into Karen's car, and she pulled back out on to the road. She filled Arnie in on her theory about the missing gold as they headed to the farm.

When she'd finished, Arnie gave her a sideways glance. 'That sounds . . .'

'Far-fetched?' Karen suggested.

'I was going to say doolally . . . but far-fetched works, too.'

'I think it makes sense.'

Arnie thought for a moment, then said, 'Say Tilda found the gold. She'd need help digging it up, perhaps, or verifying her findings, so I suppose it makes sense that she'd ask Professor Stark for help. But why Alison?'

'Maybe Alison had connections we aren't aware of yet? Or she had access to money to fund the excavation? Or perhaps simply because they were friends? Tilda referred to Alison as a kindred spirit.'

'Hmm. Sounds a bit of a stretch to me,' Arnie said as they stopped by the gate at the entrance to Price's farm. 'There's the car.'

As they got out of the car, they heard Price's dogs barking in the distance.

Arnie shuddered. 'That noise is giving me flashbacks to when I was chased by Rothwell's Dobermans.'

'Let's hope the dogs are safely inside tonight,' Karen replied, her gaze fixed on Stark's car. 'It's empty. Do you think Stark is still around here somewhere?'

Karen and Arnie walked up to the car as the wind picked up, sending leaves skittering across the lane that led up to the farmhouse. Arnie suddenly stopped, his gaze fixed on something in the distance.

'What is it?' Karen asked, following his line of sight.

'Over there, by the excavation site. Do you see those lights?'

Karen squinted. At first, she couldn't see anything, but then she noticed a faint, flickering glow coming from the field where the archaeologists had been working. As she watched, the glow grew brighter, casting an eerie light across the dark landscape.

'What *is* that?' she asked.

Arnie was frowning. 'I don't know, but it shouldn't be there. Although we've released the crime scene, Sylvie said she hasn't been able to get the insurance company to cooperate yet, so there shouldn't be anyone working on the site.'

Interesting. 'Let's go and take a closer look.'

As they approached the field, the deep rumble of an engine reverberated in the otherwise silent night. The lights were now much brighter, casting long, shifting shadows over the grass.

Karen and Arnie slowed their pace, moving quietly now, trying to stay out of sight as they drew closer to the excavation site. They crept up to the edge of the field, and from there, they could see the whole scene spread out before them.

A JCB digger was parked near the edge of the trench where Alison Poulson's body had been found. Its engine roared, and its huge metal claw was raised high in the air. It looked like it could be Professor Tom Stark sitting in the cab, but his face was hidden in the shadows. The digger's headlights illuminated the trench.

Stark was using the digger's claw to dump huge shovelfuls of dirt into the trench, filling it up. The claw clanked and rattled as it dropped each load of soil.

'What's he doing?' Arnie wondered aloud.

'He's filling in the trench.'

'Do you reckon he's trying to hide evidence?'

'Possibly.'

They watched as the huge digger dumped another basketful of earth in the trench. What was Stark so desperate to bury?

'We have to stop him,' Arnie said. He took a step forward, but Karen grabbed his arm, holding him back.

'We need to call for backup,' she said. 'There's no telling how he'll react if he sees us coming.'

Arnie hesitated, torn. Then he nodded, reaching for his phone. But as he looked at the screen, his face tightened in frustration. 'No bars.'

Karen reached for her own phone, but it was the same story – no signal.

They were on their own.

She turned to Arnie. 'All right. At least there are two of us.'

They moved quickly, staying low as they crossed the field. The digger's engine roared, the sound growing louder and more frantic as they drew nearer. Stark was working faster now.

As they reached the edge of the fenced-off area, Arnie said, 'It's definitely Stark. We can't let him destroy evidence if that's what he's trying to do.'

'And if he won't cooperate?'

'JCBs usually have an emergency stop button.'

'Where?'

'Not sure. Near the cab?'

When they were a few feet away, Karen and Arnie exchanged a tense look. Then, without a word, they both broke into a run, charging towards the digger.

Stark spotted them and sat up straight in the cab, his head whipping around.

As Karen and Arnie reached the trench, Stark was pulling levers and slamming buttons, trying to get the digger moving. But Karen and Arnie were almost upon him.

'Stop!' Karen yelled.

But Stark ignored her, his hands flying over the controls. The digger's engine screamed, and the huge machine lurched forward, the claw swinging wildly.

Stark was trying to use the digger to attack them.

Karen and Arnie skidded to a stop at the edge of the trench, just a few feet from the digger.

'Get down!' Arnie shouted.

They both dropped to the ground just as the digger's claw swung over their heads, missing them by inches. The huge metal teeth of the claw clanged together as it passed, and then it came crashing down into the trench, sending a spray of dirt and rocks flying.

Karen and Arnie were up in an instant, charging towards the digger. Stark was still trying to use the claw to attack them, but he was clearly out of his depth. The digger's arm swung around again, the claw snapping open and shut.

Karen fell back just in time as the digger's arm narrowly missed her. She felt the rush of air as it passed by. Arnie dove to the ground again to avoid being struck, rolling in the dirt and gravel.

Stark's face was contorted with rage as he struggled to manoeuvre the digger to crush them. The machine lurched forward, its treads kicking up debris as it moved. Karen and Arnie scrambled to avoid being smashed by the claw or run over by the digger.

Karen spotted an opening and made a run for the digger's cab, Arnie close behind. Stark saw them coming and tried to swing again in their direction, but his lack of experience with the machine made his movements clumsy and imprecise.

They reached the digger. Karen grabbed on to the side of the cab, hauling herself up.

'Police! Stop!' she yelled, her voice barely audible over the roar of the digger's engine.

Stark turned to face her, his expression a mix of fury and desperation. He knew he was cornered, but he wasn't going down without a fight.

Karen clung to the machine as the digger jerked and shuddered. She hung there, her legs scrambling for grip. This man had

322

brutally murdered Alison and Tilda; there was no way she was letting go. She had no doubt he'd kill her, and Arnie too, if he could.

Determined to maintain her grip, Karen's gaze met Stark's. Gone was the well-groomed academic. In his place was a wild-eyed, unhinged individual. She was staring into the soulless eyes of a killer. There was no trace of remorse or humanity in his expression, only a chilling determination to eliminate anyone who stood in his way.

◆ ◆ ◆

Arnie stepped closer to the edge of the trench, peering down into its shadowy depths. His eyes narrowed as he thought he saw something pale and still beneath the loose dirt.

He leaned forward, trying to get a better look. 'There's something down there.'

In that moment of distraction, Stark seized his chance. He swung the digger's heavy metal arm towards Arnie.

'Look out!' Karen shouted, but it was too late.

The solid steel collided heavily with Arnie's side, catching him off guard. He had no time to brace himself or jump clear. The force of the blow sent him crashing over the side of the trench.

Arnie tumbled down into the pit, dirt and rocks sliding around him. He hit the ground hard, the wind knocked out of him. For a moment, he lay stunned and gasping for breath. Slowly, he pushed himself up on to his hands and knees, spitting dirt from his mouth.

As his vision cleared, Arnie froze. There, half-buried beneath a layer of loose earth, lay Sylvie Broadbent. She was deathly pale, her eyes closed.

Was she . . . ?

Rage flooded through Arnie, hot and fierce. What had Stark done to Sylvie? He was trying to *bury* her! With a roar, Arnie hauled

323

himself to his feet. Ignoring the pain in his ribs, he clawed his way up the steep side of the trench.

Above him, the digger's engine sputtered and died.

'Got it!' Karen yelled triumphantly. She must have hit the emergency stop button.

Arnie threw himself towards the now silent digger. Stark was half out of the cab, but he froze when he saw Arnie coming.

With a bellow of fury, Arnie launched himself at Stark, tackling him to the ground. They landed hard, a tangle of fists and flailing limbs. Arnie straddled Stark, pinning him down, and let loose a flurry of punches. Stark shrieked and struggled beneath him.

'No, stop! Please!' He raised his hands to shield his face. Blood dripped from his nose. 'I didn't mean for any of this to happen!'

Arnie felt Karen's hand on his shoulder, bringing him out of the haze of rage. 'That's enough. We've got him.'

Breathing hard, Arnie slid off Stark, slowly unclenching his fists. His knuckles were split and bleeding. Stark lay limp and snivelling on the grass.

Karen quickly cuffed Stark's hands behind his back. 'You're under arrest,' she informed Stark coldly.

Arnie didn't wait to see Karen haul Stark to his feet. He was already sliding back down into the trench, his heart pounding. Dirt cascaded around him as he scrambled over to Sylvie on his hands and knees. Gently, he started brushing the earth off her.

'Sylvie? Sylvie, can you hear me?' He pressed his fingers to her throat, feeling for a pulse.

Please, don't let her be dead.

What had she been doing out here with Stark? If she was worried, why hadn't she called Arnie? But he knew why. He'd let her down.

The anger was gone now, and all Arnie was left with was heavy, unflinching guilt. Why had he been so harsh when they'd last spoken? So she hadn't told him the full story about her interactions with Alison. She probably hadn't wanted to make herself look bad. There was no malice in it. Sylvie wasn't like that.

His breath caught as he felt a pulse, faint and fluttering beneath his fingertips.

Karen's worried face peered over the top of the trench. 'I'm going to the farmhouse to call for an ambulance. Just hold on!'

He nodded then turned back to focus on Sylvie, desperately trying to dig her free and keep her alive.

'Stay with me, Sylvie,' he urged, his voice tight with fear. 'You're going to be all right. Just keep breathing.'

'I need help.' Stark's voice carried over from the digger. 'I think my nose is broken.'

'You'll shut up if you know what's good for you,' Arnie growled.

The blooming pain in his ribs made it hard to take a deep breath, but he worked feverishly, clawing away the dirt covering Sylvie's limp form. She remained terrifyingly still and silent. The only sound was the movement of loose earth and the whimpering from Stark.

Arnie had never felt so alone.

He dug frantically, his fingers raw and bleeding. But he didn't stop. He couldn't stop.

Finally, she was free of earth. He brushed the dirt away from her face, his heart pounding. She was so still, so pale. He put his ear close to her mouth.

At first, he heard nothing. But then, he felt a faint puff of air against his cheek. She was alive.

Chapter Thirty-Five

Karen saw blue lights flashing in the distance. Backup would soon be here, along with the ambulance.

Arnie was still in the trench with Sylvie. Thankfully, it seemed like they'd arrived just in time, before Sylvie was crushed to death by the weight of the earth.

Professor Stark stood slumped against the JCB, still hand-cuffed, staring at the ground. Karen had read him his rights, but he'd just kept repeating how this whole thing wasn't really his fault.

Karen approached the digger. She needed some answers.

'Professor Stark,' she said. 'I need you to tell me what happened here tonight. Why were you trying to bury Sylvie Broadbent?'

Stark looked at her. 'None of it was my fault, really,' he said, his tone calm and reasonable. 'It was all just a series of unfortunate circumstances. I didn't want to do this. I just didn't know what else to do.'

'Start at the beginning,' Karen said. 'Tell me everything.'

Stark took a deep, shuddering breath. 'It all went wrong. I never meant for any of this to happen. It's just . . . it's all been too much for me.' He looked pleadingly at Karen. 'You have to under-stand I'm not a bad person. I'm not a real murderer.'

Karen waited, saying nothing.

'None of it was my fault,' he insisted again. 'It was all just a series of unfortunate circumstances.'

'Was it to do with the missing Jacobite gold?'

Stark's head jerked up in surprise. His remorseful expression had now turned sharp. 'How do you know about that?'

'Tilda came to you, didn't she?' Karen said. 'She showed you the gold coins and asked you to verify they were real. You confirmed they were – a discovery people had been searching centuries for.'

Stark nodded, a faraway look in his eyes. 'She showed me the pendant too. She'd found them at Loch Arkaig, not far from the shore. She'd found a small box containing the coins and the pendant. There was another, bigger chest, but it was buried deep, and she couldn't dig it up alone.' A hint of excitement crept into his voice.

'It was thrilling. All those historians searching for years . . . and a director stumbled across them with a metal detector while scouting locations for a TV show.' He shook his head in amazement. 'Tilda and I were going to work together, get press attention . . . I'd finally get the recognition I deserved.' His tone turned bitter. 'But then Tilda got drunk with her new friend Alison and told her all about what she'd found.' His eyes narrowed. 'Alison hated me from the beginning – she wanted to take over.'

'So you killed her?' Karen asked.

'She used me!' Stark said, a hint of defensiveness creeping into his voice. 'Alison used me for my knowledge, then used my contact to order a shrew's fiddle replica so she could give it to Sylvie.' A slow smile stretched across his lips. 'I thought it rather fitting to use it on Alison instead – she was the biggest shrew around.'

'So you knew it was a replica all along?'

'Of course. And I admit I hoped using it might throw you off the scent. Send you off looking for a crazy person. A *real* killer. One that killed for enjoyment.'

Karen stared at him. Did he not have the self-awareness to realise he was talking about himself?

He noticed how closely Karen was observing him and quickly smoothed his features back into a remorseful expression.

'I think you enjoyed killing them, Professor Stark.'

Irritation clouded his features, and he shook his head. 'You don't know me, Detective. Anyway, I overheard her trying to persuade Tilda to get a different expert, someone whose specialism was in Jacobean history. As if my knowledge wasn't enough! She told Tilda they didn't need me. Alison was trying to push me out. But even so, I didn't mean to kill her.'

'So what happened? Because you did end up killing her, didn't you?'

'I told you it wasn't my fault. I asked her to come out here to the dig site so we could discuss things privately. She brought the shrew's fiddle along to show me. Alison was just waiting for a plaque to arrive, and then she was going to present it to Sylvie in front of the whole crew. That was horrible of her, don't you think?'

Karen didn't reply, so he continued. 'When I confronted Alison about her trying to push me out, she laughed in my face.' His voice tightened slightly, a glimpse of the rage he was trying to control beneath his calm veneer. 'She said they didn't need me anymore. That there wasn't a thing I could do about it.'

Karen's stare was stony. She could feel the rage bubbling up inside, but she knew she had to keep it in check. She couldn't mess this up. She *needed* to know. After steadying herself with a deep breath, she asked, 'You lost your temper, and you killed Alison in the trailer?'

He paused, looking Karen straight in the eye. A flash of cruelty passed over his face, but it was gone in an instant. 'Yes. I regret it, of course. But she shouldn't have laughed at me like that.' A petulant note had entered his voice. 'I was just going to apply the shrew's fiddle at first, a little reminder to show her who she was dealing with. Alison needed to learn she wasn't the one in control. But she wouldn't shut up. On and on she screeched, like an old fishwife.' He paused again, thoughtful. 'I don't think it occurred to her to hold her tongue. That's the trouble with women like her. Manipulative, conniving, and never know when to shut up. Then she fell over, hit her head on one of the tent pegs.' He shrugged. 'A sad end, but I'm not really to blame.'

'She didn't fall,' Karen said coldly. 'You're an educated man. You must know forensics will prove you hit her.'

A long, slow smile spread over his lips, and his eyes grew distant. Karen shivered. He was remembering the kill.

'How did she end up in the trench?' Karen asked.

'I put her there. I panicked. Thought it might be something a real murderer would do, so I left her in the trench. I never imagined my own daughter would be the one to find her.' He sighed heavily. 'This past week has just been dreadful for me. Christie moping around. Melissa going back to work without even asking permission. You've no idea how bad it's been.'

Stark was revolting. He was trying to paint himself as the victim, making it sound like he'd had no choice but to kill two women in cold blood and then attempt to murder a third. Karen couldn't believe he was still refusing to label himself a killer.

'What about Tilda?' she asked, her tone sharp. 'She realised you killed Alison, and it was all over your planned visit to Scotland to try and excavate the gold?'

Stark nodded, his expression pained. 'But again, that really wasn't my fault either. If she'd come to me, perhaps we could have discussed it like adults. But she went around telling other people, and I couldn't have that, could I?' Another callous smile spread across his face before he caught himself and rearranged his features into a mask of regret.

His true nature was starting to show through the cracks in his performance as he tried to justify his actions.

'You tied Tilda to the whipping post and beat her to death, Professor Stark,' Karen said with disgust. 'Why do you keep insisting it wasn't your fault?'

'But I had no choice,' he said, spreading his hands in a helpless gesture that didn't reach his cold eyes. 'Things escalated out of my control.'

'Of course you had a choice. No one forced you to kill them.'

'You don't understand.' There was a hard edge to his voice now.

He was right. Karen would never understand. 'Why the whipping post?'

'I liked the historical significance. The connection to the past. I think Tilda would have liked it, too.' A glint of satisfaction flashed in his eyes.

Tilda would have liked it? Karen's hands clenched into fists. Stark was deluded. A monster.

'And Sylvie? What exactly did she do?'

Stark's contrite mask slid fully into place again. 'I didn't want to hurt her. I couldn't believe it when she called me today asking to meet. When she started talking about Loch Arkaig, I knew I had to do something. You have to understand I'm not a bad person, but I knew I had to act . . .'

'So you tried to bury her alive,' Karen finished coldly.

'I drugged her first!' Stark said. 'She wouldn't have felt a thing. I told you. None of this was my fault.'

Karen shook her head. The man was clearly unstable – a narcissistic psychopath. Sophie had been right about the killer's attitude towards women, too. 'You tortured Alison with the shrew's fiddle. You absolutely *did* mean to do it. And you enjoyed it.' Stark tried to interrupt, but Karen pressed on. 'And Tilda? You tied her up and beat her to death with a ferocity that sickens me. These women wouldn't bend to your will, and a supposedly clever man like you couldn't use his intellect to persuade them, so you resorted to the most horrifically callous and brutal violence I've ever seen. You are a killer, Professor Stark. And what's more, I think you're inherently evil. *Everything* that happened is *your* fault.'

Stark's face tightened. He was seething with anger.

'What about your wife and daughter?' Karen said. 'Do you like to control them, too? What happens if they push back? Was it your decision for Melissa to give up journalism?'

'No,' Stark snapped. 'It was a joint decision. Melissa knew the job was too dangerous once she had a child.'

'And your daughter? Does she answer you back?'

'She wouldn't dare.' Stark's lip curled in a snarl. 'You really are the most stupid woman. They shouldn't let vindictive little shrews like you into the police. The power has obviously gone to your head.' He then added, condescendingly, 'Let me explain this in words of three syllables or fewer, so that you can understand. I reject the notion that I'm a murderer. Intent matters. I was only trying to fool you into thinking there was a real killer on the loose, so you wouldn't look too closely at me. And obviously, I did a good job, because you fell for it.'

'For a man who prides himself on his intelligence, you're a disappointment, Professor Stark. *Obviously* has four syllables. So much for dumbing it down for me.'

Stark's face went white and he spluttered with rage. He opened his mouth to reply, but Karen walked away as the ambulance and backup arrived.

She had never encountered a killer like him before – a man who was so convinced of his own importance, but who saw himself as the victim in all of this. It was chilling, and she knew that it would take a long time for her to process what had happened.

As she watched the paramedics load Sylvie into the ambulance, Karen went to stand by Arnie. She touched his arm lightly.

'You should get checked out, too. You took quite a hit from that digger.'

'You're telling me,' Arnie said, clutching his ribs. 'It even hurts to breathe.' He tried to laugh, but his face screwed up in pain. He nodded at the ambulance. 'Paramedics said she's stable.'

'That's a relief.'

'I thought . . .' Arnie trailed off, eyes on the ground, shaking his head.

'I know,' Karen said. 'You don't need to explain.'

Karen was back at work in the office on Monday, tackling her old nemesis – paperwork.

Just as she was thinking that making paper aeroplanes would be a better use of her time than filling in another form that was almost identical to the one she'd just filled in, Tim Farthing sidled in.

The sight of Tim holding a big box of chocolates like a shield made Karen do a double take.

Was he here to apologise? Karen wondered if she'd woken up in an alternate reality.

Tim plonked them on Karen's desk and then looked noncha-lantly around the office as if delivering chocolates was something he did every day.

'Are those for me?' Karen nodded at the box.

'They're for everybody,' he said, his tone betraying a hint of defensiveness. 'Sort of a *well done, congratulations on the case* type of thing.'

He looked very uncomfortable.

She supposed this was his way of saying sorry for sarcastically suggesting she wasn't suited to the role of detective when they were at Tilda Goring's crime scene.

Tim acted like he'd rather face a firing squad than admit to bringing chocolates to apologise.

'That's suspiciously nice of you.' Karen eyed the chocolates as though they might be some kind of trick.

'No big deal. They were on sale,' he mumbled, trying to mini-mise his efforts.

'I thought they might be a leaving gift.'

'Who's leaving?'

'Me. After what you said at the Tilda Goring crime scene . . . I had a long think and decided you were right. I'm really not cut out for this work.'

'What? No. I didn't mean . . . I was joking. Of course you're cut out for it. Didn't you just piece together Stark's motive single-handedly? You came up with the theory it was all connected to the missing Jacobite gold. Not many people could have done that. It was seriously impressive. Not to mention . . .' He trailed off, finally noticing Karen's smile. 'You're not really leaving, are you?'

'No, but do carry on. I'm enjoying this.'

Tim huffed. 'I suppose I deserved that. Look, I know I can be a bit . . .' He shuffled awkwardly from one foot to another. 'A bit of a pain sometimes.'

'I'd noticed.'

'But I don't mean any offence. Sarcasm is part of my lovable personality. I'd say it won't happen again . . . but that would be a lie. Just joking,' he added quickly, noticing Karen's raised eyebrows. 'It's just who I am. I can't change that.'

'Shame.'

'Hey, now you're doing it!'

'There's a time and place though, Tim.'

'Yeah, all right,' he said before gesturing towards the chocolates again. 'I've given you a sincere apology *and* chocolates; what more do you want?'

Karen tilted her head, pretending to consider his question.

'Seriously, you're making me feel bad.' His voice carried both humour and a touch of vulnerability – a rare glimpse into Tim Farthing's less guarded side.

'Hmm . . . all right then, suppose you're forgiven.'

She opened the chocolates and took one before offering the box to Tim.

He selected one and asked, 'Did they really find the gold in Loch Arkaig?'

'We've got an expert from Glasgow University looking into it now,' Karen replied after swallowing the chocolate. Hazelnut praline. Delicious. She reached for another. 'And *Britain's Biggest Treasure Hunt* is set to film there next week.'

'I suppose all this will give their ratings a boost.'

'Sylvie, the producer, has invited me and Arnie to watch the filming,' Karen said.

'You going?'

Karen nodded. 'Yes, Mike and I are heading up to Banavie next weekend with Arnie.'

'And how's Sylvie after everything that happened?'

'Stark drugged her, so she can't remember much . . . but thankfully it doesn't seem like there are any long-term effects. I think she's going to be okay. Sylvie's a tough cookie; I like her.'

'And so does Arnie – at least, that's what I hear through the grapevine.'

Karen smiled. 'Let's just say the weekend can't come soon enough for Arnie.'

Farzana approached Karen's desk. The normally cheerful officer seemed downbeat, as though the weight of the Stark case was resting on her shoulders, dragging her down.

'Karen, do you have a minute?' Farzana asked, her voice quiet, almost hesitant.

Tim, despite his usual lack of social skills, picked up on the shift in atmosphere. He excused himself with a nod to Karen and a sympathetic smile at Farzana.

Karen pushed aside the paperwork and pulled over a chair from the empty desk behind her. 'Of course. Sit down. Chocolate?' She offered the box Tim had brought.

Farzana shook her head, sinking into the chair. Her fingers twisted together in her lap. 'I missed it,' she said quietly. 'If I had realised Stark was imitating Mackenzie on the phone to give himself an alibi, then Tilda Goring would still be alive.'

Karen leaned forward. 'Farzana, listen to me. It isn't your fault. Stark is the only one responsible for Tilda's murder.'

But Farzana wasn't ready to absolve herself. 'I keep thinking, when he answered the phone as Mackenzie, did he sound odd? Was there anything I should have picked up on?'

Karen understood the self-doubt that came with their job. The endless what-ifs that haunted quiet moments. But she also knew that dwelling on those thoughts was a dangerous path.

'You were doing your job, checking his alibi. You had Mackenzie's direct number as listed on the university website; you expected the call to be answered by Mackenzie. And at that stage, we had no evidence or reason to suspect Stark.'

Farzana nodded, but Karen could see she was only half-convinced. The burden of hindsight was a heavy one.

'Stark fooled a lot of people,' Karen said. 'He had us all believing he was an innocent bystander in this. You can't blame yourself for not seeing through his act over the phone.'

Farzana took a deep breath. 'Thanks, Karen. I needed to hear that. I thought everyone might blame me for messing up. It's just hard not to wonder . . .'

'I know. But we can't let the what-ifs consume us. We did our best with the information we had at the time. That's all we can ever do.'

Farzana stood, looking a little less miserable. 'I'll let you get back to your work. And your chocolate.'

After Farzana's departure, Karen found herself once again engulfed by the seemingly endless sea of paperwork. Just as she was considering making a paper boat to sail away on, Sophie approached her desk with a bounce in her step that had been missing for too long.

She was clutching two mugs of tea.

'Thought you could do with this,' Sophie said, placing the mug within Karen's reach and pulling over a chair.

'You're an angel.' The young detective had a knack for popping up just when Karen needed a break from monotony.

'Guess who I've just seen?' Sophie said, with a grin that suggested she had new information – or gossip. Both were equally welcome distractions from the piles of paperwork.

'Who?' Karen asked, pushing aside a pile of forms.

'Professor Mackenzie. We just had an interesting face-to-face chat where he destroyed Stark's so-called alibi.'

'Oh?' Karen raised an eyebrow, her attention fully on Sophie now. The paperwork was forgotten.

They had requested that an officer from Police Scotland check up on Mackenzie. When they'd realised Stark had pretended to be Mackenzie to give himself a false alibi, the team had been worried Stark could have killed Mackenzie too, just to ensure no one could trip up his alibi.

'He was shocked to have a police officer show up at his mother's house, especially since he'd never even *met* Stark before.' Sophie took a sip of tea. 'Mackenzie was fuming that he'd been dragged into this mess without his knowledge. The weird thing was that Mackenzie really had gone up to Scotland to visit his mother. So Stark gave us a kind of mangled version of the truth.'

'The most effective lies are distorted versions of the truth,' Karen said. 'I suppose Stark thought that would make it more convincing.'

Morgan strolled into the office with Rick in tow.

'How did the debrief go?' Karen asked Morgan, knowing that such meetings could be unpredictable depending on how well you met Churchill's high expectations.

Morgan stopped beside Karen's desk. 'Not too bad, actually. They're pleased with how we handled things. Arnie's in the hot seat now.'

Karen leaned back in her chair. 'Glad I got my debrief out of the way first thing. It was quick.' She wasn't one to brag, but dodging prolonged bureaucratic encounters with Churchill felt like winning an Olympic gold medal some days. 'Not only was Churchill satisfied, but he's also convinced the case is going to get us showered with positive press.'

'That's not what we usually get showered with,' Morgan commented dryly.

Rick flopped into a chair, his expression clouding over. 'You know what's still bugging me? Lucas Black. It's like he's vanished off the face of the earth. We know he wasn't involved in the murders, so why hide?'

'I still say he's dodging Rothwell, not the police,' Morgan said.

Rick scowled. 'Rothwell – don't even get me started on him. The guy is a textbook crook. Living it up in his fancy house when he should be behind bars. Some justice.'

'I know, it's not fair,' Karen said. 'It's not a perfect world. But we need to celebrate success when we can. And we arrested Stark. That's a win.'

'We can't let Rothwell get away with it, though. We can't just give up.'

'Oh, we won't,' Sophie said. 'We'll get him eventually.'

Karen understood Rick's frustration all too well. Quentin Chapman was still out there, too, living his life as if untouched by the law. Patience was an important part of their job – biding their time until everything lined up just right.

If there was any justice in this world – and she had to believe there was – eventually, the law would catch up with both Chapman and Rothwell.

'So,' Sophie said, clapping her hands together as if she had just thought of the world's best idea. 'Who's up for celebrating the end of this case at the pub tonight?'

Morgan perked up immediately at the mention of *pub*. 'I'm in.'

'All right,' Rick said. 'But I'm not going on to karaoke this time. I'm still having nightmares about the way Arnie murdered "My Way" last time.'

Karen laughed, shaking her head. 'It was definitely an experience.'

'An experience no one wants to repeat,' Morgan said.

Karen pushed the box of chocolates towards them. 'Tim Farthing brought these for us, to celebrate a successful end to this case.'

'Tim?' Morgan frowned and looked at the pralines suspiciously.

'Must have had a bump on the head,' Rick said, selecting a chocolate and popping it into his mouth.

Karen laughed. Despite all its frustrations and dangers, the job had its good moments. It wasn't always easy – in fact, it was rarely easy – but it was moments like these that reminded her why she kept showing up every day.

Yes, there were still challenges ahead; names like Rothwell and Chapman loomed large in their caseloads. But together the team navigated successes and setbacks and supported one another when cases took their toll.

And that, Karen thought, as she reached for a chocolate, made even the most daunting mountain of paperwork just about bearable.

Chapter Thirty-Six

Lucas Black – or Mr Lucas Avis, as he was now known – had to admit life on the Cayman Islands wasn't half bad. It was a far cry from the drizzly grey skies of Scotland he'd once hankered after, but as he strolled to the local coffee shop with the sun warming his back, he couldn't find much to complain about.

Every morning started with this ritual: a leisurely walk down streets lined with palm trees swaying in the gentle breeze, a stop at a cafe that served delicious coffee and had English-language newspapers. He'd sit there, sipping his coffee, and scan the headlines that seemed a world away from his current life.

The cafe was a cosy little place, all bright colours and open windows that let in the sea air. The barista, a chap named George, knew him as Mr Avis and now greeted him with a nod and the usual 'Your flat white, sir?'

Lucas always thanked him and then found his favourite spot, a table by the window where he could watch life unfold on the street outside. He didn't miss much about his old life, not Alison's incessant demands nor her cold shoulder when he didn't deliver to her impossible standards. Not even the picture of his ex-girlfriend that had sat on his desk – a constant reminder of what could've been.

People here were friendly enough. They didn't pry or ask awkward questions about what had brought him to their shores. Lucas preferred it that way. Best not to have too many people knowing your business – especially when your business involved working for Mr Quentin Chapman.

Lucas wasn't quite sure what he was doing out here, mind you. It was mostly paperwork – shuffling documents from one pile to another, signing off on things he barely understood. He tried not to think too hard about it. Chapman had said it was all above board, and Lucas wanted to believe him. How bad could paperwork be anyway?

Chapman had also assured him that this whole 'Mr Avis' business was only temporary – a necessary measure for privacy and safety reasons. And as for Clive Rothwell? Chapman had told Lucas not to expect any contact from him for quite some time.

Not that Lucas minded being out of Rothwell's reach. The bloke had a stare that could bore through steel, and Lucas wasn't keen on being anywhere near him when his temper ignited – which it did with alarming regularity.

Yes, it was a shame about Scotland, but then again, as Lucas gazed out at the clear blue skies and felt the gentle warmth of the breeze on his skin, he had to admit the weather here was much nicer.

The cafe began to fill up as locals and tourists alike streamed in for their morning caffeine fix. Conversations buzzed around him – a blend of accents and languages that felt oddly comforting in their unfamiliarity.

All things considered, things had turned out quite well for Lucas Black. For now, at least, life was good. And in this corner of paradise where nobody knew his real name or cared about Alison Poulson or her doomed development projects, Lucas could almost believe it would stay that way forever.

But then again – this was only week one of whatever new life lay ahead of him under Chapman's employ. Only time would tell what would happen in the future.

For now, though, there were worse places to lie low than the Cayman Islands, and there were certainly worse ways to start your day than with a stroll to a nice cafe for good coffee and friendly faces.

Lucas leaned back in his chair and folded his arms behind his head with a contented sigh.

Yes – all things considered – not bad at all.

Christie Stark slouches on the living-room sofa, her legs tucked under her, a blanket pulled over her knees despite the mildness of the afternoon. It's more a comfort thing, really – a shield against the chill of reality.

A textbook lies abandoned on her lap. It's been a week since her father's arrest, and the house feels hollow. It's easy to imagine he's still here, in his study, lost in bygone times. She tries to focus on her book, but the words blur into a soup of letters that refuse to make sense.

Her mum flits about the room pretending to dust, but Christie knows she's just going through the motions. Every so often, her gaze lingers on Christie longer than necessary. She can feel the weight of those looks; they're heavy with questions and a mother's worry that her child might crumble under the pressure.

'Christie, love,' her mum starts . . . and then stops. She bites her lip, considering her next words. 'You know . . . if you want to talk or anything . . .'

She says this at least five times a day.

Christie offers a smile. 'I'm all right, Mum.'

Her mum nods, not entirely convinced but letting it go. 'We're going to be okay.'

She says that a lot now, too.

Christie's fingers turn the pages of the textbook, flicking through the outlines of graphs and diagrams she's meant to be studying. But her mind is miles away.

Her mum sat her down last night, a serious look etched on her face as she broached the subject of moving away. Starting fresh somewhere else, where their name isn't sullied by scandal and whispers. But they've decided to stick it out here, at least for now. Her mum thinks it's because leaving would mean running away, and she says neither Stark woman is that type of person. Christie goes along with that, but the truth is that if it weren't for the group of friends she's made at college, Christie would be all for running away.

She can't bear the thought of losing friends when she finds it so hard to make them. Mia – the first real friend she's ever had – along with the others who've accepted her into their little group. And there's Leo . . . he really seems to like Christie. Not that any of that is really important right now.

It's odd to think about friendships when everything else is falling apart. The irony isn't lost on Christie – her social circle coming together just as her family disintegrates.

She closes her eyes for a moment, willing away the image of her dad in a cell that keeps flashing behind her eyelids. Her dad was never violent, never raised his voice higher than what was necessary to be heard over a lively dinner debate about history or art, but Christie always knew not to answer back.

Christie swallows hard against the lump forming in her throat. She's going to see him next week if they let her. Mum will drive her there but wait in the car; her mother is not ready to face him yet, not ready to reconcile the man she married with . . . with whatever he's become, or always was beneath his scholarly exterior.

She knows her mum is struggling too – probably more than she lets on. Christie catches her staring off into space when she thinks no one's looking.

A shiver runs down Christie's spine as she considers visiting her dad. Part of her yearns for his reassurance – that there's been some colossal mistake and soon he'll be back home as though nothing ever happened. But another part dreads what seeing him might confirm.

She tries to picture what it will be like walking into the visitation room: Will Dad look different? Will he sound different? Will he still be her dad?

'Christie,' Melissa says softly, breaking into her thoughts. 'You don't have to see him if you don't want to.'

Christie flinches at how easily her mother reads her thoughts. 'No, I want . . . I need to see him.'

Her mother nods but says nothing more; words are too flimsy for what they're dealing with right now.

A knock at the door makes them both jump. Her mother moves to answer it, but Christie's already up and heading towards the hall. She needs a distraction.

Mia stands on the doorstep. She's wearing a long skirt and even more bangles than usual. They clink as she lifts an arm to push back her hair.

'Wanted to check if you're okay,' Mia says.

Christie smiles and ushers her inside. They settle into the kitchen with mugs of hot chocolate.

'It's all just . . . surreal,' Christie admits. She wraps her hands around the mug. 'And I'm dreading going back to college.'

Mia frowns. 'Because of what people will say?'

'Yes,' Christie says, tracing the rim of her mug with a fingertip. 'You know how it is – people love gossip.'

'But *you* haven't done anything wrong.'

'I don't think gossips care about that.'

Mia reaches across the table and takes Christie's hand. 'Then let them talk,' she says firmly. 'They'll have me to deal with if they give you any grief.'

Mia looks fierce. Maybe Christie will be able to get through this with Mia in her corner.

Christie's gaze flickers to the window, to the old garden shed. 'I'm worried about Caroline.' Caroline is notorious around college. Not just for her gossiping, but for the malice that often tinges her words.

'Caroline?' Mia says, her voice laced with disdain. 'She's all bark and no bite.' Mia reaches for a chocolate digestive. 'Last time she tried to start something with me, I told her I had no idea people still used such pathetic and outdated methods of seeking attention.'

Christie smiles despite herself. 'What did she say to that?'

'She tried to insult my outfit,' Mia says, gesturing at her skirt and bangles with a flourish. 'Said I looked like I raided a charity shop.'

'And what did you say?' Christie asks, already feeling lighter as she anticipates Mia's response.

Mia smirks at Christie before delivering the punchline. 'I said, *Thank you! It's actually from your mum's latest fashion line called "No one cares what you think".'*

A genuine laugh escapes Christie for the first time in a week. It feels strange but good – like stretching after a long sleep.

Mia beams, clearly pleased with herself. 'That's how you deal with people like Caroline.'

Christie wipes away a tear that's escaped down her cheek. 'You're terrible,' she manages between giggles.

They spend another hour together, Mia telling stories of college life while Christie listens, grateful for the distraction.

By the time Mia leaves, promising to check in again soon, Christie's spirits are a little higher. Maybe facing college won't be so bad after all.

It was a crisp morning, the kind that reddened your nose and made you wish you'd invested in a pair of thermals. The sky was like a watercolour of pinks and blues as dawn crept over the stunning landscape. The chill of the Scottish Highlands nipped at Karen, Mike, Arnie and Sylvie as they huddled together at the damp archaeology site beside Loch Arkaig.

A murmur of disappointment travelled through the crew of *Britain's Biggest Treasure Hunt* as Dr Edward Killian, a historian specialising in the Jacobite uprising, stood beside them, delivering anticlimactic news. 'The large chest that Ms Goring discovered has been excavated, but it wasn't filled with the treasure that she'd hoped for.'

'No gold?' Arnie grumbled, folding his arms across his chest as he squinted at the Jacobite expert.

'No Jacobite gold, I'm afraid,' Killian confirmed. 'The chest Tilda found was filled with musket balls. Interesting historically, but hardly the stuff of legends.'

Arnie huffed. 'Musket balls?'

'But Tilda found some gold coins,' Karen said. 'She brought them back with her. And what about the pendant?'

'Ah, well . . .' Killian adjusted his glasses before continuing. 'The coins were real Louis d'ors. However, they were likely just a few buried by the same person who buried the musket balls. But there's no vast hoard of Jacobite gold here. As for the pendant, our tests indicate it was made in the late 1800s. The lock of hair inside could've been taken from another earlier keepsake.'

Arnie snorted. 'So poor Tilda Goring and Alison Poulson were murdered over a fake pendant and some old musket balls?'

Turning back to the academic, Karen asked, 'What's your theory on the lost gold?'

'Like many others, I believe that after Culloden, what remained of the gold was redirected to finance Bonnie Prince Charlie's time in exile on the Continent.' He winked at her, a glint of mischief in his eyes. 'But that's not such a romantic story, is it?'

'Thanks for your time, Dr Killian,' Karen said, her words clouding in the chilly air.

Before Killian could respond, the kind of bickering you'd expect at a toddler's birthday party, not a professional film set, filled the air. From behind one of the hulking equipment trucks, Trevor Barker and Molly Moreland emerged, locked in a humdinger of an argument that seemed to be about the Loch Ness monster.

Trevor's toupee seemed to be riding too high on his forehead in his agitation, while Molly's perfect pout was marred by her scowl.

When they spotted Karen and Arnie, they paused mid-squabble and slapped on smiles so wide they looked like they were auditioning for a toothpaste advert. 'Hello, Detectives!' they chimed in unison, voices dripping with sweetness.

'Quiet on set!' someone called, and Karen, Arnie and Sylvie strolled away so they wouldn't disturb the filming.

As the cameras began to roll, Trevor and Molly slipped seamlessly into their roles, following the autocue with practised ease.

As Karen listened half-heartedly to their lines about the 'disappointing twist in the tale', her attention wandered to Mike, who was busy snapping photos of the loch on his phone.

Beside Karen, Sylvie was engaged in a conversation with Arnie, trying to persuade him to go for a hike later. Arnie looked as if Sylvie had suggested abseiling off Mount Everest rather than a simple stroll through nature; Karen wondered if Arnie had willingly engaged in any form of physical exercise since PE lessons at school.

'Come on, Arnie,' Sylvie coaxed with the patience of a saint, 'a bracing hike will do you good!'

'You know exercise isn't as good for you as people think. Just take our colleague Rick for example. Lad was doing a double workout at the gym, circuit training and a run when he hurt his ankle. He's been limping for two weeks.'

Sylvie frowned. 'Rick? The young chap who gave me a lift home from the crime scene after Alison's murder?'

Karen nodded. 'Yes, that's right.'

Sylvie burst out laughing. 'He told you he injured his ankle at the gym, did he?'

'Why? Do you know different?' Arnie asked.

'I think so. He was very kind and walked me to the door of the pub. Unfortunately, he tripped on a loose paving stone. Someone had put some empty flowerpots by the side of the path and somehow he managed to get his foot stuck in one.'

Arnie stared at her. 'Rick got his foot stuck in a *flowerpot?*'

'Yes, firmly wedged in there. Took us a while to get it off.'

It was Arnie's turn to laugh. 'The lying little . . . Just wait until I see him.'

'You should go easy on him,' Sylvie said. 'He was very embarrassed.'

'Go easy on him? Not a chance. This is too good to pass up.'

'So, you're worrying about nothing, Arnie. Exercise is perfectly safe. I've already planned our route.'

After Arnie insisted he'd rather face Nessie herself than go on a hike, Sylvie persisted with gentle enthusiasm, and something miraculous happened – Arnie's horrified expression softened into reluctant acceptance.

'I suppose it can't hurt,' he said eventually. 'But more importantly, where are we having dinner tonight?'

'The guesthouse does some very nice haggis,' Sylvie suggested.

The expression on Arnie's face suggested he was envisioning dining on raw eggs mixed with petrol rather than sheep innards. Still, wanting to please Sylvie, he conceded with an uncertain nod.

'Well . . . won't knock it 'til I've tried it,' he said, causing Sylvie to laugh.

'I'll catch up with you both later,' Karen said before walking over to Mike.

As she approached him, she felt a sense of peace settle over her. The beautiful landscape, and the companionship . . . it was almost enough to make her forget the tragic events that had brought them here.

Mike seemed relaxed, too. He'd not mentioned trying to find his biological father since Karen had found him burning the old photos. He seemed to have turned a corner, embracing the relationship with his mother and stepfather rather than chasing the shadows of his past. But Karen wasn't entirely convinced how long that would last.

But this weekend was all about unwinding and enjoying the beauty of the Highlands.

'Isn't it stunning?' Mike said, gazing at the loch when she slipped her arm around his.

'Gorgeous. Are you ready for that walk?'

Karen's breath misted in the crisp air, her cheeks flushed from both the chill and the pace Mike had set. She looked around at the serene, untouched beauty of the Scottish Highlands. The land stretched out like a postcard around them – absolutely beautiful, even if it was freezing.

'Just remember to keep your eyes peeled. If we're lucky, we might catch a glimpse of the elusive wild haggis,' Mike said, a teasing twinkle in his eyes.

Karen laughed. 'I'll keep a look out.'

He glanced around at the sprawling scenery surrounding them. 'Who could resist this view?'

She couldn't argue with that. The loch beside them was a deep blue, and the sky just a shade lighter. Though her nose was numb with cold, Karen felt warm inside.

That was when Mike stopped walking and turned to face her. His hands were in his pockets, and there was a sudden seriousness in his gaze that made Karen's heart do a funny little skip.

Was he doing what she thought he was doing?

Before she could fully prepare herself – Mike was bending down on one knee. And not gracefully either. There was a definite wobble and a grimace of pain as his knee contacted the uneven ground.

'Mike!' Karen said, laughter threatening to bubble up despite the monumental moment. 'You're kneeling on your bad leg . . . really?'

He winced, but then flashed her a grin so charming it should have been illegal. 'It's not every day I propose. Thought I'd make an effort.'

He produced a small velvet box from his pocket and took out a solitaire ring. He held it out.

'Karen, I know this is a big step . . . but I love you, and I want to spend the rest of my life with you. Will you marry me?'

Karen felt tears brim in her eyes as she stared at him. She knew what he was asking; he wasn't just proposing marriage – he was asking her to truly move on from her past, just as he had been trying to do since the loss of his own son.

A wave of emotions crashed over her as she thought about Josh and Tilly. They were her past, a past she still grieved for, but they were gone. She could never bring them back. And here was Mike, who understood the pain of losing a child, offering her a future filled with love and happiness.

And she loved him. She *really* loved him.

'I . . .' she started, then stopped as she took a deep breath.

He looked up at her hopefully. 'Is that a yes? Because I'm starting to sink a bit. Do you know if they have quicksand around here?'

'I hope not,' Karen said, alarmed, and reached to pull him up. 'Yes, I'll marry you. Get up before you sink any more!'

They laughed together then – Mike still on one knee in the muck and Karen trying to heave him up. It was funny and overwhelming all at once.

And a small part of her was still worrying, because saying yes meant leaving Josh and Tilly and her old life behind. But then again, wasn't that what she needed? To move on?

As she helped Mike up and he attempted to wipe the mud off his trousers, she thought about how right it felt. Being with him. Moving forward.

He was the man for her, soggy knee included.

He hugged her tight enough to squeeze any lingering doubts away. Yes, it was a big step; yes, it meant leaving her old life behind. But she was ready for this new chapter, with Mike at her side.

ACKNOWLEDGEMENTS

Book ten! I can hardly believe it. The fabulous editors past and present who have worked on the Karen Hart series deserve a massive thank you. It's been a pleasure to work with such a talented group of people at Amazon Publishing. Thank you to all at Thomas & Mercer who work so hard to make this series a success, including Kasim, Sammia, Eoin, Dan, Nicole, Sana and everyone else who helps get my books to readers.

Special thanks must also go to Russel McLean and Gemma Wain, for their help and invaluable attention to detail over the series.

To my family, I'm so lucky to have you – and as always, special thanks to Chris for his support.

And finally, most importantly, thank you to the readers who have read, reviewed and recommended my books. Your kind words and encouragement mean the world to me. I can be contacted through my website: www.dsbutlerbooks.com or you can find me on Facebook: www.facebook.com/D.S.Butler.Author.

ABOUT THE AUTHOR

Born in Kent, D. S. Butler grew up as an avid reader with a love for crime fiction and mysteries. She has worked as a scientific officer in a hospital pathology laboratory and as a research scientist. After obtaining a PhD in biochemistry, she worked at the University of Oxford for four years before moving to the Middle East. While living in Bahrain, she wrote her first novel and hasn't stopped writing since.

Follow the Author on Amazon

If you enjoyed this book, follow D. S. Butler on Amazon to be notified when the author releases a new book!

To do this, please follow these instructions:

Desktop:

1) Search for the author's name on Amazon or in the Amazon App.

2) Click on the author's name to arrive on their Amazon page.

3) Click the 'Follow' button.

Mobile and Tablet:

1) Search for the author's name on Amazon or in the Amazon App.

2) Click on one of the author's books.

3) Click on the author's name to arrive on their Amazon page.

4) Click the 'Follow' button.

Kindle eReader and Kindle App:

If you enjoyed this book on a Kindle eReader or in the Kindle App, you will find the author 'Follow' button after the last page.